Monaco—glam...
and s...

Monte Carlo
Affairs

Three romantic, larger than life novels
of passionate romance.

Monte Carlo Affairs

EMILIE ROSE

First published in Great Britain 2012
by Mills & Boon, an imprint of Harlequin (UK) Limited,
Eton House, 18-24 Paradise Road, Richmond, Surrey TW9 1SR

MONTE CARLO AFFAIRS © by Harlequin Enterprises II B.V./S.à.r.l 2012

The Millionaire's Indecent Proposal, The Prince's Ultimate Deception and *The Playboy's Passionate Pursuit* were first published in Great Britain by Harlequin (UK) Limited in separate, single volumes.

The Millionaire's Indecent Proposal © Emilie Rose Cunningham 2007
The Prince's Ultimate Deception © Emilie Rose Cunningham 2007
The Playboy's Passionate Pursuit © Emilie Rose Cunningham 2007

ISBN: 978 0 263 89682 4

05-0312

Printed and bound in Spain
by Blackprint CPI, Barcelona

THE MILLIONAIRE'S
INDECENT PROPOSAL

BY
EMILIE ROSE

Dear Reader,

What could possibly be more delicious than a sexy French chocolatier? I had more fun writing Franco Constantine than I have had with any hero in a very long time. Franco is a true sensualist—a man who believes he knows what he wants and how to get it. I am so glad Stacy Reeves came along to show him the error of his thinking. :)

Throw in a vicarious holiday in magical Monaco and writing this story was an absolute pleasure. I've been fascinated with Monaco since my school days when I begged my parents to allow me to go to Amherst College in Massachusetts, the alma mater of Prince Albert of Monaco. I was convinced I could make him my prince if only I could meet him. Fate had other plans. I attended college near home, but I did indeed meet my prince.

Happy reading!

Emilie Rose

Emilie Rose lives in North Carolina with her college sweetheart husband and four sons. Writing is Emilie's third (and hopefully her last) career. She managed a medical office and ran a home day care, neither of which offers half as much satisfaction as plotting happy endings. Her hobbies include quilting, gardening and cooking (especially cheesecake). Her favourite TV shows include *ER, CSI* and Discovery Channel's medical programs. Emilie's a country music fan because she can find an entire book in almost any song.

Letters can be mailed to:
Emilie Rose
PO Box 20145
Raleigh, NC 27619
E-mail: EmilieRoseC@aol.com

Bron, Juliet, Sally and Wanda,
you know this book would not have happened without
you. Thanks, ladies, for keeping me on the road.

MJ, thanks for the spark that gave me Franco.

Prologue

"Must you marry every woman you sleep with?" Franco Constantine demanded of his father. Furious, he paced the salon of the family chateau outside Avignon, France. "This one is younger than me."

His father shrugged and smiled—the smile of a besotted old fool. "I'm in love."

"No, Papa, you're in lust. Again. We cannot afford another one of your expensive divorce settlements. Our cash reserves are tied up in expanding Midas Chocolates. For God's sake, if you refuse to have a prenuptial agreement, then at least sign everything over to me before you marry her and jeopardize our business and the family properties with mistake number five."

Armand shook his head. "Angeline is not a mistake. She is a blessing."

Franco had met the misnamed harpy at lunch. She was no angel. But he knew from past experience his father would not listen when a woman had him trans-fixed. "I disagree."

Armand rested a hand on Franco's shoulder. "I hate to see you so bitter, Franco. Granted, your ex-wife was a selfish bitch, but not all women are."

"You're wrong. Women are duplicitous and mercen-ary creatures. There is nothing I want from one that I cannot buy."

"If you'd stop dating spoiled rich women and find someone with traditional values like Angeline, you'd find a woman who would love you for yourself and not your money."

"Wrong. And if your paramour loves you and not your wealth, she'll stick by you once you've divested yourself, and I won't have to borrow against our estate *again,* close stores or lay off workers when your ardor cools and her lawyers start circling."

"If you want to control the Constantine holdings so badly, then marry."

"I won't endanger the family assets by marrying again."

"And what of an heir? Someone to inherit all this when you and I are gone?" Armand's sweeping gesture encompassed the chateau which had been in the family for hundreds of years.

Something in his father's tone raised the hackles on the back of Franco's neck. "Is Angeline pregnant?"

"No. But son, you are thirty-eight. I should be bouncing grandbabies on my knee by now. Since you're not willing to provide heirs to our estate then I think perhaps I should. Angeline is only thirty. I could have several more sons and daughters by her before I die."

"You can't be serious. You're seventy-five."

His father speared him with a hard glance. "If you marry before my September wedding, I'll sign everything over to you. If you do not…" He extended his arms and shrugged. "I'll take matters into my own hands."

Franco could easily find a woman to marry. Any number of his acquaintances would agree, but the stench of his ex-wife's betrayal still clung to him. He'd been a young love-struck fool, blind to Lisette's faults and her treachery. He would never let a woman dupe him like that again. Marriage was out of the question.

He stood toe to toe with his father. "If I find one of these mythical paragons and prove she's just as greedy as the rest of her sex, then you will sign the Constantine properties over to me without a parody of a marriage on my part."

"Prove it how exactly?"

How indeed? "I'll offer her a million euros for the use of her body for one month without the pretense of love or the possibility of marriage. That amount is but a fraction of what each of your divorces has cost us."

"I accept your terms, but don't try to weasel out of this by finding an impossible woman. She must be one who you find attractive and beddable, and who you would be willing to marry if she cannot be bought."

A woman who could not be bought. No such animal existed.

Confident he would win, Franco extended his hand to shake on the deal. Victory would not only be sweet, it would be easy, and his father's most recent parasite would not get the chance to sink her fangs in the family coffers and suck them dry.

One

"*Le chocolat qui vaut son poids en or,*" Stacy Reeves read the gilt script on the shop window aloud. "What does that mean?" she asked her friend Candace without looking away from the mouthwatering display of chocolates on gold-rimmed plates.

"Chocolate worth its weight in gold," a slightly accented and thoroughly masculine voice replied. Definitely not Candace.

Surprised, Stacy pivoted on her sandaled foot. Wow. Forget chocolate. The dark-haired blue-eyed hunk in front of her looked good enough to eat.

"Would you care for a piece, mademoiselle? My treat." Monsieur Gorgeous indicated the shop door with his hand. A silver-toned, wafer-thin watch winked beneath his suit sleeve. Platinum, she'd bet, from the affluent look of what had to be a custom-tailored suit.

Nothing from a department store would fit those broad shoulders, narrow hips and long legs so perfectly.

Never mind that she'd probably dream of licking chocolate from the deep cleft in his chin tonight, Stacy had learned the hard way that when something looked too good to be true it was. Always. A seductively sexy stranger offering free gourmet chocolate had to be a set-up because sophisticated guys like him didn't go for practical accountants like her. And her simple lilac sundress and sensible walking sandals weren't the stuff of which male fantasies were made.

She glanced up and down the Boulevard des Moulins, one of the principality of Monaco's shopping streets, searching for her friend. Candace was nowhere in sight, but she had to be behind Mr. Delectable's appearance and offer. Her friend had joked about finding husbands for each of her bridesmaids before her wedding in four weeks time. At least Stacy had thought she was joking. Until now.

Stacy tilted her head, considered the man in question and gave him a saccharine smile. "Does that line usually work for you with American tourists?"

The corners of his oh-so-tempting lips twitched and his eyes glinted with humor beneath thick, straight eyebrows. He pressed a ringless left hand to his chest. "You wound me, mademoiselle."

With his fantasy good looks he had to have an epic ego to match. "I sincerely doubt it."

She scanned the sidewalks again looking for her MIA friend. Anything would be better than embarrassing herself by drooling over something she couldn't have. Namely *him* or the five-dollar—make that euro—per-piece candy.

"You are looking for someone? A lover, perhaps?"

Lover. Just hearing him say the word, rolling that *R,* gave her goose bumps.

"A friend." One who'd been right behind her seconds ago. Candace must have ducked into one of the quaint shops nearby, either to purchase something wedding-related or to spy if she was the one responsible for this encounter. After all, stopping by the chocolate shop had been Candace's idea.

"May I assist you in locating your friend?"

He had the most amazing voice. Deep and velvety. Was the accent French or native Monégasque? Stacy could listen to him talk for hours.

No. She couldn't. She was here with Candace, the bride-to-be, and two other bridesmaids to help prepare for Candace's wedding the first weekend in July, not to have a vacation romance.

"Thanks, but no thanks." Before Stacy could walk away, Candace popped out of the shop next door waving a scrap of lace.

"Stacy, I found the most exquisitely embroidered…" She trailed off as she spotted the Adonis beside Stacy. Surprise arched her pale eyebrows. "…handkerchief."

Maybe this wasn't a set-up. Stacy rocked back on her heels, folded her arms and waited for the inevitable. Candace had naturally white-blond hair and big baby-blue eyes. Her innocent Alice-in-Wonderland looks tended to bowl men over. No doubt this guy would fall at Candace's dainty feet. Stacy had never had that problem and that suited her fine. *Forever* wasn't in the cards for her. She'd never trust a man that much.

"Mademoiselle." Tall, Dark and Tempting bowed slightly. "I am trying to convince *vôtre amie* to allow me to gift to her *un chocolat,* but she questions my intentions. Perhaps if I buy you both lunch she will see that I'm quite harmless."

Harmless? Ha! He radiated smooth charm in the way that only a European man could.

A cunning smile curved Candace's lips and her eyes narrowed on Stacy. Uh-oh. Stacy stiffened. Whenever she saw that expression, someone was getting ready to try and pull a fast one on the IRS, and that meant trouble for Stacy, their accountant. "I'm sorry, Monsieur…? I didn't catch your name."

He offered his hand. "Constantine. Franco Constantine."

Recognition sparked in Candace's eyes, but the name meant nothing to Stacy. "I've been looking forward to meeting you, Monsieur Constantine. My fiancé, Vincent Reynard, has spoken of you often. I'm Candace Meyers, and this is my one of my bridesmaids, Stacy Reeves."

Mr. Wonderful's considerable charms shone back on Stacy with the heat of the noonday sun. He offered his hand. Darn protocol. She'd been warned during the hours-long etiquette session delivered by Candace's soon-to-be sister-in-law that the inhabitants of this tiny country were quite formal and polite. Refusing to shake his hand would be an insult.

Franco's fingers closed around Stacy's. Warm. Firm. Lingering. His charisma spread over Stacy like butter on hot bread. *"Enchanté, mademoiselle."*

She snatched her hand free and blamed the spark skipping up her arm on static electricity caused by the warm, dry climate. A predatory gleam flashed in his eyes, and warning prickles marched down Stacy's spine. Dangerous.

He turned back to Candace. "May I offer my congratulations on your upcoming nuptials, Mademoiselle Meyers? Vincent is a lucky man."

"Thank you, monsieur, and I would love to accept

your luncheon invitation, but I'm afraid I'll have to decline. I have a meeting with the caterer in an hour. Stacy, however, is free for the rest of the afternoon."

Stacy's jaw dropped. She snapped it closed and glared at her friend. Embarrassment burned her cheeks. "I am not. I'm here to help you plan your wedding. *Remember?*"

"Madeline, Amelia and I have everything under control. You have a nice lunch. We'll catch up with you tonight before we go to the casino. Oh, and monsieur, the hotel has already received your RSVP to the wedding and the rehearsal dinner. Merci. Au revoir." Candace waggled her fingers and departed.

Stacy considered murder. But she'd read that Monaco had a truly impressive police force. There was no way she could get away with strangling the petite blonde in broad daylight on a crowded street, and rotting away in a European prison wasn't exactly the financially secure future she had planned for herself.

A plan now in jeopardy.

Worry immediately weighted her shoulders, but she slammed the barriers in place. *Stop it. This is Candace's month. Don't ruin it for her.*

But Stacy wasn't the type to hide her head in the sand. She knew she had some difficult days ahead. *Not now. You have a more urgent problem standing in front of you.* She blinked away her distressing thoughts and examined the man problem. She hadn't missed Candace's not-so-subtle hint that Franco Constantine was close enough to the Reynards to have been invited to the intimate rehearsal dinner for only a dozen or so guests.

In other words, *play nice.*

Franco grasped Stacy's bare elbow as if he knew making a fast escape topped her to-do list. She felt those long fingers clear down to her toes, and it rattled her that an impersonal touch from a stranger could wreak havoc on her metabolism.

"If you will give me but a moment, Mademoiselle Reeves, I must speak to the shopkeeper, and then I am at your disposal."

He escorted Stacy inside the chocolate shop. The heavenly aroma was enough to give her a willpower-melting sugar rush. After greeting the clerk, Franco commenced a conversation in rapid-fire French…or something that sounded like French.

Stacy shamelessly eavesdropped while perusing the offerings in the glass cases, but she only managed to translate every tenth word or so. Despite the money-back guarantee on the box of *Speak French in 30 Days* CDs she had listened to during the month prior to leaving Charlotte, North Carolina, she wasn't prepared for natives speaking the language at Grand Prix speed.

She caught a hint of crisp, citrus cologne and the hair on the back of her neck rose. Without looking over her shoulder she knew Franco stood immediately behind her. After bracing herself against his potent virility, she turned.

"Mademoiselle?" He held a sinful morsel aloft. What else could she do but take a bite? Her teeth sank into dark chocolate and a tart cherry. Her eyes closed and she fought a moan as she chewed. Ohmigod. Yum. Yum. *Yum.*

Cherry juice dribbled on her chin, but before she could wipe it away Franco's thumb caught it and pressed it between her lips. Knowing she shouldn't, but unable to think of a way to avoid it, Stacy swallowed and then darted out her tongue. The taste of blatantly sexy male combined with the most decadently rich chocolate she'd ever sampled slammed her with sexual arousal like nothing she'd ever experienced.

She dragged a sobering breath through her nose and

struggled to fortify her quaking ramparts. Before she could make her excuses and bolt, Franco lifted the second half of the candy to her mouth. She tried to evade his touch, but his thumb grazed her bottom lip, and then, holding her gaze, he lifted the digit to his mouth and licked the remaining confection from his skin with one slow swipe.

Her pulse stuttered. *Gulp.* Seduction in a suit. The chocolate hit her stomach like a wrecking ball, and the desire in Franco's eyes rolled over her like a heat wave, intensifying the disturbing reactions clamoring inside her.

"Shall we dine, mademoiselle?" He offered his arm in a courtly gesture.

There was no way she could go to lunch with him. Franco Constantine was too…too…too *everything.* Too attractive. Too confident. And judging by his apparel, too rich for her. She couldn't afford to become involved with such a powerful man. If she did, she could very well repeat her mother's mistakes and spend the rest of her life paying for it.

She backed toward the exit. "I'm sorry. I just remembered I have a…a dress fitting."

She yanked open the shop's glass door and fled.

Stacy slammed into the luxurious four-bedroom penthouse suite she shared with Candace, Amelia and Madeline at the five-star Hôtel Reynard. There were perks in having a friend marrying the hotel chain owner's son.

All three women looked up from the sitting area.

"Why are you back so soon?" Candace asked.

"Why did you throw me at that man?" Stacy fumed.

Candace tsked. "Stacy, what am I going to do with you? Franco is perfect for you, and the sparks between the two of you nearly set the shop's awning on fire. You should have had lunch with him. Do you know who he is? His family owns Midas Chocolates."

"The shop?"

"The globally famous company. Godiva's number-one competitor. We have a store in Charlotte. Franco's the CEO of the whole shebang and one of Vincent's best friends. He happens to be absolutely yummy."

No argument there. "I'm not looking for a vacation fling."

Madeline, a nurse in her early thirties, swept her long, dark curls off her face. "Then let me have him. From Candace's description before you arrived Franco sounds beyond sexy. A short, intense affair with no messy endings sounds perfect, and I won't have to worry about getting dumped because we'll be leaving after the wedding anyway."

A vacation affair. Stacy couldn't imagine ever being so nonchalant about intimacy. Intimacy made her feel vulnerable which is probably why she avoided it 99 percent of the time. In her nomadic life she'd never had a friendship that lasted more than a few months until she and Candace had bonded over an IRS audit three years ago when the large accounting firm Stacy worked for had assigned her to Candace's case. Having a friend was a new experience—one Stacy liked—even if she did sometimes feel like an outsider with this trio of hospital workers. Madeline and Amelia were Candace's friends, but Stacy hoped they'd be hers too by the time they left Monaco. Otherwise, if Candace moved away after the wedding Stacy would have no one. Again.

But the idea of Madeline with Franco made Stacy uneasy, which was absolutely ridiculous considering she'd spent less than ten minutes in the man's company, and she had no claim on him. Nor did she want one. Could she have a vacation romance? No. Absolutely not. It just wasn't in her cautious makeup.

"So, is he sexy?" asked Amelia, the starry-eyed romantic of the group.

The women's expressions told Stacy they expected some kind of response. But what? She knew nothing about girl talk. "Yes. B-but in a dangerous way."

"Dangerous?" the three parroted in unison, and then Candace asked, "How so? Franco seemed perfectly civilized to me and very polite."

None of these women knew about Stacy's childhood. And she didn't want to share the shameful details. Not now. Not ever. From the time Stacy was eight years old she'd known she and her mother were running from something every time they packed up—or not—and moved to a new city. Stacy hadn't figured out from what or whom until it was too late.

She swallowed the nausea rising in her throat. "Franco Constantine exudes power and money. If things went wrong between you, he could afford to track you down no matter how far you ran."

The women looked as if her answer made no sense to them. But it made perfect sense to Stacy. Her father had been a wealthy man. When he'd abused his wife the authorities had looked the other way, and when she'd run he'd used his resources to track her down. It had taken him eleven years to get even.

Wealthy, powerful men bent the rules to suit their needs, and they considered themselves above the law. Therefore, Stacy did her best to avoid them.

Franco Constantine definitely fell into the Avoid column.

* * *

Franco studied Stacy Reeves from across the casino. She was perfect for his purpose, exactly the type of female his father had described. And he would have her. No matter the cost. With women there was always a cost. The question was, would she be worth it?

Without a doubt.

In all his thirty-eight years he'd never had such an instant visceral reaction to a woman before. Not even to his ex-wife. From the moment he'd caught the reflection of Stacy's expressive eyes in the shop window this morning he had wanted her to look at him the way she looked at the chocolate. Ravenously.

The contrast between her demure dress, the reserve she wore like a cloak and those hungry eyes had intrigued him. The touch of her tongue on his finger had electrified him. If she could arouse him with such a small gesture, then he couldn't wait to experience the results of a more intimate encounter.

A quick call to Vincent had garnered him a few pertinent details about Mademoiselle Reeves and had confirmed that she was suitable for his needs. Yes, playing his father's game would indeed be pleasurable.

Franco ordered two glasses of champagne and made his way toward her. She stood back from the roulette table in the Café de Paris, observing the trio of women she'd come in with, but not participating in the gambling. In fact, she hadn't made a single wager since she'd arrived half an hour ago.

Tonight she'd twisted her shoulder-length chestnut hair up on the back of her head, revealing a pale nape, a slender neck and delicate ears he could not wait to nibble. Her floor-length gown—a sleeveless affair the color of aged ivory—gently outlined her curves but unfortunately covered her remarkable legs. She'd draped a lacy wrap over her shoulders and strapped on high-heeled gold sandals.

Elegant. Subtle. Desirable.

Mais oui. They would be magnificent together. Anticipation quickened his blood as he reached her side. He paused long enough to savor her scent. Gardenias. Sultry, yet sweet. *"Vous êtes très belle ce soir, mademoiselle."*

She startled and turned. "Monsieur Constantine."

"Franco." He offered a flute and ignored her stiff, unwelcoming posture. Her blue-green eyes, as changeable as the Mediterranean, were more azure than they'd been earlier in the day. What color would they be when they made love? He had every intention of finding out.

After a moment's hesitation she accepted the drink. *"Merci, Mon—"*

He covered her fingers with his on the fragile crystal, stilling her words. He wanted to hear his name on her lips. "Franco," he repeated.

Her lips parted and the tip of her tongue glided over her plump cherry-red flesh. He nearly gave in to the need to taste her, but he restrained himself with no small effort. She was skittish. He had to move slowly if he wanted to successfully close this deal.

"Franco." She gave his name the French pronunciation not the nasally American one he'd grown to hate during his graduate studies in the U.S.

He touched the rim of his glass to hers. *"À nous."*

She blinked and frowned. "I'm sorry?"

"To us, Stacy." She hadn't given him leave to use her name, and he was taking liberties—the first of many he intended to take with the alluring American.

Her eyes darkened and rejection stamped her fine features, but her cheeks pinked. "I don't think—"

"Monsieur Constantine," a feminine voice interrupted.

He reluctantly released Stacy's hand, and forcing his lips into a polite smile, turned to the trio of women. *"Bonsoir, mesdemoiselles."*

Vincent's fiancée introduced her friends, and while etiquette decreed Franco greet each lady, every fragment of his being remained focused on the woman who would soon be his lover. He noticed each nervous shift of Stacy's body, heard the sounds of her silk dress sliding over her skin the way his hands soon would, and he relished the catch of her breath as he deliberately brushed against her when he motioned for a waiter. He ordered beverages for each of the women and then held Stacy's gaze as she lifted her flute to her mouth. He mimicked her actions, wishing it were her warm lips against his instead of the cool glass.

The brunette Madeline sidled closer, making her interest known with her direct stare and come-hither stance while the auburn-haired Amelia blushed and looked away from the other woman's bold behavior. Both women were attractive, but he only had eyes for Stacy. Eventually, the trio turned back to the roulette wheel, affording him the privacy with his quarry he craved. Or as much privacy as one could have in a crowded casino.

"Have you wagered?" He knew she hadn't. He'd been watching.

"No."

He reached in his pocket, retrieved a handful of chips and offered them to her. "Try your luck?"

Her mouth opened, closed, opened again. "That's ten thousand doll—euros."

"Oui."

Wide-eyed, she backed away. "No. No, thank you."

"You wish to play for higher stakes? We can go to the Salon Touzeta, if you like."

"That's a private room."

"*Oui.*"

She looked at her friends, as if hoping they'd rescue her, but the wheel held their attention. "I don't gamble."

The more she refused, the more he wanted her. Was she playing hard to get to torment him or to raise her price? Very likely both. But he would win. Since his wife's betrayal he always did. "You owe me the pleasure of your company at a meal."

Wary eyes locked with his. "Why me? Why not someone who's interested and willing?" A slight tilt of her head indicated her brunette companion.

He shrugged. "Who knows why a body sings for one and not the other?"

Her lace wrap slipped from her shoulder. Franco lifted his hand and dragged a knuckle along the exposed skin of her upper arm. Her shiver before she stepped out of reach gratified him. She would be a responsive lover. "Have dinner with me, Stacy."

"I don't think that's a good idea."

"Have dinner with me," he repeated. "If you choose not to see me privately again afterward, then I will accept your decision."

Her chin lifted. "And if I refuse?"

Enjoying her cat-and-mouse game, he smiled. Her breath caught audibly. *Bien.* The attraction wasn't one-sided. "Then you and your friends will be seeing me quite often."

Slightly imperfectly aligned white teeth captured her bottom lip. How had she escaped the American obsession with a perfect smile? "One dinner. That's it?"

"*Oui, mademoiselle.* Because I can take no for an answer when the woman really means it."

Her shoulders squared. "I mean it."

He could not prevent a small smile. "*Non.* Your mouth says one thing, but your beautiful eyes say another. You want to have dinner with me."

Her cheeks flushed and her kissable lips compressed. She nodded sharply. "One dinner and then you leave me alone."

A surge of adrenaline shot through him at the small success. He touched his champagne flute to hers. Victory was within his grasp.

"*À nous*, Stacy. *Nous serons magnifiques ensemble.*"

Two

Nous serons magnifiques ensemble.

"We will be magnificent together." Stacy groaned and tossed her French-to-English-to-French dictionary on the coffee table. Her flushed skin and restlessness had nothing to do with the morning sun streaming through the hotel sitting room's open curtains or her eagerness to get out and see more of Monaco. The blame for her twitchiness could be placed solely on the desire in Franco's eyes last night when he'd said the mysterious phrase before taking his leave.

She'd dreamed about him, about those hungry eyes and that deeply cleft chin. No surprise there, since the man's blatant sexiness was an assault on her senses.

Franco Constantine was pursuing her and she had no idea why. The country was full of more beautiful, more sophisticated and more available women, but for some incomprehensible reason he wanted *her.* And, like it or not, as foolish as it might be—and it was incredibly foolish—she was attracted to him too. Scary, heady stuff. Her instincts told her to blow him off, but his friendship with Vincent made that tricky. Stacy couldn't afford to be rude and risk upsetting Candace.

Stacy shifted uneasily on the sofa. Surely she could manage a meal with him without getting in over her head? One dinner and then he'd promised to leave her alone. She'd eaten with a number of clients who'd implied they wanted her handling more than their books, and she'd resisted easily enough. Of course, she'd never been tempted like this. Franco was beyond her experience, and she couldn't help feeling as if she'd made a deal she would regret.

The door to Madeline's bedroom opened and the brunette shuffled into the sitting area. Her gaze roamed over the coffee carafe Stacy had ordered from room service and Stacy's empty cup. "My God, how long have you been up?"

"A few hours. My body clock is confused."

"So are you and Franco going to hook up?"

Stacy's blouse and pants abraded her suddenly warm flesh. "We're going to have dinner and then he's all yours."

Her skin prickled anew. Why did that bother her? Franco was too rich and powerful for her and far out of her league, but that didn't mean the other woman couldn't enjoy him.

"No thanks. I met someone after you came upstairs last night, and man oh man, is he *hot*." Madeline poured herself a cup of coffee.

This was the girl talk Stacy didn't do so well. Where were the boundaries? What was she supposed to ask? What topics should she avoid? She settled for a non-committal, "Oh?"

"Oh yeah." Madeline smiled as she sipped. "He's going to act as my tour guide after we kill our diets this morning sampling the different wedding cakes the hotel chef has prepared."

Amelia glided silently into the room. "Did I hear you say you're going out today? Me too, if for no other reason than to avoid Toby Haynes."

"Who?" Stacy asked. The name sounded vaguely familiar.

Amelia grimaced. "Toby Haynes, the race-car driver for the NASCAR team Reynard Hotels sponsors. It was a fire in his pit that burned Vincent."

"Speaking of Vincent, I guess you've both met the groom since he was a patient at the hospital where you work?" Stacy hadn't—just one more reason she felt like the outsider in the group. Story of her life.

"Yes and his cocky Casanova driver is here in Monaco and determined to be a pain in my backside," Amelia grumbled.

"Perhaps you and I could do the tourist thing together," Stacy suggested somewhat hesitantly. These women barely knew her and might prefer to spend their time with someone else.

"Sounds great. I'll get dressed." The suite doorbell chimed. Amelia, already on her feet, answered. When she turned around she held a beautiful bouquet of gardenias. "They're for you, Stacy."

Stacy's heart stalled. No one had ever sent her flowers. She accepted the fragrant arrangement, extracted the card and read the slashing black script. Tonight. 20:00. Franco.

"Who are they from?" Amelia asked.

Stacy couldn't find her voice. Were the gardenias a coincidence or had he actually noticed her perfume?

Madeline read the card over Stacy's shoulder. "Her

delicious chocolatier. Monaco operates on military time. He's picking you up tonight at eight. *Bon chance, mon amie.*"

Stacy forced an unsteady smile. She'd need more than luck to resist the sexy Frenchman.

Madeline rose, stretched and yawned. "Amelia, make sure Stacy has something suitably sexy to wear. And Stace, tuck a few condoms in your purse. Be prepared."

Prepared for Franco Constantine? Impossible.

Thanks to Candace and Amelia, Stacy was as prepared as she possibly could be for her evening with temptation in the form of Franco Constantine, minus the condoms which she most definitely would not need.

After sampling enough wedding cakes to send her blood sugar into orbit, she, Candace and Amelia had attempted to walk off the calories by touring La Condamine, the second-oldest section of Monaco, this morning, and then exploring the wonderful shops on the Rue Grimald in the early afternoon. Afterward the women had returned to the hotel and turned Stacy over to the spa staff for a facial, a manicure and a pedicure.

Stacy stood in front of the mirror and smoothed her hands over the gown they'd found in a European designer clothing outlet. Claiming it would be perfect for the rehearsal dinner, Candace had overridden Stacy's polite refusal and insisted on buying it for her. The sapphire fabric skimmed Stacy's figure without clinging, and the halter top gave her enough support that she didn't need a bra. She felt worlds more sophisticated in this gown than in anything she'd ever owned.

The phone rang and Stacy nearly jumped out of her gold sandals. Her suitemates were out. She crossed her bedroom and lifted the receiver. "Hello."

"*Bonsoir,* Stacy," Franco's deep voice rumbled over her. "I am in the lobby. Shall I come up?"

Her pulse fluttered like the flag over the prince's palace in a stiff breeze. Franco in her suite? Absolutely not.

"No. I'll come down." She hung up the phone and pressed a hand over her pounding heart. "One dinner. You can do this."

She draped her lace wrap over her shoulders, grabbed her gold clamshell evening purse and headed out the door. Her stomach stayed behind as the elevator swiftly descended from the penthouse to the lobby level. The doors opened and there he was, a six-foot-something package of irresistible—correction, completely resistible—male. Franco leaned against a marble pillar looking as rich and sinful as the chocolate he'd fed her. Stacy inhaled slowly and then moved forward on less-than-steady legs.

Franco spotted her and straightened. A midnight-blue suit and a shirt in a paler shade emphasized his eyes as his appreciative gaze glided from her upswept hair to her newly polished toenails before returning to her face. Every cell in her body quivered in the wake of the leisurely visual caress. He took her hand and bent over it, brushing his lips against her knuckles in a touch so light she could have imagined it. The whisper of his breath on her skin made her shiver.

He straightened and his intensely blue eyes burned into hers. "*Vous enlevez mon souffle,* Stacy."

There was no way she could translate even the simplest sentences when he looked at her or touched her that way. "I'm sorry?"

"You take my breath away."

"Oh." *Oh? That's it? That's the best you can come up with?* She tugged her hand and after a moment's resistance he released her. "Thank you. And thank you for the flowers. They're lovely. But you shouldn't have."

"I could not resist. Their fragrance reminded me of you." He offered his elbow. Stacy couldn't think of a courteous way to decline. Reluctantly, she threaded her hand through his bent arm and let him escort her from the cool interior of the hotel into the warm evening air. The lights of Monaco twinkled around them in the falling dusk. He paused outside the entrance. "The restaurant is only a few blocks away. Shall we walk? Or would you prefer a taxi?"

"You didn't drive?" She'd pictured him as the powerful-sports-car type, the kind who careened around the hairpin turns at breakneck speed like a Grand Prix driver.

"I drove. My villa is in the hills overlooking Larvotto. Too far to walk. But there is no parking near the restaurant."

She and Candace had taken the bus to Larvotto beach yesterday before she'd met Franco. In a country covering less than one square mile how likely was she to be able to avoid him until the wedding once this obligatory date ended? The odds weren't in her favor. "Let's walk."

A breeze stirred her hair. He caught a stray strand and tucked it behind her ear. The stroke of his finger on the sensitive skin along her jaw made her hormones riot and her pulse leap. "I would like to show you the view of Larvotto from my terrace. *C'est incroyable.*"

No matter how incredible the view she had no intention of seeing it. *Get this date on an impersonal footing.* "How is it that you know Vincent exactly?"

A knowing smile curved his lips, as if he knew she wanted to tread safer ground. He turned and led her down the sidewalk. "We shared an apartment during graduate school."

She frowned up at him. "But didn't Vincent go to MIT?"

"*Oui.*"

"You lived in the States? No wonder your English is so good." They turned the corner and the smell of Greek food from a nearby sidewalk café permeated the air. Her mouth watered and her stomach rumbled, reminding her that she hadn't eaten since the cake overdose this morning.

"Midas Chocolates distributes product on six continents. It pays to be fluent in several languages. Interpreters are not always available or reliable." He turned down a narrow alley she would have missed and stopped in front of a salmon-pink building with a red tiled roof. The only signage was the address in brass script above an unremarkable wooden door. "Here we are."

"This is a restaurant? It looks like a private residence." She'd hoped for something less intimate, like one of the numerous cafés lining the streets. She still couldn't get over how people brought their pets into restaurants. Stacy pulled her arm free on the pretext of adjusting her wrap and instantly missed his body heat even on this sultry night. *Get over it.*

"It is a secret kept by the locals. Good food. Good music. Exceptional company."

She cursed the flush warming her skin. The man issued compliments too easily, and she didn't intend to be swayed by his glib tongue. She'd been burned by insincere flattery once before. The humiliating aftermath wasn't something she wanted to relive.

He opened the door with one hand. The other curved behind her waist, palm splayed. She could feel the imprint through the thin fabric of her dress as he guided her forward. She hurried inside only to stop suddenly in the tiled foyer.

This must have been someone's home once, but now a maître d's stand occupied the niche beneath a curving staircase. The dining rooms Stacy could see to the left and right were furnished with half a dozen widely spaced, candlelit tables draped in white linens. Crystal and silver glinted in the flickering light, and music played quietly in the background. Intimate, but not unbearably so. Some of Stacy's tension eased. She could handle this.

But internal alarm bells rang as the hostess led them upstairs and finally stopped in a small private room with only one table. This very likely had once been a bedroom. Any plans Stacy might have had to keep this meal impersonal by watching the other patrons or trying to translate their conversations evaporated. The same music she'd heard downstairs drifted through exterior doors left open to a wrought-iron railed balcony. A gentle flower-scented breeze stirred the sheer curtains and made the candle flames dance.

Franco seated her. She startled when his fingertips brushed her upper arms, dragging her wrap back so that it bared her shoulders. He draped the lace over her chair, and then sat at a right angle to her, his knee touching hers beneath the table. She shifted away from the contact, but that didn't stop the buzz of awareness vibrating through her.

An older man entered. He and Franco held a rapid-fire discussion Stacy couldn't understand, and then he departed. "Was that French?"

"*Non*. Monégasque, the local dialect. It's a combination of French and Italian."

"Is that what you were speaking at your shop the day we met?"

"*Oui*, but French is the language spoken most often in Monaco. Do you speak French?"

"A little. I had the required two semesters in college and then I listened to some instructional CDs before coming here."

He covered her hand with his on the table and stroked his thumb over the inside of her wrist. Her pulse bolted like a startled rabbit. "You may practice on me, if you wish."

The spark in his eyes said she needn't limit her practice to the language. Stacy pulled her hand free and tangled her fingers in her lap. Looking away, she chewed the inside of her lip and tried to ignore the tension knotting low in her belly.

Their server returned with a tray of tiny stuffed tomatoes and mushrooms, poured the wine and departed even though they hadn't ordered yet.

"There aren't any menus?"

"*Non.* Trust me. You will not be disappointed."

Trust. He couldn't possibly know how difficult it was for her to trust anyone but herself. "What if I have food allergies?"

"Do you?"

"No," she admitted, feeling slightly ashamed for being difficult. She sipped her wine, sampled a crab-stuffed tomato and struggled to find a topic that would dilute the romantic atmosphere. "I was surprised to discover that Monaco relies heavily on French laws, including the French wedding ceremony and that they've removed the promise of fidelity from their vows. Why is that? Can French men not be faithful?"

Franco sat back, the smile slipping from his face. "I was faithful to my wife."

That doused the warmth in her belly. "You're married?"

"Divorced." And bitter by the sounds of that one bitten-off word. "You?"

"I've never been married." She'd never even been in

a long-term relationship. She'd had one clumsy encounter in high school and a brief intimate relationship with a guy from work. She shoved the bad memories back into their cave. "How long were you married?"

"Five years."

"What happened?" None of her business really, but she'd never met a divorcé who didn't want to talk about the unpleasant experience, and dull as it may be, hearing about someone else's dirty laundry was better than having Franco focus his seductive charms on her.

He shrugged, but the movement seemed stiff instead of casual. "We wanted different things."

"Do you have any children?"

"Non."

Had she imagined his hesitation? "Do you keep in touch?"

"I have not seen Lisette since the divorce."

"And you're okay with that?"

"Absolument."

Absolutely. She studied Franco, trying to gauge his sincerity. His direct gaze showed no doubts, no prevarications.

Her father hadn't willingly let go. Had that been because he'd loved her mother so much or because he'd considered her a possession, as the therapists had said? Stacy shook off the questions to which she'd never have answers and focused on her date. "Have you always lived in Monaco?"

"Non. I grew up outside Avignon, France. My family home is still there. I relocated my residence and Midas Chocolates headquarters here eight years ago after my divorce." His expression turned speculative. "You are trying very hard not to enjoy our evening, Stacy. Why is that?"

He read her too easily. "You're mistaken."

"Then prove me wrong by dancing with me."

When he put it that way how could she refuse? "I'm not much of a dancer."

He rose, pulled back her chair and offered his hand. "*Pas un problème*. I will guide you. Relax. I am not going to devour you before dessert."

But after dessert, then what? She wanted to ask, but she was too overwhelmed by his proximity to form the words. He laced his fingers through hers and rested their joined hands over his heart. She could feel the steady thump against her knuckles. He looped his other arm around her waist, spreading his palm over the base of her spine and pressing his chin to her temple. He held her as close as a lover with his thighs brushing hers. *Too close.* She tried to retreat, but the muscles hidden beneath his expensive suit flexed and held fast.

Her breath quickened. His scent, a blend of tangy lime and something totally masculine filled her nostrils. Her mouth dried and her skin steamed. She could barely hear the music to which he swayed over her thudding heart. Regardless of how unwise it might be she could feel herself weakening and wanting to give in to the desire that welled inside her each time he was near.

Pressing her palm against his lapel, she angled her upper body away from his. The move had the unfortunate consequence of aligning their faces. His mouth was much too near. If she rose on her tiptoes she could—

No. She couldn't.

"Where is the music coming from?"

His indulgent half smile sent a spiral of need through her. "There is a string quartet on the terrace."

He danced her through the open doors and then raised his arm for her to spin, but instead of letting her turn a full circle he caught her with her back to his chest and held her facing the flower-filled courtyard below the balcony.

Stacy gasped at the hot length of him spooning her back and then she lifted her gaze from the couples whirling around the flagstone dance floor and the air left her lungs in a long, appreciative, "Wow."

The rocky terrain of Monaco spread out in front of her. One thing about having a country clinging to the side of the mountain was that no matter where you looked you had a postcard-worthy view. Lights twinkled on the landscape like constellations blanketing a clear night sky, and in the distance she could see a brightly lit cruise ship anchored in the harbor. "It's beautiful."

His breath stirred the hair at her temple a second before his lips touched her skin. "And so are you."

He cupped her shoulders and turned her to face him. His palms glided down her arms and then he grasped the railing on either side of her, caging her between a twenty-foot drop and temptation. Either one could leave her broken. The warmth of the iron railing pressed her back, but the heat of his hips and thighs against hers set her afire. He feathered a kiss on one corner of her mouth and then the other. Teasing, fleeting, tantalizing kisses. Insubstantial and unsatisfying.

Her insides quivered and she wanted more. She wanted him to kiss her—to really kiss her—in a way she'd never wanted any man before, and that was dangerous territory. It had to be Madeline's talk of a vacation affair making Stacy yearn for what she couldn't have.

"Come home with me tonight, Stacy. *Je veux faire l'amour avec toi.*"

I want to make love with you. Blood rushed to her head and then drained with dizzying speed to settle low in her belly. She closed her eyes, bit her lip and shook her head. "I can't."

But she wanted to. She really, *really* wanted to. Sex had never been the exciting event for her that everyone claimed it was. She had a feeling it *would* be with Franco, but he was exactly the kind of man she'd sworn to avoid.

"*Non?* Because even though your mouth tells me no, this—" his head bent and his lips scorched a brief kiss over the frantically beating pulse in her neck "—this says yes."

Torn between desire and common sense she pressed her palms against his chest and prayed for the strength to keep refusing. A flash of movement beyond his shoulder caught her eye. She sent up a silent thank-you for the reprieve. "The waiter is back."

Ever so slowly Franco straightened, but the banked fires in his eyes promised "later." He released his hold on the railing beside her, stepped back and gestured for her to precede him into the room. Her legs were almost too weak to carry her.

Close call. Good thing this was their one and only date because she doubted she could continue saying no.

And saying yes would be far too dangerous.

"What is it you want, Stacy?"

Stacy's yearning expression as she gazed at the moonless midnight sky hit Franco with the impact of a sailboat boom. Whatever it was she wanted, he wanted to give it to her. Within reason, of course. And he would reap the rewards for his generosity.

She stopped in the corner of Hôtel Reynard's garden. "What do you mean?"

Why her? Why did this woman arouse him so easily? He didn't have the answer to the question he'd been asking himself since seeing her outside Midas yesterday, but he would find it. Sipping from her soft, fragrant skin at the restaurant tonight had only whetted his appetite. "What is it you wish for when you look upon the stars?"

"What makes you think I'm wishing for anything?"

"Your eyes give you away."

She bit her lip and hesitated. "Financial security."

"Money?" He almost spat the word. It always came down to money, but he had expected Stacy to at least make an attempt to hide her greed. Disappointment dampened his satisfaction over being right about her. Had he believed Stacy was different from any of his father's ex-wives or from his own? *Non.* Life had taught him a hard lesson. All women were the same. Yes, they came in different sizes, shapes and colors, but the craving for money is what made their mercenary hearts beat. And Stacy's greed played directly into his hands.

"My mother struggled to make ends meet when I was a child. Sometimes she had to choose between rent and food. Until I landed the job with the accounting firm I wasn't in much better shape, and now I—" She turned her back abruptly and dipped her fingers into the fountain. "I don't ever want to be in that position again."

"Your father?"

Her spine stiffened and her hands fisted. "Not part of the picture."

The personal insights—of which she'd shared few during dinner—softened him and he couldn't afford sentimentality. Time to close the deal. "And if I could offer you that financial security?"

"What do you mean?" She frowned at him over her shoulder. "Are you offering me a job?"

He joined her beside the fountain. "I am offering

you a million euros to be my mistress for the remainder of your time in Monaco. One month, is it not?"

Shock parted her lips and widened her eyes. "You're joking."

"*Non.* I realize you have obligations to Candace and Vincent, but the remainder of your time would be mine. There will be no declarations of love. No false promises. Just passion and for you, profit. *Tu comprends?*"

She shook her head as if confused. "No, I don't understand. Are you offering to pay me to sleep with you? *Like a prostitute?*"

"In France, being a man's mistress is a respected position."

"I'm not French. And sex for money is still sex for money. I'm not for sale, Monsieur Constantine. Not by the hour. Or the week. Or the month." She hugged her wrap closer and backed away without taking her gaze from his.

He pursued for each step she retreated. Nothing worth having ever came easily. And contrarily, while he respected her for not accepting his first offer, her avarice angered him. She wanted him and she wanted the money. The flutter of her pulse, the rapidity of her breathing and those very expressive eyes gave her away. Why deny it? Why deny them both?

"Why not profit from the chemistry between us, Stacy? You would be doubly rewarded. With the pleasure I can give you and with the financial security you crave."

She reached the end of the path both figuratively and literally. A low stone wall blocked her escape. Franco had restrained himself all evening, but he no longer could. He lifted a hand and stroked his knuckles along her cheekbone. "I promise you pleasure, Stacy."

She inhaled a ragged breath, but she didn't jerk away.

He slid his fingers into her silky hair and held her captive as he lowered his head to sample the mouth he'd craved for hours. Her lips were as sweet and soft as he'd imagined—more so. But she stood stiffly in his embrace with her mouth closed and her arms crossed in front of her, clutching the wrap.

Franco wasn't willing to accept defeat. He dragged his fingertips over the clasp of her dress at her nape and down the ridge of her spine. She shivered and her lips parted on a gasp. He swept inside. She tasted delicious, and he couldn't help delving deeper. Pulling her closer, he eased his hand beneath her wrap and caressed the satiny skin of her back.

The tension drained from her rigid muscles on a sigh and she curved into him, nudging her soft breasts into his chest and touching her tongue to his. Her palms flattened against his ribs and then slid to his waist. Victory surged through him, mixing with the desire already pumping through his veins. He stroked downward, curving his hand over her rounded bottom and pulling her flush against his erection.

She stiffened and jerked out of his arms. Her delicious breasts rose and fell rapidly, the tight nipples like tiny pebbles beneath her bodice. "No. I— You— No. I can't. I won't."

But he could see the indecision in her eyes. Whether she wanted to admit it or not, his proposition tempted her. "I will give you twenty-four hours to reconsider. *Au revoir*. Sleep well, *mon gardénia*."

He would not.

Three

A knock on the bedroom door jarred Stacy from her dream of a deep, velvety voice whispering illicit suggestions to her in French. Groggily, she sat up, finger-combed the hair from her eyes and tried to banish Franco Constantine from her mind. "*Oui?* I mean, come in."

The door opened and Candace breezed in. "*Bonjour.* You're a sleepyhead this morning."

Stacy glanced at the clock. Ten. She'd overslept, but thanks to the thoughts tumbling through her head after Franco's insulting offer, she hadn't fallen asleep until after four. She couldn't believe she'd actually lain awake debating the pros and cons of accepting and mentally converting euros to dollars. Worse, each time she'd dozed off she'd relived his reason-robbing kiss. "Sorry."

"No problem. But I need you to rise and shine. Vincent called. He heard about a villa that's about to come on the market, and he wants me to check it out. I need a second opinion and I know I can count on you to be practical." She perched on the edge of Stacy's bed. "Property sells fast here because there's such a high demand and a limited selection. Vincent's stuck at the new hotel site in Aruba until they work out this labor problem, and he's afraid we'll miss out on a good thing if we don't act fast."

Stacy shoved back the covers. "Then the move to Monaco is definite?"

Candace sighed. "It appears so. Vincent lives here for part of the year when he's not traveling for the hotel, but he says his condo overlooking the port in Fontvieille isn't big enough for three."

Surprise superseded the sinking feeling over the confirmation that Stacy's only friend was moving away. "Three?"

Candace winced. "Oops. I didn't mean to let that slip."

"You're pregnant?"

"Yes. Almost eight weeks. So it's a good thing we're getting married soon, isn't it?"

"I guess so." Stacy rose, but hesitated. "Should I offer my congratulations?"

"Absolutely," Candace said with a grin. She snatched Stacy into a bouncing hug and then released her. "I'm so excited I'm about to burst, but could you not tell anyone? We're not ready for Vincent's family to find out yet. I really shouldn't have said anything. I've been lucky so far because my morning sickness isn't so bad that I can't hide it or claim it's pre-wedding stress, and I can blame the need for naps on our late nights."

"You can trust me to keep your secret."

Trust. There it was again. That word. The one Stacy struggled with. "Give me thirty minutes to shower and dress."

She headed for the bathroom, shed her gown and stepped into the glass shower stall and then dunked her face under the hot spray to wash the grogginess away. The shower pelted her overly sensitized skin, dredging up remnants of dreams best forgotten.

Maybe a short-term affair was the best she could hope for given her trust issues. Should she reconsider Franco's offer? It wasn't as if he'd follow her across the Atlantic to try to force her to come back to him when he wasn't in love with her. And he'd stated up front that all he wanted was a month of her time.

But sex for money is still sex for money.

She lathered, rinsed and then shoved open the etched-glass shower door to glare at the wet woman in the steamy mirror. "I can't believe you are still debating this."

Would you have slept with him if he hadn't sprung this on you? Maybe. Probably. Because when he'd kissed her, saying no had been the last thing on her mind.

She snagged a towel and scrubbed briskly. "Let it go. You're grossly underqualified to be anyone's mistress."

But a million well-invested euros could set you up for life. No more worries about poverty. No more living paycheck to paycheck. And you won't have to panic if you can't find another job right away.

"No. Too risky. I don't have to see him again until the wedding. Forget his obscene offer. Forget him." With that settled she nodded at her reflection and reached for her makeup bag.

Twenty minutes later she zipped on another one of the sundresses she'd bought before getting laid off, this one a knee-length mint green number, stepped into her walking sandals and then yanked open the door to the sitting room and spotted the one man she'd hoped to avoid. Her stomach plunged. "What are you doing here?"

Franco set down his coffee cup and rose from the sofa. His gaze raked her from head to toe in a long, slow sweep, and Stacy couldn't stop hers from doing the same to him. She hadn't seen him in casual clothing before. His white short-sleeved shirt exposed the thick biceps his suits had only hinted at and his belted khakis revealed a flat stomach and narrow hips. A swimmer's body.

"*Bonjour,* Stacy. I am your chauffeur today."

She caught herself watching his lips move as he spoke and remembering how they'd felt against hers, and then his words sank in. Alarm clamored through her. She looked from Franco to Candace sitting in a chair. "What?"

Her friend smiled smugly. "Didn't I mention that Franco is the one who told Vincent about his neighbor's decision to sell?"

"No. You didn't. So you have your second opinion. You don't need me."

"Are you kidding? No offense, Franco, but you're a man. I need a woman's opinion."

He shrugged his wide polo-covered shoulders. "None taken."

Stacy wanted to lock herself in her room. Part of being able to resist his indecent proposition depended on not having temptation shoved in her face at every turn.

"Please, Stacy," Candace wheedled.

Stacy stifled a grimace. How could she refuse when Candace and Vincent were treating her to a month in paradise? Even if she had a sneaking suspicion the request for those consecutive weeks off might have contributed to her getting laid off. "All right."

Franco's broad palm gestured to the tray of pastries on the table. "We will wait for you to eat."

If she put food in her agitated—compliments of Franco—stomach she'd be sick. Stacy poured a glass of orange juice, guzzled it with inelegant haste and then returned her glass to the tray. "I'm ready."

Franco's knowing look made her twitchy. Stacy kept her gaze averted from him as he escorted them downstairs and outside. She could feel his steady regard as they waited for the valet to bring his car around, and when Candace became distracted by something in the hotel gift shop's window and wandered a few yards away he took advantage by moving closer. Stacy's senses went on red alert.

"You slept well?" he asked quietly.

"Of course," she lied without lifting her gaze above the whorl of dark hair exposed by the open neck of his shirt.

"I did not. Desire for you kept me awake. Each breeze through my open window felt like your lips upon my skin."

Her breath caught and her pulse stuttered. She glared at him. "You said I wouldn't have to see you again if I had dinner with you."

"*Non.* I said you wouldn't have to see me alone, *mon gardénia.*"

"Stop that. I am not your anything."

"But you will be." The certainty in his voice rattled her already fragile composure. "I cannot wait to have you in my bed, Stacy."

Were Frenchmen born knowing how to talk a woman out of her clothes? "Don't hold your breath."

An expensive-looking black sedan—Maserati made sedans?—rolled to a stop in front of them. The valet hopped out and circled the car to open the doors for the women while Franco moved to the driver's side. Stacy stepped toward the back, but Candace cut in front of her. "You sit up front. The hairpin turns make me nervous, and my stomach would appreciate the back seat. It's a little dicey this morning," she whispered the last phrase.

No fair playing the morning-sickness card. "Fine."

Stacy slid into the leather passenger seat beside Franco. Even with the console between them in the spacious interior, his presence overpowered her. His hand seemed larger on the gearshift just inches from her knee and his shoulders immense in the enclosed space. She inhaled his cologne with every breath.

He turned his head and their eyes met for heart-stopping seconds. "Fasten your seat belt, Stacy."

She complied with unsteady hands, and then Franco drove away from the coast and wound his way up the rocky mountainside. Although the steep drop-offs had Stacy clutching the sides of her seat, she had to admit the view was breathtaking.

"Do you see Larvotto?" he asked a few moments later. The blue-green Mediterranean glimmered beyond the three crescents of beach.

"Yes," Stacy answered when Candace didn't, and then she twisted in her seat to see her friend's pale face. "Franco, could you open the windows a bit?"

"Bien sûr." He quickly checked the rearview mirror and then the windows silently lowered. Slowing the vehicle, he turned down a tree-lined street which appeared to have been chiseled from the mountainside. "Candace, *tu va bien?*"

"Ah…*oui.* I'm fine." She clearly wasn't. "Are we close?"

He stopped the car in the quiet roadway. "We are here, but my house is two doors over if you need to lie down."

"No. I'll be better once I get out of the car. I keep remembering Princess Grace drove off one of these roads and died."

"Not this one." He turned into a driveway leading to a cream-colored stucco house with a red tiled roof that looked like something from a Mediterranean vacation guide. Stacy climbed from the car and immediately turned to check on Candace.

"Who would have believed pregnancy would give me vertigo?" Candace whispered. She linked arms with Stacy and followed Franco down the stone path to the front entrance. He pulled a key from his pocket and unlocked the door.

Stacy balked. "There's no real estate agent?"

"*Non.* My neighbor has only recently decided to sell. He is abroad, but left me a key."

He gestured for them to precede him. Stacy let Candace go first. Franco caught Stacy's hand and held her back. Her heart stuttered. Was he going to badger her about his offer? Or kiss her again?

"Is this part of the pregnancy?" he asked.

She blinked. "You know?"

"*Oui.* Vincent asked me to keep an eye on her, so you will be seeing a lot of me, Stacy."

Not good news when her plan to resist him was already on shaky ground. She tugged her hand free before the heat of his palm against hers melted her resistance. "She claims the pregnancy is giving her vertigo."

He looked adorably confused. *"C'est possible?"*

"I have no idea. I know nothing about being pregnant."

He nodded and then escorted her inside. To Stacy, who'd lived in low-budget accommodations all her life, the home looked like something from the *Architectural Digest* magazines her accounting firm—*former* firm— kept in the waiting area. Talk about lifestyles of the rich and famous…. She couldn't even begin to guess how many millions of euros this place cost.

She trailed after Candace who'd apparently recovered enough to examine one gorgeous room after another in the spacious home. When the women returned to the living room where Franco waited, he pushed open the door to the terrace behind the house. Candace wandered off to explore every nook and cranny of the gardens.

Stacy stayed on the flagstone patio, letting her eyes devour the flower-filled landscape. She had only vague memories of the landscaped yard of the house she'd lived in until she was eight. The places she and her mother had lived afterward had been barren and devoid of color. One day, Stacy vowed, she'd own a home a fraction as beautiful as this. One terrace of the two-level lot held a large pool, and another, a maze of roses. Living here would be a fantasy come true. And the view—

"C'est incroyable, non?" Franco said directly behind her seconds before his muscular frame spooned her back. His arms surrounded her and his fingers laced through hers on the iron railing, holding her captive when she would have ducked away.

He had to stop doing that. Every feminine particle in her urged her to lean into him and relish in the novel sensations he sent bubbling through her, but her survival instincts screamed *Run, danger ahead*. The emotional push-pull left her breathless and disoriented.

"But my view is better. You will see," he added in a deep voice that stroked her skin like a caress, peaked her nipples and made her quiver. "Come, we must go. Candace looks in need of a chaise and a cool drink."

He stepped away, taking his body heat with him and leaving Stacy surprisingly chilled in the warm late-morning air. How could she be so affected by a man she barely knew?

Candace had indeed paled as she slowly climbed the

stairs to the main patio. Stacy crossed to her side, but her friend waved away her concern as they returned to the car.

Stacy struggled to fortify her resistance to Franco as they pulled onto the road, but her internal alarms shrieked when he slowed the vehicle and turned into a driveway two doors down. "Is this your house? Why are we coming here?"

"Did I forget to tell you Franco invited us for coffee?" Candace asked from the back seat.

Stacy turned to scowl at her. "Yes. You did."

"Oops." There was no *oops* about it. The bride was matchmaking and not at all subtly.

"How kind of him." Not kind. Manipulative.

The satisfied smile playing about Franco's delectable lips made Stacy seethe. He'd wanted her in his home and he'd manipulated circumstances to make it happen. The man was set on seduction, and she had a sinking feeling he wasn't thwarted often or easily. And then she spotted his house and gasped.

The large two-story rectangular villa had been painted a buttery yellow. The trim on the second-floor balcony and around the arched windows gleamed white in the morning light. "Palladian style, right? How old?"

"Correct. The original structure was built in 1868. It has been renovated many times. Most recently by me. You have studied architecture, Stacy?"

"No. I just like to read."

Candace scooted forward. "Stacy's a bit of a history buff. She devoured any research material on Monaco and the Mediterranean she could get her hands on before our trip."

A blush warmed Stacy's cheeks. "Your home's beautiful, Franco."

"*Merci.* Wait until you see the inside. And the gardens,

of course. They are lovely by moonlight." His gaze held hers and last night's invitation lingered in his eyes. She would have seen his gardens by moonlight if she'd come home with him after dinner. She still could if she became his mistress.

Her heart accelerated and her mouth dried. "Too bad we'll miss that."

The twitch of his lips as he climbed from the car said he hadn't missed her sarcasm, and then Candace poked Stacy's shoulder. "Cut it out."

Stacy twisted in her seat. "Quit matchmaking."

The car doors opened. Franco stood in the driveway. "Mesdemoiselles?"

He helped them from the car and then turned toward the house. Stacy caught herself admiring the fit of his trousers over the tight globes of his derriere as she followed him up the stone walk toward the covered front entrance. European men wore pants that fit—none of that super-baggy stuff American guys currently favored. The fitted style certainly suited Franco.

After unlocking the tall arched door he motioned for them to enter with the sweep of his arm. Candace led the way. Stacy reluctantly followed with Franco on her heels. She couldn't help feeling that by entering his domain she was crossing a point of no return.

Her first impression was one of high ceilings and sun-drenched spaces rolling on and on in acres of cool, glossy white marble floors. Wide arches divided the individual rooms, but the glass-paned doors to each stood open. To her left a suspended staircase circled upward, and in front of her a pair of round marble columns separated a foyer bigger than her den back home from a living room larger than her entire apartment.

She glanced at Franco and found him watching her intently. "Welcome to my home."

"It's um…" Gorgeous. Huge. Intimidating. "Very nice."

The million euros he'd offered her should have been a clue to Franco's wealth, but she'd had no idea he was filthy rich. Most women would find his affluence a turn-on. But for Stacy it had the opposite effect.

"We will have refreshments on the terrace." He led them through the living room. Stacy trailed Candace past the dark wooden tables that interspersed the black leather sofas and chairs. Woven carpets in shades of ivory, black and red dotted the floor.

Red. Like blood on the white floor. She shuddered and skirted around the rugs.

Curved floor-to-ceiling French doors punctuated the exterior wall revealing an expansive patio that put the last home's to shame. Franco opened one of the doors. His bare forearm brushed Stacy's as she passed through. Accidental? Doubtful. Awareness trickled over her. She moved into the sunshine to bake the goose bumps away.

Candace crossed directly to the swimming pool located at the far end of the stone terrace and leaned over the railing. "Stacy, you have to see this. The pool pours over the side of the patio in a waterfall."

"It empties into a whirlpool below," Franco told her and then he moved closer to Stacy, dipped his head until his breath teased her ear. "Half of the spa is concealed beneath the house by the falling water. I would like to make love to you there."

Stunned by his sneak attack, Stacy struggled to catch her breath and formulate a prickly reply, but her brain refused to cooperate. Her heart raced and her palms moistened. Her skin flushed hot and then cold when she realized that in the split second before reason intervened she'd wanted to make love with him too.

That kiss clearly addled your thinking.

"Make Candace sit and rest," he murmured quietly along with a brief, but electrifying caress over the curve of her waist. "I will return with refreshments momentarily." He went inside.

Shakily, Stacy crossed to the railing. Not because she wanted to see the whirlpool below and visualize the decadent scene Franco had planted in her head. No, definitely not that. She looked because the view of Monte Carlo and Larvotto Beach from Franco's patio was more beautiful than any of the postcards she'd bought as souvenirs of her trip.

To her right a stone staircase wound down to the lower level of the terraced yard. Trees and flowers dappled the lush slope of green grass with shadows and brilliant splashes of color. And fight as she might, Stacy couldn't prevent her gaze from dropping to the exposed half of the spa.

Why not? You want to.

She'd have to be crazy to risk it. From what she'd seen of his home Franco had to be ten times wealthier than she'd suspected. *And ten times sexier. He arouses you with nothing more than words. Why not give those big hands a try? It's not like you're ever going to let yourself fall in love with anyone. So why hold out?*

"Amazing, isn't it?" Candace interrupted Stacy's illicit thoughts. "I can't imagine living like this."

Stacy pushed aside the tantalizing images. "Neither can I. It must be a real power rush to have enough money to buy whatever you want. We should find a shady spot to sit and wait for Franco."

"He knows about the baby, doesn't he? Did you tell him?" Candace asked as they strolled toward the shady covered loggia.

"Yes, he knows. Vincent told him."

"I should have guessed Vincent would. He's very protective, and he would trust Franco not to betray our little secret." Candace plopped onto a rattan lounge chair covered by a deep white cushion, lay back and closed her eyes. "Wouldn't it be great to live in paradise like this only two doors apart?"

Stacy chose a chair. She couldn't relax in Franco's home—not with him stalking her like a predatory beast. And then Candace's meaning sank in. "There's nothing like that between Franco and me."

"Oh please. He undresses you with his eyes whenever he thinks I'm not looking. You can't tell me you haven't noticed."

Stacy *had* noticed, and she was ashamed to admit the desire simmering in Franco's gaze sent a reciprocal surge through her. At least she assumed that achy, itchy tension was desire. No one had ever made her feel as attractive or feminine in her life, and she'd certainly never looked at a man and wondered how his hands would feel on her body. What would it be like to experience that kind of passion? Did she dare risk it?

"Sex is all he wants."

"Honey, that's all any man wants at first." Candace yawned.

"True. But I'm not looking for a husband."

"Then why not do as Madeline suggested and enjoy what Franco's offering? Other than Vincent, Franco is unquestionably the sexiest man I've ever met. My God, his accent just melts me, and you have to admit he's not hard on the eyes. You'll never get a chance to live like this again. I confess I'm thoroughly enjoying the five-star treatment. But I wish Vincent was here."

Stacy wanted to tell Candace about Franco's insulting proposition, but she didn't dare because telling her friend meant confessing how tempting Stacy found the offer. "Doesn't Vincent's wealth ever…concern you?"

Candace rolled to her side and met Stacy's gaze. "You mean do I worry that he'll use his money and influence to hurt me? No, I don't. I trust Vincent. Stacy, you haven't said much about your past, but from the bits you've let slip I'm guessing some rich guy did a number on you. Whoever he was, you can't let him screw up the rest of your life. Not all rich men are jerks. And you know, I don't think you've dated or gotten laid since I met you. Aren't you overdue?"

"I've dated." Twice, in three years. Pitiful. But sex? No. She needed more than a couple of dates to let her guard down with someone. If she ever could. And now that she thought about it, she probably never had, which was very likely the reason her last brief relationship had ended.

"Stacy, you've heard my sob story about the visiting surgeon who wooed me, bedded me and then returned home to the wife and kids I didn't know he had. Loving and losing that jerk burned me, but then I met Vincent and realized that sometimes you have to trust your heart and move on or be stuck in the past forever." Candace yawned again. "Do you mind if I close my eyes until Franco gets back?"

"No, go ahead." Questions and doubts tumbled through Stacy's mind. Was she stuck in the past? Had she given her father and that one tragic night too much power over her life? Or was she merely being prudent? If she didn't face her fears would she continue running from them indefinitely? Running, the way she and her mother had done for eleven years of Stacy's life. After losing her mother, Stacy had sworn she'd stop running and put down roots.

Roots a million euros could buy.

She stared at the pool and the water pouring over the ledge. She'd said no to Franco's proposition and she'd meant it. Deep in her heart she knew sleeping with him for the money was the wrong thing to do, but her practical side couldn't completely dismiss the idea of a lifetime of financial security in return for a month of intimacy with a man she desired like no other.

The mental debate circled her thoughts like an annoying, persistent mosquito no matter how often she swatted it away. Was Franco's offer too good to be true or was this an opportunity to put her past to bed and secure her future?

Trusting him when she barely knew him went against everything her mother had taught her about being wary of strangers. If only she had more time to discover whether power and money had corrupted Franco, but he'd given her only twenty-four hours to make a life-altering decision. Half of those hours had already passed.

The rattle of crockery drew her gaze to Franco crossing the terrace with a tray in his hands. His biceps bulged under the weight. He paused, his gaze landing on Candace. "She sleeps?"

Candace didn't stir. Stacy shrugged. "I guess so."

He nodded toward the house, turned and retraced his path. Stacy hesitated, but then rose and followed. Franco's kitchen was a combination of old-world charm and modern convenience—a cook's dream of dark cabinetry, glossy countertops and top-of-the-line appliances.

The aroma of freshly brewed coffee filled the air. He set the tray on the table. "You did not eat breakfast. You must be hungry."

She studied the array of fruits, cheeses and chocolates. He also had a coffee carafe, a pitcher of orange juice and a couple of bottles of sparkling water. "Your housekeeper did this?"

"You think I am not capable of feeding my guests?"

"I don't know you well enough to know what to think." And therein lay the crux of her dilemma. Part of her wanted to explore the way he made her feel and part of her wanted to play it safe.

"My housekeeper comes twice a week. The rest of the time I fend for myself. Eat, please. Or would you prefer I feed you?" He lifted a candy. "These are the chocolate-covered cherries you enjoyed the day we met. I would like to taste it on your tongue."

Her breath snagged. She staggered back a step, but that wasn't nearly far enough. She needed a break from his overwhelming charisma because she was perilously close to caving. "I need the restroom."

"*Bien sûr.* This way." He popped the chocolate into his mouth and led her down a hall, through a set of arched double doors, and he then stepped aside and gestured to another door. *"C'est là."*

Stacy stood frozen in what could only be Franco's bedroom. A huge wooden bed covered in a red-and-gold nubby silk spread dominated the otherwise black-and-white space. "You, uh…don't have a guest bathroom?"

"Of course, but I wanted to see you in my bedroom, and I wanted you, *mon gardénia,* to imagine yourself in my bed and in my bath with my hands and my mouth on your skin. As I have done."

The tantalizing vision exploded in her mind in vivid

Technicolor, and a fine tremor rippled over her. Her heart hammered and her mouth dried.

Franco didn't attempt to touch her or coerce her by using the desire clearly visible in his blue eyes. He'd simply stated his wishes and left the rest to her.

One step and she'd have financial security for life and a lover who might possibly make sex enjoyable rather than endurable. And when she left there'd be an ocean between them.

She closed her eyes and inhaled deeply.

Play it safe? Or risk it all?

Four

"Okay. You win, Franco. I'll be your mistress for a month. But I have conditions," Stacy added before Franco could speak. She dodged when he reached for her. There was no way she could think with his hands on her.

Cynicism replaced the triumphant spark in his eyes. He leaned against the doorjamb and folded his arms over his broad chest. Cocky. Arrogant. Male. "And they are?"

She had to be insane to agree to this, but if she hoped to survive it then she had to maintain some control and keep the affair on a business footing. What she needed were boundaries and rules. Safeguards. With her heart racing, she dampened her lips.

"I don't want Candace, Amelia and Madeline to know about the money." Or any chance of friendship would be destroyed. She wasn't even sure she could respect herself once this was over. She hadn't had to go hungry or bail on a landlord in the middle of the night since her mother's death, but the memories of the hunger pains and furtive escapes of her childhood lingered. And then there was her current employment—*un*employment—status to deal with once she returned home. She'd had excellent reviews at work, but still, the job market was tight and hers wasn't the only company downsizing. Add in a dwindling saving account and...

Focus on the future. With careful investing you'll never be poor or homeless again.

He inclined his head. "Anything else?"

"I won't spend the night." Call her crazy, but she didn't want to let her guard down enough to literally sleep with him.

A single dark eyebrow lifted. *"Non?"*

"No. My duty is first and foremost to Candace. We begin most days going over the wedding planning stuff. My time with you can't interfere with that."

"I shall return you to the hotel before your morning meetings."

Suddenly, she felt dirty. "When and how will I get paid?"

His nostrils flared and his generous lips thinned. "Your bridesmaid duties will end when Vincent and Candace depart on their honeymoon trip following the reception. You are scheduled to leave Monaco the next day, *oui?*"

"Oui. I mean, yes."

"You will spend your last night in Monaco with me. The entire night, Stacy." It was an order not a question. "In the morning I will give you a cashier's check and drive you to the airport, but should you not fulfill any part of our agreement, then no money."

Her breath hitched and her pulse thumped as loudly as the helicopter taxi they'd taken to Monaco from the Nice-Côte d'Azur airport. "And if you decide to end it early?"

A muscle in his jaw bunched and then his lips curled in a slow, devastatingly sexy smile. "I assure you I never finish anything prematurely."

It took a second for his meaning to sink in and when it did her cheeks caught fire. "But if you do?"

"You will be paid."

"Okay." Now what? Did they shake hands over the deal or—

Franco captured her elbows and tugged her forward. His mouth slanted over hers in a hard kiss as if she'd angered him. Stacy stiffened as second, third and fourth thoughts descended like an avalanche. She was on the verge of pulling away and cancelling their arrangement when his lips softened and parted. The fingers grasping her arms loosened and swept up to sift through her hair and cradle her head in his hands.

His mouth lifted, realigned and returned, seducing a response from her with long, luxurious turn-her-muscles-to-mush kisses. She tasted a hint of dark chocolate on his tongue. Chocolate and Franco, a hot and heady combination. His hands painted warm stripes down her back, over her hips and then around to her waist, before rising until his thumbs rested just below her bra.

Her breasts ached in anticipation of his touch, and desire simmered inside her. She couldn't believe her body could respond with such abandon when she knew Franco was using her. She'd been used before. But she wasn't a lonely seventeen-year-old trying to fit in at her third high school anymore. She wouldn't expect love or forever this time, so she wouldn't be hurt.

"Hey guys, where'd you go?" Candace's voice called out from somewhere in the house.

Franco slowly lifted his head, his lips clinging to

Stacy's for several heartbeats. His passion-darkened gaze speared hers. "Tonight we begin."

She couldn't find her voice, but she managed a stiff nod.

Dear God, what had she done?

She'd agreed to trade sex for security. She couldn't help feeling she'd sold her soul to the devil, and she hoped she didn't live to regret it.

Anticipation made Franco edgy. He hated it. He was, after all, a man of thirty-eight and not a boy of eighteen. His hormones did not seem to know the difference tonight.

Impatience urged him to take Stacy directly to his bedroom, to strip away her modest black dress and cover her ivory skin with his hands and mouth, but her pale, anxious expression cooled his ardor. Standing in his foyer, she looked torn between running back into the night and fulfilling her end of the bargain no matter how unpleasant.

Where was the passionate but reserved woman he'd left at the hotel mere hours ago? The one who'd kissed him with such fervor this morning that only her friend's untimely interruption had prevented him from consummating their agreement against his bedroom door? He wanted that passionate woman back. And he would have her. Stacy would be warm and pliant in his arms and his bed before the night ended. And he would win. The woman. And the contest with his father.

He pitched his keys onto the credenza, halted behind her and curved his hands over her shoulders. She startled. "May I take your wrap?"

"Oh, um, yes, sure." She darted a quick, nervous glance at him and tension tightened inside him as an unacceptable thought pierced his conscience.

"Stacy, are you a virgin?" He'd had lovers, dozens of them, but no virgins. Experienced women understood that all he wanted was the transitory pleasure of their bodies. An innocent might expect more.

Color rushed to her cheeks and she ducked her chin. "No. But I…this…is new to me. I don't know where to begin."

His clenched muscles loosened. Nerves he could handle. Regrets and crying, he could not. He had intended to satisfy his hunger for Stacy first tonight and then his less demanding appetite for dinner afterward, but perhaps he would alter his strategy. Dinner first. Pleasure later. Anticipation would only heighten the senses. "Leave that to me."

Franco stroked the lace down her arms, caught her elbows and pulled her back against his front. Her bottom nudged his thighs. The urge to thrust his growing arousal against her gnawed at him, but he would coax Stacy until she was breathless and eager for his possession, as she had been earlier. He nuzzled through her silky hair and sipped from the warm, fragrant juncture of her neck and shoulder. She shivered.

Bien, the responsive woman still lurked beneath her pale and tense exterior. He encircled her with his arms and spread his palms over the slight curve of her abdomen. "I will ensure your pleasure tonight, *mon gardénia.*"

A little *hic* of breath lifted her breasts, and though he wanted to cup her soft flesh in his hands and stroke his thumbs over the tips pushing against the fabric of her dress, he could wait. But not long.

"We will dine on the terrace." He released her and led her through the living room, draping her wrap over the back of a chair as they passed. On the patio he seated her, lit the candles he'd placed in the center of the table and then poured the cabernet franc. After removing the lid covering the crudités and setting it aside, he sat and lifted his glass. *"À nous et aux plaisirs de la nuit."*

She made a choked sound. "I'm sorry?"

"To us and the pleasures of the night," he translated.

"That's what I thought you said," she muttered into the bowl of her glass and took a healthy sip of wine.

He removed a small box from his suit pocket and placed it on the table in front of her. He had planned to give her this after savoring her delicious body, but why wait? Stacy needed coaxing, and in his experience jewelry always made women more amenable. "For you."

The line formed between her eyebrows. "You don't have to buy presents for me."

He would make sure she wore it when she met his father. He shrugged. "Open it."

She set aside her wine, hesitantly opened the box and stared. Seconds later she snapped the lid closed and shoved the box toward him. "I can't accept that."

He stilled. "You don't like diamonds?"

"Of course, but—"

"You have a diamond bracelet?"

"No." She closed her eyes, swallowed and then met his gaze. "Franco, we already have a deal. Can we just stick to it?"

He masked his surprise and puzzlement. He had never had a woman refuse his gifts before—especially not expensive jewelry. "Perhaps I wish to see you wearing the diamonds. And nothing else."

"Oh." Her cheeks flushed. *"Oh,"* she repeated and fiddled with the stem of her glass for a moment before looking at him through her thick lashes. It was a worried glance rather than a flirtatious one. "Diamonds do it for you, huh?"

He reared back. "No, diamonds do not *do it for me.* I merely wished to give you a gift."

"And I'm telling you that you don't have to."

What game was she playing? He examined her face, her guileless eyes. Was her innocence an act? It had to be. Otherwise she never would have accepted his offer. He rose. "I will return momentarily with dinner."

In the kitchen he mechanically plated the smoked mozzarella with sundried tomatoes and peppercorns in a puddle of olive oil while mulling over Stacy's refusal. She had to have an ulterior motive. He retrieved the filet *barole* from the warming oven, divided it onto dishes and poured the cognac and mushroom sauce over it.

Was she after a bigger prize? Perhaps a diamond ring instead of a bracelet? If so, she would not get one from him. He would never marry again. His one and only failed marriage had taught him that women were selfish creatures. Nothing mattered except their wants. *Nothing.*

Not even life.

His throat tightened at the memory of the babe his wife had carelessly discarded without his knowledge or consent. Had there not been complications with the abortion, causing the doctors to hospitalize Lisette and call Franco to Paris, he would never have known her "shopping trip" was a lie or that she had conceived his child—a child she did not want. And then there were his father's costly divorces. Stacy was no different from any other greedy woman. She had revealed her true nature by accepting his terms. He set his jaw.

Non. He did not trust women. He enjoyed them *briefly* and then he moved on. But he was a generous lover both in bed and out. Stacy would have no complaints.

Stacy was not at the table when he carried the tray outside. He scanned the dimly lit terrace and found her in the shadows by the railing overlooking the garden below. Or perhaps she studied the whirlpool. His arousal stirred in anticipation.

After placing the meal on the table he joined her. "Dinner waits."

She turned slightly. A gentle breeze lifted tendrils of hair. "I'm sorry, Franco. I didn't mean to hurt your feelings by refusing the bracelet. I just don't think we should try to make this into something it's not."

Again she surprised and perplexed him. "What would that be?"

"A relationship."

His thoughts exactly, but hearing her voice them disturbed him in an inexplicable way. "We are going to be lovers, Stacy. We will have a relationship, albeit a temporary one. And if I choose to buy things for you then I do so because it pleases me, not because I expect more from you than our original agreement. Now come. We will eat and then we will pursue our mutual pleasure."

Would she be worth a million bucks?

Stacy's stomach clenched. She had absolutely no appetite and her taste buds had deserted her, but she forced down another bite of tender steak to drag out the meal as long as possible. Throughout dinner she'd watched Franco's hands as he cut his meat or cradled his wineglass, and her mind had raced ahead. Those hands would soon be on her. Cupping her flesh. Stroking her skin. Was that anticipation or dread making her dizzy?

What if after they did this Franco decided she wasn't worth the money? After all, she wasn't experienced. She could count her intimate encounters on one hand, and her knowledge was limited to the basics—which in her opinion were overrated. If he expected anything like the fancy stuff she'd read about in the women's magazines she'd borrowed from work, then he'd be disappointed.

Franco placed his knife and fork on his empty plate. "The food is not to your liking?"

Chew. Chew. Chew. Gulp. "It's delicious. Did you cook?"

His knowing eyes called her a liar. "No. It is catered. Perhaps your appetite lies elsewhere."

Her fork slipped, the tines screeching across the china. She winced. Franco had probably never encountered a more gauche female. He was sexy and sophisticated down to the soles of his shoes and she was…not. So why had he chosen her?

She abandoned her utensils, blotted her mouth with her cloth napkin and then knotted her fingers in her lap. "I guess I'm just not very hungry."

"I am ravenous." He abruptly pushed back his chair and stood. "But not for food."

Stacy's heart stalled and then raced, but Franco reached for their plates instead of her, piled them on the tray and carried them toward the kitchen.

Time's up. Time to deliver your end of the bargain.

Stacy slowly exhaled and then lurched into action, nearly overturning her glass in the process. She gathered the stemware and then followed Franco inside, wishing she'd drunk more than one glass of wine. If she had, maybe she wouldn't be so nervous. But she'd never acquired a taste for wine. She preferred girly drinks with umbrellas, and she drank precious few of those because she kept herself on a strict budget. Unfortunately, sobriety left her tense and clear-headed enough to doubt her sanity in accepting his proposition. Besides, getting drunk would be stupid. She needed to stay in control.

Whatever had possessed her to believe she was qualified to be Franco's mistress? How could she satisfy a worldly man like him? And how could she become intimate with a man she barely knew? Franco wasn't much of a talker. If he'd shared half as much conversation as he had lingering, desire-laden, toe-curling glances, then she could write an in-depth biography about him. But he hadn't. Then again, neither had she.

Details aren't necessary. This isn't about friendship or forever.

Stacy stiffened her spine. She could get through this. She'd survived attending fourteen schools in ten years, her mother's shocking and unexpected death and her father's betrayal. Four weeks as Franco's plaything would grant her the economic freedom to buy a home and to stop feeling like a visitor in her own life—a visitor who might have to pack up and leave at any moment.

But thinking about the money made her feel a little like a hooker. A lot like one, actually. So she shoved those thoughts aside and tried to focus on the man. About how sexy and desirable Franco made her feel…

When she wasn't thinking about the money. She winced.

Franco deposited the tray beside the sink and then took the goblets from her and set them on the counter.

"Let me help you wash those," she offered, hoping to buy time.

"The dishes can wait. I cannot."

Before Stacy could do more than blink, Franco's arms surrounded her and his mouth crashed onto hers. Possessive. Hungry. Demanding. He cupped her bottom, pulling her flush against the length of his hot muscle-packed body, and his tongue found hers, stroking, tasting, tangling. Arousal simmered beneath

Stacy's skin, but it couldn't completely overcome her stomach-tightening trepidation or doubts.

Franco was a wealthy, powerful man who had the money to buy whatever he wanted—including her. Would he play by the rules? She was on foreign territory here—both in Monaco and in this affair. Who would protect her if this turned ugly?

She pushed against his chest, breaking the kiss. "Wait."

"For?" His barely audible growl swept across her damp lips, and his passion-darkened eyes bored into hers.

She licked her lips and tasted him. "What if I don't meet your expectations?"

"I find that unlikely." His hand covered her breast, his thumbnail unerringly finding and caressing her nipple with a back and forth motion.

Tendrils of sensation snaked through her defenses. She had to stay clear and focused. Letting go meant becoming vulnerable. Perhaps she should just take care of him? But how? Drop to her knees and take him in her mouth? If so, she had a problem, because her one and only experience with that in high school had not gone well. She shuddered.

He gripped her upper arms and set her from him. "Stacy, what game are you playing?"

"I'm not playing a game. I just…" She bit her bottom lip. "We don't know each other very well."

"What is there to know except the pleasure we can give one another?" His fingers threaded through her hair, tugging gently and tipping her head back. "Have you never experienced immediate attraction for someone you have just met and let passion lead?"

"Uh…no."

His eyes narrowed suspiciously. "How old are you?"

"Twenty-nine. But I, um…"

"You haven't had many lovers."

Was it obvious? Heat scalded her cheeks. She wanted to hide her face, but his grip on her hair prevented it. "No."

His nostrils flared. "I will teach you what pleases me, and I will satisfy you, *mon gardénia.*"

He stated it with surety and she wanted to believe him, but why would he bother? He'd bought her whether she liked sex with him or not. "If you say so. You probably should have asked about my sexual experience before offering your bargain."

"Ce n'est pas important."

Not important? How could her lack of experience be unimportant?

He released her hair and laced his fingers through hers. "Come. The kitchen is not the best place for our first time."

Nerves twisted tighter in her stomach with each step. She knew where they were headed long before they reached the carved double wooden doors. His bedroom. Once inside the large chamber he faced her. "I have pictured you here. Sprawled on my sheets. Naked except for the flush of passion on your skin."

She wheezed in a breath at the sensual image his words painted and blurted, "Do you have condoms? Because I'm not on the pill."

"And even if you were, the pill is not protection against sexually transmitted diseases—of which I have none," he stated matter-of-factly.

Her discomfort with the current conversation further illustrated her lack of qualifications to become Franco's mistress. A more experienced woman could probably have this preliminary chat without as much as a blush. But not her. She shifted on her feet. "Me neither."

"I have protection." He turned her toward the bed,

reached for the zip of her dress, swiftly pulled it down to her hips and then flicked her bra open.

Oh God, were they going to just do it? She shouldn't be surprised or disappointed. Despite what the magazines said, in her experience, that's the way it happened. Rushed, fumbling hands followed by awkward contact and grunting. At least it would be over soon.

Air cooled her skin and then warm hands slipped inside the gaping fabric of her dress to trail down her spine with a feather-light touch. Goose bumps rose on her skin and her toes curled in her pumps.

Franco's thumbs worked upward from her lower back, massaging her knotted muscles all the way to her neck. His fingers drew ever-widening circles over her shoulders, down to her waist and back again. Her eyelids grew heavy and she shivered as unexpected pleasure rippled over her.

A hot, open-mouthed kiss on her nape surprised a gasp from her, and then her dress and bra fell from her shoulders. Startled by the swift disrobing, she grabbed at her clothing, but too late. The garments puddled around her ankles. She crossed her arms over her chest, covering her breasts.

"*Non.* Do not hide."

Her eyelids jerked open. She found her gaze locked with Franco's in the large gold-leaf mirror hanging over the dresser. Slowly, painfully, she lowered her hands and fisted her fingers beside her. Her heart pumped harder as his gaze devoured her breasts, her black hipster panties and then her legs. In her opinion, her body was okay, her breasts merely average, but if Franco was disappointed in what he'd bought he didn't show it.

Behind her, he discarded his coat and tie, tossing both toward a chair without breaking her gaze. His belt whistled free and then thumped into the chair. Each movement stirred the air around them and teased the fine hairs on her body. He unbuttoned his cuffs and then his shirt and tugged his shirttails free, but didn't remove the garment. Part of her wanted to turn and examine him as he had her, but the governing part of her stood transfixed, muscles locked and rigid.

"*Tu es très* sexy, Stacy." His hands, shades darker than her pale skin, curved around her waist.

Her lungs failed, but whooshed back into action when his palms splayed over her belly, one above her navel and one below. An unaccustomed urge to shift until his hot hands covered more intimate territory percolated through her, but she remained as still as a statue.

"Your skin is like ivory. You do not sunbathe?" he whispered against the sensitive skin beneath her ear a second before his lips made electrifying contact.

"I d-don't have the time. When I'm not working I volunteer my time mentoring at-risk teens." Kids who were lonely outsiders like she'd been.

His gaze searched hers for a moment and then lowered to the tiny birthmark above her right hip bone. He traced the small reddish splotch with a fingertip. The delicate caress made her feminine muscles clench.

His mouth opened over her skin, laving her pulse point. At the same time he pulled her back against his bare chest. She hardly had time to register the heat of him seeping into her or the tickle of his chest hair before his hands swept upward. His thumbs stroked beneath her breast once, twice, three times. Her nipples tightened painfully. She mashed her lips on a whimper.

Involuntarily, her head tipped back against him. He trailed kisses down her neck, across her shoulder and back to her jaw. She shouldn't be enjoying this. She didn't know him and wasn't certain she could trust him, but the rasp of his hands across her skin aroused her unbearably.

And then he covered her breasts. His fingers tweaked her nipples and something inside her detonated, radiating a delicious sensation from her core. A moan slipped between her teeth.

Franco murmured words in French as he caressed her, words she was too distracted to translate. Stacy squeezed her eyes shut and struggled to maintain control, to remember this was a business transaction, and then Franco's hand slipped into her panties and his fingers brushed over her most sensitive spot. Her thighs automatically clamped together against the intrusion, but Franco continued to stroke. He delved into her wetness and plied it over her flesh again and again. Circling. Tormenting. Tempting her to let go.

His foot nudged hers apart, opening her for deeper access, and his fingers plunged inside her. Her lungs emptied. Warmth expanded in her belly and her body trembled with need—need she fought to restrain. He pulled her hips flush against his. The length of his erection nudging the base of her spine fractured what little control she had maintained. And then suddenly the tension snapped and orgasm washed over her in waves of pulsing heat, buckling her knees and making her clutch Franco's arms to keep from falling to the floor. His caresses slowed, easing her though the aftershocks buffeting her.

So that's what all the fuss is about.

Winded and stunned by the intensity of her response, Stacy forced her lids open and met Franco's gaze in the mirror. Questions filled his eyes and her skin baked with embarrassment. Feeling raw and exposed, she ducked her head. He must think her totally shameless.

But then shameless is what he'd bought.

Five

Franco could not believe the evidence before him, but the wonder on Stacy's face and her current embarrassment could only have one cause. "Your first orgasm?"

She winced and dipped her chin in the slightest of nods.

Franco swiftly withdrew his hands. Not because her revelation repulsed him, but because her confession sent a volatile cocktail of emotions through him. Anger rose swiftly toward those who'd misused her, and possessiveness wasn't far behind. Stacy would be his, *certainement,* but only temporarily. The third and possibly the most dangerous reaction was understanding. Inexperience, not manipulation, explained the mixed signals she'd been sending him. None of those responses had any place in this relationship.

"Stacy." He waited until she eased open her eyes again. "Your first, but not your last."

Her lips parted and then relief replaced the surprise

in her eyes. Had she thought he would reject her because her past lovers had been selfish bastards? She might be a pawn in the game with his father, but she would not suffer for it.

He turned her in his arms and covered her mouth, gently this time. Seducing instead of taking. Sipping, suckling her bottom lip and teasing the silken inside with his tongue instead of ravaging her as he'd done earlier.

He still desired her, still hungered for her, but for her sake, he would dull the sharp edges of his need and make this good for her. Good for both of them. By the end of their month Stacy would be a sexually confident woman. She would not forget the lessons he taught her. That other men would benefit bothered him marginally, but he brushed the concern aside.

Inexperienced or not, she accepted your proposition. That makes her like all the others.

Stacy clutched his waist, bunching his shirt in her hands. He wanted her hands on his skin. He released her long enough to rip off the garment and cast it aside.

Stacy's breath caught. Her pupils expanded as her gaze explored his torso, following the line of hair to his waistband. He captured her hands and spread them over his skin and then glided their joined hands over his burning flesh. Her fingers threaded through his chest hair, tugging slightly, and sending electrifying bolts of pleasure straight to his groin. Her palms dragged across his nipples. His whistled indrawn breath mingled with her gasp as hunger charged through him. He released her hands and fisted his by his side, fighting the need to crush her to him.

She tentatively traced the lines defining his abdominal muscles, and his flesh contracted involuntarily beneath her curious fingers. His control wavered like tall trees in the hot sirocco winds.

What is this? You are no boy.

And yet he trembled like one.

"Unfasten my pants," he rasped.

She hesitated and then slipped her fingers between fabric and flesh. His stomach muscles clenched and his groin tightened as she fumbled the hook free and then reached for his zipper. Franco gritted his teeth as she lowered the tab over his erection.

Perhaps all women are born knowing how to torture a man.

When she finished the task, she paused, bit her lip and looked up at him though her thick lashes. His control frayed.

Franco moved out of reach, ripped back the covers and sat on the edge of the bed. He swiftly removed his shoes and socks, letting his gaze rove over her as he did so. Stacy did not have the stick-straight model figure to which so many women aspired these days. Her breasts were exquisite, round, the perfect size to fill his palms, and tipped with dusty-rose aureoles which he could not wait to taste. Her waist and hips curved nicely. Who would have guessed that she hid such an alluring body beneath her sedate clothing?

"Remove your panties." He didn't dare touch her. Not yet.

Her breath hitched and then her thumbs hooked into the black, shiny fabric and slowly pushed it over her hips and thighs to encircle her ankles. She toed them aside and crossed her hands in front of her dark curls. He shook his head. "Let me look at you. Next time I will taste you."

Her eyes closed. She swallowed.

Franco extended his hand. "Come."

Watching him warily, Stacy shuffled forward.

"Sit." She turned as if she were going to sit beside him on the bed, but he caught her, pulling her toward him until her legs straddled his. She slowly sank onto his thighs, her knees flanking his hips on the mattress and her buttocks resting on his lap. The position left her breasts level with his mouth and her feminine core open and exposed.

She was his, his to do with as he wanted, and at the moment he wanted her hot and wet and writhing with pleasure in his arms. He would wipe away the memory of her selfish lovers.

Franco pulled a nipple into his mouth, sucking, laving and gently nipping until her panted breaths stirred his hair. He caressed her back, her buttocks, savoring the smooth texture of her skin, the scent of her filling his lungs and the taste of her on his tongue. *"Touche-moi."*

She lifted her hands to his shoulders and then tangled her fingers in the hair at his nape.

He groaned against her breast. Need urged him to grind his hips against hers, but he settled for reaching between them to stroke her slick folds. Her short nails dug into his skin and a quiet whimper slipped free.

By the time he finished with her, she would not be shy about expressing her passion, he vowed.

His thumb found a rhythm to bring her satisfaction while he feasted on one nipple and then the other until she shuddered against his palm as *le petit mort* rippled over her. Not a moment too soon. Franco was about to erupt.

He stood abruptly, lifting her and then laying her on the bed. Just as he'd envisioned, only a passionate flush covered her skin. He swiftly removed his pants and briefs and reached into the bedside drawer for a condom. Lips parted and eyes wide, Stacy watched his every move as he donned protection. The color on her cheeks deepened and spread to her kiss-dampened breasts, and desire hammered insistently inside him.

He knelt between her legs, finesse and patience long gone, and cupped her buttocks in his hands. "Guide me inside, Stacy."

She curled her fingers around his length. He slammed his eyelids closed, clenched his teeth and stiffened his spine against the exquisite agony of her touch. She steered him toward her entrance and, muscles rigid and trembling with the effort to go slowly, Franco eased into her tight core one excruciating inch at a time. Restraint made his lungs burn and sweat bead on his skin.

When she lifted her hips to rush him the rest of the way in his control snapped. Franco surged deep, withdrew and plunged again and again and again. He fell forward, catching his weight on arms braced on the pillow beside her head. Stacy's back bowed, her arms encircled him, and her breasts teased his chest. The scrape of her nails on his back stimulated him past sanity. He gazed into her eyes and saw desire and surprise as her breath quickened and her body arched.

Her muffled cry as she climaxed again combined with the contracting of her inner muscles to hurdle him over the edge. His roar echoed off the walls as desire pulsed from him.

He collapsed to his elbows, satisfied and yet at the same time unsettled. Gasping for breath, he searched for the cause of his disquiet. And then understanding descended like a guillotine. Quick. Sharp. Cold.

He had let sex with Stacy become personal. A mistake he'd learned to avoid long ago.

It could not—would not—happen again.

* * *

Even before her pulse slowed, Stacy had regrets. What had she done? She'd had sex for money. And she'd enjoyed it.

What did that say about her?

Nothing complimentary, that's for sure.

She closed her eyes tightly and tried to distance herself from the lean, hard body of the man above her. *Inside her.* But she couldn't block out the comfortable weight of him pressing her into the mattress, his scent or the aroma of sex.

Franco rolled away to sit on the edge of the bed with his back curved and his elbows on his knees. Her sweat-dampened skin instantly chilled without the heating blanket of his body, but he was sitting on the covers. Feeling exposed and vulnerable, she crossed her ankles and hugged her arms over her breasts.

He rose and his pale backside mesmerized her. As much as she hated herself at the moment, the ashes inside her sparked to life at the sight of corded muscles rippling beneath the sleek, tanned skin as he shoved his fingers through his hair. The movement drew her gaze to the breadth of his shoulders. Had she made those scratches? Embarrassment flamed her face.

"Would you like to shower?" he asked in a flat, unreadable voice, without turning.

She blinked and looked away. "No. Thank you."

She wanted a shower. But not here. Not now. What if he decided to join her? He'd bought her. Did that mean she'd forfeited the right to say no? She hadn't yet come to terms with the pleasure he'd wrung from her tonight, so she wasn't ready for another intimate encounter. She had to keep this affair impersonal, because opening up to more than that would make her vulnerable.

But there had been nothing impersonal in what they'd just shared. At least not on her part.

Sex for money. She clutched the thought close—like a talisman. As ugly as it sounded, it was safer than trusting her heart to a man like Franco Constantine. A man with more money and probably more power than her father.

The moment he disappeared into the bathroom Stacy vaulted from the bed and snatched up her clothing. Her hands trembled so badly it took three tries to fasten her bra. In her haste she pulled her panties on wrong-side out, but she didn't dare take time to remove them and put them on again. She wanted to be dressed before Franco returned. Dressed and ready to leave.

She stumbled over her shoes—she couldn't even remember removing them—and shoved her feet inside, and then snatched up her dress and dragged it over her head. The zipper stuck in the middle of her back. Frustrated tears stung her eyes as she tugged in vain. She bit her lip, blinked furiously and willed them away.

Gentle hands nudged hers aside. Stacy nearly jumped out of her pumps. She hadn't heard Franco return. His knuckles brushed against her spine, raising goose bumps as he fiddled with the zipper, freed the fabric and pulled up the tab.

Stacy stiffened her resolve and met his gaze in the mirror. His broader naked form framed hers. Her hair was a mess and her lips were swollen, but she didn't care. "I want to go back to the hotel."

His jaw shifted. All signs of passion had vanished from his face, leaving his features hard and drawn. "I'll drive you."

"I'll wait in the living room." She bolted.

"Stacy." His voice halted her on the threshold.

Reluctantly, she turned. Her breath caught at the sight of Franco in all his naked glory standing with one knee cocked and his torso slightly angled in her direction. The man had a body worthy of the beefcake calendar someone had given Candace at her bridal shower. His chest was wide and covered with dark curls, the muscles clearly defined, but not bulky like a body builder's. A line of hair led to a denser, darker crop surrounding a masculine package any centerfold would be proud to claim, and his legs were long and strong.

"Are you all right?" The question seemed forced.

Physically? "Yes."

Mentally? She was a wreck. She'd never felt more alone or confused or ashamed of herself. She needed to reassess. Maybe financial security wasn't worth it. On the other hand, she'd enjoyed sex for the first time in her life. But sex with a man she'd known only three days. Brazen, that's what she'd been.

"I will be with you in a few moments," Franco said, reaching for his shirt.

Stacy nodded and fled. Agitated and anxious, she paced the length of the living room, skirting the red rugs and ending at the kitchen archway. She needed to do something to channel her thoughts and nervous energy. Her gaze lit upon the dirty dishes. Seconds later she had them submerged in a sink filled with hot soapy water. She scrubbed the fine china probably harder than she should have.

Franco had turned cold immediately after he'd…finished. Had she turned him off with her fumbling and in-experience? What if he drove her to the hotel and told her to forget the deal? At this moment she wasn't sure that wouldn't be a good thing. She wasn't sure about anything except that she needed to be alone.

She cleaned the second plate, rinsed and dried it and then tackled the stemware.

"Que fais-tu?" Franco asked from behind her, startling her into almost dropping the last glass.

She didn't turn. "I'm washing the dishes."

"My housekeeper comes tomorrow."

She finished drying the wineglass, set it on the counter and carefully folded the damp towel, delaying facing him until the last possible moment. When she did she focused on the cleft in his chin rather than his eyes. "It's done."

"You are my mistress, Stacy, not my maid."

Mistress. Her mother would have been appalled. Her mother, who'd always told Stacy the right man would treat her like a princess. Her mother, who'd led a secret life Stacy hadn't known about until the investigation into her mother's murder had revealed details of a life that looked like a fairy tale to outsiders, but had actually been a nightmare.

"Am I? Still?"

Franco closed the distance between them. He'd dressed in the clothing he'd worn earlier, but without the tie or jacket, and he'd left the top few buttons of his shirt open. Her traitorous nipples tightened at the memory of those dark, wiry curls teasing her breasts.

He reached out and lifted her chin, forcing Stacy to look into his eyes—eyes that no longer burned with passion, but were completely inscrutable instead. "Unless you find my touch repugnant, and I don't think you do, *mon gardénia,* then our agreement stands."

She couldn't speak and didn't know what she'd say if she could find her voice. Did she want the affair to continue? His fingers stroked down her neck, making her pulse leap and her skin tingle. Apparently, no matter what her brain said, her body was all for the affair.

He withdrew his hand. "Come. I'll drive you to the hotel."

"You look shell-shocked."

Stacy pivoted and found Madeline behind her in the hotel lobby. "Hi."

"Was that Franco I saw leaving?"

"Yes." After a silent ride from his home, Franco had insisted on walking her inside. Stacy hadn't invited him upstairs.

"Okay, Stace, what gives?"

"Nothing. I…we had dinner." He hadn't kissed her goodnight, and she didn't know whether that was good or bad.

"Uh-huh, and what else?"

Her cheeks burned. She wished she and Madeline were closer, because she needed to talk to someone, and she was certain the more experienced woman would be able to help her unravel her tangled and conflicting emotions.

"Stacy, did he hurt you?"

"No, no, it's nothing like that. We should go up. It's late."

"It's barely midnight, and we're not going upstairs until you tell me what has you fluctuating between blood-red and hospital-sheet white." Madeline hooked her arm through Stacy's and half led, half dragged her toward the bar.

Within minutes Madeline had snagged them a secluded table, an attentive waiter and a couple of fruity cocktails. "Drink and spill."

Stacy didn't know where to begin or how much to share with this woman whom she'd only met a week ago.

"Okay, let me start. You slept with him and…" Madeline prodded.

Stacy choked on her drink. "How did you know?"

Madeline shrugged. "Was it good? Because I'm going to be seriously disappointed if a guy as sexy as Franco Constantine was a lousy lay."

Lousy lay. The words echoed in Stacy's head, an unpleasant blast from the past, compliments of the high-school jock who'd wooed her until she'd surrendered her virginity. She'd thought being a popular guy's girlfriend would win her acceptance in a new school, but afterward he'd dumped her and told all his friends she was a lousy lay. That was the first time Stacy had welcomed her mother's decision to relocate.

Madeline gripped her hand. "You've gone pale again. Start talking, Stace, or I'm calling the cops, because I'm starting to think he forced you do something you didn't want to do."

"No, don't. There's no need for that. Yes, we slept together and no, it wasn't lousy. He didn't hurt me or force me. I promise." Uncomfortable with the confession, she shifted in her seat.

"Did he dump you?"

"No."

"Then what's the problem?"

She hesitated and then confessed in a whisper, "I barely know him and I had sex with him."

"So?"

So she felt like a tramp. Worse, she'd made a bargain with a man who had the power to make her repeat her mother's mistakes. Not one of her finest decisions.

"You weren't a virgin, were you?"

"No."

"Then I'm not seeing a problem. It was good, right?"

Stacy could feel a blush climbing her neck as she nodded.

"And what's wrong with being with a guy who makes you feel good as long as he's not diseased, married or committed to someone else?"

Stacy fidgeted with her napkin. "Nothing, I guess."

"Stace, there are plenty of guys out there who'll make you feel like crap. You have to grab the good ones when you can. And if it lasts, great. If it doesn't…well, you tried. As long as you're careful. STDs are ugly. Take my word on that. I see plenty of them in the E.R."

Madeline took a sip of her drink and then continued, "It's a double standard, you know? Guys are expected to be experienced and good in bed, but women are supposed to virtuously wait for Mr. Right. How will we recognize him if we don't look around? And what happens when our Mr. Right turns out to be a total jerk?"

Stacy vaguely remembered Candace mentioning a nasty breakup in Madeline's past. She tentatively covered Madeline's hand offering support, but at the same time Madeline's words lifted a load from Stacy's shoulders.

An affair with Franco wouldn't hurt anyone as long as she remembered his passion-profit-and-no-promises offer was temporary and kept her heart safely sealed off. For the first time all night she smiled. "Thanks, Madeline. I needed to hear that."

"Hey, that's what friends are for."

Friends. Stacy savored the word and nodded.

When she left Monaco behind she'd have friends, good memories of sex instead of only bad ones, and for the first time in her life, she'd have a nest egg and soon, a home of her own.

And she'd be an ocean away from the man who threatened her equilibrium.

"Everybody needs to take a nap today," Candace said as she entered the sitting room for breakfast and their usual planning session Friday morning. She placed her cell phone on the coffee table. Candace was the only one of the women who had one that worked in Monaco. Their U.S. cell phones were useless here.

"Why?" Stacy asked.

"Because Franco's taking us to Jimmy'z tonight. He says the place doesn't start rocking until after midnight."

Franco. Stacy's heart skipped a beat. She'd wondered when she'd see him again. Wednesday night he'd left her with a vague, "I will be in touch."

Because she refused to waste a day in paradise sitting in her room and waiting for him to call, she'd spent yesterday exploring Monaco-Ville, the oldest section of Monaco, alone. Her suitemates had other commitments. She'd looked over her shoulder countless times as she watched the changing of the palace guard, wondering if she'd run into Franco, but he'd have no reason to visit tourist spots like the Prince's Palace or the wax museum. He'd probably seen it all before. Besides, he was probably at his office…wherever that was.

Filled with a mixture of anticipation and dread, she'd returned to the hotel late in the afternoon. But there'd been no message from Franco. Stacy had shared a quiet meal at a sidewalk café with Candace and then gone to bed early, only to toss and turn all night.

How could she miss a man she didn't even know? She blamed her uneasiness on not wanting to violate the terms of their agreement by being unavailable. It definitely wasn't a desire to see him again. The warmth between her thighs called her a liar.

"Typical of a guy," Candace continued, "he was stumped when I asked him what we should wear."

Stacy reached for one of her three guide books, looked up the club and read aloud, "'Jimmy'z—An exclusive dance club where the jet set hangs out. Dress code—casual to formal, but wear your designer labels.'"

Stacy didn't own any designer labels.

"You three can go shopping after we tour the Oceanographic Museum and the cathedral this morning," Candace said. "But I have an appointment with the stylist for a practice session on my wedding-day hairdo."

Madeline shook her head. "Not me. I have plans for later."

"Same here," Amelia offered.

Stacy couldn't afford anything new, and she refused to let Candace keep buying things for her. "I'll find something in my closet."

And just like that Franco undermined Stacy's concentration for a second day. Every tall, dark-haired man she spotted in the distance Friday morning made her pulse spike, and no matter how impressive the sights, she kept thinking about Franco and the night ahead. Had it not been for her lack of sleep for the past three nights she wouldn't have been dead to the world when the suite doorbell rang later that afternoon. Shoving her hair out of her eyes she stumbled groggily into the sitting room, opened the door to a hotel staff member.

"A package for Ms. Reeves," he said.

"I'm Stacy Reeves." She accepted the large rectangular pewter-colored box and the man turned away. "Wait. I'll get a tip."

"It's been taken care of, mademoiselle. *Bonsoir.*"

He turned away. Stacy closed the door and leaned against it, her exhaustion totally eradicated. Only Franco would send her something. She pushed off the door and carried the package into her room. With trembling hands she plucked at the lavender ribbon and opened the box.

A folded piece of ivory stationery lay on top of the lavender tissue paper. She lifted it and read, For tonight.

No name. No signature. But the handwriting was the same as that on the card included with Franco's flowers. Franco. She inhaled a shaky breath and pushed back the tissue paper to reveal a pile of teal garments, the same shade as the Mediterranean Sea outside the hotel windows.

She pulled out the first piece, a soft, silk camisole, and laid it on the bed. The second, a sheer, beaded wrap top, matched perfectly, as did the third, a handkerchief-hem skirt with the same beading on the edges as the wrap. She held the skirt against her body. It would be fitted from her waist through her hips, but the lower half would swish and swirl about her thighs as she moved. The perfect dancing outfit, and judging by the designer label, it probably cost more than her monthly rent and car payment combined.

And then her gaze caught on two more wrapped items in the bottom of the box. She unwound the tissue from the largest first and found strappy sandals to match the clothing. She slipped one on her bare foot. Perfect fit. In fact, everything looked as if it would fit. How had Franco known her sizes? Even she didn't know the European conversions. Had Candace told him? Or was he so experienced with women he could accurately guess their sizes just by looking at them. Probably the latter.

She opened the last package, gasped and dropped the

matching bra and thong in the exact same shade of teal on the bed. Heat rushed through her.

Franco was dressing her from the skin out. He'd bought the privilege to do so, just as he'd bought the right to undress her later if he chose.

Anticipation—or was it dread?—made her pulse race.

Six

A wiser man would choose another woman, Franco told himself as he entered Hôtel Reynard a few minutes before midnight. Stacy had made him feel more than sexual relief—a luxury he no longer afforded himself. It would not happen again.

He had ignored her yesterday just to prove he could, but he had failed miserably. She had invaded his thoughts like a fever. If the family estate and the company he had sweated blood over were not at stake, he would bid her farewell. But it had taken him two months after making the agreement with his father to find a woman who met both his and his father's criteria. Stacy came with the added benefit of leaving the country after the month was up. He would not have to deal with a clingy woman who refused to accept goodbye.

Nodding to the concierge, Franco stepped into the penthouse elevator and swiftly ascended. Tonight there would be no intimate conversations. He would dance with Stacy in the crowded, noisy club. Afterward he would send her suitemates back to the hotel in the limo and take Stacy to his villa where they would have sex. And then he would put her in a cab and send her back to the hotel. Alone.

He did not want to know her better—except intimately, of course. Nor did he want to discover what had made an attractive and intelligent woman completely unaware of her appeal, for she seemed to have absolutely no vanity.

The suite's doorbell chimed when he touched the button, and seconds later the wooden panel swung open. Stacy. She took his breath away. His gaze absorbed her, from her loose shining hair to the outfit he had chosen, down her lovely legs to her pink-painted toenails in the sexy heels.

"*Tu es ravissante, mon gardénia,*" he murmured in a barely audible—thanks to the annoying thickening of this throat—voice.

Her cheeks pinked and she dipped her chin. "Thank you. And if I look ravishing it's because of the lovely outfit. Thank you for that too. But you don't have to buy—"

"The color matches your eyes when you climax," he interrupted. Ignoring her shocked gasp, he reached for her right hand and bent to kiss her knuckles. At the same time he retrieved the diamond bracelet she had left behind from his pocket and fastened it on her wrist.

He straightened. "Are your suitemates ready? I have a limo downstairs."

"Is that Franco?" Candace called from within the suite.

Fingering the bracelet, Stacy stepped back, opening the door and revealing the trio of women. "Yes. He has a limo waiting."

"Then let's go," Madeline replied. "And Stace, if that's the kind of stuff you have stashed in your closet I'm glad we're the same size."

Stacy shot him a quick glance as if warning him not to correct Madeline. "I need to get my purse."

His gaze followed her as she walked away, the uneven hem of her skirt swinging flirtatiously above her knees. Knowing her buttocks were bare save the clinging fabric of her skirt and the thin ribbon of her thong made his blood pool behind his zipper. Nor could he take his eyes from her once she rejoined them. This fascination was not good. But it was temporary. He would get over it.

In the limo he settled beside her with the other women on the seat across from them. Stacy's scent filled his nostrils and her legs drew his gaze. His fisted his hand against the compulsion to smooth his palm up her thigh.

He belatedly remembered the role Vincent had asked of him. "I have a table reserved beside the dance floor. The rules are different here than in the States. Unattached men and women dance freely without partners. If you see someone you wish to dance with you make eye contact, and if the interest is returned you move toward each other on the floor."

"You mean the guys don't ask you to dance?" Amelia queried.

"Not verbally, no. The club is safe, but if you have problems come to me. Stacy and I will be nearby."

Stacy's eyes widened. She seemed to sink deeper into the seat as her companions' speculative gazes landed on her. She had not wanted her friends to know about the money, but hiding the affair would be impossible.

Franco nodded to Candace. "Vincent says you are only to dance with women or ugly men."

His comment brought a laugh and eased the tension. "The limo is on standby. If you wish to leave, use it. Don't get into cars with strangers."

A collective groan arose from the opposite bench and Madeline mumbled, "Not my father's favorite speech."

Franco shrugged. "Vincent charged me with your safety."

The limo pulled to a stop outside Jimmy'z. The women climbed out, Stacy last. Franco followed, his gaze on her shapely bottom. The men gathered near the entrance eyed the women, Stacy in particular. Franco rested a possessive hand on her waist and bent closer. "You will dance with no one but me."

She briefly closed her eyes and then nodded.

Inside, the hostess led them to their table. The club was dark and the music loud with a driving beat. Franco wondered what Stacy thought of the retro decor, but decided it did not matter. Knowing her tastes was not part of their deal.

He arranged for their drinks and waited with impatience he had no business feeling for Stacy to consume hers while the women chatted, pointed out celebrities and acclimatized themselves to the club. An hour later even the shy Amelia had deserted them for the dance floor. Franco extended his hand. Stacy bit her lip, hesitating before she laid her palm over his and rose.

Thankful that slow songs were few and far between at Jimmy'z, he led her onto the floor. The night would be long enough without the arousing slide of her body against his. Needing the physical exertion to expend some of his caged energy, he released her hand and found the rhythm of the beat. Stacy moved self-consciously at first, but soon either the gyrating crowd surrounding them or the alcohol relaxed her. The results devastated him. A slight sheen of sweat dampened her flushed skin, reminding him of her face just before *le petit mort*. He would have been better off if Stacy had remained stiff.

His gaze slid over her. When he had chosen her clothing he'd had no idea the effect she would have on his control and his carefully planned evening. Each pirouette flared her skirt almost to her bottom. He wasn't the only man to notice. A primitive urge to mark her as his surged through him.

He cupped a hand around her nape, pulled her close and pressed a quick, hard kiss on her lips. He said into her ear, "You dance like you make love. *Très* sexy."

Shock made Stacy stumble. Could the man read minds? Franco caught her quickly, pulling her flush against the hot length of his hard body. The contact was too intense, too arousing. She jerked back, her gaze slamming into his. Suddenly the air seemed loaded with sexual tension.

For the past two hours she'd been thinking he moved like an invitation to sin—an invitation she wanted to accept more and more with each passing second. She'd believed that after a night in his bed she couldn't—wouldn't—desire him again. Wrong. Her body, already warm from dancing, flushed with heat and pulsed with a sexual awareness with which she'd been unfamiliar until Franco.

Franco moved closer, his hand curving around her waist and his hips punctuating the beat in a purely sensual dance that made her feminine muscles clench in anticipation. A mating dance. Not graphic or crude. Just devastatingly, pulse-acceleratingly sensuous. And she wasn't the only woman to notice. Since they'd arrived, each time Stacy had glanced past the cobalt silk stretched across his broad shoulders she'd caught women glaring at her or ogling Franco's behind, and who could blame them?

More than one bold woman had sashayed up to them on the dance floor and shimmied directly beside him as if trying to draw his attention. But Franco's gaze never strayed. His eyes had remained locked on hers or on the movement of her body with an intensity burning in the blue depths that made her feel incredibly attractive and yes, very desirable. Realizing she was proud to be the woman he'd chosen was a scary thought since the man *should* be her worst nightmare.

Her throat dried and her belly tightened. She blamed the discomforts on thirst and hunger. Nerves over this evening had ruined her appetite and she'd barely touched the dinner she and her suitemates had shared earlier. Hoping for a distraction, she dampened her lips and glanced toward their table, but her friends weren't there to rescue her.

Franco intercepted her look, caught her hand and led her off the dance floor without a word. He paused beside her chair, brushed stray tendrils of hair from her damp forehead and tucked them behind her ears. His fingertips lingered over her pulse points, no doubt noting the rapid tattoo not solely caused by the dancing, and then one hand traced her collar bone and dipped into the V of her top. Desire rippled over her, tightening her nipples and making her shiver.

"Another drink, *mon gardénia?*"

Maybe the alcohol was to blame for loosening her inhibitions and erasing her common sense. Whatever, she wanted him to kiss her instead of staring at her lips as if he would consume her were they not surrounded by people, and her response was both unacceptable and unwise, given what she knew of men in his position.

She cleared her throat and sat. "Water this time."

He signaled the waiter, ordered another round of drinks for their table and seated himself beside her.

Stacy gasped when his hand smoothed up from her knee and then her breath wheezed out again when his fingertips stroked along the sensitive skin of her inner thigh.

"You wish to go?"

She did. Oh boy, she did. What did it say about her that she couldn't wait to get back to his house, back to his bed? She waited until after the waiter deposited the drinks and left to reply. "We shouldn't leave before the others."

"Amelia has found someone. Madeline and Candace are coming this way."

Surprised that he'd kept track of her suitemates, she turned in her seat and searched the crowd until she located Amelia dancing with a tall, sandy-haired man. "Should we leave her with him?"

"Toby will take care of her."

"Toby? Toby Haynes? The race-car driver?"

"*Oui,* and Vincent's best man. He is also charged with your safety while you are in Monaco." He removed his hand as the women neared the table and Stacy immediately missed his touch.

Something is definitely wrong with you.

Madeline and Candace slid into their seats.

"*Merci,* Franco," Candace said. She and Madeline toasted him with their fresh drinks. "This has been a blast, but I wish Vincent were here."

Madeline scanned the crowd. "And Damon. I had hoped he'd join us tonight."

"Damon is your tour guide?" Stacy asked.

"Yes. But I guess he had to work tonight."

"Shall I call for the limo for you?" Franco asked.

"Yes," Madeline and Candace answered simultaneously.

"Excuse me." Franco left the table, headed onto the dance floor and spoke to Toby and then disappeared toward the club entrance.

Candace grinned mischievously. "I'll tell ya, Stacy, Franco is definitely a keeper. He has some seriously sexy moves, and if he's half as good in bed as he is on the dance floor, a girl could have a real good time."

Stacy's cheeks burned. She ducked her head and fiddled with her cocktail napkin. So this was girl talk. "He's a good, um…dancer."

"You're going home with him?" Madeline asked.

Stacy fought the urge to squirm in her seat. "Yes, but I'll be back for our morning meeting."

"The only thing on the agenda tomorrow is me tinkering with the rehearsal dinner and reception seating. No work for you, so stay as long as you like," Candace replied with a wink and a smug smile. "It's almost 3:00 a.m. I have a feeling we'll all be sleeping in."

Stacy had permission to spend the entire night with Franco. Did she want to? The swiftness of her answer surprised and alarmed her. She'd slid far too easily into the role of a rich man's mistress.

"Remove your clothing," Franco ordered in the darkness thirty minutes later.

Stacy's breath caught. She couldn't see anything, not even her hand in front of her face, and she didn't know where she was. Franco had led her into his home, and without turning on any lights, he'd guided her down a hall and a flight of stairs.

The click of her heels had echoed off the walls until

they'd stopped moving and now the eerie silence deafened her. Or maybe her thunderous heartbeat drowned out all sound.

Did she dare trust him? She found herself wanting to. Scary.

A mechanical whirl startled her, making her look to her right. The wall slid open like a curtain to reveal moon-washed gardens, the roar of a waterfall and a spa large enough to lie down in without touching the sides.

Half of the spa is concealed beneath the house by the falling water. I would like to make love to you there, Franco had said. Was it only a day and a half ago?

A thrill of anticipation raced through her. Anticipation. Something she'd never experienced in a relationship with a man before Franco.

Moonlight seeped around the cascading water to dimly illuminate her surroundings, and a gentle breeze wafted in, carrying the scent of flowers. The people of Monaco loved their flowers. Gardens and flower boxes abounded.

Stacy scanned the room filled with more exercise equipment than the gym in her apartment complex until she spotted Franco in the shadows. He flipped a switch and the whirlpool splashed to life, its water gleaming like bubbly champagne from the golden glow of lights beneath the surface.

With his gaze fixed on her he leaned against the wall, toed off his shoes and removed his socks. Mesmerized, she watched as he straightened and reached for the buttons on his shirt. It fluttered to the floor followed quickly by his pants and briefs. He stood before her like a finely chiseled statue. An incredibly aroused and well-endowed statue. His chin lifted. "Your turn."

She gulped and reached for the knot of her sheer wrap, but she was nervous, her fingers uncooperative.

She'd never stripped for a man before. Nor had she ever had one look at her the way Franco did with his gaze burning over her, his nostrils flaring, his fists clenched by his side. Finally, the knot gave way. She shrugged off the wrap and dropped it on a nearby weight bench.

Taking a fortifying breath, she reached for the back hook and zipper of her skirt. It swished down her legs. She stepped out of it and her shoes and turned to deposit both on the bench.

A warm hand covered her bottom, making her jump and gasp. Franco. She hadn't heard him cross the room. His other hand joined the first, stroking her buttocks, thighs and her belly, and molding her against him. The thong was no barrier to the heat of his lean flanks against her cheeks and the hard length of his erection against her spine. Desire made her dizzy.

What happened to maintaining a clear head and control?

He murmured something in French, something she couldn't translate, and then his fingers caught the hem of her camisole and whisked it over her head.

"Turn around," he ordered in a deep, velvety voice.

She pivoted on trembling legs. The sharp rasp of his indrawn breath filled her ears. He lifted a hand to outline the top of her demi-bra with a fingertip. Her nipples tightened and need twisted inside her as he retraced his path, this time delving below the lace and over her sensitive skin. How could he make her want like this?

"Take it off."

Stacy reached behind her, unhooked the bra and shrugged out of it. Franco's approving gaze caressed her breasts and then dropped to the tiny teal thong.

"And the rest."

She shoved the lingerie down her legs wondering

why she had not once considered saying no. And then she straightened. Franco tipped his head to indicate the spa. Stacy descended the whirlpool steps. The hot water swirled around her ankles, her calves, and once she reached the center of the small pool, her thighs. Franco joined her, reclined on the bench seat and extended his hand.

"Turn around."

She did and then he pulled her into his lap and flattened her back against his chest with his erection sandwiched in the crease of her buttocks. The water swirled between her legs and lapped at her breasts, but then Franco's caressing hands replaced it, massaging, tweaking, sweeping her up in a whirlpool of desire.

She let him have his way. He'd bought her, bought the right to use her any way he wanted. And she had to remember that, but it was hard to keep up the mental barriers when he touched her like this. Sure, he'd promised her pleasure, but did she really deserve it?

His teeth grazed the tendons of her neck. She shivered and tilted her head to give him better access. He stroked her breasts, her abdomen, her legs, nearing but never quite reaching the place where she needed his touch the most. She squirmed in his lap and bit back a frustrated whimper. He stood abruptly, lifting her with him, sat her on the cool tile edge of the whirlpool and then knelt between her legs.

Next time I will taste you, he'd said.

"Wait—" The touch of his tongue cut off her shocked protest with an intense burst of sensation. No man had ever licked her there. Franco laved and suckled, taking her to the brink again and again, but each time she thought she'd shatter he'd stop to kiss her thigh, nibble her hip bone or tongue her navel.

Frustration built until she unclenched her fingers from the rim of the tub and tangled them in his hair to hold him in place.

He grunted a satisfied sound against her and then found the heart of her again with his silken tongue. Seconds later climax undulated through her. Her cries echoed off the stone walls and her muscles contracted over and over, squeezing every last drop of energy from her until she sagged against Franco's bent head and braced her arms on his broad shoulders.

He straightened, reached behind her for a condom packet she hadn't even noticed and quickly readied himself. Cupping her bottom, he pulled her to the edge of the spa and plunged deep inside her, forcing another lusty cry from her lungs. She shoved her fist against her mouth.

Franco pulled her hand away. "I want to hear the sound of your passion. Better yet, I want to taste your cries on my tongue."

He covered her mouth with his.

She ought to be ashamed of herself, Stacy thought as she clung to him and arched to meet his thrusts, but she couldn't seem to rally the emotion with Franco pistoning into her core and bringing her to the brink of another climax. She yanked her mouth free and gasped for breath as her muscles tensed and she came again, this time calling out his name.

Franco plunged harder, deeper and faster until he roared in release, and then all was silent except for the rush of the water and their panting breaths.

He held her, or maybe she held him, as he sank back into the hot water, taking her boneless body with him. She drifted above him. The current swirled over her sensitized skin, teasing, tantalizing, slowing her return to sanity. Without Franco's arms to anchor her, she'd float away like a cork on the tide. She trusted him to keep her head above water.

Trust. The thought jarred her into planting her knees on the bottom of the tub on either side of Franco's hips and pushing him away so abruptly that she almost dunked him. How could she trust him? He was everything she'd sworn to avoid, but avoiding him was becoming the last thing she wanted to do.

To protect herself she'd have to learn everything she could about him. Did he have a temper? Any obsessions?

She'd learn—even if learning meant letting her guard down enough to spend the night.

"I'll call a taxi for you." Franco disentangled their bodies and stood. He stepped over the low wall separating the indoor and outdoor halves of the spa and ducked beneath the waterfall. The cooler water from the pool sheeted down on his head and splashed over Stacy's skin. Seconds later he climbed from the whirlpool.

Stacy rose on legs so rubbery it was a miracle they supported her, and wrapped her arms around her waist. "Candace said there's nothing on the agenda for tomorrow—today. I—I can stay."

Muscles rippling beneath his wet skin, he disappeared into an adjoining room without responding and returned moments later with a black towel around his hips and another in his fist. When she didn't take it from his outstretched arm he dropped it beside the spa. "I have other plans for the weekend."

Plans? With another woman? Stacy didn't care to identify the uncomfortable emotions stirring inside her. She had no claim on Franco's time. In fact, she should be glad he wanted to spend it elsewhere. But strangely, she wasn't.

"There is a change of clothing for you in the bathroom." A tilt of his head indicated the room he'd just vacated. He flicked a series of switches. The wall slid closed, the whirlpool stilled and silence and darkness descended on the room. Then overhead lights flashed on leaving Stacy feeling naked and exposed under his thorough perusal. Her damp skin quickly chilled.

"You may shower, if you like, and then join me upstairs." He gathered his discarded garments and left.

Dismissed. He'd had his way with her and now he was done. How could he be so conscientious of her satisfaction one moment and then such a cold bastard the next? Shame crept over her.

What are you doing? Falling for the first guy to give you an orgasm? So he's a good lover. He bought *you. Just because he's doing favors for Vincent and he watched out for your friends at the club doesn't make him a nice guy.*

And he has plans. *Plans that don't include you.*

Irritated with herself, Stacy climbed from the water, dried off and wound the towel around her nakedness. She grabbed her shoes and clothing from the weight bench and let curiosity lead her into a humongous tiled bathroom. A large glass shower stall took up one corner and a wooden sauna occupied the other. And was that a massage table? Did Franco have a personal masseuse?

A V-neck sundress in a muted floral print of blues and greens and a matching lightweight sweater hung in an open closet beside a white toweling robe. She ran her fingers over the dress's flirty ruffled hem. Silk, whereas her dresses were cotton. Designer instead of department store. Other than the sexy but impractical sandals in a box on the floor of the closet, the outfit was exactly the style she would have chosen for herself if she had an unlimited budget. Which, of course, she'd never had.

The dress tempted her, but she didn't want anything else from Franco, nor did she want to explain to her suitemates why he kept buying her presents.

Her reflection in the long mirror caught her eye. Ugh. Her makeup was ninety percent gone and her hair clumped in wet tangles over her shoulders. She dumped her clothes on the counter, washed her face in the sink and then finger-combed her hair as best as she could. She unhooked the diamond bracelet and left it on the long marble vanity and froze. Her heart stalled. *Her watch.* She hadn't removed it. Panic dried her mouth. Where had she misplaced it?

She backtracked, but didn't see it on the bottom of the spa or anywhere around the weight bench. It hadn't been expensive, but its value couldn't be measured in dollars. She remembered putting it on tonight. Wherever it was, she *had* to find it.

Maybe Franco could help. She returned to the bathroom and quickly yanked on her dancing outfit. The cool, sweat-dampened fabric made her grimace. After smoothing the wrinkles with her hands, she followed the direction Franco had taken earlier. The stairs led to a hallway, and while she would have preferred to explore this end of the house and perhaps learn more about Franco, she tracked his voice to the living room. With his back to her, he swore, dropped the phone on the cradle and shoved his hands through his damp dark hair.

"Is something wrong?"

He turned, his gaze narrowing over her choice of clothing. He'd changed into jeans and a black polo shirt. "The taxi is unavailable for an hour. I will drive you back to the hotel. Why are you not wearing the dress?"

"I told you. You don't have to keep buying me gifts. I accepted this one because I didn't have anything suitable to wear tonight, but otherwise…" She shrugged. "I don't need anything."

His lips compressed and a muscle in his jaw jumped. "And the bracelet?"

"I left it downstairs on the counter. It's beautiful, but not practical for an accountant. If I wore it to work people would wonder if I'd been embezzling from their accounts, and I never go anywhere dressy enough to need something like that."

Surprise flicked in his eyes. "You will continue to work when you return home?"

"Of course." As soon as she found another job. "Once I pay taxes on the money and buy a house there won't be enough left to live a life of idle luxury."

"Taxes? And what job will you list as a source for your income?"

Good question. She twisted the thin gold strap of her evening bag. "I haven't figured that out yet, but suddenly opening a bank account with more than a million dollars would red-flag the IRS. And I'm not stupid enough to keep that much cash lying around my apartment."

"Why not use an offshore bank?"

"Too cloak-and-dagger. I'd feel like a money launderer. Besides, not reporting the income would be illegal." Did he think she was crazy not to hide the money? She couldn't tell from his neutral expression. "Franco, I lost my watch. I didn't see it downstairs. Could you give me the number for the limo service, the taxi and Jimmy'z? I'll call to see if anyone found it. It wasn't expensive, but it was…my favorite. I need to find it."

"I will make the calls."

"Thank you." She agreed because the language barrier might be an issue, but then shifted in her sandals, reluctant for some stupid reason to see the night end. "I enjoyed tonight."

He folded his arms and leaned his hips against the back of the sofa. "You sound surprised."

She rubbed her bare wrist and wrinkled her nose. "I'm not a clubbing kind of person."

He studied her so intently her toes curled in her shoes, and then he reached behind him and lifted a small plastic shopping bag. "This is one gift I insist you accept. A cell phone. My numbers are already programmed into it."

She'd be at his beck and call. But that's what he'd bought. And the phone might come in handy when she needed to reach Candace or if one of the women needed to reach her. "Am I allowed to use it to call anyone else?"

"Not your lover in the States," he replied swiftly.

She took the bag from him and peeked inside to see a top-of-the-line silvery-green picture phone. "I meant Candace, Madeline or Amelia. I don't have a lover back home. If I did, I wouldn't be involved with you."

Again he looked as if he didn't believe what she said—a circumstance she was beginning to get used to. He pushed off the sofa. "Come."

She followed him outside and slid into the passenger seat of his car and waited until he climbed in beside her. "Why did you choose MIT?"

He didn't answer until he'd buckled his seat belt and started the engine. "They have an excellent Global Leadership program."

"Couldn't you get that at a university closer to home?"

He pulled onto the road and drove perhaps a half mile before replying. "My mother was from Boston and I was curious about her city."

Stacy jerked in surprise. "An American?"

Another long pause suggested he didn't want to share personal info. "Second-generation. She met my father while visiting her cousin in Avignon."

The lights of Monaco sparkled across the mountainside in the pre-dawn hour. Stacy didn't think she'd ever tire of the view, but the insights into Franco fascinated her more. "Are you close to her? Your mom, I mean."

"She died when I was three," the brusque response seemed grudgingly offered.

"I'm sorry. It's hard to lose a parent." She still missed hers, and now that she knew why she and her mother had lived such a vagabond life, she could even accept, respect and forgive her mother's choices.

A streetlight briefly illuminated his tense face. "Yours?"

A gruesome graphic image flashed through Stacy's mind. She squeezed her eyes shut and forced it away. "She…died when I was nineteen."

"And she left you enough money to attend college?"

"No. I co-oped."

"What is that?"

"I worked part-time in my field with sponsoring companies and that meant I had to take a lighter load of classes. It took six years of going to school year-round, but I finished."

"Vincent did not tell me that."

"You asked Vincent about me? What did he say?"

"That he had not met you, but that you had…how did he put it? You saved Candace's bacon in a tax audit."

Stacy laughed and Franco's gaze whipped in her direction. He acted as if he'd never heard her laugh. Come to think of it, he probably hadn't. "Candace's was my first audit, and I went a little overboard in her defense. I think the IRS agent was glad to get rid of us by the time

I finished pointing out all the deductions Candace could have taken but hadn't."

Franco pulled the car into the hotel parking area, but not into the valet lane and stopped. He turned in his seat and studied her face in the dim light. "You enjoy your work."

"I love—um, my job." She'd barely caught herself before using past tense. Being laid off had been like moving to a new school and being rejected all over again. It had hurt—especially since she hadn't done anything wrong. "Numbers make sense. People often don't."

He pinned her with another one of his intense inspections that made her want to squirm. "I will be out of town this weekend. A car will pick you up at quarter to six Monday evening and deliver you to my house. My housekeeper will let you in before she leaves. Wait for me. We will have dinner."

And then sex? Her shameless pulse quickened. "I look forward to it."

And the sad thing was, that wasn't a lie, and Monday seemed a very long way away.

Seven

"I have found her," Franco said upon entering the chateau's study.

His father looked up sharply, set his book aside and rose from the sofa to embrace him. "Franco, I was not expecting you this weekend. If you had called I could have delayed lunch."

He hadn't known he was coming. This morning's urge to put some distance between him and Stacy had been both sudden and imperative. She had clouded his thinking with incredible sex and contradictory behavior. He needed distance and objectivity to decipher her actions.

"No problem. I will raid the kitchen later. Where is Angeline?"

"Shopping in Marseille."

Ah, yes. Exactly why he was here. To remind himself that a mercenary, self-indulgent heart beat at the core of every woman.

Take his mother, for example. Although his father had never spoken a negative word against her, Franco had been curious enough about the woman who had given birth to him to investigate her death. During one of his university vacations he had researched the police reports and the newspaper stories and discovered that his mother had enjoyed her status as a rich, older man's wife. She had often attended weekend house parties without her husband, and there she'd indulged. In booze. In cocaine. And who knew what else? At one such party, a chemical overdose had killed her at age twenty-six.

His father passed him a glass of wine. "So tell me about this young lady."

"She is an American accountant, a friend of Vincent's fiancée, and she claims she counsels troubled teens in her spare time."

"And?"

"I offered her a million euros to be my mistress for a month. She accepted." But she would not accept all his gifts. That did not make sense. Her honesty had to be a ruse. Who would report a million euros windfall to the tax man and forfeit almost half in taxes?

"She is attractive? Desirable?"

An image of Stacy rising like Venus from the churning waters of the spa flashed in his mind. Droplets had streamed down her ivory skin, clung to her puckered nipples and glistened in the dark curls concealing her sex. Before he had removed the first condom he had been ready to reach for a second. He'd had to dunk beneath the cooling waterfall to regain control. "That was our agreement."

"And yet you're here and she's…where?"

"Monaco. Vincent is pampering his bride-to-be and

her attendants with an all-expenses-paid month at Hôtel Reynard while they plan the wedding. Stacy is a bridesmaid."

"Ah, yes. Vincent is another one making his papa wait for grandbabies. Has he recovered from the accident?"

Vincent had come home with Franco several times during school vacations. Franco had also visited the Reynard home in Boca Raton, Florida. It had been Vincent who had suggested Franco relocate to Monaco for the tax advantages the principality could offer Midas Chocolates. "He is completely mobile now, and through surgeries and physical therapy, has regained 80 percent use of his right hand."

"And his fiancée does not mind the scars or the handicap?"

"She was his nurse in the burn unit. She has seen him look worse." And she had stood by him. Probably because Reynard Hotels was a multi-billion dollar corporation with ninety luxury hotels spread across the globe.

"I look forward to seeing him again and to meeting his bride. I also want to meet your…Stacy, you said? You'll bring her here."

The idea repulsed him. "I do not see the need."

"I do. And is she the kind of woman you would be willing to marry if she refused the money?"

Franco cursed the wording of his agreement with his father, but it would not become an issue. "It will not happen. She has already accepted."

"You seem very certain of that."

"I am."

"When is the money to be paid?"

"The day after Vincent's wedding."

His father turned away, but not before Franco caught a glimpse of a smile. "Just remember our agreement, son."

"How could I forget?"

How indeed? When he returned to Monaco, he would show Stacy the benefits of being a rich man's plaything. Before long she would greedily beg for his gifts instead of refusing them.

And then she would take the money and run.

Alone in Franco's house.

Stacy stood in the foyer after the housekeeper left. Uncertain. Uncomfortable. Undecided. She could be a polite guest and wait in the living room as directed or she could search for signs of obsession. Being a snoop wasn't honorable, but after what she'd learned about her father… She shuddered.

Knowledge was power and she needed all the knowledge she could get about Franco Constantine. Her safety depended on it.

She turned down the hall toward the master-bedroom wing. A twinge of guilt made her pause on the threshold, but she took a deep breath and marched in. The furniture surfaces were clear of clutter. No photographs or knickknacks gave a clue to the room's owner other than big, bold wooden furniture and luxurious linens. The classic landscapes on the wall also revealed little. She would not stoop to pawing through his drawers.

The view of Larvotto through the open drapes lured her, but she ignored it and cautiously opened a door to reveal a closet as large as her apartment bedroom. It looked like a *GQ* man's dream with clothing and shoes neatly aligned on the racks and shelves. There was no sign of a woman anywhere…except for the dress Stacy had left behind the other night hanging alone on an otherwise empty rod with the shoebox beneath it.

She closed the door, returned to the foyer and looked

out the window, but there was no sign of Franco's car. The opposite hallway beckoned. Just past the stairs to the basement she found an open door and looked inside. Franco's study. A large dark-wooden desk dominated the space and tall bookshelves lined the walls on either side of the double French doors opening onto the back patio.

A pair of photographs on one shelf drew her across the room. She lifted one of Franco and another man about the same age standing in front of a picturesque castle. Vincent Reynard. Stacy recognized him from the picture Candace had shown her, but the photo had been taken before the accident that had marred half of Vincent's face. Franco looked at least a decade younger than the man she knew, and his smile was genuine and devastatingly handsome instead of twisted and cynical. Fewer lines fanned from his eyes and none bracketed his chiseled lips. Had this been taken during their grad-school days? But the setting looked European instead of American.

Stacy returned the frame to the shelf. An older man stared out at her from the second photograph. His heavily lined face couldn't conceal the same classic bone structure and cleft chin as Franco. He had Franco's thick hair and straight brows, but his were snowy white instead of coffee-bean dark, and his eyes weren't nearly as guarded as Franco's. Was this Franco's father? She'd never know. And she was okay with that. Really.

Turning slowly, she scanned the tables, sofa and bar cart, but she found no sign of Franco's ex-wife. She returned to the entrance hall and eyed the staircase. Did she dare? What if Franco came home while she was upstairs? How would she explain her snooping without revealing that she'd visited her father's house after her mother's death and what she'd discovered had given her the willies? Franco didn't need to know her tragic past or that her father most likely had been mentally unbalanced. No one needed to know. It was hard enough to make friends without people wondering if she carried her father's defective genes.

Her futile search supported Franco's claim that he was over his wife and his marriage and that he'd moved here after the divorce...unless there was something upstairs. Not that Stacy really cared about his wife, but she wanted to make sure Franco wasn't the type to use his money and power in dangerous ways.

It's not as if you're the kind of woman a man can't forget, especially a man like Franco who must have far more glamorous women than you at his beck and call all the time.

That again raised the question of why he had chosen her?

The sound of a car in the drive made her heart stutter. She hustled to the window, looked out as Franco's black sedan rolled to a stop. Her mouth dried and something resembling anticipation shot through her.

How could she be eager to see him? He was using her.

And you're using him, so don't get sanctimonious.

He climbed from the vehicle. His gaze searched the front of the house and found her in the window. For a moment he paused with one arm braced on the top of the car and just stared at her. A lump rose in her throat and her heart beat like a hummingbird's wings. He bent and reached inside. When he emerged again and started toward the villa he carried a small white bag with pink ribbon handles that looked too feminine in his big hand.

Another gift she'd have to refuse?

And why did she keep refusing? The diamond bracelet alone could be pawned to pay off her car. But they'd agreed on a price for a service and to keep tacking on extras seemed unethical…. As if there could be anything more unethical than their current agreement. The irony of her situation didn't escape her. But she had to be able to live with herself after this affair ended, and that meant setting standards and sticking to them. It wasn't easy. There had been precious few gifts in her past. And she'd lost the most important one.

She rubbed her bare wrist and then wiped her palms over her pencil-slim skirt and opened the front door. If they were truly lovers this was the point where she'd rush down the walkway to embrace him and welcome him home. Instead, as he approached she stood frozen inside the door unsure exactly what he expected of her.

The closer he came the more shallow her breathing became. While her gaze fed on his lean dark-suited form, he inventoried her lavender blouse, navy skirt and sensible low-heeled pumps. Suddenly she felt dowdy, and she wished she'd slipped into the flirty and feminine sundress hanging in his closet. That she'd even consider dressing to please him rattled her. "Hi."

"*Bonsoir,* Stacy." His arm encircled her waist. He snatched her close, taking her mouth in a ravenous kiss that bent her backward. She clutched his lapels and held tight. Their thighs spliced and the heat of his arousal nudged her belly. His tongue stroked hers and hunger suffused her with embarrassing swiftness.

By the time he released her she was breathless and dizzy, with her pulse galloping out of control. She unfurled her fingers from his suit coat and sagged against the door frame. He swept past her, set the gift bag on the credenza and continued through the living room and toward the kitchen.

Stacy stared at the bag, her curiosity piqued. Maybe

it wasn't for her. After taking a few moments to gather her composure—and to battle the urge to peek into the bag—she closed the front door on the balmy evening and followed him.

Franco had removed his suit coat and laid it over the end of the center island. He held a martini shaker in his hands. The flexing and shifting of his muscles beneath his white shirt as he mixed the sloshing liquid filled her mind with images of those bare muscles bunching and contracting beneath his supple skin as he braced himself above her. She plucked at her suddenly sticking blouse and exhaled slowly.

He poured the contents into a glass and set it on the counter in front of her. Her eyebrows rose.

"You are surprised I noticed you never drink more than one glass of wine at dinner and you ordered fruity drinks at the club?" he asked as he opened a bottle of red wine with practiced ease.

"I guess I am."

He filled his wineglass and lifted it in a silent toast then nodded toward the martini. "Try it."

Stacy lifted the glass and sipped. Chocolate, cherry and vanilla mingled on her tongue. "Very good."

"It is made with Midas Chocolate liqueur." He reached into his inside coat pocket and withdrew a handful of gilt-edged cards which he placed on the counter. "*Le Bal de L'Eté* is this Saturday. I have tickets."

There were more than two tickets in the pile. "A summer ball?"

"*Oui*, it is an annual charity event to mark the opening of the summer season at the Monte Carlo Sporting Club. Europe's *l'aristocratie*, including royalty, attend. You and your friends might even meet the prince."

She gaped. "Of Monaco?"

"*Oui.*"

She'd heard it wasn't uncommon to see members of the royal family on the street or at sporting events, but to meet them… "Will either of the two long dresses you've seen me wear work?"

He shook his head. "*Non.* I will arrange for you—"

"Then I can't possibly go."

"—and your friends to have appropriate gowns," he continued as if she hadn't interrupted.

She sighed. He had her cornered and he knew it. "And if I refuse then Candace, Madeline and Amelia will miss the ball."

He shrugged. "*Tout a un prix.*"

Everything has a price. Yes, he did seem to live by that rule. But how could she deny the other women this opportunity to rub elbows with royalty? "You fight dirty."

"I play to win."

"Okay. On behalf of my friends, I accept." Jeez. That had sounded ungracious. But she hated being manipulated.

"*Bien.* And while you are in an accepting mood…" He left the kitchen and returned moments later carrying the bag. "For you." He held up a hand to stop her protest. "Open it before you refuse."

She reluctantly accepted the bag, withdrew a small box, opened it and gasped. *Her watch.* Hugging it to her chest, she ducked her head, blinked her stinging eyes and struggled to contain the happy sob building in her chest. He couldn't possibly know how much this meant to her. "Thank you."

"You are welcome. The limo driver found it. The band was broken. I had it replaced with a similar one."

"My mother gave me this when I graduated high

school. It was the last gift she gave me before she—" Her throat thickened, choking off her words.

Franco smoothed his hand from her brow to her nape. His fingers clenched in her hair and then stroked forward to lift her chin. "I am glad we found it. Now finish your drink and then go downstairs and remove your clothing. The masseuse will be here in ten minutes."

"Masseuse?" Stacy wasn't wild about the idea of someone else seeing or touching her naked body. She hadn't joined her suitemates in the hotel spa for sea-salt massages for that very reason. But she wouldn't mind Franco's hands on her. "You're not going to, um... massage me?"

A slow naughty smile curved his lips. "I am going to watch. And after she has turned your muscles to butter and departed, I am going to take you on the massage table."

The image he painted sent a shiver of arousal over her. Stacy realized she was beginning to like not only Franco, but this mistress stuff too.

And that was definitely not good news.

My God. He had almost hugged her.

Franco fisted his hands and watched the lights of Stacy's taxi disappear into the night. What kind of fool was he to be swayed by eyes brimming with tears and gratitude? And yet when Stacy had looked at him earlier tonight, clutching that cheap watch to her breast and smiling through tear-filled eyes, he'd almost succumbed to the urge to embrace her.

He did not hug or cuddle or any of those other relationship things that would lead a woman to expect more from him than he could give. And he did not trust tears. Tears were nothing more than a weapon in a woman's arsenal. How often had Lisette used tears to get her way during their marriage? After the abortion she'd tried to soften him by crying and claiming that he'd been spending more time at work than with her, and she'd been afraid he no longer loved her and would not wish to have a baby with her.

Regret crushed his chest in a vise. He *had* spent more time at work during that final year of his marriage. His father's latest divorce settlement had forced him to borrow against the estate, and that meant finding new sources of revenue to cover the debt. Franco had not explained that to Lisette which meant if he were to believe her story, he would have to accept part of the blame for the loss of his child. And that was a burden he could not bear.

Much better to remember that Lisette, like his mother, had been selfish. She'd made a decision she had no right to make without his input, and then she'd tried to place the blame on a scapegoat—him. And of course, there had been more to her story, as he'd discovered the day the hospital released her and his replacement had arrived to carry her to her new home.

He slammed the front door. Stacy Reeves was no different from any other woman. He simply hadn't figured out her strategy yet. But he would. In the meantime, he would make use of her beautiful body and then send her back to her hotel each night until he had his fill of her. And he would sleep alone—as he always did.

"Ohmigod, is that Prince William?" Amelia asked in a hushed voice on Saturday night.

Stacy followed Amelia's wide-eyed gaze over the glittering guests gathered in La Salle Des Etoiles in the Monte Carlo Sporting Club to the tall blond with an aristocratic nose. Stacy had never been a royal watcher. She probably wouldn't recognize a prince if he walked up and shook her hand, but that didn't dilute the excitement of being in the room with the kind of people who graced the pages of the magazines in her former employer's waiting room.

"It could be. Franco said there would be royalty here." In the minutes since they'd climbed from the limo and made their way inside Stacy had spotted at least a dozen American movie stars, two rock idols and a late-night talk-show host. She was so far out of her element it wasn't even funny.

"You want to tell me how you scored tickets for *Le Bal de L'Eté?*" asked Candace, looking stunning in a platinum satin dress. Vincent hadn't been able to get away from the job site to join them, but Candace had handled her disappointment well. "Vincent said they're almost impossible to get unless you're famous or one of the super-rich upper class."

Stacy glanced at her suitemates, each wearing an evening gown Franco had purchased. He'd given Stacy the name of an elite shop on Avenue des Beaux Arts and told her the proprietress would take care of them. "You'll have to ask Franco."

Amelia fidgeted beside her in pale-yellow tulle. "So is it getting serious between you two? Because from where I stand he's looking a lot like Prince Charming and the Fairy Godfather rolled into one very attractive package."

Stacy stroked her hand over the delicate floral beading on her turquoise dress and searched for an answer that wouldn't shock her friends. Telling them the driver had picked her up Monday, Tuesday and Wednesday evenings and delivered her to Franco's villa for sex and dinner probably wasn't the best response. Just thinking about those nights made her tingle.

But Franco had been out of town since Thursday

morning, and her body, which had happily gone without sex for so many years, was having withdrawals. *And withdrawal is all it is,* she assured herself. Just because he'd shown her facets of her sexuality that she'd never known existed didn't mean she was developing an emotional attachment to him. She hadn't missed him or anything mushy like that. Besides, his absence had allowed her to spend time with her suitemates.

She was actually beginning to feel like one of the group instead of an outsider. The bonds of friendship were forming, and tonight while they'd fussed over each other's clothes, hair and makeup in preparation for the ball she'd had a hint of what it might have been like to have sisters. But she wasn't comfortable enough yet to tell her suitemates the unvarnished truth. "Not serious, no. I'm just having a holiday romance as Madeline suggested."

"Are you sure it's not more than that?" Candace asked. "You certainly jumped on that gown the moment the shop owner told you Franco had suggested she help you choose something the color of your eyes."

Heat rushed to Stacy's cheeks. So she wanted to look attractive for him. What was wrong with that? She was beginning to realize he wasn't an arrogant ass even though he did a good imitation of one quite often by pulling away immediately after making love—having sex. But if he were truly a jerk he never would have had her watch repaired or treated her friends to this Cinderella evening. He'd shown his generosity in a dozen other ways outside of bed, like the museum and theater tickets that had been delivered to their suite Thursday morning, the basket of chocolates yesterday and the flowers today. He was showering her with gifts her friends could share—gifts she couldn't refuse without depriving her suitemates.

She shrugged. "He's paying for my gown. He ought to have some say about it."

"Uh-huh," Madeline said, her disbelief clear. She'd chosen a drop-dead-sexy black dress guaranteed to make heads turn, but Madeline seemed to be searching for someone in particular and was unaware of the attention her dress garnered. "Don't get your heart involved, Stace. Remember, we go home in two weeks."

Stacy nodded. How could she forget that in a matter of days she'd either leave Franco and the most sensual period of her life behind or discover she'd repeated her mother's mistake? The first filled her with regret, the second with stomach-twisting apprehension. She forced a smile. "Don't worry about me."

She scanned the crowd searching for Franco. He was supposed to meet them here tonight, but they were a little late arriving. Her gaze collided with his across the room and her stomach took a nose-dive to her sandals. He turned and spoke to the group he was with and then headed in her direction. Her pulse skipped erratically and her mouth dried.

He looked amazing in a tuxedo. Rich. Powerful. Sexier than any man in the room. And hers. For now. The thought filled her with pride…and doubts. Why her when, judging by the heads turning in his wake, he could have any of these more sophisticated women?

Desire flared in his eyes as he climbed the shallow stairs. His gaze lingered on her décolletage before gliding to her toes and back to her face, and then he took her hand in his and bent to brush his lips over her knuckles. He straightened and looked into her eyes. *"Tu es magnifique, mon gardénia."*

Before she could find her voice he turned toward her companions and bowed slightly without releasing her hand. "*Bonsoir,* mesdemoiselles. *Vous êtes très belle ce soir.* As before, the limo is at your disposal. You will forgive me if I steal Stacy for a dance."

He didn't wait for a reply, but tucked her hand in his arm and led her away. Stacy glanced over her shoulder at the women who offered her a trio of grins and thumbs-up.

On the dance floor Franco pulled her into his arms, leaving her with the sensation of being swept off her feet and into another world—a world in which she wasn't a lonely, staid and unemployed accountant. For a few moments she could pretend to be one of the beautiful, glamorous people who attended exclusive balls, traveled by limousine, rubbed elbows with royalty and captivated a millionaire.

But this wasn't real. She had to remember that.

She laced her fingers at Franco's nape, relishing his slight shudder when she inadvertently teased the sensitive skin with her nails. Each night he'd taught her something new about giving pleasure as well as receiving it. She loved knowing she had the power to make him tremble with desire, but the downside of learning her strength was that her fear of letting anyone get too close faded more with each intimate encounter. Keeping her walls strong wasn't as easy as before—especially when his touch made her feel so alive.

The muscular length of his thighs and torso brushed hers as he swayed to the music. He nuzzled her temple and inhaled deeply, his chest rising to tease her breasts through the thin fabric of her gown. *"J'ai manqué ton parfum."*

She tilted her head back and studied him through her lashes. His passion-darkened eyes cut short any attempt at translating his words. Her skin prickled with awareness and desire smoldered within her. Only inches separated their mouths and the urge to rise on her toes and kiss him tugged at her, but this was his turf, not hers. She didn't know the rules here and until now had never been tempted to make a public display.

"What did you say?"

His lips thinned, as if he regretted speaking. Finally he said, "I have missed your scent."

Her heart stalled and her breath caught. "Me too—yours."

A muscle in his jaw bunched. His fingers flexed against her hips, urging her closer to his thickening arousal. A corresponding heat pooled low in her abdomen. "We must stay until Vincent arrives and then we go. I want you naked and hungry for me."

She gasped and jerked in surprise, but Franco held her close. "Vincent's coming? I should tell Candace. She'll be thrilled."

"It is a surprise. He should be here any moment." He tucked her head beneath his chin. "I must go to Avignon tomorrow. You will accompany me."

She wanted to see where Franco had grown up, but at the same time, her duty to Candace came first. "I don't know if I can, Franco."

"I have paperwork I must peruse. It cannot wait and neither can I." He smoothed a hand over her bottom. The song ended, but he made no effort to release her or leave the dance floor.

Stacy's pulse drummed in the silence. She glanced to where she'd left her suitemates, but they weren't there. "I'll have to check with Candace."

"I have already discussed it with Vincent. He has not seen his fiancée for a month, and he assures me he will not let her leave his bed for the next few days." A flame burned in his eyes. He tightened his arms and melded his hips to hers as the orchestra began another song. "I understand his needs."

She swallowed the lump rising in her throat. Franco wanted her and he made no attempt to hide his desire. What would it be like to have that forever?

Stop it. This isn't about forever—especially not with a man like him.

She tried to pull back, mentally, physically, but the steel band of Franco's arms held her captive. His hands and body subtly rubbed and nudged hers. The rich and famous faces around her blurred as she focused on the man who seduced her at every turn. Moisture gathered in her mouth and much lower. Dancing with him was like foreplay. Her arousal grew so intense she was tempted to find a coat closet and drag him inside. Her face burned and she buried her nose against his neck. How had he turned her from a sexually reticent woman into one who craved his touch so badly she was considering public indecency?

What seemed like eons later Franco said, "Vincent is here. Come."

She glanced toward the entrance and saw a handsome man with brown hair. He resembled the man in the photos she'd seen, and yet Franco led her in the opposite direction. That wasn't Vincent? But then the man in question turned his head to scan the room and Stacy saw the tight, burned skin on the right side of his face. Definitely Vincent. She caught her breath in sympathy. She couldn't imagine the pain he'd endured. Candace had told her about the series of surgeries he'd already undergone and those yet to come.

Franco shot her a hard look and his grip on her hand tightened. "His scars repel you?"

"Of course not. Besides, I knew what to expect.

Candace showed me a picture. She's very protective of him." And from the hard and cool tone of Franco's voice and the warning glint in his eyes, it seemed as if he might be as well. Loyalty to his friends was yet another interesting facet of Franco's personality, but reading him was like trying to decipher a foreign language. There were bits she couldn't understand. "Where are we going?"

"To retrieve his fiancée." They reached a group of women gathered on the far side of the room. "*Excusez-moi, mesdemoiselles.* I must borrow Candace."

Candace frowned. "Is something wrong?"

"*Non.* There is someone you need to see."

Candace noted Stacy's hand held tightly in Franco's and a smile curved her lips. "Having a good night?"

Stacy's face and neck warmed. "Yes."

"And it is about to get better," Franco muttered for Stacy's ears only, sending a flash fire through her.

He led them toward the entrance and stopped at the bottom of the stairs where Vincent waited with love in his eyes so intense Stacy's heart stuttered.

Candace spotted him, squealed and launched herself into his arms. Given Stacy's already erotic thoughts, witnessing their passionate kiss made her squirm and glance at Franco. His thumb stroked over the inside of her wrist and his eyes promised *soon.* Her pulse tripped.

The couple drew apart, hugged and parted again with blinding smiles. And then Vincent turned to Franco. The men embraced and exchanged a few words too quiet for Stacy to overhear in the noisy ballroom. The genuine affection between them surprised Stacy. To date, Franco had seemed somewhat aloof except when in seduction mode.

When they parted, Candace dragged Stacy forward. "Stacy, this is Vincent. Vincent, Stacy."

Vincent extended his hand. Ignoring the scars, Stacy shook it. From Candace she knew he'd come a long way in his recovery, but other people's squeamishness sometimes bothered him. "It's good to meet you, Stacy."

"You too, Vincent. And thank you for this once-in-a-lifetime vacation."

"You're welcome. Anything that keeps Candace from overdoing it with the wedding plans works for me." Vincent encircled Candace's waist and spread his left hand possessively over her still flat belly. The couple exchanged another intimate, love-laden glance.

What would it be like to have a man look at her that way?

The rogue thought staggered Stacy. Suddenly it hit her that she would never experience the bond that Candace and Vincent shared. Until now that hadn't concerned her. In fact, being alone and safe was a path she'd deliberately chosen, but now the solitary life she'd planned yawned ahead like a barren stretch of desert road.

Because of her bargain with Franco she'd soon have a home. But it would be empty.

She'd never fall in love.

Never experience the hope, joy and anticipation of having a child with someone she loved—all of the emotions written clearly on Candace's face.

Stacy would live alone. Die alone. And the world would be no different because of her time in it.

Sadness settled over her like a cold, wet blanket. Every lesson she'd learned to this point had made her afraid to let anyone get too close. But she'd found the courage to make friends. Could she also find the courage to allow a man into her life and into her heart?

Not a powerbroker like Franco. But maybe someone tamer. Someone less wealthy. Someone she could trust. If such a man even existed.

Eight

Stacy had shared intimacies with Franco that made her blush, and yet she still knew very little about him beyond the physical. She hoped a night in his family home would fill in a few of the blanks.

"Do you always buy your women?" she asked to fill the silence during the hours-long Sunday-afternoon car ride to Avignon.

Franco's jaw hardened and he shot her a chilly glance. "I have never offered a woman money for sex before you."

If that was supposed to make her feel special, it failed. "Good, because it seems a little like…prostitution."

"It is supply and demand. You have something I want and I am willing to pay your price. Relationships always come at a price, Stacy. If you do not believe that then you are deceiving yourself. I prefer to have the terms stated up front rather than be unpleasantly surprised in the end."

Would anyone willingly enter a relationship if they knew the costs going in? Stacy's fling with the high-school jock had cost her her self-respect, and her short-lived involvement with a coworker had diminished her confidence. But her mother had paid the ultimate price for loving the wrong man.

Stacy pushed the memories away and studied Franco's profile, the way he brushed his thick dark hair away from his brow, his straight nose, his sensuous lips and square chin. Beard stubble already shadowed the line of his jaw even though it was barely two in the afternoon. "As an accountant I often see the effects of costly divorce settlements. Is that what happened in your case?"

Seconds passed as Franco exited off the autoroute and onto a narrower road. She wondered if he'd avoid answering personal questions the way he usually did. She'd given up on getting an answer when he said, "Money was not the issue. My wife had an abortion. I did not know she was pregnant or that she did not want children."

No wonder he was bitter. "I'm sorry. Did you want a large family?"

"It was assumed I would provide heirs."

"You still could."

"I will not marry again."

She felt a quick stab of…something. Regret? Of course not. It didn't matter to her if Franco didn't want another wife. What he did once she left Monaco was none of her business. And she wanted it that way.

A few minutes later he turned down a long, straight tree-lined driveway. When they reached the clearing at the end of the drive Stacy mouthed a silent, "Wow."

The white stone structure with its round twin towers flanking opposite corners looked like something from a fairy tale. Flags bearing coats of arms fluttered from the conical spires. It looked familiar and then she placed it as the building in the background of the picture of Franco and Vincent in Franco's study.

"You grew up in a castle?"

"*Un château*. There is no moat, drawbridge or curtain wall."

Castle, chateau, whatever. "No wonder you were able to get tickets to the ball. You're one of them. The aristocracy."

A twinge of envy stirred inside her—not for his wealth, but for the childhood he must have had. "You and your siblings must have loved playing here."

"I am an only child."

"Me too." As a child she'd longed for someone to play with, and as a teen she'd just wanted to belong somewhere and to have someone to confide in. Always being the new kid and an outsider had been difficult.

The cobblestone courtyard circled a round multi-tiered fountain. Wanting to absorb every detail, she barely waited for the car to come to a stop before she shoved open the door and leaped out. Moments later Franco joined her beside the gurgling water. "How long has the chateau been in your family?"

He shrugged. "A few hundred years."

"A few hundred *years?*" Stunned, she faced him. "Do you have any idea how lucky you are?"

"How so?"

Regretting her revealing outburst Stacy bit her lip and stared at the parapets and then panned the acres of emerald lawn. "You've always had a home to go to. A place where you belonged."

"You did not?" he asked quietly.

"No." She turned toward the trunk. "Let's get the luggage. I can't wait to see the inside of the chateau."

He caught her arm in a firm, but not painful grip. "Explain."

She didn't want his pity, but if her past could keep him from taking this spectacular place for granted then what would it hurt to tell him? "My mother left my father when I was eight. After that we never lived in any one city for more than a year."

"They divorced?"

"No. He refused to grant her a divorce, so she ran away."

"Why did she run?" He drew mind-numbingly erotic circles on the inside of her bicep with his thumb.

"According to the diaries I found after she…died, my father was physically abusive. She wrote that she left the first time he struck me. I don't recall being hit, but I do remember my mother sending me to my room whenever my father started yelling. And I remember the fights and arguing and the sound of my mother crying. I remember kissing her boo-boos." The last phrase came out in a strangled whisper as the past descended over her like a dark, oppressive cloud.

He muttered something she suspected was a curse. "Why did she not have him arrested?"

Feeling chilled despite the sunny day and warm temperature, Stacy pulled away and hugged herself. "She tried once, but my father was wealthy and powerful. He had friends in high places and the hospital records of her injuries mysteriously disappeared, so the charges were dropped. In her diary she claims reporting him only made him angry and vindictive."

"You said earlier that your mother had to choose between food and rent. Could she not demand monetary support from your father?"

"No. She wrote that the one time she called for help he threatened to kill her if he ever found her." The memories rose up to choke her and a shudder slithered through her. She'd never confessed the full extent of her past to anyone. She didn't know why she wanted to now except perhaps she wanted Franco to understand why financial security was so important to her. For some reason it was important that he know greed hadn't been the motivating factor in accepting his proposition. "One day he did."

A moment of shocked silence stretched between them. "*Mon dieu.* What happened?"

"I came home from my first class in night school and found my mother and a man I didn't recognize dead in our apartment. The police identified him as my father. He'd found us with the help of a private investigator. The CSI guy said my father shot my mother and then himself."

She squeezed her eyes tight against the memory of red blood pooled on the white kitchen floor and having to walk through it to see if her mother was still alive, and then rib-crushing panic when she realized she wasn't.

Franco yanked Stacy into his arms and hugged her tight enough to squeeze the breath from her lungs. One big hand rubbed briskly up and down her spine. His lips brushed her forehead. She leaned into him, absorbing his strength and accepting comfort in a way she'd never allowed herself before, but then she gathered herself and withdrew, because leaning on him was a habit she couldn't afford. But she instantly missed his embrace.

The empathy in his eyes made hers sting with unshed tears. "So now you know why I accepted your proposition. I want a home. Nothing as grand as this. But a place that's all mine."

"What of your father's estate? If he had wealth, then why did you not inherit?"

A question she'd asked herself countless times

until she'd learned the truth. "He left everything to his alma mater."

"And you did not contest his will or file a wrongful death suit?"

She shifted on her feet and studied the sunlight reflecting off the windows of the chateau. "No. Either would have cost money I didn't have. And I couldn't risk running up years of legal fees and then losing and being in debt."

"Stacy, no court in the States would have denied your right to his estate after what he took from you, and a lawyer would have accepted you as a client with payment contingent upon a settlement."

She dug the toe of her sandal into the gravel drive and debated full disclosure. What did she have to lose? She lifted her gaze to Franco's. "Immediately afterward, I wondered if I could have stopped him if I'd been at home, and I said as much to the police detective. He told me that from the extra bullets in the gun and the photographs of me in my father's rental car, they suspected he had intended to kill me too."

The ultimate betrayal. A parent who wanted her dead.

"By starting school and changing my schedule I wasn't where he thought I'd be." She walked to the back of the car, struggled to regain her emotional footing and waited for Franco to open the trunk.

"After that I didn't want anything from him except answers which he couldn't give me. The executor of the estate let me walk through my father's house before the auction. Mom's makeup table looked like she'd gone out for the day and would return any minute, and all the clothing she'd left behind hung in the closet even though she'd left eleven years before. My room was the same. It was like a shrine to an eight-year-old girl. It creeped me out."

"And you had no one to turn to?"

"No one I trusted." *Trust.* There was that word again. She realized she was beginning to trust Franco and that couldn't be good. He was rich. She hadn't seen signs of him abusing his power or the law, but she'd known him less than two weeks.

"You have accomplished much by moving on instead of letting your past destroy you." The approval in his voice wrapped her in a cocoon of warmth.

"I didn't want my mother's sacrifice to be in vain. She left to protect me."

He stroked his knuckles along her cheekbone. "You have done her proud."

His words were a soothing balm she hadn't known she needed, and the tenderness in his eyes made her yearn for something, but what exactly, she wasn't sure. She stepped closer.

"Franco, Franco, Franco," a childish yell splintered the intimate spell. Stacy flinched and backed away. Close call. She couldn't afford to become dependent on him or his approval.

Franco lowered his hand and turned to the small boy bolting from the chateau. The child raced down the walk and launched himself at Franco who caught him, swung him in the air and then hugged him while the boy talked far too fast for Stacy to translate the words. Franco replied in the same language, his voice low and tender.

Stacy couldn't help but stare. Franco looked relaxed and happy. A wide smile transformed his handsome face into a knee-meltingly gorgeous one. If he ever looked at her that way she'd completely forget about his wealth and all the other reasons why he was the wrong man for her.

Who was the boy? Franco had said he and his wife

hadn't had children and yet the affection between the two was unmistakable. She guessed the child to be about six or seven.

Franco set the child on the ground and ruffled his dark hair. "Stacy, this is Mathé. Mathé, this is Mademoiselle Reeves. Speak English for her, please."

Mathé's small left hand clutched Franco's larger one as he shyly mumbled a hello and quickly shook Stacy's hand. Big brown eyes peeked at her before turning back to Franco with idolization shining in their depths. "Are you staying?"

"*Oui,* for the night. Go tell your *grandmère* we will need two rooms." The boy rushed off.

Stacy's gaze followed him back to the house. "He's cute."

"The housekeeper's grandson. He has lived here with her since his mama ran off with her lover and left him behind three years ago." The bitterness in his voice raised a number of questions.

"He's about the same age your child would have been."

Doors slammed in Franco's expression. Any remnants of his smile vanished. He extracted their suitcases and slammed the trunk. "Do not try to paint me as a hero or a sentimental fool. I am neither."

"Whatever you say. But he's clearly thrilled to see you."

"I spend time with him when I can. He has no father and mine is too old to keep up with him."

"*Entrez-vous?*" An older man called from the open front door. Stacy recognized him from the photo in Franco's study.

"*Oui,* Papa. We are coming." Franco carried the luggage toward the house. Stacy followed. "I have come to look over the documents you had drafted."

"You are staying the night?" Stacy thought he asked.

"Oui."

Her French had improved tremendously in the past two weeks, but Stacy quickly lost track of the heated rapid-fire conversation that followed. Whatever his father said turned Franco's face dark with anger.

Franco turned to her. "It appears my soon-to-be stepmother has decided to redecorate the house. All of the bedrooms except for mine and Papa's have been stripped."

"We could go to a hotel," she suggested.

"Not necessary. Stacy, is it? I am Armand Constantine. Welcome. Come in." He extended his hand. "It is not as if you and Franco are not already sharing a bed. I am old, but I am not old-fashioned or easily shocked."

Embarrassment sent a scalding wash across her skin. "It's nice to meet you, Monsieur Constantine."

She shook his hand and followed him inside. The detailed plasters, gilt-framed artwork and period furniture in the entrance hall screamed history—a history Stacy had never had as her father's house had been built after Stacy's birth. A wide staircase worthy of a romantic Hollywood movie soared upward from the center of the grand hall.

"Franco, show Stacy upstairs and then bring her to the salon for refreshments."

Franco remained motionless for several seconds and then nodded stiffly and climbed the stairs. Stacy followed, her eyes drinking in the original oils on the walls, the beautiful antiques and the endless halls. Finally, Franco shoved open a door and walked into a round room that looked as if it belonged to a teenage boy.

She quickly averted her gaze from the double bed covered in a blue spread. Her pulse skipped erratically at the thought of sharing the narrow mattress with him.

Sleeping with him—something she had yet to do. "Your bedroom's in a tower."

"*Oui.*" The clipped word drew her gaze from the boyish decor to his face.

"I guess your stepmother didn't get to your room yet?"

"My room is off-limits to her as it has been to each of my father's four wives." He dumped their bags on a large wooden trunk beneath one of the five windows punctuating the walls.

"He's been married four times?"

"Five if you count my mother. He likes to fall in love. Unfortunately, he falls out of it rather quickly. But not before each of my stepmothers has her turn at emptying the bank accounts and erasing all traces of the previous Madame Constantine from the chateau."

No wonder he thought every woman had a price. She'd learned more about Franco in the past half hour than she had in the previous two weeks. She'd thought the chateau meant Franco had enjoyed the stability and permanence she'd lacked, but apparently not if he had revolving stepmothers and his home was always being torn apart.

Shelves loaded with sports memorabilia lined the walls. The trophies and ribbons drew her to the side of the room. Bicycle racing. Swimming. Rowing. That explained those wide shoulders and muscular legs. She'd never lived anywhere long enough to join a team, and at one time she'd condemned her mother for that. Stacy had lost count of the times during the past decade she'd wished her bitter words back.

She dragged her fingers along the spines of a series of books on car racing. Franco's cologne teased her nose a second before the heat of him spooned her back and his hands settled at her waist. She leaned into him.

"I took Vincent to the Monte Carlo Grand Prix after our grad-school graduation twelve years ago. He became hooked on fast cars. When he returned to the States he convinced his father to sponsor a NASCAR team."

And last year he'd been badly injured at a race.

Stacy turned. Franco stood so close their hips and thighs meshed and she could see the tiny strain lines radiating from his eyes and lips. "You can't blame yourself for his accident. Candace said it was a freak event. Something about an equipment failure."

He hesitated. "There is a price for each choice we make."

"*Tout a un prix,*" she quoted his earlier words back to him. Everything had a price. Including her.

Would the price for this affair end up being more than she could bear?

Franco needed to get away from Stacy. *Now.*

He had broken a rule and hugged her. How could he not? She might have tried to act unaffected while telling her grisly tale, but the tremor in her voice and the deathly pallor of her face had given her inner angst away. If she was acting, she was the best damned actress he had ever seen.

But if she was telling the truth then not only had her mother walked away from money, but Stacy had as well. She could not possibly be that different from other avaricious members of her sex. Could she? Had she not already hinted that a million dollars would not be enough to give her a life of leisure?

But she plans to go back to work. She did not ask for more.

What was it about her that made him talk? He had revealed things about Lisette and Vincent that he had never shared with anyone. If he did not leave now then there was no telling what she would extract from him.

He put necessary inches between them. "I must read over the documents and spend an hour with Mathé. Can you amuse yourself?"

"Of course," Stacy replied without hesitation.

"If you are genuinely interested in history then you may explore the house. The wives are allowed to change the linens, but not the furniture or the architecture."

Excitement flared in Stacy's eyes. Any of his other lovers would have pouted if he tried to ignore them, and then they would have cajoled or attempted to seduce him into entertaining them. If he had brought his lovers here, that is. And since Lisette, he had not. Stacy would not be here if not for his father's insistence on meeting her. Franco would not put it past the old goat to have stripped the rooms himself to force Franco to share his bedroom and his bed.

"Your father won't mind if I snoop around?"

"*Non.* Papa knows the history of the house and the furnishings. I will see if he can accompany you."

"I don't want to be any trouble." She fussed with a button on her blouse and Franco struggled with a sudden urge to strip the garment from her. He had escorted her from his bed to a taxi less than twelve hours ago, and yet his desire for her had not diminished with exposure. If anything, his craving for her had intensified. Not a positive circumstance. "Your father wasn't expecting me, was he?"

"He asked to meet you."

Her eyes widened. "You told him about me? About us?"

"*Oui.*"

"The whole truth?"

"I do not lie." Her gaze fell and her cheeks darkened.

From embarrassment? Was she ashamed of the bargain they had made? Franco reached out and tucked a stray lock of hair beneath Stacy's ear. "Tonight, we will do something I have never done."

Her pulse quickened beneath his fingertips. "What's that?"

"I have never had a woman in my boyhood bed. Fantasies, *oui*. But flesh? *Non*."

Her gaze darted to the object in question behind him and the tip of her tongue dampened her lips. He could not resist bending down to capture and suckle the soft, pink flesh. Stacy leaned into him, curling her fingers around his belt and rising on her toes. Her breasts pressed his chest with tantalizing softness.

She had come a long way as a lover. In a short time she had become less reticent about her pleasure, but she had yet to initiate any contact. He was on the verge of saying to hell with the documents and tumbling her onto the sheets when she pulled away. Blushing, she ducked her head as if her ardent response embarrassed her. "Go. I'll be fine."

He didn't want to leave her, and for that very reason he escorted her to the salon where his father waited with refreshments, then walked out and locked himself in his father's study.

The documents transferring ownership of the Constantine holdings to Franco, less a lifetime annuity for his father, were straightforward. His father had agreed to sign the papers the day Stacy returned to the States with her million. Franco delayed as long as he possibly could, rereading the document and then playing with Mathé before going in search of Stacy two hours later.

He found her in the nursery, sitting in an old rocking

chair with her head tipped back and her eyes closed. Her slender fingers caressed the worn wooden arms.

His mood lightened at the sight of her. And what nonsense was that? Why did Stacy affect him so strongly? Was it because she did not try to work her wiles on him? Or did she have him completely fooled? Was her air of innocence the bait in her trap?

"Que fais-tu?" he asked, more harshly than he had intended.

She startled and her lids flew open. "I'm imagining what it would be like to rock your baby in the same chair that your mother and grandmother used. It must be comforting to know that generations of ancestors have sat here and had the same hopes and fears for their children. Any child would be fortunate to have roots that deep, Franco."

An image of Stacy rocking with a dark-haired baby at her breast—his baby—filled his mind. He rejected the possibility. No matter how logical her motivations, he'd bought her, and he could not respect a woman he could buy. "I doubt my mother ever rocked me in that chair. She was not the loving type. I had a series of *bonnes d'enfants.*"

"Nannies?"

He nodded.

"My mother was wonderful. We moved a lot and she worked most of the hours in the day, but I always knew she loved me." Stacy rose, hugged herself and walked to the window. The curtains had been removed, leaving the wide casement bare to the evening sun. "She was my best friend even though I wasn't always the best of daughters. I hated moving, and once I hit my teens we argued about it often. But that's because I didn't know why. She always told me my father loved me and wanted to be with me, but that he couldn't."

"She lied."

She abruptly faced him with her head held high, her hands fisted by her side and fire in her eyes. "To protect me, yes."

"My father lied as well, but during a school vacation I researched the newspaper archives and learned the truth about my mama. She was a spoiled party girl always looking for excitement. Shopping. Drugs. Men."

The sympathy softening Stacy's eyes made him regret the confession. Confidences would lead her to expect more from him than he was willing to give. He was a cold bastard—or so he'd been told. Stacy would do best to accept his limitations and his money and move on.

"I'm sorry. I assumed living in a wonderful place like this meant you'd automatically have a happy childhood."

"I was not unhappy." And why was he sharing that? Because he did not want her pity.

"Are you and your father close?"

"When he is not enthralled with his latest paramour, *oui*. We used to go to the races together." She was getting too personal. He had to derail this tête-à-tête.

Franco approached her, pinning her in the window by planting a hand on either side of her. He leaned closer, inhaling her unique scent and aligning his hips with hers. Desire thickened his blood. "I have not made love in this room either and we have an hour before dinner."

That he considered sex less personal than conversation was telling, he realized. The understanding he saw in Stacy's eyes took him aback. She saw through his actions, but rather than call him on his evasive tactics, she smiled and cupped his cheek. "I'm all yours."

For two more weeks. Longer would be too dangerous. Stacy had a way of breaching his defenses. He would have to find a way to stop her before he crumbled like castle ruins at her feet.

Nine

Franco's laughter stirred something deep inside Stacy.

She crossed from the luxurious en suite bathroom to one of the tall tower windows of Franco's bedroom and looked outside. Franco and Mathé were kicking a soccer ball around on the lawn below. Franco's teeth flashed in the early-morning light as he laughed again.

He'd be a good father. The kind of father she wished she'd had. And his children would have all the things she'd lacked. History. Roots. Security.

According to Monsieur Constantine, this room hadn't changed in over two decades. Franco could have had something new with each of his stepmothers' re-decorations, but instead he'd stuck with the furnishings he and his father had chosen together. That told Stacy Franco liked stability. And he might even have a tiny sentimental streak. Like her.

She touched a finger to her watch and then smoothed

a hand over the scarred wooden headboard pushed against the wall between two windows. Last night she'd slept spooned with Franco on the narrow mattress. This morning she'd awoken alone, but surprisingly well-rested. Letting her guard down enough to sleep had apparently not been an issue after all. But then again, he had exhausted her before letting her sleep. Warmth rose under her skin and settled in her pelvis. The man seemed determined to make up to her for the mediocre lovers of her past.

"You are exactly what Franco needs, my dear," Monsieur Constantine said in heavily accented English behind her.

Startled, Stacy turned and found him in the open bedroom doorway. Hadn't Franco said he'd told his father the whole truth? "How can you believe that?"

The older man shrugged. "I am sure you had your reasons for agreeing to accept money in exchange for spending time with my son. But you are not like any…how you say?…gold diggers I have ever encountered. I have met many in my seventy-five years, and I have even had the misfortune to marry a few. Between my wives and Lisette, my son has become quite bitter and distrustful of women."

Stacy nodded. "He told me about Lisette."

Bushy white eyebrows rose. "That is surprising. Did he also tell you that he continued to love her until she admitted she had married him for his money, and that she had the abortion because she was planning to divorce him?"

Poor Franco. "Um…no."

"My divorce settlements put us in financial difficulties. Difficulties over which Franco eventually triumphed, but his wife did not have the integrity to lessen her expenses and stand beside him through adversity. When one truly loves one takes the good with the bad...as I did with Franco's mama."

He joined her by the window and looked down on Franco and Mathé. "He will not tell me what Lisette said to him in that Paris hospital, but it changed him. He is not the son I once knew. He keeps much locked inside now."

The weight of his gaze settled on Stacy. "My boy has a wounded soul. It will take a special woman to heal him."

What exactly was he implying? "Why are you telling me this, Monsieur Constantine? I'm not that woman."

"I believe you are."

A choked sound of disbelief erupted from her mouth. "I'm sleeping with your son for money."

"And the agreement troubles you, yes?"

"Of course."

"And that is but one of the reasons I know you are not like the others."

Keeping up with the bizarre discussion was beyond her. He might as well be speaking a foreign language. "One of the reasons?"

"*Oui.* If you cared only for financial gain you would be garbed in jewels and designer clothing instead of your inexpensive American pieces. Franco is a generous lover. Except in matters of the heart."

True. But his loyalty to Vincent and Mathé came from the heart, so he wasn't incapable of caring. "Dare I ask if there are more reasons?"

The older man smiled. "Only the most important one. When I gave you the tour of the chateau yesterday you asked many, many questions about the history of the house and furnishings. You never once asked the value of a single item."

No, she hadn't. She'd been more concerned with the

sentimental significance than the monetary worth. "I guess I never thought about the costs."

"*Exactement.* For a woman who claims to be motivated by money, it seems to have little importance to you."

Other than the security it represented, he was right. She didn't want to be rich. She just wanted a home. Otherwise, she would have sued her father's estate as Franco had suggested. Heaven knows the lawyers had aggressively solicited her and encouraged her to do so before she'd fled Tampa and started over in Charlotte. But she hadn't wanted to be tied to blood money. She'd rather be poor than feel guilty for profiting from her mother's murder. "Okay, you have me there, but I'm still not the right woman for Franco."

"We shall see, Stacy. I am hoping my son will see what a treasure you are before it is too late." He offered his arm in the same courtly gesture Franco often used. "Now come, breakfast waits and you should eat before you make the drive back to Monaco."

"And once every inch of your ivory skin is slick with the sun-warmed tanning oil I will thrust deep into your body again and again until you cry out as *le petit mort* overcomes you," Franco resumed his tantalizing tale after they crossed Monaco's border and turned toward the harbor.

Stacy's heart raced. She licked her dry lips and squirmed in her seat, attempting to alleviate the ache between her legs.

Franco had filled the past half-hour of their trip with a lengthy, detailed description of the sensual afternoon he had planned for them on his sailboat. His verbal seduction was a timely reminder that their relationship was all about sex. Only sex. Any emotional connection she might feel with him after the personal insights she'd gained into his character at the chateau had no place in the bargain they'd struck.

His fingertips trailed up the inside of her thigh. "And I will not stop until—"

An annoying sound interrupted him and dampened her arousal. A cell phone. Hers. Stacy blinked, exhaled and dug her phone out of her purse. "Hello?"

"Candace is having a meltdown," Amelia's voice said. "Madeline and I have tried everything we know to calm her down. It's your turn."

"What do you mean?"

"She's freaking out and talking about cancelling the wedding. We can't figure out why. You have to try. Tell her how much money she'd be wasting or something. Not that money would matter if she was really unhappy, but she's absolutely crazy in love with Vincent. We can't let a flash of panic ruin that. Please, Stacy, just get over here convince her to sit tight until rational thought returns."

Alarmed, Stacy glanced at Franco. "I can be there in fifteen minutes."

She disconnected and turned in her seat. "I'll have to take a rain check on the boat ride. That was Amelia. She wants me at the hotel."

"Something is wrong?"

"Um…Candace needs me." Because he was Vincent's friend she couldn't tell him why. But she wanted to. She wanted to ask him how someone as deeply in love as Candace could have doubts.

"And what of our plans?"

Stacy had never been on a boat, but that wasn't the appeal. She wanted to spend more time with Franco, wanted to learn more about him. She'd planned to ask

questions during the car ride home, but his verbal seduction had waylaid that. Had he done it deliberately?

"Franco, I would love to spend the afternoon with
you. And making love on the boat sounds amazingly
sexy even though I'm not sure about doing it outdoors
on the deck where we might be seen by anybody with
a good set of binoculars. But when Candace needs me
I have to go, and you promised our relationship
wouldn't interfere with the wedding stuff."

His jaw hardened. "Vincent assured me your
presence would not be required for several days."

She should have tried harder to check with Candace
before leaving for Avignon, but the bride-to-be hadn't
been in the hotel suite Sunday morning or answering her
cell phone. In the end, Stacy had let her curiosity about
Franco lead the way. "Vincent was wrong."

Franco turned the car away from the marina and
toward the hotel. Moments later he stopped the vehicle
outside the entrance. A doorman opened her door and
helped her alight. She thanked him and joined Franco
by the trunk.

She reached for her bag, but Franco held it out of
reach. "I will see you inside."

Not a good idea since she had no idea what she'd be
walking into. "No need. I'll…um, call you later."

He looked ready to argue, but instead he relinquished
her suitcase and stroked her cheek. The passion simmering in his intensely blue eyes snarled a tight knot of
desire beneath Stacy's navel. "Dinner tonight. I will
send the car."

"I'll have to clear it with Candace first."

He nodded. "I will let you go, but first—"

Heedless of the hotel staff members and vacationers
around them, he took her mouth. Hard. Hot. Intimately.

His tongue delved, stroked and then he suckled hers. By the time he lifted his head Stacy clung dizzily to his belt. "Do not keep me waiting one moment longer than necessary, *mon gardénia*."

He stroked a thumb over her damp bottom lip and then left her standing in the driveway on trembling legs, torn between desire and friendship. She wanted to go with Franco, but Candace needed her.

Stacy shook off her indecision. Her friendship with Candace would continue beyond the next two weeks, but her relationship with Franco would not. And she'd better not forget it. Passion and profit were all she could expect from him. No promises, he'd said. And that wouldn't change no matter how well she understood him.

She marched inside and across the lobby. The elevator whisked her to the top floor. Stacy shoved her keycard into the lock and entered the suite in time to hear Candace ranting, "I can't believe he expected me to drop everything and spend three days in his bed."

Amelia spotted Stacy, grabbed her by the arm and dragged her into the sitting area. "Good. You're here. Tell her how crazy it would be to cancel the wedding at this late date."

Stacy let her purse and overnight bag slide to the floor. "What's wrong?"

Candace pivoted. A white line of tension circled her compressed lips. "I can't marry Vincent."

Stacy blinked. "Why?"

"Why does everybody keep asking me that?" Candace glared at them and then paced in front of the long window. "Can't you just accept I made a mistake and leave it at that?"

"No," Amelia and Madeline chorused.

"Don't you love him?" Stacy persisted.

"I wouldn't be here if I didn't."

And the love in Vincent's eyes at the ball had been impossible to miss. "Did something happen to make you no longer trust him? Did he scare you? Threaten you? Hurt you?"

"No." She sounded surprised Stacy would even suggest it, but then she didn't know Stacy's past. One day, Stacy realized, she'd have to tell her. But not today.

"Then I don't understand why you'd throw this all away. Do his scars suddenly repulse you?"

Anger flushed Candace's pale cheeks. "No. They. Do. Not."

"Then why can't you marry him? You love him and he clearly adores you."

"It's like you said. He's rich and powerful and I'm…not. I don't fit into his world. The balls, the limos, the designer gowns, they're not me."

"They're not any of us, but we've had fun faking it," Amelia said.

Stacy recalled Monsieur Constantine's words about Franco's ex. "Candace, would you still want to be with Vincent if he lost all his money?"

"Of course I would. I don't know what you're getting at, Stacy, but I am not marrying Vincent for his millions. I thought you knew me better than that."

"My point is, doesn't he deserve a woman who'll love him for who he is as a person and not for the penthouse lifestyle he represents? And doesn't the fact that you don't care about the scars or the superficial trappings and that you could live without the limos and designer clothes make you the perfect woman for him?"

And didn't Franco deserve the same thing? His father was right. It would take a special woman to appreciate the man beneath the glitz. Someone who didn't assign dollar signs to everything or mind slowly chipping away at his hard shell to discover his secrets.

Someone like you.

Stacy gasped in surprise as the thought sprouted and took root. It would be so easy to convince herself she was the woman who could heal Franco's embittered soul. But that would be foolish. Besides, he wouldn't be interested in a nobody like her when he had a continent full of glamorous, sophisticated women to choose from. And she…well, she couldn't risk it.

"Yes. No. I don't know." Candace sank onto the sofa and buried her face in her trembling hands.

Madeline sat beside her and passed her a tissue. "You have been happier this year than I've ever seen you. Do you really want to throw that away because of bridal jitters?"

"What I want doesn't matter." Candace blotted her tear-stained face. "Vincent's parents are arriving tonight. He wants to tell them about the baby, and once they find out they're going to think I trapped their precious son with a pregnancy to get my claws on their fortune."

Tension seeped from Stacy's muscles upon hearing the true reason for the panic attack. This was a salvageable situation. She glanced at her suitemates, but neither Amelia nor Madeline looked surprised about the baby news. Hmm. Maybe the baby wasn't a secret after all.

Stacy sat on Candace's opposite side and tentatively laid a hand over her clenched fist. "You're afraid to tell your future in-laws you're pregnant?"

"They're Boca Raton and I'm trailer trash. They're not going to want somebody like me raising their grandchild."

Stacy understood the feeling of not fitting in all too well, but running had never made it better. "Number one, Candace, you're not trailer trash. You're a registered nurse. Number two, I suspect the Reynards are going to want someone raising their grandchild whose love will stay strong through the good times and the bad."

"That would be you," Amelia said.

Stacy nodded. "Don't forget what you've already been through with Vincent. I'm sure they haven't."

After a moment Candace's lips curved into a quivery smile. She looked at each of them in turn and then took a shoulder-straightening breath and lifted her chin. "You're right. I am the perfect woman for Vincent, and if the Reynards don't agree, well...I'll just prove them wrong."

"We've got your back," Madeline vowed.

Stacy wished she had half as much confidence as her friend in matters of the heart. But she didn't. She was an emotional coward and probably always would be.

"Don't ever fall in love, man," Vincent groaned into his beer.

"That is not what you have been telling me for the past six months," Franco replied as he sat on the opposite end of the sofa from Vincent and pressed the remote control to his plasma television. He tuned his satellite dish into an American sports channel. "You have been singing the praises of a woman to warm your bed."

Vincent wore a besotted expression similar to the one Franco had seen on his father far too often—one Franco swore never to wear again. Lisette had cured him.

"It's more than regular sex. It's waking up beside her and watching her sleep. Or knowing she loves you enough to let you see her without her makeup on or to kiss her before she brushes her teeth."

The back of Franco's neck prickled. He shifted his shoulders to ease the uncomfortable sensation. He had watched Stacy sleep this morning at the chateau, but that had nothing to do with love. It had been lust. Nothing more. And the kiss on her brow had been an attempt to wake her and satisfy his hunger. If in the end he had elected to take a cold shower and let her sleep, it was only because he had driven her to orgasm so many times last night that he doubted her capable of coming again so soon, and he never left a woman unsatisfied in bed.

"Fifty bucks says the Marlins whip Boston," Vincent said, drawing Franco's attention back to the baseball game. "Women aren't logical. And they're full of contradictions."

"I agree, and I accept your bet." He had finally found Stacy's weakness. She could be bought but only if the gifts benefitted her friends. Such altruism had to be a pretense.

"Women are like a jigsaw puzzle with missing pieces. Frustrating. Unsolvable. And I ought to know. I must have put a hundred puzzles together during my hospital stay."

"You will get no argument from me." Each secret he uncovered about Stacy suggested she was not like the other women of his acquaintance, which only meant he needed a more complete picture to uncover her strategy. He glanced at his watch. When would she call?

Vincent had phoned immediately after Franco had left Stacy at the hotel ninety minutes ago. Watching baseball with his friend was not the sexually satisfying afternoon Franco had planned, but he could not concentrate on work, and he had been a Red Sox fan since his days at MIT.

Vincent's expression turned to one of bewilderment. "When I told you I'd keep Candace busy I honestly thought she and I would spend every spare minute of the next three days making up for four weeks' abstinence. But this morning I mentioned my parents were flying in today and that I wanted to tell them about the baby, and she freaked."

"Due to your parents' arrival or to revealing the pregnancy?"

"Don't know. That's the illogical part. Candace and my parents get along, and in another month or two she'll be showing. No point in trying to hide it. Besides, I don't want to. I spent years avoiding getting a girl pregnant, but the minute I found out Candace was carrying my baby I wanted the world to know. Candace is the one who insisted we keep a lid on it. Besides, my folks will be thrilled to finally have a grandkid on the way since my sister isn't anteing up."

Franco's father was impatient as well. Impatient enough to force Franco's hand. Franco's mind flashed back to the image of Stacy in the nursery rocking chair, her wistful expression before she'd known he was watching and the sadness in her eyes when she'd talked about her mother.

Stacy's life had been tragically difficult, but it had not broken her. He had to respect her strength even though he disliked her willingness to sell herself for financial security. How hypocritical of him, since he benefited from her mercenary streak.

Vincent swore as a Sox batter hit a grand slam. "If they keep this up I'll owe you for more than the tickets to the ball and that killer dress you bought for Candace."

"There is no need to repay me."

"Bull. You and Toby are babysitting these women at my request. I'll cover all the costs, and I'll grant you a year's lease on a Midas Chocolates location in the galleria of the Aruba hotel." He popped a handful of nuts in his mouth and washed them down with a sip of beer.

"The hell of it is, Franco, that when I was stuck in

labor negotiations, Candace is all I thought about. And I got pissed—not because the union rep was being a prick, but because he was keeping me away from Candace. It's hard to care about dollars and cents when I'm scared as hell that I'm going to blow it with her. She's the best thing that's ever happened to me, and if having my lady-killer mug back meant never having met her, I'd rather keep the face that frightens children."

Surprised by the emotional speech from a man previously not given to sentiment, Franco drained his beer. Stacy had invaded his concentration at work as well this past two weeks. No woman had ever done so—not even Lisette. The only positive in the situation was that his preoccupation would end as soon as she boarded the plane bound for the States. "The scars are less noticeable with each surgery and graft."

"Yeah, but unlike you, I won't win any beauty contests."

The doorbell rang, wiping the smile from Franco's lips. He was not expecting anyone. Normally, he would be at work on a Monday afternoon. *Stacy?* No, she would call and his cell phone had not rung. He had checked twice to make sure it was turned on. "Excuse me."

He crossed the entrance hall and opened the door. Stacy stood on the porch looking as delicious as a juicy peach. A wide-brimmed straw hat covered her chestnut hair and a pale-orange sundress outlined her curves. Her bare legs looked magnificent despite the bulky walking sandals she insisted on wearing.

The breath stalled in his lungs, but his heart raced. He caught a glimpse of a taxi's taillights turning out of the drive.

A tentative smile wobbled on her lips. She removed her sunglasses, revealing her azure eyes. "Is it too late to go boating?"

"Vincent is here." He found her fading smile and obvious disappointment surprisingly gratifying since it mirrored his own. He used his thumb to free her bottom lip from her teeth. "Come in."

"I don't want to intrude. I'll just call a cab." She reached for her cell phone, but he caught her hand.

"*Non.* Stay." He dragged his knuckles along her arm. She shivered, reminding him of last night, of tasting every inch of her delectable skin until she whimpered and squirmed. "You may sunbathe by the pool. I will drench your body in suntan oil, and when the game ends I will send Vincent in search of Candace and we will have the sybaritic afternoon we anticipated, but on dry land. My patio is private. No one will see or hear when I make you cry out in ecstasy."

Her breath hitched and her nipples pushed against her dress. "Okay."

He motioned for her to precede him. Stacy crossed the foyer and entered the den. Franco noted that she avoided stepping on the rugs. He filed the odd fact away for later.

Snapping his cell phone closed, Vincent rose. "Hi, Stacy. Rain check on the game, Franco. Candace called. I have to go."

Vincent shook his head when Franco smirked. "You're laughing now, but one of these days a woman will have you dancing to her tune."

"That will not happen, *mon ami.*"

"Just wait, bud. Your day will come. I'll see myself out." A moment later the front door closed behind Vincent. The engine of his Ferrari roared and then faded in the distance.

Franco turned to Stacy. "Remove your clothing."

She gasped and clutched her bag tighter. "Here? Now?"

"*Oui.*" He tugged his shirt over his head and pitched

it onto the sofa. He retrieved the condom from his wallet before dropping his trousers and briefs and kicking off his shoes and removing his socks. Stacy watched wide-eyed and then licked her lips as she stared at his growing erection. The slow glide of her tongue over her rosy flesh made him pulse with need.

She turned her back. Franco swept her silky hair aside, unzipped her dress, flicked open her bra and shoved both to the floor. He dragged her panties down to her ankles, pulled her back to his front and cupped her breasts. For several seconds he fought the urgency to be inside her and simply savored the feel of her warm, soft skin against his and the weight of her breasts in his palms. He inhaled her scent and his control wavered. He stepped away. "Come."

He led her outside, dropped the condom on the table and then arranged the double-width lounger to his liking. He took the straw tote which she held in front of her like a shield and set it on the tiles. Despite Stacy's apparent shyness, her nipples were erect and desire flushed her face and neck.

"Lie face down."

She crawled onto the chaise, presenting him with her delectable bottom. He fisted his hands against his rampant hunger.

"You have suntan oil?" His voice came out an octave lower than usual.

"I have lotion in my bag."

"*Pas le même chose.* Not the same. I will return momentarily, and then, *mon gardénia,* I will make you moan."

An all-over tan had never been one of Stacy's goals. She didn't even have the courage to try on one of the thong bikinis so prevalent on the beaches here. And forget going topless.

She could not believe she was naked on Franco's patio. Glancing left and right, she verified that this spot was indeed private, thanks to the vine-covered trellises at each end of the house. The sun warmed parts of her it had never seen before. And then Franco returned, striding boldly, *nudely,* in her direction. He had a pair of towels tucked under his arm, a bottle of suntan oil in one hand and one of water in the other.

Her heart pounded faster. She dampened her dry lips. If anyone had ever told her a month ago that she could become a hedonistic creature she'd have called them delusional.

"Close your eyes," he said as he dropped the items he carried beside her on the chaise and straddled her legs. Stacy did so, admitting she'd probably brought this on herself by telling him his masseuse had not turned her on. What Franco had done after the masseuse left, on the other hand…. The memory sent a delicious tingle through her. Suffice to say she would never view the long wooden benches of a sauna in the same way again. If she ever saw the inside of another sauna.

Warm oil trickled over her shoulders and back, quickly followed by Franco's firm hands. The scent of coconuts filled her nostrils as he massaged her with long, slow strokes across her shoulders and down her spine. His fingertips teased the sides of her breasts, her waist. The occasional drag of his sex against her buttocks made her breath catch. He paused, shifted and then oil dribbled onto the small of her back and over her bottom. It seeped into the crevice and between her legs to her most sensitive spot. She squirmed on the chaise.

Franco's hands stilled her hips. *"Non."*

He alternated feather-light brushes with muscle-deep massages over her back, her bottom, down her legs and across the soles of her feet. Throughout the process the wiry hairs on his legs teased her hyper-sensitive skin. And then he stroked his erection between her slickened cheeks. Stacy yearned to rise to her knees and let him take her from behind as he had once before, but he moved away. The memory of that night in front of his bedroom mirror, the way he'd cupped her breasts and nibbled her neck, the undiluted hunger on his face as he'd plunged into her again and again made her shiver.

"*Attente elle*," he ordered in a gravelly voice.

Wait for it. One of his favorite phrases. But Stacy didn't want to wait. She wiggled impatiently, but Franco didn't quicken his torturous caresses. Arousal pulsed through her. She no longer cared about prying eyes, but focused instead on the man who seemed bent on driving her out of her mind with desire. He rose from the chaise and she tensed in anticipation.

"Turn over."

Stacy hastily complied. Franco's shaft glistened with suntan oil. She reached for him, but he shook his head and pulled the brim of her hat over her face. "No peeking."

She settled back into the cushion. Oil trickled over her breasts and slowly ran down her sides like tiny, warm fingers. He poured another pool in her navel and then drizzled more over her curls. His palms covered her breasts and she gasped. He teased and tweaked, rolling the slick tips between his fingers and buffing with the flats of his palms. She shifted her legs, but that only intensified the ache. His massage continued down her torso and her legs, skipping her neediest parts.

Stacy was ready to beg when Franco bent her knees, knelt between them and stroked his shaft along her soft, slick folds and against her center. A moan slipped from her lips as she rose swiftly toward the peak. She heard a snick of sound, and then icy-cold water splashed her nipple. She squealed and tried to rise, but Franco planted a palm on her breastbone and treated the opposite side to the same cold, fizzy bath. The carbonated water teased in an unbelievably sensual way, and then his hot lips covered a cooled tip. He alternated between icy baths and hot suckling until Stacy batted her hat away.

"That was sneaky."

He sat back on his haunches, his grin unrepentant. Two could play that game. She sat up, snatched the water from his hand and drenched his erection. His howl turned into a groan when she took him into her mouth.

Franco fisted his hands in her hair, but he didn't thrust or try to gag her the way her high-school lover had. Franco let her take the lead and as much of him as she could handle. Pleased and surprisingly turned on, she released him and showered him with another splash of water and then another deep kiss. His back arched. He hissed with each splash and muttered what sounded like encouragement in French each time her lips encircled him. She smiled and repeated the process until the bottle was empty.

She had never expected to like doing this, but the tendons straining Franco's neck and his knotted muscles attested to his enjoyment. And she liked pleasing him.

"Tu es une sirène." He tugged gently on her hair, but firmly enough to make her release him.

A siren? Her? She smiled.

He reached for the condom he'd tossed on the table earlier, tore the wrapper with his teeth and then sheathed himself. Stacy reclined and opened her arms. Franco guided himself to her center and plunged deep. The sun-warmed latex over his hot shaft added yet another new dimension to his erotic play. She savored the sense of fullness, rightness, and then tangled her legs around his waist the way he'd taught her and held on tight. He took her on a roller-coaster-fast ride to the top and then she plunged over to the sound of him calling her name as he climaxed.

Their gasps filled a silence broken only by the hum of the pool filter and an occasional bird call. Stacy stroked a hand down his sweat-dampened back. "Wow."

He levered himself up on his elbows. "You have hidden talents, *mon gardénia.*"

A blush warmed her cheeks. How could she still blush around this man? "I've had an excellent teacher."

"And there is yet much to learn," he said gently as he pulled away. And then he stilled and stiffened. *"Le condom, c'est cassé."*

Stacy's heart missed a beat. Her muscles turned rigid. She prayed she'd mistranslated. "What?"

Franco's serious gaze locked onto hers. "The condom broke."

A wave of panic seized her. Her gaze dropped to the damning evidence, and her heart nearly beat its way out of her chest.

Dear God, was she going to repeat her mother's mistake?

Calendars, dates and biology scrambled in her head, and then sanity slowly invaded, making sense of it all, but leaving her cold, drained and eerily calm. She exhaled shakily. "My…um, period is due in a few days. We should be safe. I'm…um…unlikely to conceive now."

"How regular are you?" he asked without blinking.

She flinched, and feeling exposed, dragged a towel over her nakedness. Would she ever get used to these intimate conversations? "Like clockwork."

"Bien. But to be certain you will visit my doctor

before you return to the States. I will make the appointment." As if that settled everything, he straightened, crossed to the pool and dove in.

But Stacy was far from settled. She pressed a hand to her chest. Close call. Too close. She wasn't prepared to have a baby or let a man into her life.

Or was she?

Ten

A baby.

And not just any baby. *Franco's baby.*

The words reverberated in Stacy's head as the taxi carried her back to the hotel. Guilt nagged her for sneaking out while Franco was in the shower, but she couldn't calmly sit across the dinner table from him or go back to bed with him until she figured out the chaotic emotions churning inside her.

Her chances of getting pregnant today were slim. And that was good news. Wasn't it?

Absolutely.

This was the wrong time, the wrong place and the wrong man.

But there was a tiny spark of something that felt suspiciously like hope glowing deep inside her. Illogical, foolish hope. The idea of having a baby appealed, even though she hadn't once thought about having children since learning the truth about her mother's murder.

Had being around Candace activated some twisted kind of approaching-thirty biological clock?

She pressed a hand to her agitated stomach. Franco had the means to buy and sell her a hundred times over, and after his painful experience with Lisette there was no telling how he'd react if Stacy turned up pregnant.

Would he want the child or tell her to get rid of it?

"Mademoiselle, we have arrived," the taxi driver's words jerked Stacy back to the present before she could pursue that disturbing line of thought. She blinked and saw the hotel entrance outside the car window. The ride had passed in a blur.

A uniformed hotel employee opened her door. She dug the appropriate money from her wallet, paid and tipped the driver and climbed from the cab.

Standing on the pavement, she debated going up to the suite. But Madeline was far too perceptive. She'd zero in on Stacy's disquiet in seconds, and as much as Stacy longed for a dose of the savvier woman's no-nonsense advice or the support she knew her trio of suitemates would offer, she needed to get her thoughts in order first.

Stacy stepped onto the sidewalk and headed toward Monaco-Ville with no particular destination in mind. She loved the old-world charm, the sense of history and permanence in the oldest part of the principality. That it happened to be in the opposite direction to Larvotto Beach and Franco's view was an added bonus.

For the past ten years she'd focused on her safety and her financial security, but she'd completely neglected the emotional component of her life. She'd been afraid to let anyone get close and had paid for it with loneliness. Not even the teens she counseled were allowed past her emotional barriers. She cared about them, but knowing they might pack up and move without notice led her to maintain a protective distance.

But she didn't want to be alone or afraid anymore. She liked having friends, liked feeling connected and wouldn't mind having a family.

If she were pregnant, she wouldn't get rid of the baby no matter what Franco said. With his million euros she could afford to keep it, and even without his money she could manage once she found another job.

But could she deny a father his child or a child its father, live life on the run, always looking over her shoulder and never set down roots or make a home? No. She wouldn't wish her childhood on anyone. Not unless she truly feared for her own or her child's safety.

She didn't see Franco as being that kind of threat.

Didn't your mother's diary and your father's actions teach you anything? Rich men can't be trusted.

But she'd seen no sign of Franco being power-crazed or bending the laws to suit his needs. Other than buying her, that is. But as he'd pointed out, mistresses were not unusual here, and he'd shown her nothing but respect. He'd made sure that each sexual encounter left her satisfied when he didn't have to. He'd watched over the bridal party for Vincent, and he took the time to play with a fatherless boy—almost every weekend, according to Monsieur Constantine.

From everything she'd seen, Franco was a good man, and she suspected he'd be a good father.

Oh my God. Are you falling for him?

The leaden feeling in the pit of her stomach said yes.

Her steps slowed and her internal warning sirens screamed.

Had she learned enough about her own strength and resilience over the past decade to lower her walls and let a man in? Maybe. The training she'd had before and since she'd begun volunteering with the teens had taught her what constituted a healthy relationship. Surely she could practice what she preached?

A child's laughter startled her. Stacy looked around, stunned at where her subconscious had led her. The Saint Martin Garden was one of several playgrounds Monaco had set aside for children. She'd walked past it the day she'd toured the Prince's Palace. Sinking down on a bench in the shade, she studied the happy faces of the mothers and children.

Monaco would be a wonderful place to raise a family. According to her stack of guide books, the schools were good and the police force was second to none. Education and safety had been her guideposts in recent years.

Whether or not today's encounter resulted in a baby, would Franco want more than the agreed-upon month? Would he be interested in her staying in Monaco to see if their relationship had a future after the other brides-maids flew home? She and he were both wounded souls who feared trusting and being hurt. Could she heal him and in the process learn to trust again?

Could he be happy with her? She couldn't compete with the elegant women at the ball, but the remarkable chemistry between them had to account for some-thing, didn't it?

Confidence swelled within her. She could do this. She would face her fears and ask him to give their rela-tionship a try.

Her cell phone rang. Stacy checked the number on the caller ID. Franco's. Her heart raced and her palms dampened. She couldn't talk to him right now. Her decision was too new, too raw, so she silenced her phone.

Tomorrow she'd be ready to take that colossal leap.

A baby.

The idea didn't repulse Franco as much as it should have. In fact, having a child with Stacy could solve many problems. If he provided an heir, his father would not feel the need to impregnate the tramp plotting to empty the Constantine coffers. And Stacy wanted financial security. They could each benefit from continuing their relationship.

He tried Stacy's cellular number again and once more received her voice mail. He disconnected rather than leave a third message. Why had she left without saying goodbye? And why would she not return his calls?

By the time he had finished working out his tension by swimming laps, she'd been in the lower-level shower. He could have joined her, but he had needed a few moments alone to consider the ramifications of their situation. In all his thirty-eight years he had never had a condom break. He had retreated to his bathroom, and when he had exited his shower Stacy had been gone.

Had Candace phoned? Had Stacy's wedding duties once more taken precedence over her agreement with him? Was she having a relaxed dinner with her suitemates at this very moment while he paced his living room?

He looked forward to his evenings with Stacy more than he should, and he would not mind spending more time with her. She was attractive, intelligent and an extraordinary lover. She did not cling or make demands on his time that he was not willing to offer.

She is getting too close. And if you do not quit focusing on her absence you will be no better than your besotted friend.

He turned on the TV, but not even a baseball game tied in the bottom of the ninth inning with bases loaded could hold his attention. His thoughts kept straying to Stacy, her belly growing round with his child. But he could not afford to be deluded by a woman's false promises again.

What if Stacy were pregnant? Would she, like Lisette, choose to abort his child? Could he stop her?

He wiped a hand over his face. No. He would not engage in a legal battle to force a woman to carry a child she did not want. His only options lay in convincing her she wished to continue the pregnancy and in coming to an agreement satisfactory to them both regarding the child.

Stacy could not possibly be as pure-hearted as she pretended. He would prove it. And once he did then perhaps she would quit monopolizing his thoughts.

"I want you to have my baby," Franco said Wednesday night.

Stacy's heart and lungs stalled at the bald statement. She stared into his somber eyes across the secluded table in Le Grill, the ritzy rooftop restaurant at the Hôtel de Paris.

Her heart lurched back into motion and she dragged oxygen into her deprived lungs. Warmth and cautious optimism trickled through her.

Franco must have spent the forty-eight hours since the broken-condom incident thinking about a future together—as she had. She'd barely been able to concentrate on her bridesmaid's duties. She'd lost track of the number of rehearsal-dinner place cards she'd messed up yesterday and how many times the seamstress had asked her to stand still during her final dress fitting today.

"Your baby?" The words filled her with a tingly sensation. He offered her more than she'd ever dared hope for. Financial security. A home. The possibility of a family. A man who would treat her like a princess the way her mother had promised.

"*Oui.*"

"I might not be pregnant."

"A circumstance we can easily rectify."

Was this a proposal? It had to be. Why else would he bring her to this romantic restaurant where the roof retracted to allow the patrons to dine beneath a blanket of stars? But Franco didn't pull out a ring or get down on bended knee. Maybe the French didn't follow that custom? "I've, um…been thinking about that too."

"You would have to leave your job—a job you claim to love."

She clenched her napkin in her hand, looked away from his intense gaze and confessed, "No, I won't. I was laid off the week before we left for Monaco. I didn't tell Candace because I didn't want her worrying about me when she had a wedding to plan."

Franco's jaw hardened. "You are unemployed? You said you would go back to work when you returned to the States."

"I plan to search for a job, but there are a lot of companies downsizing right now. Not knowing how long it would take for me to find another position is another reason I accepted your offer. But now I don't have to worry about that. I wouldn't mind working here until the baby comes. Afterward—"

"I will pay the expenses on your apartment in Charlotte until you return. And of course, you will be compensated."

Confused, she blinked and frowned. "What?"

"I will give you another million euros upon the birth,

and I will cover all the medical expenses you and the baby incur."

Dizziness threatened to topple her. She grasped the edge of the table and studied his face, but she didn't see any trace of emotion or romance. In fact, he looked as if he were closing a business deal. "A-are you asking me to marry you, Franco?"

He reared back in his chair. "*Non.* I need an heir. You want financial security. I am offering a solution to fill both our needs. A second million will give you the life of leisure you claim the first would not."

The delicious shrimp appetizer she'd consumed turned to molten lead in her stomach. Her chest felt so tight she could barely breathe. "You want me to have a baby...and hand it over to you? Gr-grant you sole custody?"

"*Oui.* As you have seen, I can provide many advantages for a child."

The horror of his words chilled her to the bone and pain speared through her like shards of glass. Oh my God. She'd fallen in love with the arrogant bastard.

Impossible. She hadn't known him long enough to fall in love with him. But merely liking him and being disappointed in him wouldn't hurt this much.

"You don't want me? You only want to buy my baby?" For clarity's sake she rephrased her questions. The words burned her throat. She had to be wrong. He couldn't be asking that.

"*Tu es très* sexy, Stacy. I will enjoy sharing your bed for however long it takes to produce a child. But I have no desire for a wife."

He had clearly stated that he would never marry again on their ride to Avignon. Why hadn't she listened? Franco was alone by choice. He would never allow a woman to get close to him. And he would never change.

She might be willing to lower her walls and risk her heart, but he wasn't.

How could she be so stupid? She'd been falling in love with him and he'd been setting her up. She shoved back her chair and stumbled to her feet. "No."

Franco rose. "I will give you twenty-four hours to reconsider."

Déjà vu. "Don't hold your breath. This time I won't change my mind. You can take your two million euros and shove them up your fine French a—"

"*Y a t'il un problème, mademoiselle?*" an anxious waiter asked.

"Yes, there's a problem. I feel ill. I'm leaving." She turned back to Franco. "I don't ever want to see you again."

"Stacy, if you end this now you will forfeit the money."

And she'd be right back where she started. Nearly broke and out of a job. Too bad. There were some things money couldn't buy.

"Your price is too high. I could never have a child and let it go." A chill swept over her when she realized what she'd said and that she meant it to the bottom of her soul. There was more of her father in her than she'd ever realized. She gulped down a wave of nausea. "And I could never respect a man who would ask me to do so."

She gathered her wrap and her purse and raced for the exit before her tears could escape.

"You were right about Angeline."

His father's voice drew Franco from his contemplation of the Fontvieille harbor far below his thirtieth-floor office window. He swiveled his chair to face the door and the desk and the profit and loss statement he had been neglecting. "What happened to her?"

"I told her I was considering transferring ownership

of the Constantine holdings to you and she left." Pain, disappointment and resignation deepened the lines on his father's face.

"I am sorry." But good riddance.

Armand sank down into the leather visitor chair. "She reminded me of your mother. They all do. Young. Vibrant. Beautiful."

"My mother was unfaithful. Why would you want another woman like her?"

"Francesca was always faithful to herself. I made the mistake of believing my love would transform a party girl who needed to be the center of attention into a loving wife and mother. But true love does not require change. And giving her free rein in hopes that she would be happy and always come home to me was not fair to you. I should have put a stop to the drugs the moment I found out about her habit, but I was afraid doing so would drive her away."

Franco digested the surprising insight into his parents' relationship.

"You were right about Stacy," he admitted reluctantly.

He had waited eight days for her to call and tell him she'd changed her mind. Eight days of being unable to concentrate or sleep well. But the only communication he had received from her was a box delivered via courier containing the gifts he had given her—except for the watch band. She had kept the gift he could buy with pocket change.

Where was the greed, the sense of entitlement that his other lovers had had?

His bed was empty. And there was a barrenness to his days and nights that had not been there before. Even Vincent's bachelor party last night had not lightened his mood.

"Stacy refused the money?"

"She walked away from our agreement when I offered her another million to have my baby."

"I assume that was a proposal."

"*Non.*"

"You asked her to bear a child and then relinquish it to you?"

"*Oui.*"

His father shook his head sadly. "For someone who is worried about our liquid assets you are throwing around a lot of money."

An accurate charge. "It was a test."

"To see if she was…what did you say? Ah yes, a duplicitous and mercenary creature who would sell you anything you wanted to buy?"

Franco nodded.

"And she refused."

"She said my price was too high."

"That would explain why our employees have been ducking for cover for the past week." Franco arched an eyebrow and his father shrugged. "I may have retired, but I have my sources."

Armand tapped the file against the sharp crease of his trousers. "So you have finally found a woman you cannot buy. What are you going to do about it?"

Franco fiddled with his pen and remained silent. He did not have an answer. He'd had confirmation this morning from a physician that Stacy was not pregnant. The news did not bring him any relief from the edginess riding his back.

"Our agreement was that you choose a woman you would be willing to marry if she could not be bought. I will not hold you to that because a marriage should never be based on anything but love." His father stood and tossed the file folder onto the desk in front of Franco.

"The documents are signed. You do not have to marry to gain control of the Constantine holdings. It is yours. But perhaps you wish to marry to regain your heart."

Taken aback, Franco stared at his father. "I do not wish to marry again."

Armand planted his fists on Franco's desk and leaned forward. "She is not like Lisette, Franco. This girl cares nothing for your net worth."

No. Stacy was nothing like his selfish ex-wife. But opening himself up for another evisceration held little appeal. "I know, but the risks—"

"Bah. When did you become a coward? Love is a gamble, but when it is true the rewards far outweigh the costs. Being alone and right is a poor substitute for being happy and in love—even if that love is imperfect." He straightened. "What will it cost you to let Stacy get away? Can you live with always wondering who is putting the smile on her face? Who is warming her bed? Think about that, hmm?"

His father turned for the door without waiting for an answer, but paused on the threshold. "I will see you at Vincent's rehearsal-dinner party this evening. Perhaps by then you will have your answers."

After his father left, Franco opened the document folder. The signature on the bottom line made Franco the sole owner of the Constantine holdings, including the chateau and Midas Chocolates. He had more to lose now than ever before.

In two days Stacy would return to the States. A wise man would let her go. Only a besotted fool would beg her forgiveness and ask her to stay.

"He's here," Madeline whispered.

Stacy's stomach clenched into a tight knot, but she kept

her back to the entrance of the private dining room in the upscale Italian restaurant hosting the rehearsal dinner.

She'd known Franco would be here tonight, but that didn't mean she was ready to face him. Only Madeline knew the full truth of Stacy's situation, and that was because she'd caught Stacy in a weak moment, dragged her for another late-night meeting in the bar and pried the sordid story out of her. Stacy didn't want to dampen Candace's happiness so she'd sworn Madeline to secrecy.

"Want me to keep him away from you?"

A smile tugged Stacy's lips at the mother-hen tone of her suitemate's voice. "I don't think that will be necessary. But thanks."

If Franco had missed her or discovered any feelings for her at all, he would have called. But Stacy hadn't heard from him since she'd left him in the restaurant last week. She swallowed to ease the tightening of her throat.

She, on the other hand, kept second-guessing her decision. She loved him more than she'd ever thought she could love anyone, but he obviously expected every woman to leave him as his mother, his father's exes and Lisette had done. If Stacy stayed with him but delayed getting pregnant, could she convince him in time that she wasn't like the other women in his life?

Her gaze shifted to Candace and Vincent's love-struck faces. Franco had never looked at her that way—with his heart and his soul in his eyes. She yearned for him to.

Technically, the bride and groom had been married earlier this evening in a private civil ceremony the way French and Monegasque law required, but they were waiting until after the church service tomorrow morning to actually begin their lives as husband and wife.

"What's he doing here? He's not on the guest list," Madeline said in a panicked whisper.

"Who?" Stacy turned toward the door. Her gaze landed on Franco in a dark, custom-fitted suit and her heart ached. She quickly looked away before meeting his gaze and spotted the man who'd posed as Madeline's tour guide—a man who'd turned out to be anything but the humble tour guide he'd led Madeline to believe he was.

The color completely drained from Madeline's face. She squeezed Stacy's hand. "Stacy, I don't want to abandon you, but I cannot face him right now. Go with me to the ladies' room?"

Stacy squared her shoulders. She would not run. Her running days were over. "No. Go ahead. I'm okay. Franco is seated at the opposite end of the table from me. I can avoid him until after dinner. Longer, if I'm lucky."

If not, she'd survived her mother's murder and her father's betrayal. Facing Franco couldn't be worse than that. Or could it? She felt as if her heart were being ripped out all over again.

Needing a few minutes to bolster her defenses, she slipped out onto the colonnade. In forty-eight hours she would not have this magic view of Monaco, but no matter what happened she would always be grateful for her time here. She'd learned that despite her dysfunctional youth she could fall in love, but she could let go—unlike her father.

"Why do you not tread on my rugs?" Franco asked from behind her.

Stacy winced and wished she'd had a few more minutes to prepare for this encounter. She took a bracing breath and turned to find him a few yards away. He stepped out of the shadows and her lungs emptied again when she noted the lines of stress marring his handsome face. She shook off her concern. If he was stressed, it was no more than he deserved. He'd tried to buy her baby.

"I had to walk through pools of blood on our white kitchen floor when I found my mother and father. Your red rugs on white marble remind me of that night."

"I will throw the rugs out and replace the floor if you will come back to me."

Her heart stuttered. "What?"

He closed the distance between them. "I was wrong, Stacy. All the money in the world cannot buy the one thing I desire most."

"An heir? I'm sure you can find some woman who'll jump at the chance."

His unwavering blue gaze held hers and something in their depths made her pulse skip. "I desire you, *mon gardénia*."

His velvety deep voice sent a tremor rippling over her. She held up a hand to halt his approach. "Don't do this, Franco."

But he kept coming until her palm pressed his chest. His warmth seeped through his silk shirt into her fingers and snaked up her arm. She jerked her hand away and fisted it by her side.

"I was afraid to trust what my eyes—what my *heart*—told me. I offered to buy your baby as a test. If you had accepted the money, then I would know you were like every other woman I have known. But you are nothing like them."

She couldn't comprehend what he was saying, but that look in his eyes was beginning to fan that ember of hope she thought he'd extinguished. "Why me?"

A smile flickered on his lips. "Besides your incredible legs and the contradiction between the siren in your eyes and your cloak of reserve?"

"Huh?"

"Because my father challenged me to find a woman I could marry if she couldn't be bought."

Had someone slipped something into her drink? "I'm sorry?"

"Papa suggested I stop dating spoiled rich women and find someone with traditional values if I wanted to find a woman who would love me for myself and not my money. I told him I would prove him wrong by finding one of the mythical paragons he described and buying her."

Stacy flinched. She'd thought she couldn't possibly feel worse, but she did. Had she been nothing more than a bet? He lifted a hand to stoke her cheek, but she jerked out of reach. "So taking me to the chateau was just flaunting me in front of your father to show you'd won?"

"*Oui.* That was my original goal. But then you told me about your parents. You had compelling reasons for accepting my offer. Reasons which I could not condemn. And you refused to let me spoil you with meaningless gifts. I found myself falling in love with you." He extended his arms, palms up and shrugged. "I had to push you away."

Falling in love with her? She pressed a hand over her racing heart. "I would have slept with you without the money, Franco."

"And I would have offered you more." He stepped closer and trapped her by planting his hands on the railing beside her. "So much more."

He really had to stop doing that. She told herself to duck out of the way, but her legs seemed numb. He bent and teased the corners of her mouth with tantalizing, but insubstantial and unsatisfying kisses.

"*Je t'aime,*" he whispered against her lips and her world stopped. Taking advantage of her shocked gasp, he captured her mouth in a deeply passionate kiss. And then he slowly drew back, his lips clinging to hers for a heartbeat longer.

The emotion in his eyes washed over her, but she was afraid to believe what she saw.

"I love you, Stacy, and if you can find it in your heart to forgive me, I want to marry you. I will add fidelity to my vows, because I never want you to doubt that my heart and my soul belong only to you. And whether or not we have children, the money I promised you is yours because you have given me so much more than money can buy."

Her eyes burned and her throat clogged. Happiness swelled inside her. Only a man who truly loved her would offer her everything she'd ever dreamed of and at the same time open the door to set her free and provide her the means to escape.

He loved her enough to let her go.

"You don't have to buy my love, Franco. It's freely given."

"Tout a un prix."

A smile wobbled on her lips. She cupped his cheeks and stroked her thumbs over his smooth warm skin. "Not this time. I love you, and if you lost everything today, I would still love you tomorrow and every day thereafter. Yes, Franco, I will marry you."

His chest rose on a deep breath. "I swear you will never regret it, *mon gardénia.*"

* * * * *

THE PRINCE'S
ULTIMATE DECEPTION

BY
EMILIE ROSE

Dear Reader,

Like many American girls, I grew up hearing fairy tales and dreaming of my own prince. In my teens I switched to reading romance novels, and just like the fairy tales of my childhood, those stories carried me away, filled me with hope and instilled in me a belief in happily ever after.

I hope you enjoy *The Prince's Ultimate Deception*, my modern-day version of Cinderella, as much as I enjoyed creating a magical kingdom and a prince worthy of his princess.

Happy reading,

Emilie Rose

PS Stop by my website at www.EmilieRose.com for updates on my books!

To Christine Hyatt for sharing your wisdom
and showing me the path.

You helped me make my dreams come true.

One

"Please. You *have* to help me."

A woman's desperate plea caught Prince Dominic Andreas Rossi de Montagnarde's attention as he and his bodyguard Ian waited for the elevator inside Monaco's luxurious Hôtel Reynard. He observed the reflected exchange between a long-haired brunette and the concierge through the gilt-framed mirror hanging on the wall beside the polished brass elevator doors.

"Mr. Gustavo, if I don't get away from all this prewedding euphoria I am going to lose my mind. Don't get me wrong. I am happy for my friend, but I just can't stomach this much romance without getting nauseous."

Her statement piqued Dominic's curiosity. What had soured her on the fairy-tale fantasy so many others harbored? He had never met a woman who didn't wallow in wedding preparations. Each of his three sisters had dragged out the planning of their weddings for more than a year, as had his beloved Giselle.

"I need a tour guide who can work around my brides-maid's duties for the next month," she continued. "One who knows the best places for day trips and impromptu getaways because I don't know when I'll need to escape from all this—" she shuddered dramatically "—happiness."

American, he judged by her accent, and possibly from one of the Southern states given her slight drawl.

The concierge gave her a sympathetic smile. "I'm sorry, Mademoiselle Spencer, but it is nearly midnight. At this hour I cannot contact our guides to make those arrangements. If you will return in the morning I am sure we can find some-one suitable."

She shoved her fingers into the mass of her thick, shiny curls, tugged as if she were at her wit's end and then shifted to reveal an exquisite face with a classical profile. Her bare arms were slender, but toned, and she had a body to match beneath the floor-length green gown subtly draping her curves. Nice curves deserving of a second glance which Dom-inic willingly took. Too bad he couldn't see if her legs were as superb as the rest of her.

His gaze slowly backtracked to the reflection of her lovely face and slammed into mocking and amused emerald eyes the same shade as her dress. She'd caught his appraisal and repaid him in kind with a leisurely inspection of her own. Her gaze descended from his shoulders to his butt and legs. One arched eyebrow clearly stated she intended putting him in his place. He fought a smile over her boldness, but he couldn't prevent a quickening of his pulse. When her eyes found his once more he saw appreciation but no sign of recognition.

Interesting.

She returned her attention to the concierge. "In the morning I have to ruin two years' worth of dieting and exercise by stuffing myself with wedding cake samples. Please, I'm begging you, Mr. Gustavo, give me a guide's name tonight so I'll at least have the promise of escape tomorrow."

Escape. The word echoed in Dominic's head as he pondered the elevator's unusual slowness. He needed time to come to terms with his future, to marrying and having children with a woman he didn't love and might not even like, without the paparazzi shoving cameras in his face. In a word, he needed to escape—hence the lack of his usual entourage, dying his blond hair brown and shaving the mustache and beard he'd worn since he'd first sprouted whiskers.

This would in all likelihood be his last month of peace before all hell broke loose. Once the paparazzi caught wind of the proceedings at the palace they would descend on him like a plague of locusts, and his life would no longer be his own. He could see the headlines now. Widowed Prince Seeks Bride.

Apparently the American needed to escape, as well. Why not do so together? Looking at her would in no way be a hardship, and discovering how she'd willingly divorced herself from romance would be an added bonus.

He glanced at Ian. The bodyguard had been with him since Dominic's college days and sometimes Dominic swore the older man could read his mind. Sure enough, warning flashed in Ian's brown eyes and his burly body stiffened.

The elevator chimed and opened, but instead of stepping inside the cubicle Dominic pivoted toward the concierge stand. Ian hovered in the background, silently swearing, Dominic was sure. "Perhaps I could be of assistance, Gustavo."

Gustavo's eyebrows shot up, not surprising since the man often arranged Dominic's entertainment.

"Pardon me for eavesdropping, mademoiselle. I could not help but overhear your request. I would be happy to act as your guide if that meets with your approval?" Dominic waited for recognition to dawn in her eyes. Instead a frown pleated the area above her slim nose. From her smooth porcelain skin he guessed her to be in her late twenties or early thirties—far too young to have forsaken love. As was he. But what choice did he have when duty called?

Her gaze traveled over his white silk shirt and black trousers and then returned to his face. "You work here?"

Surprise shot through him. Was his simple disguise so effective? He had hoped to throw off the paparazzi from a distance, but he hadn't expected to fool anyone up close, and yet she apparently didn't know who he was. Admittedly, he'd lived as low profile a life as any royal could in the past few years, and he avoided the press more often than not, but still… Was this possible?

Dominic made a split-second decision not to enlighten her. He'd had a lifetime of cloying, obsequious women due to his lineage. Why not enjoy being a normal man for as long as it lasted? "I don't work for the hotel, but I am here as often as I can be. Hôtel Reynard is my favorite establishment."

She looked at Gustavo. "Can I trust him?"

Gustavo seemed taken aback by the question. As he should be. Dominic, as next in line to the throne of Montagnarde, a small three-island country four hundred miles east of New Zealand, wasn't accustomed to having his integrity questioned.

"*Certainement,* mademoiselle."

Her thickly lashed emerald gaze narrowed on Dominic's. "Are you familiar with Southern France and Northern Italy?"

His favorite playgrounds, and in recent years, prime examples of the types of tourist meccas he intended to develop in his homeland. "I am."

"Do you speak any languages other than English, because

I barely scraped by in my college Latin class, and I only know health-care Spanish."

"I am fluent in English, French, Italian and Spanish. I can get by in Greek and German."

Her perfectly arched eyebrows rose. Amusement twinkled in her eyes and curved her lips, rousing something which had lain dormant inside him for many years. "Now you're just bragging, but it sounds like you're just the man I need, Mr.…?"

He hesitated. To continue the masquerade he'd have to lie openly not just by omission and he detested liars. But he wanted to spend time with this lovely woman as a man instead of a monarch before fulfilling his duty and marrying whichever woman the royal council deemed a suitable broodmare to his stud service. What could it hurt? He and the American were but ships passing in the night. Or in this case, one small corner of Europe.

"Rossi. Damon Rossi." He ignored Gustavo's shocked expression and Ian's rigid disapproving presence behind him and extended his hand. Dominic hoped neither man would correct the hastily concocted variation of his name or his failure to mention his title.

"Madeline Spencer." The brunette's fingers curled around his. Her handshake was firm and strong and her gaze direct instead of deferential. When had a woman last looked him in the eye and treated him as an equal? Not since Giselle. Unexpected desire hit him hard and fast and with stunning potency.

A similar awareness flickered on Madeline's face, expanding her pupils, flushing her cheeks and parting her lips. "I guess that only leaves one question. Can I afford you?"

Caught off guard by her breathless query and by his body's impassioned response, Dominic glanced at Gustavo who rushed to respond for him. "I am sure Monsieur Reynard will cover your expenses, mademoiselle, since you are an *honored* guest of the family and a *dear friend* to his fiancée. Hi— Monsieur Rossi should not accept any money from you."

Dominic didn't miss the warning in Gustavo's statement.

Madeline's smile widened, trapping the air in Dominic's chest. "When can we get together to set up a schedule?"

If he weren't expecting a conference call from the palace with an update on the bridal selection process momentarily he would definitely prolong this encounter. "Perhaps tomorrow morning after your cake sampling?"

He realized he hadn't released her hand, and he was reluctant to do so. Arousal pumped pleasantly through his veins— a nice distraction from the disagreeable dilemma which had driven him into temporary exile.

Madeline was apparently in no rush, either, as she didn't pull away or break his gaze. "That'd be great, Damon. Where shall I meet you?"

Dominic searched his mental map for a meeting place not haunted by the paparazzi. The only option his testosterone-flooded brain presented was his suite, but the tour guide he'd implied himself to be could hardly afford penthouse accommodations. Already his lie complicated the situation.

Gustavo cleared his throat, jerking Dominic back to the present. "Perhaps *le café* located in the lower terrace gardens, Your—Monsieur Rossi?"

Dominic nodded his thanks—for the recommendation and for the conspiracy. He was used to being a leader and making decisions, but even a future king knew when to accept wise council. "A very good suggestion, Gustavo. What time will you finish, mademoiselle?"

Straight, white teeth bit into her plump bottom lip and Dominic struggled with a sudden urge to sample her soft pink flesh. "Elevenish?"

"I shall count the hours." He bent over her hand and kissed her knuckles. Her fragrance, a light floral mingled with the tart tang of lemon, filled his lungs, and his libido roared to life like the mythical dragon island folklore decreed lived beneath Montagnarde's hot springs.

Dominic had not come to Monaco with the intention of having a last dalliance before beginning what would in all likelihood be a passionless marriage. But he was tempted. Extremely tempted. However the lie, combined with his duty to his country meant he had nothing to offer this beautiful woman except his services as a guide. He would have to keep his newly awakened libido on a short leash.

It wouldn't be easy.

Madeline Spencer's fingers squeezed his one more time and then she released him with a slow drag of her fingertips across his palm. A sassy smile slanted her lips. "Until tomorrow then, Damon."

With a flutter of her ringless fingers she entered the penthouse elevator—the one he'd just abandoned. The doors slid closed.

Dominic inhaled deeply. For the first time in months the sword of doom hanging over his head lifted. He had a short reprieve, but a reprieve nonetheless.

"Oh. My. God." Madeline sagged against the inside of the penthouse suite door and pressed a hand over her racing heart. "I think I'm in lust."

Candace and Amelia, two of Madeline's three suite mates, straightened from their reclining positions on the sofas of the sitting room. They'd already changed from the evening gowns they'd worn to the casino earlier into sleepwear.

"With whom?" Amelia, wearing a ruffled nightgown, asked.

"I have just hired the most gorgeous man on the planet to be my tour guide."

"Tell all," Candace ordered. The bride-to-be was the reason Madeline, Amelia and Stacy, her bridesmaids, were sharing a luxurious suite in the five-star Hôtel Reynard. The quartet had been granted an all-expenses-paid month in Monaco compliments of Candace's fiancé, Vincent Reynard, to plan the couple's wedding, which would take place here in Monaco in four weeks.

"His name's Damon and he has the most amazing blue eyes, thick tobacco-brown hair and a body that won't quit. He's tall—six-three, I'd guess. It was nice to have to look up at a guy even when I was wearing my heels."

"Are you sure it's not *love* at first sight?" Amelia asked with a dreamy look on her face.

Madeline sighed over her coworker's die-hard romantic notions. "You know better. Love is not a fall I intend to take ever again."

Thanks to her lying, cheating ex-fiancé.

"Not all men are like Mike," Candace said as she stacked the tourist pamphlets she'd been perusing neatly on the table.

For Candace's sake Madeline hoped not. Vincent seemed like a nice guy and he truly doted on Candace. But Mike had done the same for Madeline in the early days, and therefore Madeline no longer trusted anyone carrying the Y chromosome.

"No, thank goodness, but my jerk detector is apparently broken, and there are enough guys out there like Mike that I've decided to focus on my career and avoid anything except brief, shallow relationships from now on. Men do it. Why can't I?"

Not that she'd had time for any kind of relationship lately, meaningless or otherwise, given the extra shifts she'd volunteered for at the hospital and the rigorous exercise program she'd adopted during the two years since Mike split.

"Sounds like you're hoping for more than guided tours from this guy," Candace guessed.

Was she? She couldn't deny the electricity crackling between her and Damon when they'd shaken hands, and when he'd kissed her knuckles her knees had nearly buckled. The man might be a tour guide, but he had class and charisma out the wazoo. She'd bet he could turn a shallow affair into a momentous occasion.

"Maybe I am. Maybe I want to have a wildly passionate vacation fling with a sexy foreigner. If he's not married, that is. He wasn't wearing a ring, but—" Their pitying expressions raised her defenses. "What?"

Amelia frowned. "This is about Mike showing up at the hospital last month with his child and pregnant wife in tow, isn't it?"

"It's not." *Liar.* But hey, a girl had her pride and Madeline planned to cling tightly to the ragged remnants of hers.

Mike had made a fool of her. He'd led her on with a six-year engagement, and then he'd dumped her on her thirtieth birthday when she'd jokingly suggested they set a wedding date or call it quits. As soon as he'd moved out of her town house and left his job as a radiologist at the hospital where they both worked, coworkers she'd barely known had rushed to inform her that while she'd been planning her dream wedding he'd been sharing his excellent bedside manner with other women. And judging by the family he'd brought by the E.R. last month, he'd married someone else and started pumping out babies as soon as he'd dumped her.

The lying, conniving rat.

Love? Uh-uh. Not for her. Never again. And she hoped reality didn't slap Candace in the face. But if that happened Madeline would be there to help her friend pick up the pieces—the way Candace and Amelia had been there for her.

Candace rose and crossed the room to wrap Madeline in a hug. "Just be careful."

Madeline snorted. "Please, I am a medical professional. You don't have to lecture me about safe sex. Besides, I'm on the Pill."

"I wasn't referring only to pregnancy or communicable diseases. Don't let that dickhead Mike make you do anything reckless you'll regret."

Candace and Amelia had never liked Mike. Maybe Madeline should have listened to her friends. But not this time. This time she wouldn't be blinded by love. This time she was looking out for number one. "That's the beauty of it. Assuming Damon is interested in a temporary relationship, he can't lead me on, dump me or break my heart because I'll be leaving right after the wedding. I mean, what can happen in four weeks?"

Amelia winced. "Don't tempt fate like that."

Candace sighed. "I know each of us has different things we want to see and do in Monaco, but don't spend all of your time with him. We want to see some of you, too."

Madeline bit her lip and studied her friend. How could she explain that being immersed in all the wedding hoopla brought back too many painful memories—memories of planning her own aborted wedding and wallowing in every intricate detail to make the day perfect? All for naught. She couldn't, without hurting Candace's feelings.

"I promise I won't abandon my friends or my bridesmaid's duties—no matter how good Damon is at guiding or anything else."

She looped an arm around each woman's waist. "Friends are forever and lovers—" she shrugged "—are not."

Good grief, she was as nervous as a virgin on prom night, and at thirty-two Madeline hadn't seen either virginity or prom night in a *long* time.

Her heart beat at double time and it had nothing to do with the sugar rush from sampling too many wedding cakes this morning.

Was her hair right? Her dress? And wasn't that just plain ridiculous? Nonetheless vanity had caused her to pull on a dress with a deep V neckline in the front and back and to don the outrageously sexy shoes she'd bought at the designer outlet down the street. She'd even French braided her unruly hair and added her favorite silver clip.

She scanned the partially open-air café for Damon. He rose from a table in the shadowy back corner, looking absolutely delicious in dark glasses, a casual, short-sleeved white cotton shirt and jeans. Wide shoulders. Thick biceps. Flat abs and narrow hips. Yum.

The glasses were a tad affected given he wasn't seated in the sunny section of the café, but so many people in Monaco sported the same look that he didn't seem out of place. Still— she tipped back her head and looked up at his handsome face—she'd rather stare into his pale blue eyes than at her own reflection.

"*Bonjour,* Mademoiselle Spencer." He pulled out her chair.

She tried to place his accent and couldn't, which was pretty odd since her job exposed her to an assortment of nationalities on a daily basis. And then there was the intriguing way he occasionally slipped into more formal speech....

"Good morning, Damon, and please call me Madeline." His knuckles brushed the bare skin between her shoulder blades as he seated her. Awareness skipped down her spine, startling a flock of butterflies in her stomach. *Ooh* yeah. Definitely a prime candidate for her first string-free fling.

She tugged a pen and pad of paper from her straw purse. "I thought we'd discuss possible outings today. Perhaps you could give me a list of suggestions, and I'll tell you which ones interest me."

"You will not trust my judgment to choose for you?"

As she'd done with Mike?

"No. I'd prefer to be consulted. I'm not sure how much you overheard last night, but I'm here with a friend to help plan her wedding. I'll have to be available for her morning meetings Monday through Friday and whenever else she or the other bridesmaids need me. So you and I will have to snatch hours here and there and not every day. Are you okay with that?"

"I am." He leaned back in his chair and steepled his fingers beneath his square jaw. He really had wonderful bone structure. His blade-straight nose had probably never been broken, and his high zygomatic arches allowed for nice hollows in his lean, smooth-shaven cheeks. Straight, thick, dark hair flopped over his forehead, making him look boyish, but the fine lines beside his eyes and mouth said he had to be in his thirties.

"Last night you said romance made you nauseous. I have yet to meet a woman who did not revel in romance. What happen—"

"Now you have," she interrupted.

His lips firmed and his eyebrows lowered as if her interruption annoyed him, but her sorry love life was not up for discussion.

The last thing she wanted to tell a prospective lover was that she'd been an idiot. She'd been so enthralled with the idea of love and being part of a couple that she'd given in to whatever Mike wanted, and in the process she'd surrendered part of her identity. What ticked her off the most was that even though she'd been trained to assess symptoms and make diagnoses, she'd missed the obvious signs that her relationship was in trouble. Not even the twenty pounds she'd gained over six years while "eating her stress" had clued her in to her subconscious's warnings.

"What happened to make you so wary?" he asked in a firm voice that made it clear he wasn't going to drop it.

She stared hard at him for several moments, trying to make him back down, but he held her gaze without wavering. "Let's just say I learned from experience that planning a perfect wedding doesn't always result in happily ever after."

"You are divorced?"

"Never made it to the altar. Now, about our excursions… Despite what Mr. Gustavo said about Vincent Reynard picking up your tab, I don't want to go overboard with expenses."

"I will keep that in mind. Are you more of an outdoor person or the museum type?"

She said a silent thank-you that he accepted her change of subject. "I prefer to be outside since I spend most of my waking hours inside."

"Doing…?"

Who was interviewing whom here? He didn't act like any potential employee she'd ever questioned. He was a little too arrogant, a little too confident, a little too in charge. But that only made him more attractive. "I'm a physician's assistant in a metropolitan hospital. What kinds of outings do you suggest?"

"There are numerous outdoor activities within a short distance that would cost little or nothing. Sunbathing, snorkeling, sailing, windsurfing, hiking, biking, fishing and rock climbing."

He ticked off the items on long ringless fingers bearing neatly trimmed, clean nails. She had a thing about hands, and his were great, the kind she'd love to have gliding over her skin.

"If you have more than a few hours we can go river rafting or spelunking in the Alpes-Maritimes or drive across the border into Italy or France to explore some of the more interesting villages."

"I'm not a sun lizard. Isn't that what they call the people who lay on the rocks of the jetty? I prefer action to lazing about, and cold, dark places give me the creeps, so let's skip the sunbathing and the spelunking and go with everything else. You'll arrange the tours and any equipment rental and provide me with the details?"

"It will be my pleasure."

She'd bet he knew a thing or two about pleasure, and if she was lucky, he'd share that knowledge. She slid a piece of paper across the table. "Here's my tentative schedule for the next month. I've blacked out the times when I'm unavailable. That's my suite number in the top corner. You'll have to call me there or leave a message for me at the front desk since my cell phone doesn't work in Europe."

She couldn't remember the last time she'd gone somewhere without a pager or cell phone, usually both, clipped to her clothing, and she couldn't decide whether she felt free or naked without the familiar weight bumping her hip.

A breeze swept into the open-air café, catching and ruffling the paper. She flattened her hand over it to keep it from blowing away. Damon's covered hers a split second later as he did the same. The heat of his palm warmed her skin. Electricity arced up her arm. Judging by the quick flare of his nostrils, she wasn't the only one feeling the sparks, but she couldn't see his eyes to be sure and that frustrated her.

She tilted her head, but didn't withdraw her hand. He didn't smile as he slowly eased his away, dragging his fingers the length of hers and igniting embers inside her.

"You know, Damon, if you're going to flirt with me it would be much more effective without the glasses. Hot glances don't penetrate polarized lenses."

He stilled and then deliberately reached up to remove his sunglasses with his free hand. "Are you interested in a flirtation, Madeline?"

The one-two punch of his accented voice huskily murmuring her name combined with the desire heating his eyes quickened her pulse and shortened her breath. "That depends. Are you married?"

"No."

"Engaged?"

"I am not committed to anyone at this time."

"Gay?"

He choked a laugh. "Definitely not."

"Healthy?"

His pupils dilated. He knew what she meant. "I have recently received a clean bill of health."

Excitement danced within her. "Then, Damon, we'll see if you have what it takes to tempt me."

Two

"This is a mistake, if I may say so, Dominic." Only in the privacy of their suite did Ian dare use Dominic's given name. Seventeen years together had built not only familiarity, but friendship.

"Damon. Damon Rossi," Dominic corrected as he packed for his first outing with Madeline Spencer.

"How am I to remember that?"

"D.A. Rossi is the name I sign on official documents, including the hotel registration. Damon is but a combination of my initials and an abbreviation of our country."

"Clever. But if the paparazzi catch you with a woman on the eve of your engagement…"

"As of this morning there is no engagement. A woman has not been selected, and if the council continues to argue as they have done for the past four months over birthing hips, pedigrees and whatever other absurd qualities they deem necessary for a princess, they will never come to an agreement, and I will not be forced to propose to a woman I know or care nothing about."

The council members had dehumanized the entire process. Not once had they asked Dominic's preferences. They might as well be choosing animals to breed from a bloodline chart.

Dominic had been nineteen when the council had chosen Giselle as his future bride, and he had not objected for he'd known her since they were children. His parents and hers had been friends for decades. He had convinced their families to postpone the marriage until after he obtained his university degree, and in those intervening years he and Giselle had become friends and then lovers before becoming husband and wife.

In the nine years since her death he had not met one single woman who made an effort to see the man behind the title and fortune.

And now once again the council would decide his fate as the traditions of his country decreed, a circumstance which did not please him, but one he was duty-bound to accept. But this time the idea of the group of predominantly old men choosing a stranger to be his wife did not sit well.

Dominic threw a change of clothing on top of the towels, masks and fins already in his dive bag. "Mademoiselle Spencer wishes to see Monaco. I wish to explore the tourist venues as a vacationer instead of as a visiting prince. Perhaps I will see a different side to the enterprises than I have seen before. The knowledge will benefit Montagnarde's tourist development plan which, as you know, I will present to the economic board again in two months. This time I will not accept defeat. They will back my development plan."

He had spent the years since he'd left university studying successful tourist destinations and laying the groundwork to replicate similar enterprises in his homeland. He wanted to model Montagnarde's travel industry after Monaco's, but the older members of the board refused to accept that the country had to grow its economic base or continue to lose its youth to jobs overseas. His father had sworn to lend his support in return for Dominic agreeing to marry before the end of his thirty-fifth year. With sovereign backing Dominic's plan would be passed.

"You know nothing about this woman," Ian insisted.

"A circumstance I am sure you have already begun to rectify." Any acquaintance with whom Dominic spent more than a passing amount of time was thoroughly investigated.

"I have initiated an inquiry, yes. Nevertheless, an affair would not be wise."

"Not an affair, Ian. A harmless flirtation. I cannot have sex with a woman to whom I am lying."

We'll see if you have what it takes to tempt me.

His heart rate quickened at the memory of Madeline's enticing banter and vibrant eyes. He would very much like to be her lover, but for the first time in years he found himself savoring the idea of being merely a man whom a beautiful woman found attractive. He didn't want to ruin that unique experience by revealing his identity, but he couldn't sleep with Madeline until he did. "I am aware of the risks."

"How will you explain my presence?"

Dominic zipped the bag and faced Ian, knowing his decision would not be a popular one. "The Larvotto under-water reserve is well patrolled by the Monaco police. No other boats or watercraft are allowed in the area. You can rest easy knowing the only dangers I face while snorkeling are that of the fish and the artificial reef. You will wait on the shore and keep your distance."

"I am charged with your well-being. If something should happen—"

"Ian, I have not given you reason to worry about my safety in years, and I won't now. I am a skilled diver. I have tracking devices in my watch and my swim trunks, and no one knows our plan. I will be fine." He hefted the bag. "Now come. I wish to see if Mademoiselle Spencer looks as good in a swimsuit as I anticipate."

Getting practically naked with a guy on your first date certainly moved things right along, Madeline decided as she removed the lemon-yellow sundress she'd worn as a cover-up over her swimsuit and placed it on the lounge chair beside her sandals and sunglasses.

Her black bikini wasn't nearly as skimpy as the thong suits so popular on the public beach around them. She scanned the sunbathers, shook her head and smothered a smile. The women here thought nothing of dropping their tops on the beach, but they didn't dare lie in the sun without their jewels. *Bet that makes for some interesting tan lines.*

To give him credit, Damon had stalked right past the bare breasts on display without pause. When his attention turned to her, raking her from braid to garnet-red toenail polish, she said a silent thank-you for the discounted gym membership the hospital offered its employees and the sweat and weight she'd shed over the past two years. Her body was tight and toned. It hadn't always been. But she wished Damon would lose the sunglasses. The thinning of his lips and the flare of his nostrils could signify anything from disgust to desire. She needed to see his eyes.

In the meantime, she did a little inspecting of her own as he untied the drawstring waist of the white linen pants he'd worn over his swimsuit due to Monaco's strict rules about no beachwear, bare chests or bare feet on the streets.

Damon's white T-shirt hugged well-developed pectorals and a flat abdomen. And then he dropped his pants. *Nice.* His long legs were deeply tanned, muscular and dusted with burnished blond hair beneath his brief trunks. "You must spend a lot of time outdoors."

He paused and gave her a puzzled look.

"The sun has bleached your body hair and the tips of your lashes," she explained.

"I enjoy water sports." He handed her a snorkel, mask and fins that looked new. "You have snorkeled before?"

"Yes, off the coast back home."

"And where is home?"

"North Carolina. On the eastern coast of the U.S. I live hours from the beach, but I used to vacation there every summer." She missed those boisterous vacations with Mike's family more than she missed Mike. The devious, dishonest rat. How could such a great family spawn a complete schmuck?

She dug her toes into the fine grains beneath her feet. "Is it true that all this white sand is brought in by barge?"

"Yes. That is the case for many of the Riviera beaches. Of the nations bordering the Mediterranean Sea, Monaco has the cleanest and safest beaches because the government is the most eco-conscious. Thanks to the Grimaldi family, the country is almost pollution free. In recent years the government has expanded its territory by reclaiming land from the sea. The underwater reserve we are about to explore was built in the seventies to repair the damage of overfishing and excessive coral gathering. The reefs are home to many fish species and red coral." He indicated the water with a nod. "Shall we?"

He'd certainly studied his guidebook. "Don't you want to take off your T-shirt?"

He tossed his shades on the chair beside hers. "No."

"Do you burn easily? I could put sunscreen on your back." Her palms tingled in anticipation of touching him.

"I prefer to wear a shirt, thank you."

Did he have scars or something? "Damon, I see shirtless men at work every day. If you're worried that I can't control myself…"

His chest expanded, and this time she received the full effect of those hot blue eyes. Arousal made her suck in her breath and her stomach. "It is not your control I question, Madeline. Come, the reef waits."

She'd never get used to the way he said her name with a hint of that unidentifiable accent. It gave her goose bumps every time. And speaking of control, where was hers? She wanted to jump him. Here. Now. "Where did you say you were from?"

"I did not say." He flashed a tight white smile and strode toward the water, where he dunked his fins and mask before donning both.

She mimicked his actions and then stared at him through the wet glass of her mask. "You like being a man of mystery, eh?"

He straightened and held her gaze. "I like being a man. The mystery is all in here." He gently tapped her temple. "Stay close to me. Watch for jellyfish and sea urchins. Avoid both."

Admiring the view of his taut buttocks and well-muscled legs, she followed him deeper into the water. For the next hour she swam and enjoyed the sea life. Each time Damon touched her to draw her attention to another sight she nearly sucked the briny water down her snorkel. Miraculously, she managed not to drown herself. By the time he led her back to shore her nerves were as tightly wound as the rubber band ball the emergency room staff tossed around on slow nights.

"That was great. Thanks." And then she got a good look at the shirt adhered like shrink-wrap to his amazing chest, the tiny buttons of his nipples and his six-pack abs. An even better sight and definitely one she'd like to explore.

"I'm glad you enjoyed it." He dropped his mask and fins on the chair, donned his sunglasses and ruffled his hair to shake off the excess water and then finger-combed the dark strands over his forehead.

"What made you decide to become a tour guide?" She dried off as he bagged their diving gear.

"When a country has few natural resources and limited territory, its people and the tourism industry become its greatest assets."

Surprised by his answer, she blinked. She'd expected a simple response such as he enjoyed meeting new people or the flexible hours, not something so deep. "Studied that, have you?"

"Yes."

She dragged her knit sundress over her head. "Where? I mean, are there tourism schools or what?"

Holding her gaze—or at least she thought he was, beneath those dark lenses—he hesitated so long she didn't think he'd answer. "I have a Travel Industry Management degree from the University of Hawaii at Mānoa."

He seemed tense, as if he expected her to question his statement, and she should. If he had a college degree and spoke four languages fluently then why was he acting as a tour guide? It didn't make sense. She reminded herself that not everyone was as career driven as she was, but Damon didn't seem the type to kick back and let the fates determine his future. She'd seen enough type A guys to recognize the signs and he waved them all like flags. But that was his business. A string-free affair—if they had one—didn't give her the right to interfere.

"The States? No kidding. What brings you to Monaco?"

"I am studying their tourism industry."

"And then what?"

"I'll apply what I've learned to my future endeavors." He zipped the dive bag and grabbed the handles. Eager to go, was he? Before she could ask what kinds of endeavors, he said, "If we leave now we'll have time to stop at the hotel café for a snack before I leave you. You have missed lunch."

"I'm in no rush. I had hoped we could spend the rest of the afternoon together. Maybe play some beach volleyball or jump on the trampoline at the far end of the beach? And this place is surrounded by restaurants. We could grab a bite here."

"I have another appointment."

She tried to hide her disappointment. While she had enjoyed the day, it hadn't gone quite as she'd hoped. Admittedly, she wasn't a practiced seductress, but if she wanted a vacation romance it looked as though she'd have to work harder for it.

Time to initiate Plan B. First she freed and finger-combed her hair while trying to build up her courage, and then she reached beneath her dress, untied her damp bikini top and pulled it through the scooped neckline.

A muscle at the corner of Damon's mouth ticked and his throat worked as he swallowed.

"You may change in one of the dressing rooms, as I will," he said hoarsely. His Adam's apple bobbed as he swallowed.

"No need. Besides, I didn't bring a change of clothing." Her nipples tightened when he didn't look away. Well, *hallelujah.* He'd been so professional and distant she'd begun to think she'd imagined the sparks between them.

And then in an act more brazen than anything she'd ever dared, she reached beneath her dress and shucked her bikini bottom. She twirled the wet black fabric once around her finger before tucking it along with her top in her tote. *Take that, big guy.* If Damon insisted on hustling her back to the hotel and dumping her, then he'd have to do so knowing she was naked except for a thin knit sheath.

Never let it be said that Madeline Spencer wouldn't fight for what she wanted, and in her opinion, Damon Rossi was the perfect prescription to mend her bruised ego and heart. A few weeks with him and she'd return home whole and healed.

"I wonder what all the commotion's about?"

Madeline's question pulled Dominic from his complicated calculations of hotel occupancy rates as the taxi approached Hôtel Reynard. He'd been attempting to distract himself from the knowledge that she was completely nude beneath her dress and failing miserably.

A camera-carrying group of a dozen or so paparazzi stood sentry across the street from the hotel with their zoom lenses trained on the limo parked by the entrance. Dominic silently swore. His escape route had been sealed. He leaned forward to speak to the driver. "Rue Langlé, *s'il vous plaît.*"

Madeline's eyebrows rose in surprise. "Where are we going?"

"I do not wish to fight the crowd. We'll dine in a quiet café instead of the hotel." Ian would not like the unplanned detour, and Makos, the second bodyguard who kept in such deep cover that Dominic rarely spotted him, would like it even less.

"I thought you were in a hurry to get to another appointment."

"It can wait." There was no other appointment. He merely needed time away from the tempting woman beside him before he grabbed her and kissed that teasing smile from her lips. Even in the cool water, touching the wet silkiness of her skin had heated his blood. He'd wanted to flatten his palms over her waist, tangle his legs with her sleek limbs and pull her flush against him. A maneuver that probably would have drowned them both, he acknowledged wryly.

Dominic faced a conundrum. With each passing moment his desire for Madeline increased, and yet his lie stood between them. He ached for her, but he was reluctant to lose the unique relationship they had established. She looked at *him,* flirted with *him,* desired *him.* Not Prince Dominic. He was selfish enough to want to enjoy her attentions a while longer.

She twisted in her seat to stare out the taxi's back window at the paparazzi as the driver took the roundabout away from the hotel. The shift slid her hem to the top of her thighs. A few more inches and he'd see what her bikini bottom should be covering. He gritted his teeth and fisted his hands against the urge to smooth his palm up her sleek thighs and over her bare buttocks.

"It's probably just another celebrity," she said. "Amelia says the hotel is crawling with them."

"Who is Amelia?"

"My friend and one of the other bridesmaids. She's a huge fan of entertainment magazines and shows. She claims the security inside the hotel makes it a celebrity hot spot. Supposedly paparazzi aren't even allowed on the grounds, which would explain why they're staked out across the street."

He'd have to avoid her friend. "You are not interested in star gazing?"

She settled back in the seat and faced him. "No. I don't have time to watch much TV or read gossip rags. I work four or five twelve-hour shifts each week, depending on how much overtime the hospital will allow me, and I usually go to the gym for another hour after work."

That could explain why not even a flicker of recognition entered her eyes when she looked at him—not that he was a household name, but he was known unfortunately, thanks to a couple of wild years after Giselle's death when he'd tried to smother his grief with women and parties. "Your diligence at the gym shows."

She tilted her head, revealing the long line of her throat and the pulse fluttering rapidly at the base. "Is that a compliment, Damon?"

"I am sure you are aware of your incredible figure, Madeline. You do not need my accolades." The words came out stiffly.

Her eyebrows dipped. "Are you okay?"

"Shouldn't I be?"

"You seem a little…tense."

His gaze dropped pointedly to her hiked hem.

She glanced down and her eyes widened. A peachy glow darkened her cheeks, making him question whether the siren role was a new one for her. And then the hint of a smile curved her lips as she wiggled the fabric down to a more respectable level. The woman was driving him insane and relishing every moment of his discomfort.

"Monaco is small enough that we could have walked to the café, you know," she said.

"You have had enough sun." And he was less likely to be recognized in an anonymous taxi. The driver pulled over in the street and stopped. Dominic paid him and opened the door. He noted Ian climbing from a taxi a half a block away. Dominic subtly angled his head toward the Italian café as a signal.

Madeline curled her fingers around Dominic's and allowed him to assist her from the car. She joined him on the sidewalk, but didn't release his hand. The small gesture tightened something inside him. When had he last held hands with a woman? Such a simple pleasure. One he hadn't realized he'd missed.

She tipped back her head. "Monaco has strict protocol. Are you sure we're dressed appropriately?"

One of us is. He had pulled on trousers and a polo shirt before leaving the beach. His attire was acceptable, as was Madeline's if one was unaware she wore nothing beneath the thin yellow sundress. The driver retrieved the dive bag from the trunk. Dominic took it from him. "The café is casual. I recommend the prosciutto and melon or the bruschetta."

He'd prefer to feast on her, on her rosy lips, on her soft, supple skin, on the tight nipples pushing against her dress.

Wondering when his intelligence had deserted him, Dominic led her inside and requested a table in the back. Madeline didn't release his hand until he seated her. He chose a chair facing away from the door. The fewer people who saw his face the better and Ian would cover his back.

The entire afternoon had been an exercise in restraint and a reminder that he was not an accomplished liar. He had been so distracted by his unexpected attraction to Madeline that he had almost blown his cover. Had she not commented on his blond body hair he would have removed his shirt and his secret would be out.

Your secret is keeping her out of your bed.

Without a doubt, he desired Madeline Spencer, but getting women to share his bed had never been difficult. Getting one to see him as a mere man, however, was nearly impossible. He would have to reveal his identity soon for he did not think his control would last much longer, and then if he could be certain Madeline could be happy with a short-term affair, he would explore every inch of her. Repeatedly.

But before he revealed *his* secret he needed to discover *hers*. Why had she renounced love?

After placing their orders Dominic asked, "Did you love him?"

Her smile wobbled and then faded. Her fingers found and tugged one dark coil of hair. He wanted to wind the spirals around his fingers, around his—

"Who?"

Her pretended ignorance didn't fool him. The shadows darkening her eyes gave her discomfort away. He removed his sunglasses and looked into her eyes. "The man who disappointed you."

She fussed with her cutlery. "*Pfft*. What makes you so sure there is one?" When he held her gaze without replying she bristled. "Is this twenty questions? Because if it is, you'll have to give an answer for every one you get."

Risky, but doable if he chose his words carefully. He nodded acceptance of her terms. "Did you love him?" he repeated.

"I thought I did."

"You don't know?"

She shifted in her seat, reminding him of her nakedness beneath the T-shirt thin layer of cotton. "Why don't you tell me what you have planned for our next outing?"

"Because you are a far more interesting topic." His voice came out in a lower pitch than normal as if he were dredging it up from the bottom of the sea. "Why do you question your feelings?"

She sighed. Resignation settled over her features. "My mother was forty-six when I was born and my father fifty.

They were too old to keep up with a rambunctious child. I wanted to do things differently when I had children, so I made a plan to get married and start my family before I turned thirty. I met Mike right after college. He seemed like the perfect candidate and we got engaged. But it didn't work out."

"One failed relationship soured you?"

Another squirm of her naked bottom made him wish he could take the place of her chair. "My parents divorced. It wasn't pretty. Have you ever been in a long-term relationship?"

"Yes."

Her arched brows rose. "And?"

"My turn. Why did your relationship end?"

She frowned. "Lots of reasons. First, I spent too much time trying to be the woman I thought he and society expected me to be instead of the one I wanted to be. Second, he found someone else."

"He is a fool."

A smile twitched her lips. "Don't expect me to argue with that brilliantly insightful conclusion."

The waitress placed their meals on the table and departed.

"Have you ever been married?" Madeline asked before biting into her bruschetta.

"Yes."

Her body stilled and her emerald gaze locked with his. She chewed quickly and then swallowed. "What happened?"

"She died." The words came out without inflection. He'd learned long ago to keep the pain locked away behind a wall of numbness.

Sympathy darkened her eyes. "I'm sorry. How?"

"Ectopic pregnancy."

She reached across the table and covered his hand. Her touch warmed him and surprisingly, soothed him. "That must have been hard, losing your wife and child at the same time. Did you even know she was pregnant?"

How could this virtual stranger understand what those closest to him had not?

"Yes, it was hard, and no, we didn't know about the baby." It had infuriated him at the time that many had been more concerned with the loss of a potential heir to the throne than the loss of his wife, his friend, his gentle Giselle. Only recently had his anger subsided enough for him to agree to another marriage. If his sisters had produced sons instead of daughters, he probably never would have.

They finished the meal in silence. He waited until Madeline pushed her plate aside before asking, "You do not wish for another *affaire de coeur* or the American dream of a house with a white picket fence and two-point-something children?"

She straightened and put her hands in her lap. "No. I'm over my urge to procreate. It's time to focus on me. My wants. My needs. My career. I don't need a man to complete me. And I don't need marriage to find passion."

Passion. Arousal pulsed through him. "You can be happy with brief liaisons? Without love?"

"Absolutely. In fact, I prefer it that way. If I want to take a promotion, a trip or stay out late with my friends, then I don't have to worry about anyone's ego getting bent. So, Damon…" Her fingertips touched his on the table. "What you said on the beach about your control…? Losing it with me would not be a problem."

He inhaled sharply. Her meaning couldn't be clearer. She wanted a lover. And he would be more than happy to oblige. The question was should he reveal his identity beforehand, or since she wanted nothing more than a brief affair, did he have to reveal anything at all? Did he have to ruin this camaraderie? For he knew with absolute certainty that the knowledge would change their relationship.

He stood and dropped a handful of bills on the table.

Her hand caught his and the need to yank her into his arms surged through him. "You paid for the taxi. Shouldn't I get this?"

"No." He pulled back her chair. She rose and turned, but Dominic didn't back away. Her breasts brushed his chest. His palm curved over her waist. "I know of a back entrance to the hotel."

Her quick gasp filled his ears and temptation expanded her pupils. "What about your other appointment?"

His gaze dropped from her emerald eyes to her mouth. "Nothing is more important at the moment than tasting you."

Her tongue swiped quickly over her bottom lip and he barely contained a groan. "We could go to your place."

Again the lie complicated matters. He shook his head. "I share with another man."

She grimaced. "And I'm sharing a suite with the bride-to-be and two other bridesmaids. I have my own bedroom, but I wouldn't feel right taking a man to my room."

And he had to avoid her celebrity-watching friend. He clenched his teeth to dam a frustrated growl and laced his fingers through hers. He led her outside the restaurant, passing by Ian on a nearby bench. Dominic scanned the area, for there was one thing that couldn't wait. A narrow flower-lined alleyway beckoned. Dominic ducked in, pulled Madeline behind a potted olive tree and into his arms.

"Wha—"

His mouth stole the word from her soft lips. Desire, instantaneous and incendiary, raced through his bloodstream at the first taste of her mouth. He sought her tongue, stroked, entwined and suckled. Madeline's arms encircled his waist, pressing her lithe body flush against his.

Her flowers and lemon scent filled his nostrils and her warmth seeped deep inside him. He tangled the fingers of one hand in her silky curls, caressed the curve of her hips with the other and pressed the driving need in his groin against her stomach.

A horn sounded in the street, reminding him of where they were and the omnipresent possibility of paparazzi. Except for a few insane months, he'd spent a lifetime carefully avoiding the press, and yet Madeline made him forget. Reluctantly, he lifted his head.

Madeline opened dazed eyes and blinked her long, dark lashes. Her lips gleamed damp and inviting as she gazed up at him. "That was worth waiting for."

For the first time in ages Dominic felt like a man instead of a dynasty on legs or an animal expected to breed on command. "I will arrange privacy for our next outing."

Three

Pain burned Madeline's throat Thursday morning, but she'd be damned if she'd let Candace know it. She gritted her teeth into a bright smile.

Watching the *couturière* fuss and flutter around her petite blond friend reminded Madeline of the wedding dress her mother and aunts had sewn for her. The trio had dedicated a year to creating a gorgeous gown and veil with intricate seed pearl beading and hand-tatted lace. Neither would ever be worn.

It should have been a clue that Madeline's engagement was doomed when her dream dress included a full cathedral train, and yet Mike had claimed he wanted an informal backyard wedding, or better yet, a Vegas quickie—if she'd pay for the trip. Her fiancé had been loaded, and yet he'd been a total miser.

She shook off the memories and widened her smile. "You look gorgeous, Candace. That dress couldn't be more perfect if it had been custom-made for you."

"You think?" Her friend smoothed her hands over the silk douppioni skirt beneath a hand-beaded bodice and twisted this way and that to see her reflection in the three-way mirror. "I'm not showing?"

Another twinge of regret pinched Madeline's heart. If she'd stuck with her plan, she probably would have had several babies by now. But since Mike couldn't keep his pants zipped most likely they would have been divorced and playing tug-of-war with innocent children. Not a pretty picture. She ought to know. Her parents' divorce when Madeline was ten had been rough.

Breaking up with Mike had been for the best, and luckily his paranoia over the two percent failure rate of the Pill had led him to use condoms as a backup every single time. Otherwise, there was no telling what the two-timing louse would have brought home from his extramural adventures.

Candace's expectant expression dragged Madeline back to the present. "Candace, no one will know you're pregnant unless you tell them. The empire waist covers everything—not that there's anything to hide yet. You're only eight weeks along."

Candace had confided her pregnancy to Madeline and sworn her to secrecy before they'd left North Carolina. She'd wanted Madeline's medical assurance in addition to her obstetrician's that traveling in her first trimester wouldn't endanger the baby.

"Okay, this is the dress. *Je voudrais acheter cette robe,*" Candace told the seamstress.

The seamstress rattled off a quick stream of French while she unfastened the long line of silk-covered buttons down Candace's spine, and Candace replied in the same language. Madeline didn't have a clue what either of them said. She should have borrowed those French lesson CDs her suite-mate Stacy had used.

The heavy fabric swished over her friend's head. With the dress draped over her arms, the seamstress departed. Candace quickly pulled on her street clothes, crossed the dressing room to Madeline's side and took her hands. "You had a lucky escape. You know that, right?"

Madeline winced. She should have known her friend would see through her fake merriment. They'd been through a lot together in the past twelve years: college, their engagements to Mike and Vincent and the deaths of Madeline's father and Candace's brother. "I know, and trust me, I am not missing that two-timing dud."

"But the wedding preparations are hard for you." It was a statement, not a question. "I'm sorry. But I couldn't do this without you, Madeline."

"I love seeing you this happy."

"Your turn will come." Candace squeezed her fingers and released her.

Not as long as I have a functioning brain cell. God forbid I ever go through that again. "This month is all about you."

"When will the rest of us get to meet your gorgeous guide?"

"I'm not sure. I'll have to ask. I won't see him again until Saturday." Two days. It seemed like an aeon.

After kissing her into a stupor yesterday Damon had put her in a cab with the promise of passion to come. If that kiss was a sample of what she could expect, then it would be passion unlike any she'd ever experienced. She couldn't remember Mike's embrace ever making her forget where she was.

Last night after dinner with Candace at the world-renowned Hôtel Hermitage she'd returned to the suite and found a message from Damon telling her he had arranged a sailboat for the weekend. He'd found a place for them to be alone. Her mouth dried, her palms moistened and her pulse bounded like a jackrabbit. She felt wild, reckless and free. A first for her.

"Maybe Damon will sweep you off your feet, and we'll have a double wedding in three weeks," Candace interrupted Madeline's illicit thoughts.

Madeline groaned. "Don't start your matchmaking here. It's bad enough that I suffer through your blind date matchups at home. Besides, I'd never be stupid enough to marry a guy I'd known such a short time."

She hitched her purse over her shoulder and opened the door, hoping Candace would leave the topic behind in the dressing room of the chic boutique.

Candace followed her out. "That's just it. When you love someone you don't want to wait. The only reason I waited to marry Vincent was because he insisted on being able to put the wedding ring on my finger himself. The day he reached that point in his physical therapy we set the date."

Which reminded Madeline of the crazy year her friend had had. Vincent had been severely burned along the right side of his body just over a year ago in a freak pit accident at the local race track. Madeline had treated him in the E.R. when he'd first arrived at the hospital and then Candace had been his nurse throughout his months-long stay in the burn unit. Before he'd been released the two had fallen head over heels in love.

Madeline had to give Vincent credit. He'd tried to convince Candace she deserved a man who wouldn't be scarred for life, but Candace didn't care about his scars. Love truly was blind.

A fact you know all too well.

Candace handed her credit card to the clerk and then turned back to Madeline. "The fact that you dated Mike for almost a year before you became engaged and you didn't push him to set a date for six years tells me you weren't in a rush to tie yourself to him till death do you part."

Good point. She hated it when others saw something that should have been obvious to her. "When did you become a shrink? I thought you were a nurse."

Candace shrugged. "Nurse. Shrink. Most days they're one and the same in the burn unit. But I don't need to be a psychiatrist to know that Mike didn't treat you well. You deserve a guy who will, Madeline."

"I'm strictly a love 'em and leave 'em gal from now on."

"That's a knee-jerk reaction to the dickhead's lies. You'll get over it, Ms. Monogamy. You're the one whose only lover was a man you thought you were going to marry."

Madeline's cheeks flashed hot. She glanced at the *couturière*. If the woman understood English—and most people in Monaco did apparently—she gave no sign of being interested in their exchange.

Having older parents meant Madeline's values were from a bygone era, and she'd waited to fall in love before falling into bed. But that was because her father had been a tough, no-nonsense vice squad detective with a habit of scaring off his teenage daughter's potential suitors and later she'd been too busy with school and a part-time job to have the energy to date.

But she had every intention of sowing the wild oats she'd been hoarding—starting with Damon Rossi. "My inexperience is a circumstance I intend to remedy as soon as possible."

"I still think there's more to your instant attraction to Damon than lust. I've never known you to get gaga so fast."

Madeline didn't reply until the shop door closed behind them. She faced her friend on the sunny sidewalk lined with designer shops and wrought iron lampposts. "Candace, I'm not gaga. I'm horny. And that's all it is. I have a two-year itch to scratch. Nothing more. Nothing less."

"Right. It took you ten months to sleep with Mike. You wanted to jump Damon after ten minutes. Listen to your sub-conscious, Madeline. It's trying to tell you something."

"You're wrong. Completely. Totally. Unequivocally wrong. And I'll prove it. Just watch."

She'd live it up in Monaco and then leave in three weeks' time with her sexual urges satisfied and her heart intact.

This had to be a mistake.

Madeline stopped on a long stretch of sunbaked dock in the Port de Monaco. Over a hundred boats bobbed and swayed around her in neat rows, and because it was Saturday, a number of other boaters were out and about, chatting in a musical chorus of foreign languages. The boats in this line were big. None resembled the small craft she'd expected Damon to rent. She double-checked the slip number on the note the hotel desk attendant had given her. Whoever had taken the message must have misunderstood.

No problem. She slung the strap of her beach bag over her shoulder and started walking. She'd check out slip one-eighteen just in case there was a smaller sailboat tucked behind the big ones. If there wasn't, she'd return to the hotel and wait for Damon to call with the correct instructions. Surely he'd guess something had gone awry when she didn't arrive on time?

Sun warmed her skin. Boat parts clanged and creaked beside her and birds cried overhead. A breeze teased tendrils from her braid and molded her skirt and cropped sleeveless top to her body. She'd only made it past a half-dozen yachts when a familiar dark-haired figure in white pants, a loose white shirt and sunglasses stepped onto the planks from a boat about five car lengths long. Her heart and steps faltered. The hotel hadn't made a mistake. Damon had rented a boat with a cabin. Make that a *yacht* with a cabin.

And because Candace didn't have a morning meeting tomorrow, Madeline was free to spend the night if she chose. She moved forward, one step at a time. Her lungs labored as if she'd sprinted from the hotel instead of ridden in the cushy hired car Damon had arranged for her. She'd never had a wildly passionate no-strings-attached affair, but if she boarded the boat, there would be no turning back.

This is what you wanted.

Maybe so, but that didn't keep her from being nervous. The distance between them seemed to stretch endlessly.

Damon didn't smile, didn't move toward her. Hands by his side and legs braced slightly apart, he waited, looking as if he belonged at a yacht club. But then she supposed a good tour guide should fit into his surroundings. He'd said he enjoyed water sports so he probably had the sea legs to handle a gently undulating dock and a boat that probably cost more than her condo.

She reached his side, shoved her sunglasses up onto her head and waited, poised on a knife edge between tension and anticipation. Her reflection in his dark lenses looked back at her, and his cedar and sage scent teased her nose.

She bit her lip and eyed the yacht. "I'm going to hate billing Vincent for this rental. I'll cover it. If I can afford it."

"The boat is borrowed. There is no charge." Damon took her bag. Their fingers touched and sparks swirled up her arm and settled in a smoldering pile in her stomach. His palm spread across the base of her spine, upping her body temperature by what felt like a dozen degrees. "Come aboard, Madeline."

Still, she balked. "It's only fair to warn you that I've never been on a sailboat. I don't know the bow from the stern."

A hint of a smile flickered on his lips. "You have nothing to fear. I won't ask anything of you that you're not willing to give. Our only task is to enjoy the sail and each other."

Her breath shuddered in and then out. He'd read her pretty easily. It wasn't the sail making her jittery. It was the prospect of being alone with him, of giving in to these foreign and over-whelming feelings and embarking on an uncharted sensual journey. "Okay."

He guided her onto the boat's back deck. A hip-high wall surrounded an area about ten feet square. He descended through a door into the cabin below and then turned and offered his hand. "Watch your step and your head."

Her fingers entwined with his and the heat of his palm spread through her making her knees shaky. At the base of the stairs she paused and blinked, allowing her eyes to adjust to the dimmer interior. Once she could focus, what she saw dazzled her. The luxury of stained wood cabinetry and bisque leather upholstery surpassed anything she'd ever seen—even her plush hotel suite.

Without releasing her hand Damon led her through a sitting area and a kitchen. He stepped through another door and moved aside for her to enter. A bed dominated the spacious stateroom—a bed she'd soon be sharing with him. Her heart thumped harder. The room seemed to shrink in size and the oxygen thinned. Her skin dampened, but her mouth dried.

Long, narrow horizontal windows let in sunlight, warming the cabin. Or maybe it was the knowledge of what lay ahead making her hot. She plucked at her suddenly clingy shirt.

"You may change in here or in the head." He dropped her bag on a bed and indicated a bathroom by tilting his head, and then he removed his sunglasses and tossed them on the mattress. Holding her gaze with desire-laden eyes, he cupped her shoulders. "Need help changing?"

"I, um…no." She swallowed the lump in her throat. She'd wanted adventure and she'd found it. Nerves, excitement and expectation vied for dominance inside her. Nerves won.

His hands coasted down her arms in a featherlight caress and then encircled her waist. He edged his fingers beneath the hem of her top and found the sensitive skin above her skirt. A shiver worked its way outward from the circles he drew on her abdomen with his thumbs. Mike's touch had never affected her this way—not even in the early days when the sex had been good.

"I have been waiting for this." He lowered his head and briefly sipped from her lips.

She didn't want to talk, didn't want to do anything to lessen the intoxicating effect of his lips and hands on her. She wound her arms around his neck and sifted his soft hair through her fingertips. "Me, too."

With a groan he pulled her closer, fusing the length of his body to hers and kissing her hungrily. His torso was hot and hard against hers, his tongue slick and skilled. A gentle tug on her braid tipped her head back, allowing him to delve deeper, kiss harder. Madeline held him close, savoring the sensations whirling through her. She clenched and unclenched her fingers in his hair and then swept her palms over his broad shoulders and down his back.

Footsteps above her startled her into jerking out of his embrace. "What's that?"

"Our crew is casting off. We'll stay below deck until we clear the harbor."

There were strangers on board? She'd thought they'd be alone. Uneasiness prickled her spine. "Why?"

"To stay out of their way while they navigate the channel."

"No, I mean why do we have a crew?"

"Because my attention will be focused on you and not on sailing. Change into your swimsuit and then join me in the galley." He swept his thumb over her bottom lip, grabbed his sunglasses and then left the room, closing the door behind him.

Madeline stared at the wooden panel. Her father had been overprotective—a hazard of his occupation dealing with the seamier side of life. Were his frequent warnings the cause of her uneasiness?

Lose the paranoia. Enjoy your weekend. It makes sense to have a crew on a boat this large, especially since you know nothing about sailing.

Tamping down her misgivings, she reached for her bag.

Seduction on the Mediterranean Sea. Damon had delivered nothing less in the hours since they'd left Monaco behind.

Madeline stood beside him on the front—*bow*—of the anchored sailboat with the deck rocking gently beneath her feet. She sipped her wine and feigned calm when every cell in her body quivered with eagerness for the night ahead. Lights on shore flickered on the ink-dark horizon. She didn't know from which city or even which country.

She turned her head and found Damon's blue gaze locked on her face in the pale moonlight. Sexual energy radiated from him. The entire day had been one long session of foreplay. She'd been wined and dined and tantalized from the moment she'd joined him in the kitch—*galley*. He'd massaged sunscreen into her skin and painted erotic designs on her body with the end of her braid. But he hadn't allowed her to return the favor. He'd kept his shirt on and insisted she keep her hands to herself. Whatever blemishes he was hiding beneath that fabric, she'd prove to him that they didn't matter.

Damon opened his mouth and took a breath as if preparing to speak, but closed it again as he'd done a few times today. He stared at the wine he swirled in his glass, finished it in one gulp and looked at her again.

He wasn't getting shy on her, was he? She never would have pegged him as the reticent type. But then what did she know about him except that he was drop-dead sexy, could drive her to the brink of orgasm without touching the usual parts and that the concierge trusted him?

She slipped an arm around his waist, rose on tiptoe and kissed his chin because she couldn't reach his lips. Damon dipped his head and covered her mouth, parted her lips and swept inside. He tasted like wine, sunshine and the promise of passion. And then he pulled away, cupped her face and pressed it to his shoulder. "Not here. Let's go below."

He laced his fingers with hers and quickly led her inside. There was no sign of Ian and Makos, the crew, in the sitting area or galley. The men must be in their cabin at the rear of the boat. Her worries about them had been unfounded. They'd efficiently done their jobs without encroaching on her and Damon's privacy although she'd been aware of their presence. How could she not be when both men were built like football defensive linemen?

Damon deposited their wineglasses on the counter before leading her into the bedroom at the front of the craft and closing the door behind them. Moonlight seeped through the narrow windows, bathing the room in silvery light. He didn't turn on the lamp and she wondered if that was because of the scars or whatever he hid under his shirt. She could scarcely hear the smack of the waves against the hull over her thundering heart.

Damon's expression turned serious and he seemed a little uneasy. He cupped her shoulders. "Madeline—"

She pressed her fingers to his lips. "It's okay. I'm nervous, too."

He opened his mouth to speak again, but she shook her head and traced his soft bottom lip with her fingertip. "Would you believe I am thirty-two years old and I've only had one lover?" His eyes widened and she cringed. "I'm not telling you that because I want a proposal or anything. I don't. This affair is about here and now and that's all. I just want you to know I might be…limited skillwise. But I'm a fast learner. Now please, kiss me. You've driven me insane all day. I want to do the same for you and I can't wait another second."

But he made her wait ten seconds before banding his arms around her and hauling her close. He took her mouth in a hard, hungry kiss, shifted his head and stole another and another until she clung to him because her legs no longer felt steady. She broke the connection to gasp for air. Their gazes locked and panted breaths mingled.

After a day of not being allowed to touch him, Madeline seized the opportunity to run her hands over him. His shoulder and arm muscles flexed beneath her fingers, and then she shaped his broad back, his narrow waist and finally, his tush. His groan vibrated over her like thunder. He splayed his hands over her bottom and yanked her against the ridge of his erection. Whatever deficiencies he thought he had, that wasn't one of them.

He shoved off the jacket she'd put on after dinner and then bunched the fabric of her top in his hands and whisked it over her head. Her white lace bra glistened in the moonlight and then with a flick of his fingers that, too, was gone and his warm hands shaped her breasts. With a whimper of delight, she closed her eyes and let her head fall back. Pleasure radiated from the nipples he buffed with his thumbs and coalesced into a tight, achy knot of need beneath her navel.

He dipped his head and circled her aureole with his tongue. Hot. Wet. Her knees weakened. She fisted her hands in his shirt and held on. And then he suckled and she whimpered as currents of desire swirled wildly inside her.

"Hurry. Please." She'd never been so aroused in all her life, and he'd barely touched her. She blamed it on the drawn-out foreplay of the day, his scent, his heat, his unique flavor. Her fingers fumbled on the buttons of his shirt, and then finally the last one separated and she pushed the shirt out of her way. The room was too dim to see more than a shadow of chest hair, but his muscles were taut and tight and rippled beneath her questing fingers. No raised or puckered scar tissue marred his supple skin. Nothing to be ashamed of. She found the fastening on his waistband.

He captured her other nipple with gentle teeth, hastily unzipped her skirt and pushed it to the floor. Frantic with need, she sent his shorts and briefs on the same path. She wanted him naked and inside her before she came without him. She'd never been a multiple-o's girl, and she wasn't wasting her one and only on a solo trip. His hand covered the satin front of her panties, stroked, teased. She clenched every muscle and fought off climax, but she was close, too close.

Slapping her hand over his to still him, she gasped, "Condoms. In my beach bag. Now."

His smile gleamed white in the near darkness. "Impatient?"

"Yes."

"I want to taste you."

"Next time. Please, Damon. I'm about to come unglued."

His smile vanished. He hesitated a second before reaching

for her beach bag and handing it to her. She dug until she found the new box of condoms, dropped her bag on the floor and ripped the box open. He reached to take the packet from her.

"No. My turn." She tore the wrapper and reached for him, encircling his thick erection with her fingers and stroking his hard, satiny length. A deep growl rumbled from him.

Mike, the twit, would have a serious case of penis envy if he knew how much better endowed Damon was.

But then Damon tweaked her nipples and thoughts of Mike evaporated in a hot rush of desire. She applied the protection, yanked the covers from the bed and scooted backward toward the headboard. Damon followed, crawling across the mattress like a stalking panther. Impatient for him to pounce, she shimmied her panties over her hips. Damon hooked them with his fingers and tugged them the rest of the way down her legs and tossed them over his shoulder.

"Loosen your braid." His raspy voice against the inside of her knee gave her goose bumps.

She did as he ordered. The moment she finished he plowed his fingers into her hair, cradled her head and devoured her mouth, demanding a response which she was more than happy to give. His body lowered over hers, and hot skin melded to hotter skin from her ankles to her nose. The sheer eroticism of his hair-spattered flesh against hers sent a shiver of delight over her. His masculine scent filled her nostrils, his taste made her crave more. She hooked a leg behind his hip. "Please."

He angled to the side. His fingers parted her curls, found her wetness. And then he did the unforgivable. With only three strokes he made her come. *Without him.* Damn it, she railed even as ecstasy convulsed her body and emptied her lungs.

Before she could protest he filled her with one deep thrust. She'd scarcely caught her breath before he withdrew and returned. Harder. Deeper. Again and again he pounded into her. Instead of relaxing and cooling down the way she usually did after climax, her heart continued to race and her muscles coiled tight again.

She couldn't. Could she?

Not believing what her body was telling her, she dug her nails into his hips and her heels into the mattress and urged him to go faster. And then it happened. Orgasm broke over her like the waves that had crashed over the bow this afternoon, sprinkling sensation on her skin like droplets of seawater.

Smiling with surprise and delight, she buried her face in his neck and then nipped his earlobe. Damon groaned against her temple. His back bowed and he thrust deeper as his climax shook him. And then he collapsed on top of her.

She savored his weight, his warmth, his sweat-slickened skin against her chest and beneath her palms. The sound of water smacking the hull slowly replaced the roar of her pulse.

"Wow," she whispered. "Thank you."

Damon braced himself on his elbows and lifted, his satisfied gaze locking with hers. "Good?"

"Oh yeah." Had her responsiveness been a fluke? She couldn't wait to find out. "Wanna do it again?"

Life didn't get any better than this.

With anticipation dancing across her skin Madeline opened the bathroom door and eased into the bedroom. She lifted a hand to shield her eyes from the blinding sunlight flooding through the cabin windows.

Damon rolled over looking smug, sexy and disheveled beneath the rumpled covers. He'd earned the right. They'd made love three times last night, and he'd made a multiple-o's girl out of her each time. In fact, he'd made her wish for a few fleeting moments that this could be more than just a vacation fling. She liked him, and the man was divine in bed.

His hungry gaze raked her nakedness, inflaming her and making her feel sexy, desired and special. He flipped back the sheet and patted the mattress. "Come here."

Something wasn't right. Madeline's steps faltered. The hair on Damon's head was a rich tobacco-brown, but the curls on his chest and surrounding his impressive erection were dark golden blond.

Like the beard stubble on his chin.

Like the hair on his arms and legs.

Not sun bleached.

Huh?

"You're a natural blond?"

Guilt flashed in his eyes. "Yes."

"Damon, why would you—"

He grimaced and shook his head. "Dominic. My name is Dominic. Not Damon."

Warning prickles danced along her spine. She wrapped her arms around her naked middle. "Your— What?"

"I can explain." He swung his long legs over the side of the bed, stood and stepped toward her.

She held up a hand to halt him and backed away from his rampant masculinity while she struggled with the facts. One corner of her mind registered that he had a body worthy of the cover of a fitness magazine or a centerfold, but the other…

"You lied to me?"

"Other than my name, everything I've told you is true."

The man who'd given her the most incredible night of her life was a liar?

Shades of Mike.

"You expect me to believe that?"

"Yes." He exhaled. "Madeline, I am sorry for the deception, but I wanted a chance to be with you as a man instead of—" his chin shifted, his shoulders squared and resignation settled over his face "—instead of a monarch."

Confused, she blinked. "As in 'butterfly?'"

A smile twitched his lips. "As in Prince Dominic Andreas Rossi de Montagnarde at your service." He bowed slightly.

"Huh?" What in the hell did that mean? He thought he was a prince? Was he certifiable?

His eyes narrowed as he straightened. "The name means nothing to you?"

"Should it?"

"My father is the King Alfredo of Montagnarde, a three-island nation in the South Pacific. I am next in line to the throne."

Fear slithered through her, making her heart blip faster. She was somewhere in the Mediterranean Sea at least a mile offshore with a delusional guy. "Sure you are. A prince, I mean."

Where were the survival instincts her father had drilled into her from an early age? Why had she ignored the warning prickles when she found out there were strangers on board? And why had she ignored the voice that said Damon was too good to be true?

Adrenaline flooded her veins, making her extremities tingle and her heart pound. Medical professionals called it the fight-or-flight response. Her father had called it live-or-die instinct, and he'd credited it with saving his life on more than one occasion. She'd put herself in danger, but she was going to get out of it. There was no other option.

Without taking her eyes off Damon, she reached for the skirt she'd discarded last night, yanked it on and zipped it. "Take me to shore."

"Madeline—"

"Now." She fumbled on her bra and then her shirt. Where had he thrown her panties? She couldn't afford to be vulnerable in any way, shape or form. She located the scrap of lace and donned it.

"I can't do that. Not yet."

She stilled and alarm raced through her. "Why not?"

"You must listen to me first. I wish to explain."

She didn't know why Damon had lured her onto a yacht, but she wished like the devil she'd paid more attention to the grim warnings of white slave trade and crime outside Monaco that Candace's future sister-in-law had shared along with etiquette lessons, but Madeline had written the woman off as an obsessed alarmist.

Wrong.

Inhaling deeply, she tried to recall what she'd been taught about handling unbalanced people and hazardous situations in the E.R. It didn't happen often, but there had been a few times when she'd had to protect herself and the other patients until security arrived.

Rule one: be aware of your surroundings. "Where are we exactly?"

"Off the coast of France."

Rule two: don't alarm the suspect. Keep him calm.

She forced a smile, but it wobbled. "Damon, I'd really like to go ashore."

"That's impossible. You don't have your passport."

Good point. But wouldn't the authorities understand just this once?

He moved closer. "Madeline—"

"Stop. Stop right there."

Rule three: when all else fails use the weapons at hand. There were knives in the kitchen. She'd seen them last night when she and Damon had prepared dinner together. Damon had cooked. What prince cooked? Royalty had servants for that kind of thing. Therefore, he was no prince.

She shoved her feet in her shoes, jerked open the cabin door and scanned the kitchen—*galley. Dammit, who cares what it's called?* She had to get off this boat. Ian and Makos sat at the table. Would they help her? Or were they in on this, too? She could take one guy. But three would be tricky.

She opened drawers until she found the one containing a razor-sharp filet knife with a nine-inch blade. And then Damon—Dominic…whatever the hell his name was—entered the small kitchen and reached for her. Using one of the self-defense moves her father had taught her she grabbed his right arm, ducked and turned and twisted his wrist up behind his back. She pressed the knife to his throat.

"Tell your friends to take me to shore. Now."

She heard an ominous sound and looked up to see two handguns pointed at her from across the room. Big, black ugly weapons. The crew members were in on this and armed.

My God. She was being kidnapped.

Four

"Ian, Makos, lower your weapons," Dominic stated calmly. Neither man complied. "That is an order."

"But Your Highness—" Ian protested.

"Do it. Madeline isn't going to hurt me." Dominic honestly believed it. He could feel the frightened quiver of her tense body pressed against his bare back and see the fine tremor of the hand at his jaw—the same hand that had brought him indescribable pleasure last night.

"That's what you think, buster. I'm a trained medical professional. I know where to cut to take you down instantly." The hand clamped around his wrist might not be completely steady, but her grip and voice were strong. She honestly believed her life was in danger—a circumstance he deeply regretted.

His bodyguards had lowered their guns, but raised them again upon hearing her threat.

Dominic subtly shifted a couple of inches to his right to

prevent the men from getting a clear shot at her. "Perhaps I should mention that Ian and Makos are my bodyguards. It is not wise to provoke them."

A slight shake of his head had the guards returning the weapons to the holsters concealed by their jackets with obvious reluctance.

He didn't doubt Madeline had the skill to kill him, but he doubted she had the nerve, and he wouldn't give her reason to find it. "If you incapacitate me, you will lose not only your human shield, but also your bargaining power. As a medical professional you took an oath to do no harm. Release me before someone gets hurt."

"Right." Disbelief colored the word. "And then what? You and your goons sell me? Ransom me? What?"

"I have no intention of ransoming or selling you. We'll return to port. Ian, give Madeline your phone so that she may call the hotel. Gustavo will vouch for me."

Her breasts nudged his back and her breath puffed against his nape as she snorted. "The concierge is probably in on this…this kidnap attempt. He told me I could trust you. If I call anyone, it'll be the police."

"You haven't been kidnapped. You boarded this yacht of your own free will as any of the other marina patrons will attest. And you will be returned unharmed. Call the authorities if you must, but doing so will be time consuming and embarrassing once the press gets involved."

"What press?"

"The ones I had hoped to avoid with my disguise. I colored my hair and shaved my beard because I wished to vacation without being hunted by the paparazzi. That's why I avoided the hotel after our swim at Larvotto. I did not wish to be recognized by predators with telephoto lenses."

A half minute passed. Although he'd never needed to use his skills, he'd been trained from an early age for situations like this. If he weren't concerned about hurting Madeline, he could escape her hold. An elbow here. A head slam there. He could easily hook one of her legs out from under her with his and send her tumbling to the floor. But she might impale herself as she fell. So he wouldn't. He'd already violated her trust by deceiving her. He wouldn't add physical injury to his crimes.

"Put the guns on the counter and slide them this way. Grips first," she demanded. "The phone, too."

He signaled with his free hand for Ian and Makos to do as she ordered. Both men looked at him as if he'd lost his mind but after a tense silence complied.

She edged closer to the weapons, towing him along with the knife still at his throat. The sad truth was her strength and bravery impressed him and turned him on. Luckily, he'd donned his pants before coming after her or she and his crew would see exactly how strongly she affected him.

He'd never met a woman like Madeline Spencer. Each time he thought he had her figured out she threw a new and intriguing puzzle piece at him—one that didn't fit his image of her.

Who was this woman who didn't hesitate to defend herself? And what had her ex-fiancé done to disillusion her so about love and to make her so distrustful? It had to be more than merely ending the relationship or finding someone new. And why did the knowledge fill Dominic with rage and a thirst for revenge on her behalf?

She halted a yard from the counter. To use the cell phone she'd have to have at least one hand free. He waited for her to choose between releasing him and putting down the knife, but evidently she came to the same conclusion. "I want to go ashore."

"Then you must allow Ian and Makos to go on deck. We can

be back in Monaco in an hour." That would give him time to convince her to trust and forgive him. He'd had every intention of telling her the truth before making love to her. Each time he'd opened his mouth to do so he had looked into her eyes and considered what he stood to lose. Her sassy, confident smile. Her relaxed yet seductive grace. The easy flow of conversation between a man and a woman who were equals. He'd lived with stiff formality for too many years. She'd given him a taste of what he'd been missing, of what a relationship should be, but what his future marriage would very likely not entail.

Last night when she'd stopped his words with gentle fingers on his lips he'd been weak enough to let desire overrule his conscience, but this morning he hadn't been able to stomach having her call him by the fictitious name. He wanted her crying out his name next time she climaxed.

And there would be a next time. He was more determined than ever to enjoy his last days of freedom in Madeline's company and in her bed. Whatever experience she might believe she lacked as a lover she more than made up for with an earthy sensuality that had brought him pleasure more intense than any he'd ever experienced. He wasn't ready to let her go. Not yet. But soon, unfortunately, he would have to.

She jerked his wrist upward with enough force to get his attention, but not enough to do permanent damage. "How stupid do you think I am? They could sail anywhere."

"You can see the GPS screen from here and know if they sail away from port. You'll have the phone, a pair of handguns and me as your hostage if they head in the wrong direction. And Madeline, my passport is in the cabin. Check it."

Another snort. Another brush of her breasts against his back. Another spark of arousal below his belt. "As if you couldn't fake that."

"Then pull me up on the Internet."

"Gee whiz. I forgot to pack my computer in my beach bag," she drawled sarcastically.

"When we get back to Hôtel Reynard then. I have a laptop in my suite."

"Do you think I'll follow you anywhere after this? And what do you mean 'your suite?' You're staying at Hôtel Reynard?"

"Yes. On the same floor as you, but at the opposite end of the hall in the Royal Suite. We are temporary neighbors. Why else do you think I was waiting for the penthouse elevator the night we met?"

She frowned as she considered that and then growled in anger and shifted on her feet behind him. Each movement rubbed her breasts against his naked back, a distraction he didn't need if he wished to avert disaster.

"Your henchmen can go on deck, but we're locking the door behind them and if they try to come through, I'll shoot because I think you're full of sh—"

"You know how to handle a gun?" Most shooting accidents happened at the hands of the inexperienced and he would prefer to avoid bloodshed. Particularly his.

"My father was a vice cop. I can not only handle a gun, I'm a damned good marksman. He made sure of it."

Ian caught Dominic's attention and tapped his thigh, indicating the smaller weapon Ian kept strapped above his ankle. Dominic signaled the negative and maintained eye contact long enough for the man to understand Dominic would handle the situation. Ian clearly didn't like it, but he accepted Dominic's silent command with a slight nod.

"Pull up anchor and return to port." Dominic's order contradicted every oath his bodyguards had taken. Members of the royal guard had to be willing to die for their country. That meant not leaving one of their leaders with a knife at his throat. But Ian and Makos did as he requested, climbing the ladder and closing the cabin door behind them.

Madeline pulled him toward the hatch and latched it.

"Sit." She shoved him toward the sofa.

Flexing his shoulder, Dominic sat because not fighting would serve his purpose better than asserting his authority or his physical dominance.

Poised on the balls of her feet, Madeline kept the knife at the ready and her eyes fixed on him as she quickly closed the blinds on each window. Smart move. Being unable to see inside the cabin would prevent Ian from trying anything heroic.

To make her feel less threatened Dominic propped his feet on the coffee table, crossed his ankles and leaned back, linking his fingers over his belly. As soon as he did Madeline backed toward the galley and collected the guns.

She handled the firearms comfortably, competently, checking the safeties and the clips of each weapon before shoving the knife back into the drawer. His respect for her climbed another notch. She was smart, resourceful, strong and calm in a crisis. Not to mention sexy as hell.

If a little misguided.

"My passport is in my bag. I'm blond and have a beard in the photo, but you've known me for a week and spent the night in my bed. You should be able to see past facial hair and a temporary dye job."

She kept the width of the room between them. "I don't care about your stupid and probably forged passport. You're still a liar."

Guilty as charged. "I didn't originally intend to conceal my identity, but Madeline, when you looked at me that night by the elevator I saw a woman who desired *me,* not a woman who wanted to land a prince. Do you have any idea how rare that is? It has only happened one other time. With Giselle, my wife."

"Spare me the sob story. I'm sure that was fiction, too."

"Sadly, it is not. I had known Giselle since we were children. We became engaged when I was nineteen and she sixteen."

Her nose wrinkled in distaste. "That's positively feudal."

He shrugged, but didn't waste time trying to explain a bridal selection process he knew she would neither like nor understand. "I agree. She was too young. That is why I insisted we postpone the marriage until I graduated from the university. And then as I told you in the café, she died two years into our marriage along with our first child."

"I don't want to hear it."

He ignored her words and kept talking to keep her calm and to get her to let down her guard. "My country is raw and largely untamed due to the royal advisory council's fear of change."

She rolled her eyes. "Uh-huh."

"It is believed that Montagnarde was once a massive volcano, but sixty million years ago the ocean breached the walls and extinguished the fire. There are three islands now surrounding an inland sea of crystal clear water."

"What a great imagination. You should write a book."

He smiled at her acid tone. She didn't believe him. Would she, like so many others, become deferential, obsequious and more interested in what his wealth and power could do for her once she accepted his identity? Undoubtedly. And when she did he was certain his fascination with her would end. "My youngest sister is writing a history of the islands. I have three sisters. Danielle, Yvette and Brigitte.

"Each generation of monarchs must have an agenda. My great-grandfather's was to protect our borders from outsiders and pests which might devastate our crops or wildlife. My grandfather focused on building a first-class transportation system within and around the islands, and my father on exporting our products. I am determined to introduce the world to the beauty of Montagnarde. Like Monaco, we should maximize our tourist potential. That is why I focused my degree and the past ten years' study on tourism. I intend to implement change and put my country on the map."

"So you admit 'your country' isn't on the map." More sarcasm.

"In terms of global recognition, not yet. But our wines, olive oils and organic produce are beginning to find success in foreign markets. As for our tourism development potential, we have mountains suited to skiing or climbing, depending on the season, blue seas perfect for sailing, sport fishing or surfing, underwater caverns to explore and hot mineral springs for rejuvenation. The natural reefs off our shores put the man-made ones in Monaco to shame and the species of fish and marine life are incredible."

The urgency to share the beauty of his country with her was unexpected and unwelcome, not to mention impossible. "The emeralds mined in Montagnarde are almost as lovely as your eyes, Madeline."

She snorted. "Save your breath. I am *so* over your flattery and so over you."

Frustration rose within him. He had power and wealth at his fingertips and yet the one thing he wished for he couldn't have. He wished for more time with Madeline. But time was a luxury he did not have….

Unless he could turn this disaster to his advantage.

A gurgle of disgust erupted from Madeline's throat. "You are really something."

"So you told me last night. I believe *magnificent* is the word you used."

She wanted to smack that confident smirk off Damon's face. A shocking fact, since she'd never been one prone to violence. Her cheeks burned hot. She'd been a fool for swallowing his garbage the way she had Mike's. Just how stupid was she to let two handsome faces override her common sense?

"Keep it up, bucko, and I might just shoot you for the fun of it. I don't like being made a fool of."

"Is that what your ex did? Made you look foolish?"

She very deliberately released the safety on the gun. "It's not smart to piss off an armed lady."

Damon held up his hands as if in surrender. "Then I will tell you more about my homeland instead." He lowered his arms and linked his fingers over his navel. She could not believe she had nibbled her way down that lying rat's goodie trail last night.

Worse, the proof of Damon's deceit had been right in front of her. Only she'd failed to see the signs because the lights had been out. Sort of like her relationship with Mike. She'd only seen what she wanted to see until he'd forced her to acknowledge the truth.

She hated feeling stupid. Clueless. Duped.

"Each of the islands of Montagnarde has one or more glacial lakes with water pure enough to bottle. The streams and rivers are a fisherman's paradise. Like New Zealand, we have no poisonous snakes or spiders."

Blah. Blah. Blah. She focused on the GPS screen and tried to tune out his words. Whatever he said would be more lies anyway. She could hear the men above them moving about and raising the sails.

Trapped on a yacht with a trio of lunatics. What had she done to deserve this? And would she live to tell the tale?

Yes, dammit, you will. Your mother's depending on you.

"My country was discovered in the 1700s by the Comte de Rossi, a Frenchman searching for a shorter route to the spices of India," he continued. "His ships veered off course in a storm. He landed on the main island searching for food and to make repairs. He decided to stay and explore."

"Right. And the natives just let the French drop anchor and take over?"

"Initially, the islands' inhabitants were bribed with the luxuries on board the ships, but sadly, within the first year the majority of them were decimated by European diseases—also on board de Rossi's ships. The Comte, owner of the fleet, declared himself king and named the islands Montagnarde for the peaks that pierced the clouds. During his lifetime he selectively allowed his countrymen and the finest craftsmen to immigrate, and it is said his advisors kidnapped the most beautiful woman in all of France to be his bride and queen."

Until he uttered the last part his tall tale had *almost* sounded plausible. Her mouth dried. "You'd better not be thinking along the same lines."

"I regret that our affair must end when I leave Monaco."

"In case you missed the bulletin, our affair is already over." Her stomach growled. She glanced at the coffeepot and inhaled the aroma of the strong brew. Her racing heart didn't need the caffeine jolt, but she did need something in her empty stomach to counteract the light-headedness caused by an adrenaline rush combined with not replacing the large number of calories she'd burned off in the past twelve hours.

Naked and entwined with the dishonest snake.

With a gun in her right hand she found a mug with her left and mounded a diet-wrecking amount of sugar inside, and then she poured a stream of coffee on top and swished it around to mix it. She didn't risk taking her eyes off Dominic long enough to search for a spoon or cream. She sipped the syrupy brew. *Eeew.*

"There are pastries in the cabinet to your left and eggs, sausage, fruit and cheese in the refrigerator."

His words made her salivate, but blocking her view of her captive to search the fridge was out of the question. "You'd love it if I'd drop my guard, wouldn't you?"

"I would enjoy breakfast more. We worked up quite an appetite last night."

Her body flushed all over. "Jerk."

She opened the cabinet, found the croissants and hurled one at him with enough force to break a window had it been a rock.

He snagged it out of the air. "Thank you. I am fond of Ian's coffee, as well."

She almost flung her mug at him. Instead she extracted another from the cabinet, filled it and shoved it to the far end of the bar. He was out of luck if he wanted cream or sugar.

He rose and slowly approached. "You don't need the gun, Madeline."

She cursed him, using the one four-letter word she *never* used and he grinned.

"I believe you did that last night. Three times. And with extremely satisfying results."

She gaped. Did the man have an ounce of sense? She had a loaded gun in her hand and he insisted on provoking her.

He moved around the end of the bar. Good God, she didn't want to shoot him. She didn't take lives. She saved them. And until he'd betrayed her she'd liked him. Maybe she could just maim him. But where? She considered her artery-avoiding options. "Don't even think about it."

He stopped his advance and leaned his hip against the counter.

"I can think of nothing but the softness of your skin. Your scent. Your taste. That voracious mouth. The slick clench of your body as you drove me out of my mind. I have never desired a woman as I do you, Madeline. And we could be rediscovering that passion at this moment if you would put the gun down."

Damn him and his low-pitched seductive voice. Arousal tumbled through her. How was that possible in this situation? She briefly closed her eyes—no more than a blink—as the images of last night inundated her, and in that split second Damon lunged forward. His long fingers latched around her wrist. He shoved her gun hand toward the ceiling and slammed his body into hers, backing her against the refrigerator door and forcing the breath from her lungs. The gun exploded with a deafening sound and bits of ceiling rained down.

She struggled, but Damon had her pinned like an insect on a collector's board with his broad chest, his muscular hips and rock-hard thighs grinding against hers.

"Release the gun, Madeline," he ordered calmly.

The hatch door rattled viciously.

"Release the gun," he repeated this time with his warm breath and prickly morning stubble against her jaw. "I promise you are in no danger."

There was nothing remotely sexy about wrestling for a gun, and yet there wasn't an inch of him she couldn't feel imprinted on her skin. Her traitorous brain remembered being this close to him just hours ago with nothing but a thin sheen of sweat between them. How dare her body betray her at this moment. She stiffened her softening muscles.

"As if I'd believe anything you say," she muttered and tried to bow her spine to earn some breathing room.

"You have no choice." There was a hard, commanding edge to his voice that hadn't been there before.

Her hand started to go numb from the pressure he exerted on her radial nerve. Her grip loosened at the same time as the hatch splintered open. Over Damon's shoulder she saw Ian charge in, leading with a small pistol.

"Stand down," Damon called out. His big body blocked hers from his henchmen. He held up his hand, displaying the weapon he'd taken from her.

The other gun lay on the counter out of reach.

Damn. Damn. Damn. She'd let her guard down. Had her father been alive he would have been disappointed in her. Determined she would never be a victim of the kind of crimes he investigated, he'd drilled self-defense techniques into her once a week from the day he'd moved out.

"Ian, Makos, retrieve your weapons. Mademoiselle Spencer will be joining me in the captain's cabin."

"In your dreams, *prince*." She practically spat his fake title.

"Give us a few moments and then we would like breakfast." He grasped each of her arms and then lifted his weight and yanked her forward before transferring her wrists to one big hand behind her back. His long fingers compressed like a vise.

"Don't make me tie you up," he murmured in her ear. "Although we might enjoy that another time."

"Bite me."

"I would be more than happy to in the privacy of our cabin." He turned her and steered her toward the cabin. Try as she might she could not wriggle free. Man, the guy was strong. And then he closed the door and locked it behind them. Damon released her.

She hustled to the far side of the room, scanning the surfaces for weapons and finding none. Not even a vase to crack over his head. But even if she incapacitated him she'd still have to deal with the two armed thugs in the other room.

He reached into his luggage, withdrew something and tossed it onto the bed. His passport fell open to the picture and her breath caught. As handsome as Damon was as a brunette, he was drop-dead gorgeous as a blond with his hair slicked back to reveal his amazing bone structure and those pale blue eyes.

She inched closer and snatched up the booklet. It named him as Prince Dominic Andreas Rossi de Montagnarde. Hair: blond. Eyes: blue. Height: six feet three inches. She did the math and came up with his age: thirty-five. She flipped through the pages and read stamped ports of entry from across the globe.

But the "passport" was a fake. It had to be. Princes didn't pretend to be tour guides. They traveled with an entourage of toadying staff, and they didn't hang out with commoners like her. She knew that much from *CNN*.

Was Damon some sort of charlatan who connived his way around the globe with a false title? With his looks, charm and sexual prowess he could swindle big-time. But he should focus on women with money. Maybe he thought she was loaded because she'd told him she'd be in Monaco an entire month.

"Recognize me now?" he asked.

"No. And it doesn't matter anyway because once we dock I don't ever want to see you again unless it's to ID you in a police lineup." She flung the documentation back onto the tangled sheets and tried not to recall how the linens had become so mussed.

"I am very sorry to hear that. Because I have not had my fill of you, Madeline. I find your company quite refreshing."

"Too bad." She paced the length of the cabin. "Okay, here's the deal. Put me ashore and I'll forget this ever happened. I won't report you or your thugs."

Not exactly the truth, but—

"Good try, but no." Damon sat on the bed, stretched his legs out before him and leaned back against the headboard, looking as comfortable as he had in the middle of last night when he'd sat in the same spot and watched her shower through the open bathroom door. The memory of how he'd taken the towel from her and lapped the water from her skin afterward shortened her breath and tightened her nipples. She turned her back and stared out the narrow window. Better that than look at his naked chest and remember what an idiot she'd been last night and what an idiot she was being right now by getting distracted by sex.

Wasn't it just her luck that the best lover she'd ever had was a step lower on the slug meter than Mike? Her ex might have been a liar and a cheat, but as far as she knew he'd never broken the law or stooped to kidnapping.

Twenty tense, silent minutes later a knock on the door brought Damon to his feet. He let Ian and breakfast in and then relocked the door after the man left. Food was the last thing she wanted, but if she had to swim or run for it then she'd need whatever fuel she could get. She inched toward the tray while Damon pulled on a blue shirt with a gold crest on the pocket and traded his wrinkled pants for clean briefs and a pressed pair of khakis. He buttoned the shirt and tucked it in, adding a leather belt, and then he stepped into rubber-soled boat shoes. As a final touch he raked his hair back off his forehead with his fingers, exposing his aristocratic bone structure. In that getup he looked like one of the rich and famous. Very "yacht club" and a far cry from her tour guide-lover-kidnapper.

"You realize you have threatened the life of a monarch?" Damon asked casually as he spread cherry preserves on a croissant.

How long was he going to persist in that fairy-tale garbage? Grabbing a pastry with one hand, she flipped him a rude gesture with the other. She bit through the flaky crust and into the moist croissant, chewed, swallowed with inelegant haste until she'd consumed most of her breakfast-fuel supply.

He finished his with less speed, poured a cup of coffee and sipped. "The offense is punishable by imprisonment or death in my country."

She nearly choked on her last bite of pastry and then gulped down the formerly butter-rich now tasteless wad. It hit her stomach like lead. His threat wasn't funny. She'd been worried before, but this ratcheted up the tension in her muscles another ten notches. What exactly was she dealing with here? Because she didn't believe for one second that he actually was royalty.

She eyed the coffee carafe and considered whacking him with it. Did it have enough weight to knock him out? And then what would she do? "We're not in your country."

"The Monaco authorities will be even less lenient."

Other than a sick churning in her stomach she had no answer for that. She wished she'd used Ian's cell phone to call Candace and Amelia and ask them to send the harbor police or whatever they were called.

Who would look after her mother if Madeline ended up not making it back to Charlotte? May Spencer wasn't in fragile health yet, but she was seventy-eight. She didn't travel well and flying made her seriously ill. Would she be able to handle a trip overseas to search for her missing daughter?

Don't think like that. Damon hasn't hurt you. In fact, he stepped between you and the goons' guns twice. Surely if he intended to harm you he wouldn't have?

Or maybe she was worth more alive than dead.

"What do you want from me? I don't have any money. My father is dead and my mother lives on a cop's and a retired teacher's pensions. Trust me, that's a pittance. And I hear the U.S. doesn't negotiate with terrorists."

"I am neither a terrorist nor a kidnapper. I merely wish to continue our…assignations."

Her mouth dropped open. Was he nuts? *Of course he is. He thinks he's a freaking prince.* "You want to remain my tour guide?"

"I would prefer to be your companion and your lover for the remainder of your vacation and mine."

The man had balls of steel and a pea-size brain. "I don't do forced sex."

His bearing snapped military straight and his aristocratic nose lifted. He had the arrogance thing down pat, and he even looked like royalty for a minute there. "I am neither a rapist nor an extortionist. When you return to my bed, Madeline, it will be because you desire me as much as you did last night."

How ungentlemanly of him to mention her enthusiasm. "Not going to happen."

"Would you care to place a wager on that?" One corner of his mouth slanted upward.

Foot stomping overhead followed by the boat's engine rumbling to life preempted her scathing reply—which was a good thing since she couldn't think of one. She moved back to the window and saw the port of Monaco in the distance— swimmable distance if she could get out of this cabin and past the thugs who sounded like elephants overhead. She eyed the skylight in the ceiling, but there was no way she could reach it let alone get through it before Damon could grab her legs.

"We have reached the marina," Damon stated.

Fifteen minutes later the sound of voices—more than had occupied the dock when they'd left—filtered through the closed windows. Damon looked outside and cursed. "Paparazzi. Along with the Sûreté Publique. Ian must have called for assistance."

The police? Thank God. She pressed a palm to her chest.

He caught her shoulders and her gaze. "You will do exactly as I say when we disembark. I would not like to see you inadvertently injured."

"And if I don't?"

"I will press charges."

Jeez, how long was he going to play this gig?

All she had to do was agree. She'd be screaming for help the second she got outside, but he didn't need to know that. She'd report him to the authorities, and she'd tell Vincent Reynard and have the imposter kicked out of the hotel—maybe even banned from all of Reynard's hotels worldwide. Maybe the Monaco Sûreté Publique would haul Damon off in handcuffs. After the scare he'd given her she'd enjoy watching that.

"Okay. I'll do what you say." The lie didn't even make her twitch.

The boat bumped against the dock. Heavy footsteps immediately boarded, rocking the craft.

"Follow my lead and do not say anything to incriminate yourself."

Incriminate herself? That was a riot coming from a con man.

Keeping her behind him Damon opened the cabin door and rattled off something in French. Madeline ducked under his arm, intending to sprint for the hatch, but she skidded to a halt at the sight of the overcrowded galley.

Police. Six of them. With weapons drawn. They fired off commands—commands she couldn't understand and moved toward her in a threatening manner. She backed into Damon.

"English please." Damon's hands encircled her waist and

then he shifted her to his side and draped an arm across her shoulders as if they were friends. Or lovers. "Mademoiselle Spencer does not speak French. And the weapons are unnecessary. She is unarmed."

"You are under arrest, mademoiselle, for assaulting Prince Dominic," one of the officers said.

She gaped. "Me? What about him and his henchmen? They kidnapped me!"

Two of the men reached for her but Damon stopped them with an outstretched and upraised hand. "I apologize for wasting your time, officers. My bodyguards misunderstood the nature of our—" he paused to stare intently into Madeline's eyes "—love play."

He compounded that lie by kissing the tip of her nose.

Her cheeks caught fire over the insinuation while confusion tumbled through her brain. "That's not what hap—"

"*Madeline.*" Damon cupped her shoulders and gave her a gentle shake. "The game is over. You do not want the police to arrest you. Do you?"

She looked from the officers to Damon and back again. The cops had handcuffs, guns and attitude. Enough testosterone crackled in the air to fill a Super Bowl team's locker room. She had encountered hundreds of law enforcement officers through her father and in the E.R.—enough to recognize the real deal when she saw it. These guys weren't pretending. And apparently Damon—*Dominic*—whatever he called himself, wasn't, either.

Her stomach lurched. She gulped back the breakfast rising in her throat and turned to the nearest uniformed man, a fox-faced guy about her age. "He's really a prince?"

The man blinked in surprise. "*Oui,* mademoiselle. Prince Dominic is a frequent and welcome visitor to Monaco."

Uh-oh.

"If you would give us a moment to gather our belongings," Damon said in more of an order than request, "I would be most grateful if you could assist us through the paparazzi outside."

A man whose name tag read Inspector Rousseau said, *"Certainement,* Your Highness. We are happy to be of service."

Numbly, Madeline allowed Damon to steer her back into the cabin. She closed her eyes and locked her jaws on a groan.

Oh, spit. She really had assaulted a member of royalty.

This was *so* not how she'd planned to spend her vacation.

Five

"I guess 'Oops, I'm sorry' won't cut it?" Madeline asked Dam—Prince Dominic in a barely audible voice. She glanced over her shoulder at the officers watching diligently from outside the open door.

"That depends on whether or not you agree to my terms," he replied as quietly.

Her stomach knotted. "Continue the, uh…relationship?"

Dominic nodded once—sharply—with his gaze drilling into hers. Funny how regal he looked all of a sudden. "And you will keep details of our affair private. I have no wish to read about my Monaco mistress in the tabloids."

The Prince's Monaco Mistress. She could see the headlines now. Ugh. She'd never wanted to be famous—certainly not famous for stupidity. Being humiliated by Mike in her small corner of the world had been more than enough exposure, thanks very much.

Spending time with a man who'd lied to her and tricked her into bed under false pretenses ranked low on her to-do list. But it beat incarceration. She knew nothing about Monaco law except the country had an extremely low tolerance for crime. There were cameras on every street corner as a deterrent. Even if she could convince a judge or whoever was in charge of the legal system here to understand her side, she couldn't afford to worry her mother, and she'd prefer not to ruin Candace's wedding with a scandal. And then there was the likelihood that getting arrested would probably jeopardize her job.

"Fine," she bit out ungraciously. "But remember, you are not the prince of me. I'm not doing anything illegal, immoral or disgusting no matter what you threaten."

His lips twitched. "Duly noted. You have two minutes to make whatever adjustments you wish to your appearance before we face the paparazzi."

She ducked into the bathroom and quickly cleaned up, then returned to the bedroom.

"Put on your hat and sunglasses," Da—Dominic ordered. The new name would take some getting used to.

Madeline complied. The last thing she wanted her mother or her coworkers at the hospital to see was her face on *CNN* or *Entertainment Tonight*.

"Your hair is easily recognizable. You might wish to conceal it beneath your hat."

She twisted it into a rope and shoved it beneath the cap.

"Once we exit the yacht keep your head down and do not answer any questions no matter how provocative."

Once they had their bags packed he took hers from her and turned back to address the police through the open door. "Officers, once again I apologize for the misunderstanding.

Should you require it, I will be more than happy to come down to the station and make an official report after I return Mademoiselle Spencer to the hotel."

"That will not be necessary, Your Highness," Rousseau said.

The youngest officer offered to carry their bags. Dominic handed them off and strode toward the hatch.

Where had her sexy, laid-back tour guide gone? The man in front of her stood straight, tall and regal as he followed half of the officers from the cabin.

How could he follow and still give the impression of leading?

He paused at the top of the ladder and turned to help Madeline ascend. The wall of voices and the whir of cameras slammed her as soon as her head cleared the cabin. She pulled down the bill of her cap. From the dock, dozens of camera-toting reporters shouted questions in a variety of languages. Dominic ignored them.

No, *ignore* wasn't quite the correct word. He acted as if he didn't see or hear them, as if they didn't exist.

"Head down. Let's go," he said into her ear and then he grabbed her elbow and half led, half dragged her over the planks in the wake of three officers who cleared a path. Ian and Makos followed with two other officers behind them. One remained on the boat—to guard it, she presumed. Or to write up a damage report. She winced. No telling how much paying for those repairs was going to set her back.

The crush of sweaty, smelly bodies jostling to get a picture of Dominic nearly overwhelmed her. The only other time she'd seen something even remotely close to this was when Vincent, Candace's fiancé, had been brought to the E.R. after being badly burned last year at a NASCAR race. The press had crowded into the lobby of the E.R. and security had struggled to keep them out.

A white Mercedes limo waited by the curb. An attendant opened the door as they approached. Dominic urged her to enter first. He quickly followed, choosing the seat directly across from hers. The door closed and silence and blessedly cool air-conditioned air enfolded them. The trunk thumped shut, presumably on their bags.

She looked at the milling crowd outside the tinted windows. The police kept them away from the car. "You live like this?"

"Yes. Now do you understand the need for a disguise?"

She could see how it might appeal, but still— "You should have told me who you were before we slept together."

He nodded acknowledgment. "Agreed."

She waited for him to make excuses. He didn't.

The driver climbed in. Ian joined him in the front seat. Their doors shut with a quiet *thunk* that shouted expensive car.

"The hotel, Your Highness?" the driver asked through an open black glass panel between the front and back seats.

"Yes." The glass rose and the car moved forward.

Angry and confused, Madeline shifted uneasily on the leather seat and then ripped off her sunglasses. "What game were you playing? Slumming with the commoner who didn't have the sense to know who you were? Were you laughing at my ignorance the entire time?"

"I have never considered you ignorant. Nor did I laugh at you. I enjoyed your lack of pretense. Revealing my identity would have changed that."

"You think I'm going to suck up to you now?"

He studied her appraisingly from behind dark lenses. "In my experience I find it likely."

"In your dreams, bucko." And then she recalled the protocol lessons from Candace's future sister-in-law. *Never address royalty by their first names.* "Do you expect me to call you 'Your Highness?' Because I have kissed your butt—literally. I'll be damned if I'll start bowing and scraping—"

His low chuckle winded her. "I would prefer you did not."

"Okay then. Now what? I can't imagine our outings will be any fun if we have to contend with that." She nodded toward the crowd they'd left behind—the one now scurrying along the sidewalk like a fat millipede trying to keep up with them. She couldn't imagine the dates would be fun period since she'd be participating under duress.

"We will have to be more resourceful."

"Where's your entourage? Every bigwig I've seen on TV has one."

"I left them behind. This was supposed to be a quiet, incognito vacation. Ian will arrange for additional security."

At least with security men around there wouldn't be any more intimate encounters. "How long before you accept my apology and let me off the hook?"

"Not until I tire of your company." He leaned forward and splayed his palms across her knees and lower thighs. Heat shot upward from the points of contact. "And, Madeline, I don't think that will happen anytime soon."

The sensual promise in his voice and his touch melted her anger frighteningly fast. She abruptly shifted her legs out of reach and struggled to rally her flagging ire. "Just don't expect me to sleep with you again."

He sat back and looked down his aristocratic nose at her. "You have issued that challenge once already. Repeating it only makes me more determined to prove you wrong."

"We will have lunch in my suite," Dominic announced as they exited the elevator on the hotel's penthouse floor.

"I don't think so." Eager to escape, Madeline turned in the opposite direction and marched toward her suite.

He followed, along with his bodyguards. "I insist."

She stopped outside her door and glared at him. "Insist all you want. But the answer's still no. You don't own every minute of my time. That wasn't part of our deal. I want a shower and a few hours away from you. In case you haven't noticed, I'm still ticked off."

She swiped her electronic key card. The latch whirred and the green light winked. She extended her hand. "Give me my bag."

"Give me your passport."

"Are you nuts?" *Isn't that becoming a familiar refrain?*

"I will not allow you to flee Monaco and escape fulfilling your end of our bargain."

The idea appealed. Immensely. "I can't leave. I have a friend's wedding to help plan and to be in. *I* would never screw someone who trusted me."

From the tightening of his lips she guessed he hadn't missed her implication that he had. "Regardless, I will take your passport as insurance."

The door opened and Amelia stood in the threshold, her hazel eyes cautious as she took in the foursome in the hall. "Is everything okay?"

"No, everything is not okay," Madeline informed her.

Dominic bowed slightly, turning on the charm and flashing a high wattage smile. The action made Amelia's cheeks flush and Madeline seethe. "*Bonjour,* mademoiselle."

"Um, hi." Amelia's gaze flicked back and forth between the men and Madeline.

Madeline grimaced. She'd have to make introductions even though she'd prefer to keep starry-eyed Amelia away from His

Royal Pain in the Butt. Amelia was waiting for a prince to sweep her off her feet. But not this prince.

"Amelia Lambert, my friend, suitemate and coworker. This is Da—Dominic— How in the hell am I supposed to introduce you?"

Dominic's eyes twinkled as if she'd asked a loaded question, and Madeline's pulse tripped.

Stop that. You are immune to him now.

He offered his hand to Amelia. "Dominic Rossi."

Madeline waited, but he didn't offer his title. "He's a freaking prince. And my former tour guide."

Amelia snatched her hand from Dominic's. "Excuse me?"

"The lying snake in the grass omitted telling me he's royalty. The big guys are his bodyguards, Ian and Makos." She jerked a thumb toward the lurking men.

Amelia blinked uncertainly. "Um, nice to meet you?"

"I'll explain later. Just let me in."

Amelia stepped back, opening the door wider. Madeline jerked her bag from Dominic's hand and squeezed past her friend. Dominic, damn him, followed. Ian and Makos remained in the hall like big totem poles flanking the door.

"Your passport, Madeline," Dominic reminded her. "Or I can call the Sûreté Publique."

"Go to he—"

"Why does he need to call the police?" Amelia interrupted. "Did something happen?"

Madeline fought the urge to squirm and glared at Dominic. "We had a misunderstanding, which, of course, was entirely *his* fault."

"It is hardly my fault you chose not to believe the truth," he replied in an infuriatingly calm voice.

"Since you'd been so honest up until that point?" she drawled sarcastically.

He had the decency to flush.

"The prince of what?" Amelia, bless her peacemaking heart, interrupted again.

"Montagnarde," Dominic replied, directing another one of his ligament-loosening smiles her friend's way.

"*Really?*" she whispered in an awestruck voice.

Surprised, Madeline stared. "You've heard of the place?"

"Absolutely. It's southwest of Hawaii. All the burn unit nurses want to go there—if we ever win the lottery, that is. The queen's books about an adventurous dragon are immensely popular with the children on the floor."

Madeline's gaze bounced from Dominic to Amelia and back. Was she the only one without a clue about him or his homeland? "You said your sister was the author."

"Brigitte is writing a history of the islands, but my mother writes children's books. They're the stories she told my sisters and me when we were young."

She did not want to picture him as a boy curled up in his mother's lap for a bedtime story. He'd probably been disgustingly cute then, too.

Amelia frowned and narrowed her eyes on Dominic. "Forgive my impertinence, Your uh, Highness? But I thought you were a blond and you…" She pointed at her jawline.

"Dominic, please." He pulled out his wallet, extracted a business card and offered it to Amelia. "I was incognito until Madeline broke my cover. E-mail the hospital address to me and I will have Mama send a box of autographed books to your hospital. If you would like, you may include the first names of the children currently residing on the floor so she can personalize them."

Wide-eyed, Amelia clutched the card to her chest. "I'll do that as soon as I get back to Charlotte. Thank you."

Madeline clenched her teeth. She did not want him doing nice stuff. She'd rather remember him as the sneaky, lying bastard forcing his company on her.

And he hadn't given *her* a card. Not that she wanted one. Nope. She'd be happy if she never laid eyes on him, his card or his henchmen ever again.

His blue gaze caught Madeline's. "Perhaps Mademoiselle Lambert would like to join us for lunch in my suite."

The moment she saw the pleasure bloom in Amelia's face, Madeline knew she should have killed Da—Dominic while she had the chance. The conniving opportunist had set the trap so smoothly she hadn't seen it and she'd stepped right into it. If she refused to eat with him now Amelia would be crushed.

Madeline flipped him a rude hand gesture behind her friend's back.

His smile turned wicked. "I'll take that as a yes."

Grrr. "May I see you in my room for a moment?"

"My pleasure."

"You wish." She turned her back on Amelia's dreamy sigh, stomped into her bedroom, tapped her toe impatiently until he crossed the threshold and then shut the door behind him with a restrained click. Slamming it would have been much more satisfying. She settled for heaving her overnight bag onto the bed and then planting her fists on her hips.

"Leave Amelia out of this."

"Your friend is charming."

"And off-limits to you." If the lift of his eyebrow was any indication, her tone had sounded a tad too possessive. Or protective. Or bitchy. Probably all three. "Should I expect more underhanded maneuvering from you?"

"Only if you make it necessary. I am usually quite straight-forward in my desires. And at the moment I desire your company...and you, Madeline."

Her pulse tripped over the raspy edge of his voice and her body heated at the memory of exactly what fulfilling his desires had entailed. He hadn't neglected one single inch of *her* body last night while taking care of *his* needs.

"Can't say the same about yours and you," she lied with only a pinch of discomfort.

His smile turned predatory. "Another challenge?"

She almost snarled, but settled for a glare.

He extended his hand. "Your passport, please."

"What if I want to cross the border on a sightseeing trip?"

"You will be with me, and I will have your passport. Tomorrow morning we'll go to the Rainier III Shooting Range. I wish to see how good you are with a weapon."

She ungraciously dug her passport out of the dresser drawer, slapped it into his hand and then studied her nails. "I might be busy."

"You're afraid I'm a better marksman?" He slipped the booklet into his pants pocket.

"Don't try reverse psychology on me. It won't work."

He moved closer. The dresser behind her prevented her escape. He lifted his hand and dragged a fingertip along the skin fluttering wildly over her carotid artery. "Would you prefer I stroke your erogenous zones instead? As I recall, that made you quite amenable last night."

She cursed her weakening knees and the revealing goose bumps marching across her skin. Last night his caresses had turned her mind and body to mush. She would have agreed to practically anything he asked.

But that was then. Now she knew he was the kind of guy

who'd lie his way into a woman's bed. She clenched her teeth jerked her head out of reach and folded her arms across her tattletale breasts. She ought to plant a knee in his crotch.

He must have read her mind because he lowered his hand and stepped back. "I will expect you and Mademoiselle Lambert in my suite in an hour. And Madeline, do not disappoint me."

A stranger opened the door. A gorgeous, blond-haired blue-eyed, freshly shaven stranger expensively attired in a dove-gray suit and a stark white open-collared shirt.

Dominic. Madeline's mouth dried and her heart stuttered She'd recognize that incredible bone structure anywhere. He'd been handsome as a brunette, but now... *Wow.* He'd brushed his hair back from his forehead, setting off his pale blue eyes and tanned skin.

But his phenomenal looks didn't matter. She had a zero tolerance policy for liars. "You have a hairdresser at your beck and call?"

Her waspish question didn't faze him. "Hôtel Reynard is quite accommodating. Come in, mesdemoiselles."

The layout and opulence of his suite resembled the one she shared with Amelia, Candace and Stacy, but whereas theirs was light and airy, his was decorated in jewel-tone fabrics and darker woods. The dining room table had been set with enough silver, crystal and china to buckle the legs of a less substantial piece of furniture. Afternoon sunlight streamed through the floor-to-ceiling windows overlooking the Mediterranean, making the wine and water goblets sparkle like diamonds scattered across the ivory linen tablecloth.

Rich. Formal. Elegant. Dominic's world. She was only a visitor—and a reluctant one at that. Better not forget it.

She felt the weight of Dominic's gaze on her as she studied

the setup. He believed his having loads of money would impress her. But he was wrong. She worked with dozens of consulting doctors and surgeons through the E.R. Some were incredibly wealthy, certainly not in Dominic's heir-to-the-kingdom league, but a money surplus didn't keep them from being jackasses. A seven- or eight-figure net worth meant nothing if no one liked, respected or trusted you.

Self-satisfaction was more important than mucho bucks any day. She wanted to work where she could help the largest number of people and maybe even catch a few lost souls before they slipped through the bureaucratic health-care cracks. A county hospital provided the best venue. And when her head hit the pillow each night she could rest easy knowing she'd made a difference that day. The way her father had as a cop. The way her mother had as an inner-city schoolteacher.

She glanced at her friend. Amelia seemed a little ill at ease around *Prince* Dominic. Or maybe it was the four waiters lined up like a firing squad on the far wall or the stone-faced Ian over in the corner making her uneasy.

"He doesn't like me much, does he?" Madeline asked sotto voce so the bodyguard in question wouldn't overhear.

"Would you expect otherwise? You threatened to slit my throat," Dominic replied in an equally quiet tone—but not so quiet she missed the amusement tingeing his voice.

"Madeline!" Amelia squeaked.

Madeline winced. She'd escaped telling Amelia what happened by ducking into the shower and dawdling over dressing for lunch. The extra care she'd taken with her appearance had absolutely nothing to do with impressing Dominic. She didn't care if he liked her slim-fitting lime-green sundress or her strappy sandals. She'd chosen this outfit because it complemented her eyes and showed off her hard-earned shape.

Right now she needed the confidence booster of looking good because she felt stupid. Not an emotion she enjoyed or one she experienced often, thank goodness. She had a reputation at work for thinking fast on her feet and being good in a crisis. That would be worthless if this debacle slipped out. Talk about jumping to erroneous conclusions… She'd taken a dive into the Mariana Trench.

"Rest assured, Mademoiselle Lambert, Madeline had reason to question her safety. But that is something we shall not discuss around outsiders." Dominic indicated the waiters with a slight inclination of his head.

His defense surprised Madeline as did the reminder that others would be interested in his life.

"Please be seated." He touched his hand to the base of Madeline's spine and sparks skipped up her vertebrae like stones skimming across a pond's surface. Her breath hitched. She didn't look at him as she crossed the long room to the lavishly laid table.

Frankly, the entire episode, or rather her lack of perception, was embarrassing. How could she have believed him to be a simple tour guide? From his fluency with languages to his expensive clothing, his regal bearing and complete acceptance of the waiters rushing forward to pull back their chairs, everything about Dominic screamed wealth and privilege.

Dominic stood behind the seat at the head of the table, waiting for the staff to seat Madeline on his right and Amelia on his left. Once the women were settled he sat and commenced a wine tasting ritual that launched a meal more elaborate than any Madeline had ever experienced. Each mouthwatering course arrived hot and fresh from the kitchen, and then finally, what seemed like forever later, the waiters placed dessert in front of them. Dominic dismissed the servers. Only Ian remained in watchful silence.

Madeline stared at the confection in front of her. She didn't even want to think about how many calories she'd consumed or how many extra hours she'd have to spend in the hotel gym to make up for this meal. But that didn't stop her from sampling the warm chocolate tart topped with Bavarian cream mousse. She'd never tasted anything as rich, decadent and delicious. Her mouth practically had an orgasm. Her eyes closed and a moan sneaked past her lips.

Embarrassed, she pressed her napkin to her lips and peeked at Dominic only to find his attention riveted on her face. His pupils dilated and his intense gaze shifted to her mouth. His lips parted slightly and he moistened them with his tongue. A slowly indrawn breath expanded his chest.

The raw passion in his eyes torched her body like dry kindling. Memories of his lovemaking licked through her. His touch. His taste. His incredible heat. The powerful surge of his body into hers.

Her skin flushed and dampened. The fabric of her dress abraded her suddenly sensitive breasts and desire pooled and pulsed in her pelvis.

So much for pretending indifference or forgetting even one second of last night. If a single desire-laden glance from his bedroom blue eyes could bring it all rushing back, then staying out of his bed wasn't going to be nearly as easy as she'd hoped.

Well, dammit, she'd just have to try harder. Failure wasn't an option.

She makes the same sound when she climaxes.

Madeline's moan hit Dominic like a sucker punch. Memories of their passionate night erupted inside him with the force of a volcano. Desire coursed through his veins like streams of molten lava. He instantly recalled the slick, tight heat of her body, the scrape of her nails on his back as she arched beneath him and the band of her legs around his hips urging him deeper.

She scowled at him and flicked back her hair. Remembering the sweep of her soft curls across his belly as she took him into her hot, wet mouth made him shudder. From the toes curled in his shoes to his clenched jaw, each of his muscles contracted. Sweat beaded on his upper lip.

He had spent the past two hours waiting for Madeline to become cloying, obsequious and more interested in what his wealth and power could do for her. As soon as she did he was certain his fascination with her would end.

The elaborate luncheon had been but a small sample of the luxuries he could shower upon her now that his identity had been revealed. But instead of using her position as his lover as leverage, other than an occasional unsuccessful attempt to derail the conversational path he'd chosen, she'd been unusually reticent.

She'd barely contributed to the discussion about the sights and clubs she and her suitemates had already visited or the upcoming wedding—the reason for her presence in Monaco. Her friend had been more forthcoming, but Amelia's comments had only led to more questions about the puzzling Madeline Spencer.

Finally, Amelia pushed her dessert plate away.

"You enjoyed lunch?" He hoped his impatience didn't show.

"Yes. Thank you so much for including me, Your Highness."

"Dominic. And it was my pleasure."

Her cheeks flushed. "Dominic."

He should be polite and linger over coffee, but he had lost

ground to recover and a limited time in which to do so. He stood. "Ian, please escort Mademoiselle Lambert to her suite."

Madeline shoved back her chair and rose. "I'm going, too."

Dominic caught her wrist and held firmly when she tried to pull away. Her pulse quickened beneath his fingers. "You and I have unfinished business to discuss."

She made no attempt to conceal her displeasure as she plopped back into her chair, forcing him to release her. She picked up her fork and stabbed it viciously into her dessert. No doubt she'd rather plant the tines in him.

Looking between him, Madeline and Ian, Amelia hesitated. Dominic suspected she'd stay with the slightest encouragement from her friend, but Madeline waved her away. "It's okay. I'll be right there."

Moments later the door closed behind Ian and Amelia. Dominic refilled Madeline's wineglass and then his own. "How long did your engagement last?"

"None of your business." She shoved a bite of confection between her lips and the urge to taste it on her tongue swelled within him. Normally he didn't care for sweets, but licking the rich cream from Madeline's skin appealed. Immeasurably.

"Shall I call back your friend? She seemed quite willing to provide information."

"And you were not in the least bit subtle in prying my personal data out of her."

He couldn't stop a smile. "I don't think she noticed."

"*I* noticed."

"How long?"

She huffed out a breath and pushed away her plate. "Six years."

"Six *years?*" What man could possibly allow such an eternity to pass without claiming Madeline as his own? He and Giselle had waited three years, but that was because Giselle had been too young when their engagement began. "Your fiancé had commitment issues?"

"Aren't you a smart guy to figure that out so quickly. It took me a lot longer."

"So you once believed in love? And now you don't."

"Nice analysis, Dr. Freud. Can I go now?"

"How did you make the transition?"

She blinked. "Huh?"

"How did you make yourself accept the idea of a life without a connection or bond with someone who actually gives a damn about you?"

Her lips parted and her eyes widened. "Holy moly. You're a romantic."

He debated telling her about the sterile selection process underway at home, but what point would that serve? It certainly wouldn't aid his cause in getting Madeline back into his bed and stockpiling his need for passion before he commenced a life without it. And since their relationship was temporary, what happened in Montagnarde would not affect her.

"I am tired of one-night stands. I wish to have someone share my bed for reasons other than duty, greed or fleeting attraction."

"Why bother? You'll just get disappointed in the end."

"My parents have been married for almost forty years and each of my sisters for nearly a decade. Their marriages are strong and happy."

"For now." She grabbed her wine and took a healthy sip. "My parents were married for thirty-five years before my father walked out."

The pain and sadness in her eyes tightened his chest. "Why did he leave?"

She rose. "Does it matter?"

"Apparently it matters to you. I've heard children often blame themselves for their parents' divorce."

"There you go again. Practicing psychology without a license. Don't they have laws against that in Monaco?"

But the sudden rigidity of her posture told him he'd hit a nerve. "Do you blame yourself?"

"Of course not," she replied too quickly. "I was only ten."

He captured her chin, lifted her face until she met his gaze, and repeated, "Do you blame yourself?"

She glared at him for a full thirty seconds before her lids lowered and her shoulders sagged on a sigh. "They were married twenty-five years before I came along. A menopause surprise baby. So yes, for most of my life I wondered if my arrival had upset the balance."

She shook off his hand, and hugging herself, moved to the window. "After my father died I finally found the courage to ask my mother what really happened. According to her they split because of indifference. They just fell out of love. Neither cared enough about the other to fight for their marriage, but they fought about anything and everything else. I was actually relieved when Daddy moved out and the shouting stopped."

She was tough, a fighter, and yet at the moment she seemed fragile and lost. Struggling with the urge to take her in his arms, for he doubted she would welcome his comforting embrace, Dominic joined her by the glass.

"Did you feel the same indifference for your lover?"

"What!" She pivoted to face him with her mouth agape.

"You did not love him enough to push forward with your wedding plans, and yet you did not dislike him enough to end your engagement. It appears he suffered the same indifference." He shrugged. "I would not wish for such a passionless relationship."

"It wasn't passionless," she said through clenched teeth.

"No? Did you not say last night that you had never had so many orgasms in one night nor found such pleasure? Tell me, Madeline, did you hunger for his touch the way you do for mine?"

A white line formed around her flattened lips and her face turned red. "My relationship with Mike is none of your business."

"I have heard most women choose men like their fathers."

The color drained from her cheeks and she actually staggered back a step. "What does that have to do with us? Because you sure as heck aren't looking for anything long-term with me."

He'd be damned if he knew why understanding Madeline Spencer was so important when she would be gone from his life in a matter of days. "No. As I have said before, I regret that here and now is all I can offer you."

And for some reason that left him feeling more dissatisfied and trapped by his life than he had in a very long time.

Six

Madeline stumbled midjog Tuesday morning when she saw her face on the cover of a tabloid paper.

She jerked to a halt on the cushioned running track along Boulevard du Larvotto and stared in dismay at the newsstand rack. Not one, but two papers carried photos of her and Dominic on their covers. She moved closer to examine the pictures of the two of them leaving the boat. With her hair tucked beneath her hat, her sunglasses covering part of her face and her profile angled away from the cameras, only her mother and closest friends would recognize her beside Dominic, who looked tall and commanding and royal.

Boy, had she misread him.

The captions were in French…or maybe Italian. She had no idea what they said. She reached into her shorts pocket for the euros she'd brought along to buy a bottle of water at the end of her run and picked up a copy of each paper. Her hands shook as she paid the man at the newsstand and accepted her change.

Hopefully Candace or Stacy would be able to translate. But were they awake yet? Despite their late nights here in Monaco, Madeline couldn't seem to break her wake-at-dawn habit.

With her plan to burn off the surplus of calories she'd consumed recently with a long morning run derailed, she rolled the papers into a baton and jogged back to the hotel. She let herself into the suite. Silence greeted her. None of her suite-mates were awake. But she couldn't wait. She had to know what the articles said now.

So much for avoiding His Royal Hemorrhoid today by ducking out of the hotel early.

Returning to the hall she marched the length of the plushly carpeted corridor to Dominic's door and mashed the doorbell long and hard. He'd gotten her into this mess. It would serve him right if she woke him.

The door opened. "Good morning, Ian. Where is he?"

She tried to enter, but Ian's bulk blocked her way. "Prince Dominic is unavailable."

"Make him available."

The burly chest swelled. "Mademoiselle—"

"Let her in," Dominic's deep voice called from inside.

Five heartbeats later Ian stepped aside. Could he be a little more obvious that he didn't want her here? Madeline plowed past him only to jerk to a halt at the sight of a black-robe-clad Dominic sitting at the table with coffee and a newspaper. The silky fabric gaped as he rose, revealing a wedge of tanned chest dusted in golden curls. Below the loosely tied belt his legs and feet were bare.

Was he naked under there?

Get over it. You've already seen him naked and you see naked men at work every day.

With no small effort she pried her gaze upward. Burnished stubble covered the lower half of his face. His hair was mussed and his pale eyes curious. Her mouth dried and her pulse quickened. Clearly her body had not received the message from her brain that she was totally and completely over him and that there would be no more nookie.

"Good morning, Madeline. You are eager for my company today. That bodes well for our time together."

The devil it did. Her hands fisted. Paper crinkled, reminding her why she'd come. *The tabloids.* She crossed the room, thrust them at him and then after he took them, she retreated to the opposite end of the table.

His gaze traveled from her hastily braided hair to her chest in a snug tank top and breast-flattening jog bra and then down her bare legs to her running shoes. She'd dressed the way she always did for a workout, but suddenly she became uncomfortable with her skimpy attire and lack of makeup. Maybe she should have changed before coming here.

No. You are not trying to attract him anymore.

Tugging at the hem of her very short shorts, she cleared her throat. "What do they say?"

He unrolled the papers, scanned one and then the other, his lips compressing more with each passing second, and then his gaze returned to hers. "Our affair has become public knowledge. The good news is they haven't printed your name which means they don't know it yet. There is only speculation as to whom I'm seeing."

"But what do they say *exactly*?"

His frown deepened. He gestured to first one tabloid and

then the other. "The Prince's Paramour and The Prince's Playmate. Shall I translate the articles for you?"

"No." Her stomach churned. Why had she insisted on knowing what the tabloids said? Because she'd never bought into the ignorance is bliss theory—especially since Mike. But suddenly she wished she did. Gulping down rising panic she asked, "Why would anyone care about me? I'm a nobody."

"When you became a prince's lover you became a person of interest."

She felt as if she'd swallowed a gallon of seawater. A little queasy. A *lot* uncomfortable. "I did not sign on for that."

"Would you like coffee?" He gestured to the tray on the table. A second cup already had coffee in it. A third remained empty. She glanced at the frowning, dark-suited Ian. Was he more than an employee? And what about the missing Makos? Was the third cup for him?

Who cares? This is all about you, remember? Your mistake. Your humiliation. Your fraying credibility.

She turned back to Dominic. "I don't want coffee. I want to be left alone. By the paparazzi. And by you. I have things to do and places to see and a reputation to protect."

"Too late, I'm afraid. I will arrange for someone to guard you, but until he is in place you might wish to avoid crowded tourist attractions or risk being cornered by the paparazzi."

Guard her? Oh, please. "*Hello.* I am a tourist. I want to see the sights. I still haven't found a gift for my mother, so I *will* see them. And I don't want anyone shadowing me." She tugged at her braid. "What can we do?"

One shoulder lifted in a shrug. "Ride it out."

How could he be so laid-back? "I don't want to be branded as your mistress in the papers."

"I would have preferred to avoid it, as well, but what's done is done."

"Fix it, Dominic. Make them print a retraction or something."

"Demanding a retraction would only draw more interest. I am sorry, Madeline. We will do what we can to conceal your identity from the press so you will not be bothered once you return home, but I can offer no guarantees."

She groaned and a heavy weight settled on her chest. This could *not* follow her back to Charlotte. The whispers, abruptly stalled conversations and questions about her judgment had barely stopped from the Mike debacle.

"Your Highness, we could return to Montagnarde," Ian suggested.

Madeline's muscles tensed. Why? She wanted to be rid of Dominic. Didn't she?

She turned on Ian. "You called him Damon on the boat. Why get prissy now?"

When Ian remained silent Dominic explained, "That was before you knew my identity. Ian is a stickler for protocol in public."

"One, I have slept with you, so I'm not 'the public.'" She marked the words with quotation marks in the air. "Two, if he hadn't called the cops then we would not be having this conversation."

Dominic flung the papers on the table and closed the gap between them in three long strides, stopping so close she could smell his unique scent, feel the heat radiating from his body and see each individual blade of morning beard on his jaw and upper lip.

"Three," he continued, "if I had not misled you then four, you would not have threatened me, and Ian would not have called the police. We come full circle. Protecting me is his job.

We all share the blame, but the lion's share is mine because I am the one who began the masquerade."

Good point. And as much as she hated to admit it, Dominic's willingness to accept part of the blame surprised and impressed her. She was used to guys who shucked responsibility for their mistakes whenever possible. For example, the way Mike had blamed her for his cheating.

She pressed her fingertips to her temple. This was not turning out to be a good day. "What are our options?"

He caught her hand and carried her fingers to his lips. A shock wave of awareness swept over her before she snatched her hand away. "We could remain sequestered in my suite for the remainder of your stay in Monaco."

Temptation swamped her. It took a second to force her lungs to fill and oxygenate her brain enough for reason to return. "Not going to happen. I didn't come to Monaco to hide out in a hotel. And since I may never get back to Europe I plan to see some of it—which is why I wanted a tour guide."

"Then we will keep as low a profile as possible and continue as we had originally planned once additional staff is in place."

"Is that doable?"

"It is the way I live my life. Being watched or followed is unavoidable. In the future you might wish to consider that before venturing out alone, and I would suggest you not sunbathe topless unless you want the paparazzi to enjoy your beautiful breasts as much as I do."

His compliment was lost in a tidal wave of heart-sinking, skin-prickling panic. She hugged her arms across her chest. Had anyone been watching her this morning? What about yesterday when she'd sneaked out of the hotel at the crack of dawn and hidden out in a cybercafe until she could tour the

Monaco Porcelain Factory? Had someone been watching last night when she'd returned to the hotel and been immediately whisked up to Dominic's suite by Makos? The thought gave her the creeps.

"Join me for breakfast, Madeline."

The way he voiced the invitation, low and husky and intimate, caused her pulse to spike despite her concerns.

Good grief. Haven't you learned anything?

"I have to get back for Candace's morning meeting and to get the details of some ball thing from Stacy."

The doorbell chimed. His long fingers curled around her upper arm, infusing heat into her chilled muscles. "Come into my bedroom."

She tried and failed to yank free. "Have I been too subtle? I'm. Not. Interested."

"Breakfast has arrived. Would you prefer the server report that you were in my suite when I was not dressed?"

Ugh. "That kind of thing happens?"

"Yes. Hôtel Reynard is one of the best chains in the world for screening employees, but it is wise to be cautious."

"You mean paranoid." She shook off his hand and reluctantly accompanied him to the adjoining room. A king-size bed covered in tangled tan sheets dominated the space. The burgundy-and-gold paisley spread lay crumpled at the foot. They'd left the bed on the boat in a similar condition. Her body flushed hot and her clothing clung to her dampening skin.

Excuse me. You're over him. Remember?

He closed the door, leaned one shoulder against it and folded his arms over his chest. The move separated the fabric of his robe. "Tell me about the ball."

She forced her eyes away from the triangle of skin and the barely tied knot at his waist. "Not much to tell. I found a note from Stacy this morning saying there's going to be a ball Saturday night and that Franco is buying our gowns. That's all I know."

"Le Bal de L'Eté, a charity event which opens the season at the Monaco Sporting Club, is this weekend. Who is Franco?"

"Stacy's...friend." Her suitemate was having a passionate vacation fling, the kind Madeline had hoped to have, but—

"I don't like another man buying your dress."

"Tough." Through the door she heard the sounds of the room service cart being rolled into the dining area, the rattle of dishes and the low hum of voices, and then the cart leaving.

"I'll purchase your gown."

"And won't that look great in the tabloids? I'm no man's kept woman."

"And yet you would let this Franco pay for your dress."

She'd only met the sexy French chocolatier a couple of times, and normally she wouldn't let a stranger buy her clothing, but Franco only had eyes for Stacy. "He doesn't expect anything in return."

"You believe I would buy gifts for you to coerce you back into my bed?"

"We both know you want me there." And she was just as determined not to return. If he'd lied about one thing, he'd lie about another.

"Yes, I do. What's more, you want it, too."

Right.

Wrong! "That's quite a large ego you have there. Does Ian help you lug it around?"

Dominic's lips twitched and humor sparkled in his eyes. "I'll escort you to the ball."

"Oh yeah. That's being discreet. Forget it. I'm going with my suitemates. A girls' night out. And I plan to dance with every handsome man there." She cringed inwardly. That had sounded childish. But Dominic didn't own her and he'd better stop acting as if he did.

His nostrils flared and frustration thinned his lips. "You cannot evade me or the passion between us, Madeline."

"Watch me." Intent on a quick escape, she turned and reached for the doorknob.

In a flash his palm splayed on the door above her head, holding it shut. He leaned closer until the warmth of his chest against her back sandwiched her against the wooden panel. His breath stirred her hair seconds before his lips brushed her nape. Her lungs stalled and a shudder racked her. His morning beard rasped the juncture of her neck and shoulder, and then he traced a spine-tingling line down her backbone with one finger. Her senses rioted.

How can you still want him?

"You can't forget that night any more than I can," he whispered against her jaw.

The words scraped over her raw nerves and she swallowed hard. Almost every part of her being urged her to turn, wrap her arms around him, drag him to that rumpled bed and revel in the passion he offered. All she'd have to do is turn her head and their lips would touch.

The man's kisses could cause a nuclear meltdown.

But a lone brain cell reminded her of the hell she'd already lived through, of being made to look foolish and losing the respect of her coworkers and the uphill battle to regain it.

She squared her shoulders and tightened her fingers on the cool knob. "I might not have forgotten, but neither am I willing to become a topic of gossip again."

She yanked on the door. This time he let her go. "Be ready to leave for the shooting range as soon as your meeting ends."

She stopped halfway across the sitting room and pivoted to face him. "And if I'm not?"

"Have I ever mentioned Albert and I are well acquainted?"

Albert. Prince of Monaco. And he and Dominic were apparently on a first-name basis.

She was sunk.

"Hey, this isn't the way to the hotel," Madeline protested later Tuesday morning.

On the seat beside her in the hired car driven by Ian, Dominic angled to face her. His thigh touched hers. Touching meant sparks and sparks meant instant heat which she couldn't seem to control no matter how hard she tried. She inched away.

"You wished to purchase a gift for your mother."

Darn him for remembering that. "You could have asked if I wanted to go shopping."

He captured a dark curl, wound it around his index finger and tugged gently. She felt the pull deep inside. "You would have refused."

He had her there. But she'd just spent an hour matching him shot-for-shot at the shooting range and having more fun with their competition than she should have in the she'd-decided-to-hate-him circumstances. The man had a competitive streak that rivaled her own and a willpower-melting grin whenever he bested her. She needed a break from his magnetism.

"I also told you I'm having dinner with Candace at Maxim's tonight. So whatever you have planned had better be short and sweet."

"That's why we're taking a helicopter to Biot instead of driving."

A helicopter. She swallowed.

"I'm not crazy about helicopters." Not since a turbulent toss-her-cookies ride on a Life Flight chopper. Sure, she'd taken the helicopter taxi to Monaco from the Nice airport, but she'd been overexcited about being on foreign soil for the first time in her life and she'd had Dramamine in her system.

"I will be more than happy to distract you during the flight." His gaze dropped to her lips and her abdominal muscles contracted. She'd bet he would. She could guess how. But she wasn't kissing him again. Ever. Because his kisses sent her self-control AWOL.

"Would saying no make any difference?"

A smile teased his lips. "No. We'll land in time for lunch and then tour and shop. I'll have you back before dinner."

She sighed. It would serve him right if she barfed all over him. "Okay, you win."

"Always."

He really should try to rein in that cocky attitude. But darned if that smug smile didn't look good on him.

"What's so special about Biot?" she asked to distract herself as she reclaimed her hair. Each time he twined a curl around his finger she remembered the other things he liked to wrap it around and that wasn't good for her willpower.

"It's a small French village known for its pottery and hand-blown glass. Their earthenware production dates back to the Phoenicians, but since the 1960s Biot's bubble glass has gained international acclaim. My mother collects it. I thought yours might like it."

His mother. She didn't want to think about someone somewhere loving him. And she didn't want him to be thoughtful. He was a lot easier to dislike when he was arrogant, dictatorial and throwing his royal weight around. "You can force me to go with you, but you can't make me enjoy it."

"Have I mentioned how much I delight in your challenges?"

Five hours later Madeline stood in the shadows beneath a pointed archway of Biot's Place des Arcades and admitted she'd have to eat her words. Pleasantly tired and carrying a bag containing several carefully wrapped brightly colored pieces of bubble glass, she leaned against a sun-warmed stone wall and reluctantly looked up at Dominic.

He'd been an intelligent and amusing companion during this unwanted outing, and he'd taken her not to tourist traps, but to authentic out-of-the-way shops and a restaurant frequented by locals. His language and bargaining skills had been invaluable, and he wasn't exactly hard on the eyes. What more could a woman ask for in a date? If it hadn't been for his fib and his princeliness she could almost wish this idyllic period didn't have to end so soon.

"At the risk of inflating your already gargantuan ego, I have to confess, I enjoyed today. Lunch, the galleries, the museum…all of it."

"I'm glad." Dominic braced his shoulder on the wall beside her. He stood too close, but she couldn't seem to muster the energy to widen the gap between them.

He won points for not gloating.

They hadn't been bothered by paparazzi, and she'd only spotted Ian and Makos skulking in the background a few times. She hadn't even become ill on the helicopter flight because Dominic had applied acupressure to the inside of her wrist. A secret from the Montagnarde natives, he'd told her. Well, she'd studied acupressure, too, but she must have missed that chapter. Or maybe Dominic's touch had worked magic.

He slowly reached up and removed his sunglasses and then hers. Their gazes locked and held. The smile in his eyes faded and his pupils dilated with desire. Her pulse quickened and her mouth dried. After warning her to be on the lookout for paparazzi, surely he wouldn't—

His mouth covered hers. Tenderly. Briefly. Before she could react he swooped in again, cradling her jaw in his palm and settling in for a deeper taste. His tongue parted her lips and tangled with hers.

Need coiled tightly inside her, sending heat spiraling from her core to her limbs. She shouldn't be kissing him, shouldn't be savoring the hint of coffee on his tongue or the scent of his cologne. She shouldn't be curling her fingers into the rigid muscles of his waist or leaning into the warmth of his chest.

You definitely shouldn't be considering dragging him to the nearest inn.

Where was her remarkable willpower, her vow to keep their lips forever separate? Turning her head aside, she broke the kiss and gasped for air. She craved the man more than she did carbohydrates when PMSing. And that was saying something.

She gathered her tattered resistance and backed away. "We should go. I have to get ready for tonight."

And she had to brace herself for their next encounter, because she couldn't afford to let Dominic Rossi slip beneath her guard again.

Even if she could overlook his fib, a prince and a commoner had no future.

Not that she wanted one.

Seven

Time was running out.

Dominic snapped his cell phone closed Saturday night, shoved it in his tux pocket and inhaled deeply, but the constriction of his chest tightened instead of loosening.

"News?" Ian asked from beside him on the limo seat.

"The list of bridal candidates has been narrowed to three." Which meant Dominic's days of passion and freedom were numbered. He had to get Madeline back into his bed.

"This is not unexpected, Dominic."

That didn't mean he had to like it. "No."

"Perhaps your outings with Miss Spencer have spurred the council to make a decision."

"We have been discreet." As much as he hated sneaking in and out of back doors and service entrances, he'd willingly done so to spend time with Madeline. But this week she'd avoided all but the most casual of touches.

"The council won't give you the women's names?" Ian asked.

"No. They don't want me to interfere with the selection process." The council would make the decision, negotiate the diplomatic agreements, and then he would meet the woman and propose for formality's sake. The way it had been done for three centuries.

The car stopped in front of the Monaco Sporting Club. Ian climbed out first. Dominic remained seated. He didn't want to waste an evening rehashing the same shallow conversations or battling the predatory females whom he could not afford to offend. He would prefer to be alone in his suite—in his bed—with Madeline. But Madeline would be here, and her vow to dance with every male present chafed like an over-starched shirt. Absurd since once his bride-to-be was chosen he would have no claim on Madeline. He would tell her goodbye and immediately fly off to fulfill his duty to his country and his promise to his father to continue the tradition and the monarchy of Montagnarde.

The weight of his obligations had never weighed as heavily on his shoulders as it did now.

Ian's face appeared in the open door. "Your Highness?"

Dominic climbed from the car and entered the gala. The upper echelons of European society were out in full force at the charity ball. These were the very people he needed to court and attract to Montagnarde. At the moment he couldn't care less. He scanned the crowd, searching for Madeline, but didn't see her. An acquaintance greeted him. Dominic forced a smile and commenced his job as businessman and ambassador for his country.

But as he worked the room, politely fending off unwanted advances, some subtle, some not, he wondered if his future bride was among the women in attendance tonight, for this was very likely the pool from which she would be chosen. He found the prospect unappealing since none of the women attending the ball attracted him in the least.

Three-quarters of an hour later movement at the entrance drew his attention. Madeline and her suitemates had arrived. Urgency made his heart pump harder.

Madeline had pulled her dark hair up, leaving her shoulders bare. Her drop-dead sexy black dress molded itself to the curves of her exquisite figure. When she stepped forward a slit opened almost to the curls concealing her sex to reveal one sleek, tanned leg. She turned as a dark-haired man claimed the woman beside her, and Dominic stifled a groan. Other than straps encircling her shoulders in a figure eight, the back of her dress left the smooth line of her spine completely bare to just above the crease of her bottom.

Beautiful, seductive Madeline. He had to have her. Tonight.

"Prince Dominic," a high-pitched voice said nearby.

He blinked and looked back at the woman whose red talons gripped the sleeve of his tuxedo jacket. He couldn't recall her name. "Yes?"

"I asked if you'd like to see me home tonight." She followed the words with an inviting pout and a flutter of false eyelashes which did nothing for him.

"I am honored, mademoiselle, but I must decline. I have a previous engagement. Excuse me." He bowed and made his way toward Madeline only to be delayed again and again. His frustration grew. He had to reach Madeline before another man claimed her.

She was his.

For now. And he would have his fill of her before his desolate future consumed him.

* * *

How hard could it be to *not* kiss a guy? Madeline silently fumed as she stood near the entrance of the exclusive La Salle Des Étoiles.

She "not kissed" guys every day. Dozens of them. Coworkers, patients, paramedics, her letter carrier, for Pete's sake. So what was the big deal about not kissing one more? But that was her goal.

She'd succeeded Monday night, thanks to dinner with Dominic being interrupted by an urgent call from the palace which he'd had to take.

She'd blown it Tuesday in Biot, but she'd managed to keep her lips from straying on Wednesday when he'd surprised her with a behind-the-scenes tour of the Prince's Palace, including rooms not open to the general public. She'd stuck to her guns again on Thursday because Candace and Amelia—bless 'em—had run interference by accompanying her on the visit Dominic had arranged to Princess Grace Hospital. Afterward, her suitemates had dragged her out for a night at the theater sans Dominic.

But resisting him hadn't been easy. Each day his hungry gaze had gobbled her up bite by bite, leaving her more than a little ravenous and close to bingeing on the taste, scent and feel of him.

Thank God for Friday when she'd had the good fortune to avoid Dominic completely. She hadn't been hiding *exactly*. She'd kept herself busy away from the hotel by shopping and doing wedding minutiae with her suitemates from breakfast until bedtime.

She'd been so happy to evade temptation that she hadn't even minded the reminders of her own aborted engagement. In fact, she'd barely thought of Mike, the mistake. But that was because another man had planted his flag in her subconscious and claimed her thoughts. Damn Dominic Rossi for that.

Her gaze collided with Dominic's across the haute couture and jewel-encrusted crowd of Le Bal de L'Eté and her breath caught. Speak of the devil. Her luck had apparently run out.

With his regal bearing, aristocratic bone structure and wealth of confidence, no one looking at him now would ever doubt his royal lineage. The man commanded attention without even trying, and he turned wearing a tux into an art form.

A blonde so thin the wind could blow her away stood beside him with a rapt expression on her immobile Botox-filled face. He flashed a smile at her, said a few words then broke free and headed in Madeline's direction only to be side-lined by a squinty redhead and then a big-toothed brunette whose invitation to dance horizontally as well as vertically was obvious from clear across the room.

Madeline gritted her teeth and turned her back on the prince and his fawning females. She was not jealous. Nope. Not her. He could do the mattress merengue with every other woman in the room for all she cared.

"See anybody you recognize?" she asked wide-eyed Amelia. If there was a celebrity or royal in attendance, Amelia would be able to name him or her.

"Are you kidding? This place is a who's who smorgasbord. And I'm sorry to say, that includes Toby Haynes. I cannot believe Vincent sent that race car Casanova to babysit us."

"Vincent meant well, and Toby is his best man." Vincent had been working overseas, but moments ago he'd surprised Candace by arriving at the ball unexpectedly. He'd quickly swept his bride-to-be onto the dance floor where the two gazed at each other with so much love in their eyes it made Madeline uneasy. She'd once believed herself that much in love, and how she'd survived the aftermath was still a mystery. She could guarantee she'd never let herself care like that again.

"He should know we're old enough to stay out of trouble."

Amelia's comment made Madeline shift guiltily in her stiletto heels. The edges of her heavy black sequined dress abraded her skin. She hadn't managed to stay out of trouble, but she'd neglected to fill her suitemates in on the embarrassing details. Amelia knew nothing more than what Dominic had told her—that Madeline had threatened him. Her friend didn't know the threat involved an actual knife against his princely throat or firing a gun over his royal head.

Madeline followed Amelia's disgusted gaze toward the NASCAR driver who'd been a thorn in her friend's side since their first day in Monaco. Thanks to Candace's misguided matchmaking attempts, Madeline had dated Toby a couple of times back in Charlotte. She'd quickly labeled him a player and lost interest. The attraction—or lack thereof—was mutual.

Toby was a nice enough guy and definitely good-looking, but as far as she could tell he was serious about racing and little else. Amelia, on the other hand, had taken an intense dislike to Toby during Vincent's hospital stay last year when Toby had been a frequent visitor to the burn unit. No amount of prying—subtle or otherwise—on Madeline's part had uncovered the reason for the tension between those two.

"Do you see those women drooling over him?" Amelia grumbled. Amelia was the most easygoing woman Madeline had ever met, and seeing her friend bristle and hiss like an angry cat was totally out of character. There had to be a reason.

The back of Madeline's neck prickled, and it had nothing to do with Toby spotting them and extracting himself from the women clustered around him to head in their direction. "What is it with these chicks and their sycophantic admiration? Do they have no pride? And don't even get me started on how these guys are sucking up the adulation as if it's their due."

"Good evening, Amelia, Madeline." Dominic's baritone behind her confirmed the reason for her uneasiness. Her bones turned soupy. She cursed her wilting willpower. So much for her plan to avoid the man who had the power to kiss her right out of her clothes.

"Dominic, Amelia would like to dance," she said as she turned. She tried to keep her gaze on his blue eyes, but she couldn't help soaking up the breadth of his shoulders.

"Madeline!" Amelia protested.

"It's either Dominic or Toby. Take your pick." Madeline indicated the approaching driver with a tilt of her head.

Amelia's eyes widened with panic. She looked beseechingly at Dominic and even curtsied. "I would love to dance, Your Highness."

With a polite smile Dominic inclined his head and offered Amelia his arm. "Dominic, please. I would be delighted, Amelia."

But his eyes promised Madeline retribution as he led her friend away.

Ha! He couldn't get even if he couldn't catch her. She'd make a point of dancing in the arms of other men all night— even if she had to ask them herself. She'd chosen a dress which guaranteed their answers would always be yes.

Toby reached Madeline's side moments later. His appreciative gaze zipped from her upswept hair down her black form-fitting dress to her silver sandals before he met her gaze. "If your goal is to bring these European guys to their knees, I'll bet my new engine you'll succeed. You look good enough to make me reconsider making a run for you myself, Madeline."

A girl—this one anyway—liked to have her ego stroked even

if she suspected the compliment generated from habit rather than genuine interest. "Thanks, Toby. You look sharp, too."

Toby Haynes might be blond-haired and blue-eyed and of a similar height and athletic build to Dominic, but that's where the likeness ended. Even though both men wore what were probably custom-tailored tuxes, Toby had rough edges aplenty whereas Dominic was smooth, polished perfection. But Toby didn't trip her hormonal switches. Dominic, regrettably, did.

"Who's the stiff?"

She didn't pretend not to understand Toby's question. How could she, since his eyes practically shot fire toward the man in question? "Prince Dominic Rossi of Montagnarde."

"Montag—what? Never heard of the place. Must not have a race track."

Nice to know she wasn't the only geographically challenged one present. "Montagnarde. It's a country somewhere between Hawaii and New Zealand."

"Wanna dance?"

Not the smoothest invitation she'd ever had, but it beat standing near the entrance like a wallflower. "Sure. Why not?"

Toby led her onto the floor and swept her into the flow of other dancers with skill she wouldn't have expected from a car jockey. "You're pretty light on your feet."

He grimaced. "Comes with the territory. For the most part NASCAR drivers only drive two days a week. Qualifying and race day. The rest of the time we're on the road schmoozing for the sponsors. Reynard Hotels loves swanky parties like this."

And Vincent Reynard's hotel chain sponsored Toby's racing team. "You don't?"

"Depends on the reason I'm there." He drew alongside Amelia and Dominic. "Hey, buddy, switch?"

Madeline's insides snarled. She should have known a competitive guy like Toby would have an agenda. But it was too late to escape the man she'd hoped to avoid.

Dominic stopped and released Amelia. "Certainly. Thank you for the dance, Amelia."

He bowed slightly.

Darn, she liked that stupid little bow.

Toby whisked her none-too-happy friend away.

Madeline stood in the middle of the floor and met Dominic's gaze while the other guests drifted past them. "I don't want to dance with you."

"The floor is the best place for us unless you are ready to leave." Dominic's hand captured hers. The only way to escape his unbreakable grip was to cause a scene—not part of the plan if she wanted to avoid more publicity.

"Are you kidding me? I just got here."

He pulled her into the circle of his arms and spread his palm on her naked back just above her buttocks. Her pulse tripped. She hoped her feet wouldn't embarrass her by doing likewise.

She searched for a distraction from the heat of his hand on her skin and tried to ignore the slide of his thighs against hers as he guided her across the floor. "Where's the towering twosome? Did you check your bodyguards at the door?"

"Ian and Makos remained outside as did Fernand."

"Who is Fernand?"

"Your protection."

She stumbled then and fell into his broad chest. His arm banded around her waist, welding her to the hot, hard length of his torso and keeping her there. He continued dancing without missing an orchestral beat. "My what?"

"You have had security since Wednesday."

"You've had someone following me?" The erotic rasp of

his tuxedo jacket sleeve against her back tightened her throat, making her words come out in a husky whisper.

"I told you I would."

"Yes, but…" She rewound the reel of events in her head. Had she done anything she wouldn't want reported back to Dominic? Because she'd bet his spy guy was doing exactly that. "I haven't seen him."

"You weren't supposed to." His smooth-shaven chin brushed her temple as he executed a series of quick turns that required her to cling to him or fall on her face. Ballroom dancing had never been her thing, but she had to admit following his lead was easier than expected. Good thing, since sprawling on the floor given her attire, or lack thereof, would be humiliating.

"Why do I need a shadow?"

"There are those who might believe that because you're my lover—"

Stumble. "I'm not anymore."

"—you might be a valuable negotiating piece," he continued as if she hadn't interrupted.

Fear crept up her spine like a big, hairy spider. She leaned back to look into his eyes. Unfortunately, that pressed their hips together. "I'm in danger because I slept with you?"

"Probably not. As you pointed out, Montagnarde is off the radar for most, but I prefer to be proactive rather than reactive. And while you are mine I will protect you."

The possessive words made her skin tingle. And then she remembered to object. "I. Am. Not. Yours."

The hand on her back lifted, giving her a momentary reprieve and an opportunity to fill her wheezy lungs, but then Dominic traced the edge of her dress from her shoulder to the base of her spine. The tips of his fingers slid just beneath the fabric and his short nails raked lightly across the top of her cheeks. She shivered, cursed her traitorous hormones and sent out a mental SOS to her willpower. Wherever it might be.

"You look lovely tonight. Very sexy. Come back to my suite with me, Madeline," his deep voice rumbled in her ear.

Stumble. He caught her even closer—something she would not have believed physically possible five seconds ago. Even through the heavy chain mail weight of her dress she could feel his thickening arousal against her belly. Flames of desire flickered through her and her resistance softened like warm candle wax. She was so close to melting it wasn't even funny.

But the man had broken rule number one. He'd lied to her.

And still…she wanted him. Shamelessly.

Girl, you are absolutely pitiful.

But she couldn't help remembering how good it had been between them, how amazingly wonderful he'd made her feel or how he listened to every word as if she were going to utter the secret to world peace in her next sentence.

You are in serious trouble.

"Get me off this floor," she said through clenched teeth.

"Or else what?" A smile played on his lips as he pulled her into another series of complicated make-her-cling-to-him steps. "You'll pull a weapon? Because I don't see where you could possibly conceal one beneath that dress. It caresses your curves the way I want to."

Stumble. Help. She could not argue and concentrate on fancy footwork at the same time. She planted her feet, shoved his rock-hard chest and yanked free of his hold. "Do you really want to test me here and now, Dominic?"

Ignoring the curious stares of those around her, he held her gaze as if considering calling her bluff, but then inclined his head and led her toward the edge of the floor. They had barely stepped out of the crowd when a woman wearing a take-me-I'm-yours smile appeared in front of him.

"*Bonsoir,* Your Highness. Remember me?"

Dominic made introductions, but Madeline only half listened to the simpering blonde's chatter about past parties and people Madeline knew nothing about. She scanned the well-heeled guests looking for her suitemates and a possible rescue. She spotted Stacy and Franco and Vincent and Candace, but both couples were totally wrapped up in each other. There was no sign of Amelia and/or Toby.

"…come by my apartment later?" the blonde said.

Huh? Madeline blinked in disbelief and tuned back into the conversation. Had that she-cat just propositioned Dominic despite his hand planted firmly on Madeline's waist?

Hello! What am I? Invisible?

"Excuse us, Dominic was about to get me a glass of champagne." She grabbed his arm and urged him toward the bar and then jerked to a stop. *Argh. Is your brain on hiatus?* She'd wanted to escape him, and she'd just wasted a perfect opportunity. She should have let the she-cat have him.

So why didn't you?

She had a feeling she wouldn't like the answer.

"Thank you," he said.

Before she could tell him to take his gratitude and shove it, the catty incident replayed itself again and again and again. Different woman. Same pounce. Every three yards. Jeez, fighting off the felines was exhausting. Forget champagne. At the rate they were going she'd need an entire bottle of gin to wash down the fur balls by the time they reached the bar.

Patience deserted her and she yearned to scratch a few

overly made-up eyes out. While Dominic clearly did not enjoy or encourage the attention, he remained unfailingly polite each time. Most men would have been ecstatic to hear so many come-ons in a single evening, but not him. Why was that? Was his little black book already full? Or did he consider Madeline a sure thing?

She found the encounters pretty darn insulting since it meant these pedigreed felines didn't consider her competition, and she'd had enough.

"Excuse me. I guess you missed the fact that he's with me," she interrupted a woman about to spill from her rhinestone-studded collar—um, dress.

"Dominic, *dahling*," Madeline purred in a throaty voice similar to the ones his accosters had used, "I could use that double martini you promised me right about now."

Laughter lurked in his eyes as they said their goodbyes, and then Madeline nudged him not toward the bar but toward a quiet corner. "Is there some kind of contest to see who carries home the richest prize at the end of the evening?"

The first genuine smile she'd seen in an hour curved his lips. "You have discovered the secret."

"Is that why you wanted to stay on the dance floor? To avoid the stalking women?"

"An apt description."

"Why don't you just tell them to get lost?"

He glanced toward the gathering and then back at her. "I can't."

"Some princely code or something?" But she didn't wait for his answer. "If it's always like this, then why do you come to these things?"

"Usually I come because I want to entice their business to Montagnarde." His blue gaze held hers as he lifted her hand to his lips. "Tonight I came because I wanted to hold you in my arms."

Her knees weakened and the bottom dropped out of her stomach. The room seemed to fade until all that remained was him and the desire burning in his eyes. For her. In this room full of beautiful, elegant, worldly, predatory women, he wanted her.

"Good answer," she wheezed.

And why are you resisting?

She mentally smacked a palm against her forehead. She'd wanted a man to help her heal her fractured ego and rebuild her confidence. Dominic did that. He made her feel feminine and desirable. He gave her multiple-o's.

He'd reminded her more times than she could count that here and now was all they'd have. But that was okay. More than okay. A brief vacation fling was exactly what she wanted.

It wasn't as if she'd let herself fall in love or imagine marrying him. Just as well since Dominic, like Prince Charles, probably had to marry a virgin. And she wasn't one. Not even close.

Between tonight, the incident with the paparazzi and having to sneak in and out back doors all week she could even understand Dominic's motivation for concealing his identity. But he was selling himself short if he truly believed these women wanted him only for his title and fortune. Dominic Rossi, Prince of Montagnarde, was a gorgeous piece of work, and every time she looked at him she recalled the perfection of his naked body and the way he made her body sing.

She'd bet the drooling females wanted a chance to do the same. Knowing she knew something the other more sophisticated women didn't made her feel just a teensy bit superior.

And you're wasting time here when you could be getting your hands on all that perfection.

Her pulse quickened and her mouth dried. She tightened her fingers around his. "Get me out of here, Prince, and you can hold me in your arms without a ten-pound dress between us."

The flash of heat in his eyes nearly consumed her on the spot. "As you wish."

Eight

Apparently the wealthy didn't wait for cabs or even valet service.

Within seconds of her shameless declaration Dominic had hustled her out of the gala and into a waiting limo which he'd summoned with one touch on his cell phone. She chose the bench seat facing the limo's rear window.

Dominic joined her instead of sitting across from her. From shoulder to knee the hot length of his body pressed her side as hot and hard as an iron. The door closed, sealing them in darkness and near silence, and then the car pulled away from the club.

She risked a glance at him and found his jaw muscles knotted and his gaze burning into hers. Hunger stiffened every line of his body, inspiring a similar tension in hers.

She'd never wanted anyone this badly. Digging her fingers into her tiny beaded purse and hoping to slow her racing pulse, she focused on the passing lights of Monte Carlo outside the window as the driver carried them toward the hotel. No luck.

She squirmed impatiently, but the only thing her wiggling accomplished was to make the slit in her dress part, revealing her leg from ankle to hip. Before she could adjust the gaping skirt she heard Dominic's sharply indrawn breath, and then his hand covered her knee. Ever so slowly his warm palm glided upward, his fingertips slipping beneath the edge of the heavy, sequined fabric. Her insides clenched. She'd very likely leave a puddle of desire on the seat if she didn't stop him.

She slapped a hand over his and leaned toward him to whisper in his ear. "What are you doing? Ian and the driver are right behind us."

"The privacy screen is closed and the speaker turned off. They can see and hear nothing." His fingers inched higher and his masculine scent filled her lungs with each shaky breath. "You wish me to stop?"

"Yes. No. Yes. I…don't know." She struggled to bring order to her scrambled thoughts. "Do you, um…do this often?"

A short nail scraped back and forth along the top of her thigh, each pass drawing closer to the spot aching for his touch. "I have never made love in a limo."

"Me, neither." But she was tempted. Seriously tempted. She forced her heavy lids to remain open. "We're almost at the hotel."

"Then I'd better hurry." His hand rose another inch and he found her wetness with the tip of his finger. Their groans mingled. "You're not wearing panties."

"Dress. Too. Tight," she whispered brokenly as he circled her center bringing her closer and closer to the brink. How did he do that so quickly? Arousal made it difficult to think and tension made her tremble. She covered his hand with hers, intent on stopping his audacious behavior…in a minute. "Dominic—"

"Shh. Come for me, Madeline," he whispered hoarsely.

"H-here?" Their hotel was less than a block away and privacy screen or not, Ian and the driver were only inches away.

"Now. I want you so wet that I can be inside you the moment we reach the suite."

His throaty words and talented fingers sent her flying. Her back bowed and her tush lifted off the seat as wave after wave washed over her. She bit hard on her bottom lip and fought to remain silent as her pleasure went on and on and on. When it finally ended she leaned heavily against his side.

His breathing sounded as harsh as hers in the insulated passenger compartment and she hadn't even touched him. To anyone who happened to glance in the rearview mirror or through the tinted windows, they probably looked like any other couple riding home from a ritzy party. No one would guess she'd just crash-landed from a trip to the stars.

"Your turn." She spread her palm on his thigh, but he stopped her wandering hand by lacing his fingers through hers and carrying her hand to his lips.

"Hold that thought." The limo stopped outside Hôtel Reynard's back entrance. Her body seemed heavy, melded to the upholstery. Dominic released her hand and straightened the folds of her dress. He squeezed her thigh and then released her. "Ready?"

"Are you kidding me? I don't think I can walk."

His low chuckle aroused her all over again. His breath teased her bare shoulder a second before his teeth lightly grazed her skin. In her hypersensitive state the brief contact sent a bolt of lightning straight to her womb. "If I carry you inside we'll definitely draw unwanted attention. Shall I ask the driver to circle the block?"

She sucked air into her deprived lungs and grappled for sanity. "No. I can't wait that long to have you inside me."

Dominic's breath whistled through clenched teeth. "Nor I."

Dominic had had sex before. Hot, sweaty, animalistic sex.

He'd even had sex with Madeline. But he'd never been as close to saying to hell with propriety and taking a woman regardless of their location. The limo. The elevator. The carpeted hallway outside his suite. He shook with need, and he couldn't remember the last time that had happened. Only Ian's scowling presence prevented him from taking action. Here. Now.

Madeline stood beside him in the hotel hallway without touching him. But her scent filled his lungs with every breath. Flowers. Lemon. *Sex.* He waited impatiently for Makos to do a security sweep of the suite. The moment the man gave the all's clear signal Dominic grabbed Madeline's hand and dragged her over the threshold, through the sitting room and into his bedroom. He shut the door in his bodyguards' faces, backed Madeline against the panel and slammed his mouth over hers.

She opened for him instantly, suckling his tongue and curling her fingers into his shoulders. She shoved at his tuxedo jacket and then tore at his tie and the buttons of his shirt without breaking the kiss. The garments landed on the floor behind him. With their lips still fused he raked his hands over the cool sequins of her dress searching feverishly but fruitlessly for the zipper. He gave up and tried to lift her skirt, but the fitted fabric clung stubbornly to her hips. He considered ripping it—this dress another man had bought—from her.

He wanted skin. Her skin. Against his. Now.

Madeline's nails scraped over him, drawing a line from his

Adam's apple to his navel, and then she palmed his erection through the fabric of his pants. Arousal detonated inside him. He released her mouth long enough to gasp, swear and demand, "Zipper."

"Here." She carried his hand across her breasts to her underarm. His fingers fumbled, found the tab, and tugged it to her hip. At a loss as to how to remove the seductive dress, he stepped back.

"Over my head."

He fisted the fabric, uncaring if he damaged it. He'd buy her another. A dozen. The weight of the garment surprised him. The moment the hem cleared her head he twisted and tossed it on a nearby chair. And then he turned back to Madeline and his heart slammed into his ribs like an airplane hitting a mountainside. He staggered back a step, two. His jaw went slack.

Naked, save a pair of silver high heels sharp enough to be classified as lethal weapons, she lifted her arms to pull pins from her hair. His lungs seized. He'd never seen a more seductive sight than Madeline, with her back arched and her breasts offered like a banquet. She stood with her long, lean legs slightly parted. Moisture glistened in the dark curls between her legs—moisture he'd created.

And he was about to lose it like a teenage boy.

He snapped his jaw closed and swallowed once, twice. But it did nothing to ease the constriction in his throat or the tightness in his chest. Need, painful in its intensity, clawed through him. One by one, long, dark ringlets fell over her shoulders as she released her hair, concealing her tightened nipples from his view. A criminal offense.

He captured a silky coil and painted a pattern over her puckered flesh and then brushed her hair aside to cup and caress her warm, satiny skin. Her breasts filled his hands, the nipples prodding his palms. He rolled the tips between his fingers until she whimpered and leaned against the door.

"Please, Dominic, don't make me wait." She reached for the waistband of his trousers.

He kissed her again, relishing the sharp bite of desire and the hunger fisting in his gut beneath her tormenting fingers. The moment she shoved his pants over his hips and curled her fingers around him he lifted her leg to his waist with one hand, cupped her bottom with the other and drove into her welcoming wetness. Her body clenched around him and her cries of pleasure filled his ears. He thrust again and again and again. More. Deeper. Harder. Faster. The heel of her shoe stabbed his buttocks. That little jab had to be the most erotic thing he'd ever felt.

Pressure built. He fought to hold on until her nails bit into his shoulders and she tore her mouth away from his to gasp his name. She shuddered in his arms and her internal muscles contracted. He could no more stop his own release than he could dam a volcano. His passion erupted, pulsing through him in mind-melting bursts. He muffled his groans against her warm, fragrant throat, and then sapped and sated, he fell against her.

When he recovered an ounce of strength, he braced his forearms on the door beside her head and lifted his sweat-dampened body scant inches from her torso. The arms she'd looped around his neck kept him close—not that he intended going anywhere. He stared into her beautiful face. A smile curved her moist, swollen lips, and her lashes cast dark crescents on her flushed cheeks. He absorbed the image, imprinting it on his brain to drag out during the long barren years ahead.

Two more weeks won't be enough.

It must be.

Madeline deserved more than to be a prince's paramour. She deserved a man who would look past her prickly exterior to the soft heart she fought so hard to protect. She'd once believed in love, and the right man would make her believe again. But that man wasn't him, for no matter how empty his marriage might be he would abide by his vows and his duty to his country.

Chilling arrows of regret pierced him. Madeline deserved to be happy. Even if he couldn't be.

"Wow." Her lids fluttered open and her satisfied gaze met his. And then noting his expression, she stiffened and pleasure drained from her face. She pushed against his chest and uncoiled her leg from his hip. "What's wrong?"

He slipped from her body and then it hit him. "We didn't use protection."

His pulse kicked erratically. With hope? Of course not. His fate was sealed and he'd accepted it.

But what if he, like Albert of Monaco, fathered a child out of wedlock? Would paternity and a potential heir excuse him from an arranged marriage? No. Tradition and the council demanded a bride of royal lineage. A pedigreed princess.

But a child would tie him to Madeline and give him an excuse to see her in the future even if he could not continue the affair.

She averted her face and wrapped her arms around her waist. "I'm on the Pill. So we're in the clear unless you lied about your health."

Why didn't that revelation fill him with relief? And why did the reminder of his dishonesty still sting? He'd had good reason for his deception, hadn't he?

No. If he'd learned anything from this it was that there was never a good reason for deceit. He would have to tell Madeline about his impending marriage. She deserved to know why he must let her go—this woman who'd brightened his days. But not now. When he said goodbye would be soon enough.

"I'm clean." He'd been poked and prodded, examined from top to bottom, inside and out, by the royal physicians. His health records would be provided for perusal to the family of the woman the council chose as his bride.

They could examine his vital statistics as they would a prize stallion. And like a stud for hire, he'd have no say over his mate. His obligation to provide heirs to the throne was a burden. Or was it a curse?

Madeline Spencer, jet-setter. Who would have believed it?

Madeline stared at the man standing beside her in the noonday sun in the tiny seaside town of Ventimiglia, Italy. She tried not to drool as sexy Italian words rolled off his tongue. Her tour guide extraordinaire and lover *magnifique*. Dominic.

He switched languages as easily as blinking whereas she'd struggled to pick up the necessary French phrases he'd taught her. He was probably discussing something as mundane as the weather with the merchant, but whatever he said made her want to jump him despite having left his bed just hours earlier.

She hated creeping from his suite every morning at sunup to sneak back to her room, but that was a small price to pay to keep their affair private and her name out of the tabloids. Thus far it had worked. Beyond those first couple of pictures there hadn't been more.

Curling her fingers against the urge to trace the veins on the thickly muscled arm closest to her, she focused her attention on the gold jewelry for sale. She'd already bought necklaces for her mother and Amelia and earrings for Candace and

Stacy from another vendor. Dominic, bless him, had handled the haggling and she'd ended up paying far less than she would have in the States.

An intricately engraved wide cuff bracelet caught her eye. She picked it up, saw the price and quickly put it down.

"You like it?" he asked.

"It's beautiful, but even if you talked him down to a fraction of what he's asking it would still be too expensive."

"I'll buy it for you."

She caught his hand as he reached for his wallet and stared at her floppy-hat-wearing reflection in his dark lenses. "It's bad enough that you won't let me split expenses for our outings. I'm not letting you spend more."

His jaw set in the stubborn line she'd come to recognize whenever she tried to insist on paying her way. She hadn't won a single one of those arguments, and she knew better than to expect to win this one, so she changed the subject. "What were you and the vendor discussing?"

His lips compressed, letting her know he hadn't missed her attempt at distraction. He said a few more words to the merchant and then placed his palm against Madeline's spine and guided her away from the table. He glanced over his shoulder—checking to see if Ian and Fernand followed, she suspected. It would be easy to lose them in the market-day crowd—even with her brightly colored hat, which had been chosen specifically to make her easy to track.

"I asked about market conditions. What improvements could be made and which features were absolute requirements. Montagnarde has many craftsmen. A marketplace like this would be a desirable asset to my tourism plans."

"But first you have to get the rich to visit Montagnarde and hemorrhage money." Normal people plotted to buy or pay off their homes. Princes, apparently, dreamed on a bigger scale. One night as they'd lain in the dark after making love, Dominic had told her about his development plan and his determination to move forward despite the elder council's refusal to support him.

"What did your American movie say? 'If you build it they will come?' It's the trickle-down theory. Each tourist generates income for the working class by creating multiple service jobs. Attract the big spenders and everyone will benefit. My investors and I are already constructing luxury hotels on two of the three islands. I would be interested in speaking with Derek Reynard about his family's chain constructing a third."

"I can probably arrange a meeting with Mr. Reynard, but Vincent, his son, is the director of new business development. And since I'm one of Vincent's wedding party, I know I can hook you up with him."

"I accept your offer and promise to reward you handsomely." His wicked grin sent a heat wave tumbling through her.

Dominic would make a great king one day. It made no sense for her to be proud of him and his forward-thinking agenda to bring tourists and jobs to his country. What he did once he left Monaco *and her* behind was none of her business. But there was no denying the pride swelling in her chest.

A gentle sea breeze caressed her skin as they walked hand in hand along the narrow street. She scanned the postcard view of red-roofed homes clinging to the hillside like pastel-colored building blocks. Ventimiglia was a combination of ancient history and New World charm, and she would have missed it without Dominic.

She'd never been happier than she had in the week since the ball. She'd spent the greater part of each day with Dominic. He'd taught her to windsurf and shown her bits of France: the carnival atmosphere of the summer jazz festival in Juan Les Pins; Grasse, the perfume capital of the world; and the blooming lavender fields and craft galleries in Moustiers Ste. Marie. Today when she'd only had a few hours to spare between brides-maid's duties he'd surprised her with this jaunt to the Friday open-air market only twenty minutes from Monaco.

He thought nothing of day trips via helicopter or private jet, claiming the impromptu excursions to out-of-the-way places kept the paparazzi off their tails. She didn't want to tell him that she no longer needed to escape the wedding hoopla. Funny how the preparations didn't hurt anymore.

The only bacteria growing in the petri dish of Madeline's life was not knowing when Dominic would have to return to Montagnarde and when her time with him would end. He'd promised to show her Venice and Paris in the coming week—if he was still here. And that "if" kept her on a knife edge. Apparently, there was something pending in his country which required a nightly call from home—a call that left him increasingly tight-lipped and broodingly silent.

Madeline had learned a few techniques guaranteed to erase the frown from his face like the one currently deepening the worry lines on his forehead. She smiled and considered dragging him into an alley to distract him with one of those methods now, but a quick glance behind her revealed their bodyguards shadowing them.

Dominic lowered his sunglasses. His gaze found hers and the passion gleaming in his bedroom blue eyes made her steps falter. His fingers tightened around hers. "Do we need to take a siesta?"

Her heart skipped a beat. He read her so easily.

I could get used to this.

No, you can't. This is temporary and don't you forget it.

But there'd been a few times this week when a hint of yearning for more time with Dominic had slipped through her defenses. On each occasion she reminded herself that she no longer wanted forever with anyone. No more laying her heart on the line for some guy to trample. She'd abandoned dreams of children and a home in the suburbs the day Mike walked out.

Besides, Dominic was a prince, and even if she wanted more with him she couldn't have it.

"No can do. I have to get back for that thing with Candace's future in-laws."

His fingers stroked the inside of her wrist and her pulse quickened. "Too bad."

She didn't want to go to the dinner or the engagement party that followed and couldn't care less that the festivities would take place on the largest privately owned yacht in the world, which just happened to be docked in Monaco's harbor. Her reluctance had nothing to do with avoiding the reminders of her own aborted wedding and everything to do with not wanting to waste one moment of her remaining time with Dominic. "I could probably finagle an invitation for you."

He shook his head, adjusted the bill of his baseball cap and steered her away from a group of tourists studying him a little too intently. "The bride and groom should be the center of attention. You've seen what happens when I make an appearance."

She had and the surplus of kiss-up attitude nauseated her. But still, she didn't want to go without him.

Alarm skittered through her. Was she getting in too deep?

No. Dominic made her head spin in bed and out, but her growing attachment to him over the past three weeks could be blamed on the surreal circumstances of living the lifestyle of the rich and famous. Here she was a fish out of water. She clung to him because he made her feel as if she fit in and he smoothed her language difficulties. Once she was back in Charlotte and on familiar ground she wouldn't need him as a crutch or interpreter.

But she'd miss him.

Her heart beat faster and a peculiar emptiness spread through her like chilling fog. She was greedy for his company and she resented the interruptions. That's all it was.

She nibbled her lip as they approached the lot where they'd left the car. Maybe she should start weaning herself from him.

He leaned closer to murmur in her ear. "Come to my room after the party. Call my cell. No matter how late. I'll let you in."

Her mouth dried. "I was supposed to spend the night on the boat. Promise to make leaving worth my while?"

The glasses came off and his hungry gaze locked on hers. "I will make you beg for mercy."

And he could do it. Her breaths shortened and her skin dampened. The area between her legs tingled. "Deal."

Best-case scenario she had one more week with Dominic and wise or not, she intended to enjoy every second of it. Next Friday Candace and Vincent would have their civil ceremony followed by the church service on Saturday. Her friend would marry Vincent in the same church where Prince Rainier had shocked the world by marrying his commoner bride, Grace Kelly.

So royalty marrying a nobody could happen. It just wasn't going to happen to Madeline. And she was okay with that. Really.

She glanced at the man beside her and hoped she wasn't fooling herself, because on Sunday—only eight short days away—Madeline, Amelia and Stacy would fly back to the States. Madeline's days of living like a princess would be over, and soon all she'd have left were her memories of *Once upon a time in Monaco.*

Nine

"I thought you were known for speed," Madeline complained to Toby as she tried in vain to hurry him away from the yacht.

He'd graciously offered to walk her back to the hotel. No doubt when he'd made the suggestion he'd believed Amelia would be leaving with her. There was definitely something going on with those two, but her friend wasn't talking.

"I knew there was a reason we never slept together. You insult a guy's car before he even pulls it out of the garage," he replied in a teasing tone. He gripped her elbow and slowed her to his own leisurely pace. "Sweetheart, I always take it slow when it counts."

She snorted and rolled her eyes. "Oh please. Save the car jockey chatter for someone dumb enough to fall for it. You're lagging behind now, Haynes. Get the lead out."

He ignored her. She could have covered the next twenty yards of the jetty faster on her hands and knees. He must have sensed her impatience. "You have a hot date at midnight?"

Thinking of the night ahead, of hot embraces and even hotter kisses, Madeline's body heated. "I don't kiss and tell."

"Do your friends?"

The edge in his voice stopped her. "Should they? Because I swear, Toby, if you hurt Amelia—"

A darkly dressed figure separated itself from the shadows at the end of the jetty. Madeline's fight-or-flight response kicked in. She turned, ready to defend herself, but before she could act Toby hooked an arm around her waist and shoved her behind him so fast she almost fell off her four-inch heels. Her heart skipped for an altogether different reason when she recognized their "assailant."

Tension drained from her muscles. "Dominic. What are you doing here?"

"Waiting for you." Dominic's hair was slightly mussed and beard stubble shadowed his jaw. His gaze took in Toby's protective stance and his eyes narrowed.

Was that a possessive glint in his eyes? Darn the darkness. She couldn't tell. And it didn't matter anyway. Never in her life had she been more conscious of the countdown on her days with Dominic.

She stepped around Toby. "I don't think you two were introduced the night of the ball. Dominic, this is Toby Haynes, an American NASCAR car driver and team owner. Toby, Dominic Rossi, Prince of Montagnarde."

After a moment's hesitation, Dominic offered his hand. Madeline glanced from Dominic to Toby and back as the men shook hands. Had the testosterone tide swept in? And then with a sharp nod each man released simultaneously. Had she missed something?

Madeline touched Toby's forearm and Dominic stiffened beside her. For Pete's sake, he couldn't be jealous? Could he?

She knew Dominic cared about her. No man could be as passionate and unselfish a lover without some feelings for his partner, but love? Of course not. They both knew this was a dead-end relationship.

So why did a thrill race through her? She blinked away her irrational thoughts and blamed them on that last glass of champagne—the one she'd had to try because someone told her a single bottle of Krug Clos du Mesnil cost more than her monthly mortgage payment.

"Toby, I'm going to take a rain check on your offer of an escort back to the hotel."

"You're sure?"

"Absolutely. Good night and thanks. See you tomorrow."

After a moment's hesitation, Toby pivoted and headed back toward the yacht.

"Why will you see him tomorrow?"

"A wedding thing. Why are you really here, Dominic?"

"I was impatient for your company."

"Good answer."

His gaze caressed the deep décolletage of her halter-neck gown. "You look lovely. Very sexy. Very beddable."

Her nipples tightened in response to the desire in his eyes and his voice. "Thank you."

She glanced around. "I don't see Ian. Usually, I can spot him."

Was that a guilty flush on his cheekbones? "He's not here."

Surprise and concern rippled over her. "Voluntarily? Because the guy hates to let you out of his sight. I swear he'd be in the bedroom with us if given a choice. He still doesn't trust me."

Dominic's teeth flashed white in the moonlight, but his tight smile didn't completely erase the strain deepening the lines on his face. "He feels he failed me where you're concerned and it disturbs him."

He took her hand in his and guided her away from the harbor. "I used to be very good at giving Ian the slip. I decided to see if I still could."

"Hmm. So you have a few drops of rebel in your blue blood. I like that. And Fernand?"

"I informed him you'd been invited to spend the night on the yacht."

"I was. But I declined. As you well know." Amelia, Candace and Stacy had accepted. She glanced up and down the uncrowded area. Parts of Monaco rocked late into the night. This wasn't one of them. "Is it safe—for you, I mean—to wander the streets alone?"

Dominic shrugged. "Monaco is the safest country in the world. And I'm wearing tracking devices and carrying a panic button."

"So what's the plan? I'm guessing you didn't sneak out just to sneak back in again."

"Have I mentioned that I find your intelligence a turn-on?"

Her pulse spiked. "At least a dozen times. So what gives?"

"I'd like to walk through Monaco-Ville and enjoy the musicians and magicians of the Midsummer Night's Festival." He studied her shoes. "Or should we find a piano bar and sit?"

"Lucky for you, my shoes are not the kamikaze kind despite the stiletto heels." What had he told her? He wanted to feel like a man instead of a monarch? There weren't many gifts she could give a prince, but she could handle that request. She looped her arm through his. "Let's walk—if you're sure it's safe."

His hand covered hers on his forearm. He held her gaze. "I would never do anything to endanger you, Madeline."

"I know. You're a prince of a guy," she replied tongue in cheek. "Besides, you know you'll get lucky if you get me back to the hotel safely."

Dominic choked a laugh, dragged her into a shadowy alcove and covered her mouth with his. She *mmmphed* a protest through smiling lips, but dug her fingers into his waist and pulled him closer. Her smile faded as the heat of his body seeped into hers and hunger for Dominic took control of her brain. His lips were firm and his kisses hard and desperate with a dangerous edge that stopped just shy of being too rough.

The unusual aggression turned her on like nobody's business. By the time he lifted his head her heart raced and her legs quivered like a marathon runner's after crossing the finish line.

He leaned his forehead against hers and sucked in deep breaths. "Your puns are terrible. Stick to medicine."

"Your wish is my command, Your Royal Buffness," she replied with a wink and curtsied as she often had during the past five days. She only did it because she'd discovered how much kowtowing irritated him. As usual her smart-aleck quip made him chuckle. Good. She wanted to ease whatever somber mood had taken hold of him.

They strolled through the streets of Monaco-Ville for over an hour enjoying music, magic and sharing vendor foods like any other couple. But that was the catch. They weren't like any other couple and never could be. Tonight was a stolen moment—one they'd never repeat. The realization saddened Madeline enough to make her eyes burn and her chest hurt.

Dominic must have misinterpreted her silence as tiredness, for he waved down a taxi to carry them back to the hotel. When they arrived he silently escorted her inside, and then backed her against the wainscoted elevator wall, cradled her face in his hands and looked deep into her eyes.

"I will never forget our time together." The gravity of his voice made the fine hairs on her body rise.

"Neither will I."

And then he kissed her. She knew she was in trouble because she couldn't hold him tight enough, couldn't burrow close enough. And she didn't want to let him go.

Oh, my God. I'm falling for him.

Her stomach plunged as if the elevator had dropped to the basement. She gasped and broke the kiss.

The doors opened on the penthouse floor. Dominic threaded his fingers through hers and stepped toward the doors, but Madeline's muscles refused to engage. Had she been fooling herself by believing she could have an affair without her heart getting involved?

No. No. It's not love. It's only a crush. A crush due to circumstances, romantic settings, a man larger than life and a surplus of sexual satisfaction.

"Madeline?"

She blinked and swallowed. She wasn't dumb enough to fall for a prince. Was she?

Nope. Not love. Her rapid pulse, quickening breaths and the tension swirling in her belly were by-products of sexual arousal. Nothing more. And her chest ached only because Dominic had become a friend—a friend she'd soon have to say goodbye to.

Mentally kick-starting her muscles into motion, she traveled down the corridor beside him, tiptoed into the suite and then his bedroom. The covers looked rumpled, as if Dominic had been in bed but unable to sleep before coming after her. The bedside lamp cast a dim glow over the room. The digital clock read 2:00 a.m. She'd been up since 5:00 a.m. and should be exhausted, but energy hummed through her veins.

Behind her, the door lock clicked. She turned her head.

Dominic leaned against the panel with his hands behind his back. "Undress for me."

"Is that a royal command?"

"Need it be?"

"You first."

His lips twitched. He shook his head, but kicked off his shoes and reached for his belt. "Some man needs to tame you."

"*Pfft*. That'll never happen."

"I know. It's part of your charm." The belt slid free. He tossed it aside. "Your turn."

The longer this took the more time she'd have with him. Tomorrow—today—was Saturday. Candace didn't have a meeting and Madeline didn't have to be anywhere until noon. She and Dominic could sleep the morning away if they wanted. She kicked off her shoes and removed the silver clip from her hair.

Dominic removed his watch. She mirrored the action.

Without a word Dominic fisted his shirt, yanked the tails free and then reached beneath the fabric to unfasten his pants. His trousers slid to the floor. He kicked them aside.

All she could see was his great legs beneath the shirttail hem. "Tease. Two can play that game."

She reached beneath her dress and removed her panties. She shot them toward him like a rubber band. He caught the scrap of black lace, crushed it in his hand and stroked it across his cheek. He dropped her panties and shoved his briefs to the floor. A kick piled them on top of his discarded pants.

She released the button fastening the halter top of her dress at her nape and squared her shoulders. The black satin fabric fell to her waist, revealing her breasts.

Dominic's sharply indrawn breath broke the silence of the

room. He swiftly unbuttoned his shirt, fumbling with a few of the buttons as if his fingers refused to cooperate, and then ripped it off and flung it aside, leaving him naked. His thick arousal rose from a tangle of dark golden curls. A bead of moisture glistened on the tip.

She wet her lips, curled her fingers against the need to stroke him and turned her back. "Zip?"

She didn't hear him approach. Her first inkling that he had was the touch of his lips on her shoulder, and then his hands spanned her waist and slid up to cup her breasts. He rolled the tightened tips in his fingers. Desire coiled tightly between her legs. She leaned against him. His hard, hot erection pressed against her spine and his beard stubble erotically rasped her neck as he sipped a string of kisses on her skin. He murmured something in a language she couldn't understand.

She lifted a hand to cradle his face, stroke his bristly jaw and trace his soft, parted lips. She turned her head and whispered against his lips, "No fair. Speak English."

He ignored her request, lowered her zipper and pushed her dress from her hips. And then he pulled her flush against him and bound her close with his strong arms.

She'd miss this. His strength. His gentleness. His passion. The radiator-hot warmth of his hard body against her, surrounding her.

He stroked and caressed her, her breasts, her belly, her bottom and finally, the knot of need between her legs. Her muscles quivered with each deft stroke. She could barely stand. And then he scooped her into his arms and carried her to the bed. Madeline gasped. She'd never had a man literally sweep her off her feet. And she liked it.

She roped her arms around his neck and pulled him down with her. His thigh parted hers, but instead of taking her he lay beside her, burying his erection against her hip instead of inside her where she wanted it, needed it, craved it. She wanted him to hurry, but his hands mapped her body with slow precision, tracing each curve and indention, circling her aureole, her navel, her sex. She arched against him. He released her and twisted toward the nightstand.

Finally.

She expected to see a condom in his hand. Instead, the bracelet she'd admired at the market rested on his palm. Her heart clenched. "Dominic, you shouldn't have. But how did you…?"

"Ian purchased it for me. Accept this as a reminder of our time together."

How could she refuse? "Thank you."

She lifted her wrist. He slipped it on and then kissed each of her knuckles.

This feels like goodbye.

A knot formed in her throat and her pulse skipped with alarm. "Dominic, are you leaving tomorrow?"

"No departure date has been set." He sipped his way to her elbow, her shoulder, her neck. Madeline shoved aside her disquiet and lost herself in his passionate possession of her mouth. His hands seemed to be everywhere, arousing her, coaxing her, stroking her. She returned his embrace, sculpting the muscles of his shoulders, his back, his buttocks. His soft lips traveled over skin made more sensitive by the rasp of his evening beard.

Need spiraled inside her, coiling tighter and tighter until she squirmed beneath him. "Please."

He rose over her and eased inside her one tantalizing inch at a time. No condom, a corner of her mind insisted. But condoms didn't matter. She was protected. And she wanted to be as close to Dominic tonight as she possibly could be.

He withdrew and thrust deep. She countered his every move again and again until the tingles of orgasm, headier than that glass of expensive champagne, bubbled through her, racking her body with pleasure.

Dominic groaned her name against her neck and then crashed in her arms.

She held him tight.

And wasn't sure she ever wanted to let him go.

Madeline jolted upright in the bed.

Dominic's bed.

She shoved her tangled hair out of her face and blinked, trying to clear her groggy mind and her vision. What had woken her? She looked around. No clue.

Dominic's side. Empty. She smoothed a hand over the pillow. Cool. Checked the clock—11:00 a.m. She'd overslept. Oops.

A smile flitted across her lips. She'd had good reason for snoozing late. But now she'd have to hurry. Candace had a noon appointment with the bishop at St. Nicholas Cathedral and she wanted her wedding party to be there. That included Madeline.

Why hadn't Dominic woken her as he'd done every other morning? With kisses and caresses and slow and easy lovemaking? Because she'd forgotten to tell him about the church thing and it wasn't on the calendar she'd given him.

Unfamiliar masculine voices penetrated the closed bedroom door. She snatched the covers up to cover her nakedness.

Dominic had company. She had to get dressed.

Her dress lay draped across the back of the chair instead of puddled on the floor where he'd dropped it. Her panties, hair clip, purse and shoes sat in the chair. She tossed back the covers, raced toward her clothing, scooped up the bundle and ducked into the lavish bathroom only to skid to a halt.

Eeek. Her hair resembled a frizzy string mop and the remnants of her makeup looked hideous. She dumped her stuff on the counter, quickly braided her hair and then bent to wash her face. She brushed her teeth with her finger and a dab of Dominic's toothpaste. Better. Not great. Will have to do.

The bathroom light glinted on the bracelet. Her quick smile turned into a frown. Should she hide in here or leave?

Leave unless you want to arrive at the church looking like last night's leftovers.

She tugged on her clothing and stepped into her heels. The ensemble might have been fabulous last night, but at eleven in the morning it looked exactly like what it was—the outfit of a woman who'd spent the night.

"So," Madeline mumbled to herself, "how are you going to get out of the suite?"

The only entrance lay through the sitting room. Past Dominic and his visitors. In last night's wrinkled dress. Ugh.

She returned to the bedroom. She could still hear the voices, but it sounded as if the men had moved to the balcony—the balcony spanning the entire suite, including the bedroom. Her gaze darted to the window. Curtains closed. Whew.

The balcony. That could be good. She could slip out the front door while they were outside and maybe they wouldn't see her. Still, she listened at the bedroom door for a few seconds before daring to slowly twist the knob and ease the panel open a couple of cautious inches.

"Wedding preparations will begin at once," a male voice pronounced.

Wedding? Madeline peeked out the door. Dominic and two older men stood on the balcony. One, of perhaps sixty, had a thick head of silvered blond hair, Dominic's erect posture and bone structure. The other was older, more wizened looking. A little bent. Bald.

She scanned the rest of the room and slammed into Ian's dark stare. Her heart stuttered. He stood stiffly on the far side of the room. Uh-oh. Unless Dominic had told him, Ian hadn't known she was here. She put a finger to her lips in the universal "be quiet" symbol. He didn't respond with as much as a blink.

"And if I'm not ready to return?" Dominic asked. He wore last night's clothing, but his black shirt and pants didn't look as out of place as her cocktail dress. He hadn't shaved and his hair looked as if it had only been finger-combed.

"You knew that as soon as your bride was chosen you would have to return home," the thick-haired one replied.

Bride?

Madeline's world slowed to a standstill.

Bride? Her heart bolted into a racing rhythm. Dominic was getting married? To whom? Warmth—*hope*—filled her chest before she could stymie it.

Whoa. Where had that come from?

"I'm not ready. I need more time." Dominic again.

"Why? So you can play here with your paramour? I have seen the papers and heard the reports. Do you think I don't know where you were last night and with whom?" the regal guy asked.

Paramour. Madeline's brain snagged on the word and her stomach plunged.

Paramour. *Her.*

Not the bride in question. The strength seeped from her limbs. She leaned weakly against the doorjamb and closed her eyes. The tremor started deep inside and worked its way to her extremities.

What is your problem? You knew he wasn't going to marry you.

"I have promised to do as you wish, Father. I will take a bride. One of the council's choosing. But I need more time."

A bride of the council's choosing? Her confused brain couldn't make sense of that.

"Her family awaits your arrival," baldy said. "Promises have been made and agreements signed. The jet will fly you to Luxembourg this afternoon. Your father has brought your grandmother's engagement ring. You will propose tomorrow. A gala to announce and celebrate the engagement will take place next Saturday evening."

Nausea. Dizziness. Rapid heart rate. Cold, clammy hands. Shock, Madeline diagnosed. She struggled to inhale, but it hurt too much. Pain sliced through her like an explosion of surgical blades.

What had Dominic said that day in the café? He wasn't *committed to anyone at this time?* She remembered the exact words because she'd thought it an odd answer. As odd as him saying he wanted to share a bed for reasons other than duty, greed or fleeting attraction. She hadn't understood then. She did now.

He'd been planning to marry all along. A woman of some mysterious council's choosing.

She'd never been more to him than a way to pass the time while awaiting the name of his bride.

God, she hurt. Which made absolutely no sense.

Why? Why does it hurt so much?

Because, fool, you fell in love with him.

You knew this was temporary and that he was out of your reach. And you fell for him anyway.

She bit her lip to stop a whimper of pain. She loved him.

Did you expect him to marry a commoner like Prince Rainier did?

And what about virgins? Did you conveniently forget that Dominic, like Prince Charles, might have to marry a virgin?

Her hands fisted and her nails dug into her palms. At some point her subconscious must have started believing in fairy tales. Otherwise she wouldn't be feeling as if she'd been shoved off the deck of an ocean liner. Adrift. Drowning. Lost.

Ian. She suddenly remembered the unfriendly bodyguard. Her gaze found his. How often had he witnessed the crash of a woman's world? A woman who'd fallen in love with his unattainable boss.

Hurt and humiliated, she silently closed the door, staggered back into the bedroom and braced her arms on the desk. How could she sneak out when she could barely walk?

She couldn't face Dominic. Couldn't look into his eyes and know that the man she loved was destined to marry someone else.

One more pertinent fact he'd neglected to mention.

She'd been nothing more to him than a vacation fling. A no-strings-attached affair.

A half laugh, half sob burst from her lips. She shoved her fist against her mouth to stifle the pitiful sound. He'd given her *exactly* what she asked for. And it was breaking her heart.

He may have avoided full disclosure, but she was the one who'd set up the parameters and then screwed up and broken the rules by falling in love. Sucking in a fortifying breath, she squared her shoulders. She would never let him know how badly he'd hurt her.

She sank into the chair, yanked open the desk drawer and extracted a piece of hotel stationery and a pen. The pen slipped from her fingers. Twice. Her hands shook so badly she could barely put the tip to the page.

Pull it together before Dominic comes in here and finds you wrecked.

Gulping deep, painful breaths, she struggled for calm, the way she did when a heinous accident landed in her E.R.

She would not act like those shameless women who'd flung themselves at him at the ball. She wouldn't beg for crumbs of his attention. She had too much pride for that. And she would cling to what was left of her tattered pride until her last breath.

What she needed was a cool, emotionless, nonnegotiable goodbye. A final goodbye. Because she didn't want him to come looking for her. She couldn't bear a face-to-face encounter because she didn't think she could hide her feelings, and he would pity her if he figured out her secret. Or worse, he'd be patient and polite and detached—the way he'd been with the other women who'd made their availability so obvious.

Gritting her teeth, she formed each letter, each word, each painful phrase until she had nothing left to say. At least nothing she could or would print. And then she folded the stationery and rested her head on the desk.

Empty. She felt completely drained and empty inside.

As far as Dear Johns went, hers sucked. But she didn't have time for another draft. She straightened and shoved the note into an envelope. Her mouth was too dry to lick the seal, so she tucked in the flap and earned herself a paper cut for her trouble. She sucked the stinging wound.

How fitting that her goodbye left her cut and bleeding. Dominic had cut out her heart without even trying.

She stared at the bracelet. Should she leave it with the note? No. She wanted something to remind her not to put her trust in men. Each time she'd done so she'd been hurt.

The bedroom door opened. Startled, she sprang to her feet and spun around, clutching the letter to her chest.

Ian stepped inside and closed the door. His face showed no emotions. "I will show you out."

How many times had he said those words? "Do you always clean up his messes?"

"Dominic doesn't make messes."

She blinked in surprise. The man rarely spoke to her. She hadn't expected an answer. And Ian had used Dominic's name instead of his title. Progress. But too late.

He noted her cut, opened a dresser drawer, withdrew a white handkerchief and offered it to her.

Dominic's handkerchief. She carried it to her nose and inhaled a faint trace of his cologne and then wrapped it around her finger in a compression bandage. "How are you going to get me past Dominic's guests?"

"The Royal Suite has a hidden escape exit. Come with me." He stalked into the walk-in closet, bypassed Dominic's neatly hanging clothing and perfectly aligned shoes and twisted a fleur-de-lis at the base of the sconce light on the far wall. A panel slid sideways to reveal a dimly lit space beyond.

She edged forward, leaned in and looked at the shadowy area. "Where will this take me?"

"Follow the hall to the fire stairs."

So this was it. She was being shuffled out the back door like…a mistress. She gulped down tears of shame and loss and looked at the note in her hand. She should have left it on the desk.

"Would you give this to him?" She stabbed it toward Ian. After a moment's hesitation he accepted it. The guy didn't like her. Would he deliver her message?

Madeline cupped his hand with hers and looked into his dark eyes. "And, Ian, please, *please,* keep him safe."

Ten

"She's a child." Dominic stared at the photograph in dismay. "What will I have in common with such a baby?"

"She is nineteen. The same age as your first wife when you married," Ricardo, the Minister of State and senior council member said as he laid three more photographs of the pale blonde on the glass-topped balcony table. "Young enough to bear many heirs."

Disgust rolled through Dominic. It wasn't the girl's fault. She was attractive enough, but far too young for his tastes. He preferred mature women. Women who weren't too shy, insecure or inexperienced to speak their minds. Women like Madeline.

He looked over his shoulder at the closed bedroom door. Time had run out. He'd have to tell Madeline the truth and then say goodbye. He wouldn't get to show her Paris or Venice as planned. An odd sensation of panic bound his chest, making it difficult to breath.

His gaze returned to the picture in his hand. He'd always known his obligations to Montagnarde took precedence over his personal wishes. He led a privileged life, but those privileges came at a price. "Have I ever met her?"

"Twice, she says."

He had no recollection of either occasion. This young woman had made no impression on him whatsoever. That did not bode well for their future. And yet he was expected to marry her, bed her, impregnate her. The sooner the better.

His father placed a hand on his shoulder. "Love will come, Dominic. It did for your mother and I and for each of your sisters. It did with Giselle." His fingers tightened, released. "Ricardo and I are in need of sustenance. We will adjourn to the dining room downstairs. Clean up and join us."

The pair left, the suite door clicking shut behind them. Their bodyguards would be waiting outside. Only Dominic's insistence had kept Ian present for this confidential meeting. Matters such as this required the utmost discretion.

Dominic faced the bedroom door with a growing sense of dread. When Ian's knock had awoken him this morning, Dominic had not suspected the upheaval about to take place. And then Ian had informed him that his father was in the elevator and on the way upstairs. The weight of Dominic's responsibilities had crashed down on him. His father's arrival had been a surprise—an unpleasant one. For the king's arrival could only indicate two things. The end of Dominic's freedom. The end of his days with Madeline.

He glanced at his wrist and realized he'd failed to don his watch in his haste to dress and get out of his room before his father entered. Since Giselle's death his father had adopted the habit of sitting in Dominic's room at the palace and discussing the upcoming day's events while Dominic dressed.

Dominic hadn't wanted to expose Madeline to the embarrassment of his father barging into the room.

He shoved a hand through his hair. He wouldn't be able to wake Madeline with leisurely lovemaking this morning as he had each day for the past week. And once he told her the truth the best interlude of his life would be over.

Over.

His future committed to someone else.

The choking sensation intensified. He tugged at his already loose collar to no avail. Loss mired his steps as he approached the bedroom. He braced himself, turned the knob, pushed open the door.

The bed was empty, the bathroom dark. He entered, searching for her hiding place. "Madeline? You can come out. They're gone."

"She is not here, Dominic," Ian said behind him.

Dominic glanced at the digital clock on the nightstand and exhaled. She usually sneaked out at dawn, but not this morning. He smiled, but the smile vanished when he realized there would be no more sunrises with Madeline.

"She's gone."

The finality of Ian's words made the back of Dominic's neck prickle and his stomach tense. "How?"

"There is an emergency exit. I showed her the way."

"Why have I never been told of this exit?"

"I feared what you would do with the knowledge." Ian offered him an envelope bearing the Hôtel Reynard insignia in the upper left corner. "She overheard your conversation with your father and the Minister of State."

Dominic closed his eyes, clenched his teeth and let his head fall back. She should have heard the words from him. Exhaling a pent-up breath, he extracted the letter and read.

Dominic

Thank you for making my vacation memorable.

I'll be swamped with wedding duties over the next week. No time for fun and games or distractions.

You were great. Just what the doctor ordered. But like any prescription, this one has run its course.

I hate goodbyes, so this is the only one you'll get. Goodbye.

I wish you the best.

Madeline

Pain swamped him like a tsunami. He called on numbness, his familiar companion in years past, but it refused to come. He swallowed once and then again. His hands fisted, the letter crumpling in his grip.

Madeline deserved the truth. The whole truth. She needed to know how important she was to him. How magnificent a lover. How good a friend. And he had to explain why he must say goodbye. She would understand. He would make her understand. "Where is she?"

"I don't know."

"What do you mean you don't know?"

"Fernand was excused from his duty while Mademoiselle Spencer *supposedly* spent the night on the yacht. In my urgency to remove her from the suite this morning I did not call him to track her when she left this room. I assumed she would return to her suite. She did not."

"She can't have gone far. I have her passport."

"It appears both of you went missing last night which proves my point about the secret exit. I am too old for she-nanigans like this, Dominic."

Censure tainted Ian's voice. Censure Dominic deserved. "She treats me like a man, Ian. Not a future king."

Ian nodded sympathetically. "I know, but you have your destiny. And if you insist on putting yourself in danger I will not be able to do what Mademoiselle Spencer asked of me. Keep you safe."

Dominic's head jerked up. He searched Ian's eyes. "She didn't leave cursing me for my deception?"

"I cannot read the woman's mind. But she was not swearing or throwing things."

"Find her."

"Dominic, perhaps it is best to let things be."

"Find her." And when Ian didn't move, Dominic added, "That is a royal command."

Ian snapped to attention, pivoted sharply and headed toward the door. Dominic had never spoken to him as harshly.

"She ran," Dominic called after him. Ian stopped without turning. "Why did she run, Ian? Madeline Spencer is no coward. She is courageous and mouthy and she fights back. The Madeline I've come to love would have been in my face and reprimanding me for another lie of omission."

His heart slammed against his ribs like a ship against an iceberg, winding him, chilling him. *Love.*

He loved her.

He loved her sassy mouth. Her earthy sensuality. Her refusal to kowtow. He loved the way she listened to his plans for Montagnarde and added her own suggestions.

He loved her. And he couldn't have her. Agreements had been signed. Promises made. Breaking them could cause an international incident.

Ian slowly turned, looking as if he, too, were shocked by Dominic's discovery.

"Why would she run?" he repeated.

"Perhaps she does not wish to engage in a losing battle, Your Highness."

Dominic didn't believe that. There had to be more. But what? He straightened the crumpled page and studied it more closely. What wasn't she saying? Despite the bland note, he knew she had feelings for him. She'd shown it in countless ways in bed and out. She'd ended things far too easily.

Dominic rubbed a hand over his bristly jaw and tried to decipher the puzzle of Madeline Spencer. Too courageous to run, replayed in his head. And then the pieces of the puzzle slid into place.

She'd only had one other lover. A man she'd believed she loved. Could she possibly love him, Dominic wondered? He could not leave Monaco without finding out.

"She would only run if it hurt too much to say goodbye," he told Ian. He ripped off his shirt. "I must shower and join my father. I want Mademoiselle Spencer found and in my suite when I return. If she wants to say goodbye, then she'll have to say it to my face."

"I need you to hide me," Madeline said as soon as she, Candace and Vincent reached the shadowy alcove of the cathedral.

"What?" Candace asked.

"Just for the rest of the day." She fussed with the buttons on the dress she'd bought in a nearby boutique rather than risk returning to her suite.

"Come again?" Vincent stood to her right presenting her with his unscarred left side. Candace said the wounds he'd sustained in the pit fire still bothered him despite the numerous plastic surgeries which had reduced the severity of his scars.

"I need to hide from Prince Dominic of Montagnarde and his henchmen," she whispered.

Candace straightened to her full five feet three inches. "Did that jerk hurt you because if he did, I'll—"

"Have you done something illegal?" Vincent interrupted.

How like a man to cut to the chase, dealing with the fact rather than the emotions. "I haven't broken any laws, and Dominic didn't hurt me. He did exactly what I asked him to do. He gave me great sex and a memorable vacation."

"But?" Candace prompted.

Madeline scrunched her eyes. Candace possessed the stubbornness of a mule. If Madeline wanted her cooperation it would cost her. The truth.

"I fell in love with him."

Candace squealed and bounced in her sandals.

"Keep it down, for crying out loud. We're in a church," Madeline whispered. "And do not say 'I told you so.' I'm a little too raw for that right now."

"But this is great!"

Vincent shifted on his feet and looked back toward the others gathered in the cathedral as if he'd rather be anywhere except the middle of a girlie tête-à-tête.

"No, it's not great. He's flying off to meet his fiancée this afternoon."

Candace's smile morphed into a fierce scowl. "He's engaged? The lying two-timing royal rat."

"He wasn't committed to anyone else until today." Madeline honestly believed that. "From what I overheard I gather some committee or other has been searching for an acceptable princess-to-be. Now they've found her. And he's going to marry her." Just saying the words made her throat feel as raw as if she had a full-blown case of strep.

She grabbed Candace's and Vincent's hands. "I won't let you down with my wedding duties, but until Dominic is gone I need to stay out of sight. And I can't do that by myself. I don't know the language and I don't know the country."

"I'll handle it," Vincent said without hesitation.

"Thank you." Madeline's eyes burned, but she blinked back the tears. If one seeped through she feared a torrent would follow.

One day. She only had to get through one more day. And then Dominic would be gone and she could lose herself in Candace's wedding preparations until she returned home.

She would have laughed if she weren't afraid it would turn into hysteria. She'd come to Monaco wanting to avoid the wedding preparations. Now she wanted to bury herself in them and occupy her every thought with marriage minutiae so she wouldn't have time to think of what she'd never have with Dominic or anyone else. Because this time her heart had sustained too much damage to ever recover.

The dining room was crowded. Too crowded for what Dominic had to say.

He stopped beside his father's table, but waved away the waiter who rushed forward to pull back his chair. Instead he slipped him a large tip and asked him, "Would you please have our luncheon served in the suite?"

"Certainly, Your Highness." The man hustled toward the kitchen.

"Dominic, what is the meaning of this?" his father asked.

"I have something to say and you don't want me to say it here."

"Your Highness," Ricardo began, but Dominic silenced him with a frown. The councilman, who'd risen at Dominic's approach, shifted on his feet and looked to his king for guidance.

Dominic's father rose. "Very well, son. If we must."

The return to the suite passed in tense silence due to the presence of other hotel guests in the elevator. Dominic recognized Derek Reynard, the owner and CEO of the world-renowned Reynard Hotel chain, and his wife. It was the perfect opportunity for Dominic to introduce himself and ask for a meeting to discuss the construction of a Hôtel Reynard in Montagnarde, but he had more important matters to deal with at the moment. The couple turned toward Madeline's suite. He wanted to follow, but first he had to deal with more critical issues.

The moment Ian closed the suite door behind them, Dominic faced his father. "I cannot marry the girl the council has chosen."

The minister sputtered. Dominic feared the septuagenarian might have a heart attack.

Dominic's father tensed, but otherwise showed no reaction. "Why not?"

"Because the woman I love is here in Monaco."

"And what of your duty to the crown?"

"I willingly serve my country, but I should not be cursed with an indifferent marriage due to a three-hundred-year-old custom. That custom, like our economy, needs modernizing."

"What of the agreements, Your Highness?" Ricardo asked. "The negotiations?"

"I'll renounce my title, if my decision causes difficulties for Montagnarde, but I will not marry that child or any other the council selects. I would rather live in exile than spend my life with a woman I care nothing about. I'm not a stud whose sole purpose is to service a mare."

"You would leave your family and your country for this woman you've been consorting with during your stay in Monaco?" his father asked.

"Yes, sir. I prefer to live happily elsewhere with Madeline than miserably at home without her."

"Doing what, Dominic? How will you support yourself and your wife if you leave your title and fortune behind?"

"I have the qualifications and connections to find work in the hotel industry."

His father's eyebrows rose. "You would work as a commoner? Draw a salary. Pay a mortgage?"

"Yes."

"What of your plans to develop Montagnarde's tourist potential?"

"I would mourn the loss of my dream, but not as much I would regret losing Madeline. I have dedicated the past fifteen years of my life to the betterment of Montagnarde. My plan is a sound one, and with or without me you should pursue it. But I would walk away from it all in an instant for her."

"What makes you think she's worthy of becoming a queen?"

"She's intelligent and courageous and doesn't have an obsequious bone in her body. She doesn't care about my title or wealth, and she fights me for the check after dinner. She calls me the most hideous names." Your Royal Beefcake, His Serene Sexiness and Sir Lickalot were but a few. The memories brought a smile to his lips.

His father's eyes narrowed speculatively. "She's never married?"

Dominic sucked a surprised breath at the question which cracked open the door to possibility.

Ian cleared his throat, drawing the king's attention. "Your Majesty, if I may speak?" He waited for acknowledgment. "I have the full report on Mademoiselle Spencer if you wish to peruse it."

The king made a go-ahead motion with his hand and Ian

left the room and returned with a folder. He opened it and read, "Madeline Marie Spencer, thirty-two, has never married although she has had one long engagement. She has no children, graduated near the top of her university class and is currently employed as a physician's assistant in a trauma center in Charlotte, North Carolina, U.S.A., where she is well-respected by her peers. Her credit rating is excellent, her personal debt minimal, and she has no criminal record. Not even a parking ticket. Her father, a policeman, is deceased and her mother is a retired schoolteacher."

"Where is she, this paragon?" Dominic's father asked.

"She has not been located, Your Majesty, since she left the hotel this morning. At Prince Dominic's request, we are searching."

Dominic's frustration level rose. He had to find her.

"I would like to meet this woman who has mesmerized my son in such a short time. When she's found bring her here." His attention returned to Dominic. "This will not be without complications, you understand?"

Adrenaline pulsed through Dominic's system at his father's acceptance. "I do."

"She has accepted your suit?"

"I have not been free to state my intentions."

"But, Your Majesty, the agreements... This could cause a diplomatic scandal," Ricardo protested.

Dominic's father held up a hand to silence him. "My son has had enough unhappiness in his life, Ricardo. Dominic and I will deal with the agreements. We will fly to Luxembourg this afternoon to personally make our apologies and any reparations required." He turned back to Dominic. "You're sure she's the one?"

"I've never been more certain of anything in my life."

"And do you believe she will accept your proposal?"

Tension invaded his limbs. "I don't know, Papa. But if I can't have Madeline I don't want anyone else."

"I don't know why you couldn't just use your passkey and take Madeline's passport from Dominic's room safe," Candace whispered to Vincent in the hallway of the American Consulate on Tuesday afternoon.

"Because it's stealing," Vincent replied patiently for the third time. "The hotel cannot afford the reputation of violating its guests."

"But it's *hers*."

"Stop," Madeline interjected. "As much as I love you, Candace, Vincent's right. We can't go digging around the safe just because we *think* my passport might be there. I've reported it lost and the consulate guys have promised to put a rush on it. I should have a replacement before I fly home on Sunday."

Madeline leaned against the wall beside the exit while Vincent stepped outside and signaled the waiting car. She slid on her new oversize Jackie-O sunglasses and covered her hair with a silk scarf. Disguised like a fugitive and her only crime was falling for the wrong guy.

She grimaced. "I can't believe Dominic didn't check out of the hotel. Why is he keeping the suite? Is he coming back? I can't go on riding in the floorboard of Vincent's car and hiding at his apartment."

Candace squeezed her hand. "You have no choice. Dominic had that Fernand guy following you. You had to disappear. You'll only be riding in floorboards and sneaking up service elevators for a few more days."

"But you had to reschedule everything except the wedding and rehearsal party because Dominic had my schedule."

"Like that's the worst catastrophe to ever befall a bride. Jeez, get over it, Madeline. I've said it's not a big deal."

But it was a big deal. Candace had enough stress dealing with planning a wedding in a foreign country. She didn't need the additional pressure of shuffling times and meeting places at the last minute because of Madeline's mistake.

"Maybe I should just see him and get it over with when he returns. *If* he returns."

She hoped it wouldn't kill her. God knows, losing Mike had never hurt like this. But then she'd realized in the three days since her affair with Dominic had ended that Mike's defection had hurt her pride not her heart. She'd been more concerned with what her coworkers thought of her for being so easily duped than with Mike's leaving.

She hadn't loved Mike. Not the way she loved Dominic.

Not once had she pictured herself growing old with Mike. She'd focused more on the house and children they'd have and thought more about being a mother than a wife. Not so with Dominic. She'd miss waking up beside him, making love with him and listening to his aspirations in the darkness. She'd miss his stupid little bows, the way he could melt her with his smile and his loyalty to the hulking Ian. Children? Oh yeah, a few little princes and princesses would have been nice, too, but Dominic was the main attraction.

"No, you won't confront him," Candace interrupted her pity party. "There's no reason to put yourself through that. And he might have *her* with him."

Madeline flinched. Good point. She didn't really want to come face-to-face with the woman who would be living *her* dream.

"Your Dear John generously gave him an easy out—which is more than he deserved, if you ask me. I think you should have skewered his nuts and roasted them over the barbecue." Candace held up her hands. "I know. I know. He made no promises. I got the stringless affair part the first time you explained it. And even though I thought it was a dumb idea, I really thought he was the right guy for you, Madeline. I've never seen you as happy. And I'm seriously peeved over being wrong."

At Vincent's signal Madeline and Candace raced to the car stopped by the curb and scooted in, and then Vincent turned around and looked at Madeline over the back of the seat. Her stomach sank at his serious expression.

"The hotel called. Rossi's back."

Eleven

Twenty-four more hours and she'd be gone.

Madeline kept to the outer fringes of the large private garden housing the wedding reception. An hour ago she'd completed her bridesmaid duties. The happy couple had danced their first dance and cut the cake. By this time tomorrow Madeline would be winging her way back to the States.

She didn't understand why Dominic was still looking for her unless it was to return her passport—an item he could easily leave at the hotel's front desk. Last night he'd shown up uninvited at the posh Italian Restaurant where the dinner following Candace and Vincent's civil service had been held and demanded to speak to her. Luckily, Madeline had spotted him before he'd seen her, and she'd been able to make a hasty exit out a side door through the kitchens and into the back alley.

Today she'd been so tense during the religious ceremony

at the cathedral that she'd barely heard the service. She'd kept expecting Dominic to burst through the doors, and she'd startled at every sound. She felt guilty as hell for tainting her friend's special event with unpleasant thoughts, but Candace, bless her, was taking Madeline's distraction in stride.

During the past week Madeline had adopted Amelia's habit of watching entertainment TV and reading the English tabloid papers. She kept waiting for news of Dominic's engagement to break.

Wait a minute.

Madeline dropped the leaf she'd been folding like sloppy origami. According to what she'd overheard in Dominic's suite last Saturday, the official announcement of his engagement would be made tonight at a gala in Luxembourg. Loss weighted her stomach and goose bumps crept over her skin despite the sunny day and comfortable temperatures. She hugged her silk stole around her bare shoulders.

If Dominic was there, he couldn't be here. Right?

Right.

So she didn't need to hide out here in the dappled shade of the lemon trees. She could rejoin the party and celebrate her friend's happiness.

She could even find it in her battered heart to be happy for Mike because he'd deserved more than the indifferent emotion—Dominic had diagnosed her failed engagement well—Madeline had offered. And her feelings for Mike had been indifferent, she admitted, because she'd held back and never fully committed her heart. He was still a jerk for cheating, but part of the failure of their relationship rested squarely on her shoulders.

Picking up her discarded bouquet from the stone bench, she made her way back across the flagstones to the center of the patio and stopped by Candace's side. Her friend's radiant smile faded and a worried look took its place.

Madeline hugged her. "Don't look like that. I am happy for you. Both of you."

And she meant it. Just because her dreams hadn't come true didn't mean she couldn't be thrilled her friends' had.

Candace took her hand. "You know I love you, right?"

Madeline stiffened. The back of her neck prickled. Why did that sound ominous? "Candace…?"

Madeline shot an anxious glance toward the château and spotted Makos. Her breath left in a whoosh. She turned toward the back corner of the garden where she'd been hiding, and saw Fernand yards away from her hiding spot. She then saw Ian in the opposite corner. Panic fluttered in her belly and squeezed her lungs. She spun left, right, searching for an exit, but every escape route had been blocked by a bodyguard. Members of the royal security team wore blank faces and had stiff bearings. Her years of exposure to law enforcement officers made them easy for her to pick out of the crowd.

Gulp.

"Dominic's here," she croaked.

Candace's fingers tightened. "Yes."

Bewildered, Madeline stared at her friend and tried to comprehend the betrayal.

She had to get out of here.

Toby blocked her path, parked a big paw on her shoulder. "Hear him out, Madeline. And then if you still want me to, I'll beat the crap out of him."

Madeline scanned the faces around her. Amelia and Toby, Candace and Vincent, Stacy and Franco. Were they all in on this? She clenched her teeth on a panicked, furious cry.

The bodyguards closed in until she was surrounded by a circle of dark-suited men. Three she could handle. A dozen? Probably not. Her heart raced, her mouth dried and adrenaline flooded her bloodstream.

Run, her conscience screamed.

No, dammit, I am no coward. I am through running.

But I can't let him know how much he's hurt me.

Madeline closed her eyes, inhaled deeply and exhaled slowly, fighting to still the tremors racking her. When she lifted her lids Dominic stood inside the circle and only two yards away. He wore a black suit with what she now recognized as Montagnarde's gold crest on the breast and a white open-collared shirt. His brushed-back hair accentuated his smooth-shaven jaw, but beneath his tan his face looked pale. A thin, white line rimmed his mouth and his blue eyes stared somberly into hers.

The silver-haired man, Dominic's father, stood to Dominic's right, the bald guy to his left.

"Why aren't you in Luxembourg?" she choked out.

"Father, this is the woman who held a knife to my throat and threatened my life," Dominic announced clearly, distinctly and loud enough for the crowd surrounding them to hear.

The guests' gasps barely registered. Why would he cause a scene? He knew how much she hated publicity. Madeline lifted her chin. "Tattletale. You asked for it."

Dominic's father stepped forward. "Mademoiselle, in Montagnarde threatening the life of a monarch is a serious offense."

That wasn't news. She narrowed her eyes. She looked from one man to the other. Why were they replaying this?

"There is only one way to commute the sentence," the bald guy said. "The accused must look the victim in the eye and swear she doesn't love him."

Her heart stopped. In a second someone was going to have to start CPR. But then her heart spontaneously jolted back into rhythm which meant she had to live through this instead of conveniently dying of mortification.

She sought Dominic's gaze. How could he ask that of her? How could he publicly humiliate her this way? "And if I refuse to participate in this ridiculous charade?"

Posture erect and looking totally regal, he closed the gap between them, stopping a foot away. "You stole from me, Madeline Spencer."

Confused, she blinked and shook her head. "Ian gave me that handkerchief and you bought me this bracelet. I never took anything else."

"You took the most important thing." His eyes and mouth softened. "You took my heart."

She gasped and struggled to make sense of his words. Was this a cruel joke? Was he going to marry his princess and ask Madeline to be his mistress or something? She glanced at Candace and saw tears streaming down her friend's smiling face.

She turned back to Dominic. "What about your bride-to-be? The one the council chose? The one who's supposed to wear your grandmother's ring? The one you're supposed to get engaged to tonight, for Pete's sake?"

Dominic's gaze didn't waver. "I agreed to marry without love because I never believed I would find it again."

A smile lifted one corner of his mouth. He lifted a hand and cradled her face. She wanted so badly to lean into his touch that it took all her strength to jerk away.

"When you held that knife to my throat you changed my life, Madeline. I have never known a woman with your courage. No other woman treats me like a man instead of a monarch. And no other woman loves me as completely and unselfishly as you do."

She flinched. *He knew.* A lie of denial sprang to her lips, but the intense emotion in his eyes made her forget the words.

"Tell me I'm wrong, Madeline. Tell me you don't love me, and I'll walk away."

She wanted to believe. God, she wanted to believe what she thought he was saying. Her breath shuddered in and then out.

"I'm not a virgin. And you know it," she whispered.

His eyes twinkled with laughter. "Good thing that's not a requirement."

Her eyes and chest burned. She blinked rapidly to keep the tears—happy, hopeful tears—at bay and extended her arms, wrists together. "I guess you're going to have to cuff me and take me into custody. Because I can't lie."

Dominic's eyes widened. Surprise and happiness filled their depths and a brief smile flashed across his lips before he once more donned the serious mask. "Then I hereby sentence you to life, Madeline Spencer. Life with me."

He dropped to his knee and bowed his head. For a moment it looked as if he said a silent prayer. Then Dominic's gold-tipped lashes lifted and his bedroom blue eyes found hers. "Marry me, Madeline. Be my friend. My lover. My wife. And one day, my queen."

He reached into his pocket and withdrew an exquisite emerald ring in an antique-looking gold setting.

She pressed her trembling fingers to her lips. A warm tear slid over her fingertip. "You forgot your handcuffs?"

He grinned. "I promise I'll find them later if you say yes."

She looked at Dominic's father and found acceptance and even approval in his face. "You're okay with this? Clearly, I'm not princess material."

"I beg to differ, mademoiselle. Now give my son the answer he desires."

She stared into the face of the man she loved, the man who'd stolen her heart in a matter of moments. "I always thought I wanted an on-your-knees proposal. But I was wrong."

Uncertainty flickered in Dominic's eyes.

"It's not how the proposal is delivered that matters. It's who's asking the question." She caressed his cheek, cupped his smooth jaw and stroked a finger over his lips. "Get up, Dominic. I refuse to have this discussion unless we're eye-to-eye, face-to-face and heart-to-heart."

He slowly rose.

"You are such a romantic. I love it. And I love you." She rose on her tiptoes and brushed her lips to his. She tasted tears. "Yes, Dominic, I'll marry you."

His arms banded around her with crushing force and he lifted her off the ground. The crowd surrounding them let out a deafening cheer.

Dominic set her down and kissed her so gently her heart swelled to squeeze the air from her lungs. He pulled back a fraction and braced his forehead against hers. "I love you, Madeline."

He cradled her face, brushing her tears away with his thumbs. "I hope you know what you're getting into. Royal weddings are extravagant affairs."

Madeline laughed. She never thought she'd be grateful for those six wasted years. "I have a little wedding planning experience. As long as I have you, I can handle it."

* * * * *

THE PLAYBOY'S
PASSIONATE PURSUIT

BY
EMILIE ROSE

Dear Reader,

It's not often a secondary character makes a lasting impression on me, but Toby Haynes would not go away. Even though he didn't get the girl in *Exposing the Executive's Secrets* I couldn't get him out of my head. He seemed larger than life each time he swaggered onto the page, and I wanted to get to know him better. When an opportunity presented itself, I begged my editor to let me resurrect him for this Monaco series. Lucky for me she agreed.

The problem was that, despite growing up in North Carolina, the home of many NASCAR teams, I knew next to nothing about race-car driving. Toby, as previously established, was a NASCAR driver. My research into stock-car racing opened new doors, and I became a budding fan.

Hope you enjoy Toby's book and…I'll see you at the races. :)

Happy reading,

Emilie Rose

This book would never have happened
without Wanda Ottewell, my super-cool editor.
Thanks for loving Toby as much as I did
and for letting me bring him back to life.

Thanks go to Roxanne St. Claire for trying to guide me
through the steep NASCAR learning curve.

One

Please don't let it be him.

Panic seized Amelia Lambert's heart, and then the organ lurched into a rapid, thundering rhythm like thoroughbreds breaking from the Kentucky Derby gate. Her gaze locked onto the back of the man standing at the registration counter, and a cold hard lump of dread formed in her stomach.

That sandy-blond hair, those wide shoulders, the muscular tush and long legs could only belong to one person. Someone she never wanted to see again.

Toby Haynes. Her dumbest mistake.

Why was he in Monaco *now?* She was supposed to have time to prepare for his arrival. Twenty-four days, to be precise.

She considered ducking behind one of the fat marble pillars in the glitzy Hôtel Reynard lobby until he left, but before she could translate thought into action he turned away from the desk and his gaze plowed right into hers. And then he smiled. That cocky, slightly crooked half smile had earned him the title of NASCAR's sexiest driver five years running.

She *hated* that smile.

Hated what it did to her. Hated how it made her skin tingle and flush. Hated how it made her toes curl. Hated how it tangled and heated her insides and anesthetized her gray matter.

Focusing on her as if she were the only other person around for miles, he sauntered toward her with a hotel key card in one hand and a black leather bag in the other. He stopped an arm's length away. An Atlantic Ocean too close, in her opinion.

"Hello, sweet Amelia," he drawled.

Her lungs failed at the intimacy of his leisurely I've-seen-you-naked inspection.

The man had enough magnetism to screw up compasses from here to Timbuktu. Throw in the fact that he possessed a risk-taking adrenaline-junkie personality that spelled doom for any relationship, and Toby Haynes was bad news all around. Never mind that he was every woman's dream lover in bed. A woman would have to be a masochist to get entangled with him.

Luckily she'd wised up.

Unfortunately not soon enough.

She tipped her head back to look into his silvery-blue eyes and tried to swallow the barge beached in her dry throat with only minimal success. "What are you doing here, Toby?"

"Vincent asked me to shadow you and your girlfriends until the wedding. Never cared much for following, but for you I'll make an exception."

Her stomach landed in her sandals, and chaos erupted in her brain as she scrambled to make sense of his words. Vincent was Vincent Reynard, heir to the Hôtel Reynard chain and one of Toby's race-car team's sponsors, as well as the groom-to-be to Amelia's best friend, Candace. Vincent happened to be footing the bill for Candace and her three bridesmaids to spend a month in Monaco planning the dreamiest wedding ever. The ceremony was scheduled to take place in four weeks.

"Why you?"

"I'm the best man. But then, you already know that. I recall you saying so. More than once." His Georgia roots oozed into his gravelly voice and over her skin like a humid southern breeze.

She could not believe she'd been dumb enough to feed his already Herculean ego with compliments.

But he had been that good.

And she had been that stupid. Being tipsy was no excuse.

And then she remembered Neal, her dearly departed fiancé, the man she loved with all her heart, and she felt like a traitor. Again. The same way she had that morning when she'd rolled over and spotted Toby's handsome face on her pillow.

Wait a minute. Panic knocked guilt aside. "*You're* Vincent's best man?"

"Yes, ma'am."

She would wring her friend's neck for withholding that crucial piece of information. "I'm Candace's maid of honor."

"Guess that means we'll be rubbing fenders. All those shared duties. We're gonna be tight."

This was bad. Very, very bad. Nauseating, in fact. She barely managed to contain her groan.

Toby slouched against the marble pillar beside her and

slid his key into his front pocket. The action drew Amelia's gaze over the taboo terrain of a generous masculine package encased in blue jeans so worn and faded she could tell which way the, um, *landscape* lay.

She suppressed a shiver as memories assailed her and gritted her teeth against the images burned on her retinas of how he looked naked, of what he felt like hot and bare and pressed against her, of how alive he'd made her feel on a day when she'd wanted to crawl into a dark cave and hide.

Her body smoldered and her hormones launched into a chorus line of kicks and spins. Those same stupid hormones had landed her in bed with him ten months ago, but that was a mistake she'd never repeat. Toby Haynes, like her father, was bent on burning a destructive trail along the fastest route to the grave.

Her journey climbed back up his flat stomach and broad chest and eventually reached his gorgeous tanned face, his let-me-at-you mouth and sexy bedroom eyes—eyes currently twinkling with satisfaction over her thorough inventory of his anatomy.

Darn. "Shouldn't you be driving in circles somewhere?"

His smile slipped but only for a millisecond. Had she not been staring at him like a deer caught in the headlights, she would have missed it. He blinked, raked a hand through his short, already disheveled hair and then hooked his thumb through his belt loop. His casual stance contradicted the tension carving shallow lines around his mouth.

"I have some free time. And it's ovals or tri-ovals or—"

"In the middle of the NASCAR season?"

"Yeah." He forced the word through a clenched-teeth smile.

Admittedly Amelia didn't follow car racing, but working as a nurse in a Charlotte, North Carolina, hospital near a speedway meant caring for several race-car drivers each year, and she'd learned a little about the sport whether she'd wanted to or not. Time off midseason was neither desirable nor good. It cost the driver points or money or... *something* that pushed most of the fools to check out of the hospital sooner than they should and often against doctor's orders. To earn an entire month off meant Toby had broken a major rule or been injured.

She took another quick appraisal of his muscle-packed body. He didn't look injured. He looked firm and fit and virile—*ahem*.

"What did you do?"

He shifted his jaw. "What makes you think I did anything?"

"Because you're a hardheaded, risk-taking daredevil. You drive like a maniac. And you don't miss races."

The corners of his mouth curled up—and so did her toes. "Been watching me, have you?"

Her face ignited into a ball of flame. She'd only watched part of one race. After the first wreck she'd had to turn off the TV. But Toby made the network news highlight clips every week and he'd done commercials both on TV and in print. She couldn't avoid seeing his handsome mug even though she tried.

She scowled and lifted her chin. "I have better things to do than watch grown men try to kill themselves."

"Like what?"

"None of your business. Go home, Toby. Candace, Madeline, Stacy and I can look out for each other. We don't need a babysitter. All you have to do is show up for the rehearsal and the wedding."

"No can do. My buddy asked and I owe him."

His buddy. Vincent.

She'd met Toby last year after a freak accident in his pit had burned Vincent over twenty percent of his body. Vincent had been airlifted to the hospital where Amelia and Candace worked in the burn unit. During Vincent's stay, he'd met and fallen in love with Candace. Toby had been a frequent and irritating visitor. Amelia had seen too much of him then and she'd already seen too much of him today.

"Vincent said the accident wasn't your fault."

The grooves beside Toby's mouth deepened. "I'm responsible for my team and anyone behind my wall."

If she had a dollar for every time she'd heard similar words, she could buy a private island in the Bahamas. She'd learned from her firefighter father and from her job dealing with the results of disaster that when the adrenaline kicked in, risk takers thought of nothing but the thrill of their daring deeds. They needed that rush the way a junkie needed a fix.

Toby lifted a hand to her cheek. She flinched out of reach but not quick enough to avoid a brief electrifying touch. "Like it or not, I'm going to be drafting you until after the wedding."

The fine hairs on her body rose in warning. She took a step back. "You said you didn't like to follow anyone."

His gaze rolled down her body and slowly back up. Her skin tightened and her nipples peaked. She folded her arms across her chest to hide the evidence.

"Depends on the view and the reason. Trust me, I won't be complaining."

How dare her pulse skip. She silently cursed her traitorous body. "Don't expect to take up where we left off."

"Tell me something, Amelia." He stretched out her name, long and low, the way he had when he'd groaned it during climax, and a heat wave engulfed her. "It was good between us. If I had any doubts, hearing you moan my name over and over deafened 'em. So why would you sneak out on a guy like that? And what's with the cold shoulder since?"

She squashed a trace of guilt and quickly glanced around to make sure none of the other hotel guests were listening. She'd refused Toby's gifts and hadn't returned his phone calls because she'd been afraid he'd sweet-talk her out of her common sense—and her clothes—again. The risk of falling for a guy just like dear ole Dad had been too high. She didn't intend to end up like her mother—stuck in a miserable marriage.

She wanted a man like Neal. Kind, gentle Neal, the fiancé she'd loved and lost to leukemia three years ago. She did not want a guy who'd haul his banged-up body home for her to put back together time and time again. Most marriages couldn't survive that kind of stress—a circumstance she witnessed on the job every day. With divorce rates at fifty percent, she had to use your brain to choose a partner or she'd end up in the wrong statistical column.

"Toby, what happened that night shouldn't have happened. You caught me at a weak moment. I'd had a rough week and too much to drink and I made a mistake. It won't happen again."

From the flare of his nostrils she suspected he didn't like being called a mistake. "You'd had two drinks."

"I'm not a drinker. I have a low tolerance level."

"You might call the first time a mistake, but that doesn't explain the next three. Sugar, you were hot for me—and not just that night. We'd been circling each other for months. You can't deny you wanted me. I caught you checking me out more times than I can count."

The accuracy of his words shot flames through her veins. "Then you can't count very high. And for your information,

I also crave éclairs 24-7. However I don't indulge often because too much isn't good for me. Neither are you."

"I was very good for you—every time. Granted, the first one was a little fast. But I didn't hear you complaining." The combination of his husky drawl and intense passion-darkened eyes nearly buckled her knees.

She stiffened her weak limbs and shaky defenses. She would not think about that night. Bad enough that the memory still invaded her dreams, she refused to let it take over her conscious hours. "Toby, I've heard about your conquests. Women are like races to you. You win one and then you pack up and fly to the next. You had me. It's time to move on."

"Can't do that, sugar. We're not finished."

The conviction in his words sent a shiver of desire rippling through her. He had her hot and bothered and weakening with only words. If she didn't scare him away, then she was going to be in serious trouble. Shock tactics might work. "Are you looking for a wife?"

He flinched. "No."

"Well, I'm looking for a husband and children, the white picket fence, the dog, the cat and the whole package. I won't deny you were an enjoyable interlude, but I am looking for Mr. Right and someone to share a porch swing with thirty years from now. You are nowhere close to qualified for the position, and I don't want to waste any more time on you. So back off."

She turned on her heel and beat a hasty retreat toward the elevator.

Waste time on him?

Toby fisted his hands and gnashed his teeth. Women didn't walk away from Toby Haynes. He loved 'em and left 'em on his terms and he always—*always*—left 'em wanting more.

Forget the bet. This had nothing to do with the wager he'd made to keep Vincent entertained during rough months of countless skin grafts and painful rehab and everything to do with Amelia Lambert—the first woman to mess up his foolproof system.

She'd left *him* wanting more. Nothing permanent like her fantasy house in the suburbs and happy ever after, mind you, because he didn't believe in permanence. He'd seen too many women walk away when times got tough and too many men blow when the pressure got too high. But he wanted more of her particular brand of five-alarm-fire sex. They'd combusted every which way including sideways that night, and having her dismiss the potent chemistry between them—dismiss *him*—chafed worse than sucking exhaust from the back of the pack.

He wanted her back. What's more, she wanted him, too. He'd seen the hunger in her green-and-gold eyes as she'd visually stripped him a few minutes ago, and his body had responded. Give him a few more laps around the mattress and then he'd be ready to drop the checkered flag on their relationship.

He took a minute to admire her slender figure and lean legs in a short white skirt and frilly, sheer peach-colored blouse over a fitted camisole instead of her usual shapeless hospital scrubs. Her hair, a wavy cinnamon curtain, swished between her shoulder blades with each step. His blood took a pit stop in his south end at the memory of the silky strands gliding across his belly and thighs—an experience he intended to repeat soon. *Very* soon.

He knocked himself out of neutral and straightened to tail her sweet, swaying behind. The sudden movement made the floor shift beneath his feet. Damn. He planted a steadying palm on the cool column. The vertigo vanished as quickly as it had appeared, but it reminded him why he was here.

Concussion. Couldn't drive. The doc claimed that by the time the wedding passed Toby should be back behind the wheel. Missing five races meant that, short of a miracle, he and his team would be eliminated from this year's chase for the championship. He didn't believe in miracles.

He'd been in the top ten for the past eight years and he didn't like losing. Every win proved his daddy wrong. Toby Haynes wasn't a worthless piece of crap. Too bad the old bastard hadn't lived long enough to eat his words.

Toby covered the ground between him and his target in long strides. "Hold up, sugar. We have to make plans. What in the devil is a Jack and Jill shower anyway?"

Amelia stopped abruptly and turned. "Why?"

"Because Vincent wants one and he put me in charge of it. And Candace sent me a link to a wedding Web site that says you and I are supposed to host some brunch thing together, too. I have the e-mails. C'mon up to my room and we'll go over 'em."

He'd done his research and he knew exactly what his best-man duties were. Back when he'd thought he'd be racing every weekend and blowing in only for the wedding, he'd intended to hire the best party planner in Monaco to set up a pair of bashes the bride and groom would never forget. Money was no object. But since he was stuck here he might as well use the situation to lure Amelia back into the sack.

Amelia folded her arms and gave him that prissy in-your-dreams look—the one that fired every cylinder in his engine. Nothing he liked more than a challenge, and the sweet little nurse had been a challenge from day one when she'd tried to bounce him from Vincent's hospital room after visiting hours ended. She hadn't stood a chance of ditching him then and she didn't now. What Toby wanted, Toby got. He hadn't made it from white trash to multi-millionaire by letting a few obstacles stop him.

He held out his hands and shrugged. "Hey, if you're not interested, I'm sure I can pull something together. They sell kegs in Monaco, right? And I bet the concierge can recommend a good stripper or two for the bachelor party."

Amelia's raspberry-red lips dropped open in horror. Bull's-eye. He'd missed riling her and bit the inside of his lip to stop a grin.

"You don't have beer kegs at bridal showers, Toby, and Candace would not appreciate strippers."

No kidding. But he loved Amelia's shocked whisper. Kinda reminded him of how she'd sounded when he'd dipped his head between her legs and licked her that first time. "No?"

She huffed out an exasperated breath. "Give me your list and go back to the States, back to your races and your bimbos and…whatever. I'll take care of everything."

If only he could go back.

"Nope. Gave my word. Never break it." If his good-ole-boy act made people underestimate him, that wasn't his problem. And if Amelia thought he'd give up his pursuit just because she played hard to get, then she'd seriously miscalculated how much he liked to win.

"Speaking of teamwork, I could use your help. Airline lost my luggage. Let me dump my bag upstairs and then you can take me shopping and do your worst." The airline had promised to have his bag to him within twenty-four hours, and he had a change of clothes in his carry-on. But he didn't have to share that information.

"I am not your personal shopper."

No, but she was one of those women who always helped out someone in need, a real sucker for a sob story. He'd learned that in the months of chasing her up and down hospital corridors.

"Admit it, you'd love to get me out of my pants. Again." He winked and she bristled predictably. "You've been here a day already. I know you women have scoped out the stores."

The glint in her eyes warned him he wouldn't score an easy victory. "I'm sure Gustavo, our concierge, can give you a map. If you want to discuss shower and brunch arrangements, then I'll make time to meet you in the café by the gardens later this afternoon. But right now I have plans."

Plans that didn't include him.

He ought to be frustrated by his lack of success. Instead the temporary setback only made him more determined to succeed.

The express elevator to the penthouse floor opened. She whirled around and stepped inside. Toby followed.

Her eyes widened. "Where are you going?"

"My suite."

She folded her arms and abruptly faced the doors. He was glad, because the swift ascent left him reeling. He braced a shoulder against the wall and widened his stance. The moment the brass panels opened again, Amelia bolted down the thickly carpeted hall. Toby straightened carefully, found his balance and followed more slowly, scanning the space to get his bearings.

Nine doors opened off the penthouse level. Two emergency exits. Six suites. One rooftop pool and hot tub for the private use of the penthouse-level guests. Amelia stabbed her key card into the door at the far end and a grin tugged Toby's lips. His room was next door. Convenient. *Thanks, Vince.*

He inserted the key into his electronic lock. "Knock on the wall when you're ready for me, sugar."

"Don't hold your breath." Amelia ducked into her room.

Toby's grin widened. Being sidelined for a month from the sport he lived and breathed no longer seemed like a fate worse than death. In fact, he could even say he was looking forward to it.

Two

Amelia slammed the suite door behind her—as hard as one could slam a door designed to operate silently.

She stalked into the luxurious sitting area and confronted her best friend. On second thought, maybe her *former* best friend. "Is there something you forgot to tell me?"

Candace tucked a lock of pale blond hair behind her ear and blinked her big blue eyes innocently. Too innocently. "Like what?"

"Like Toby Haynes is Vincent's best man and he's going to be a pain in my neck for the *entire* month, not just the weekend of the wedding."

"Oh, that." Candace made a show of straightening the pages of whatever wedding project she'd been working on.

"You knew. And you didn't warn me." Just as Candace had known about that miserable mistake Amelia had made ten months ago. Candace was the only one Amelia had told, and then only because she'd had to offer some explanation for suddenly switching to the Thursday-Sunday shifts—days when Toby would be at a racetrack somewhere.

"I didn't know until a couple of days ago. But it's been months since you two hooked up and split up, Amelia. You should be able to be civil to each other. Or if there's still something between you, maybe you can see where it leads."

Realization dawned and the betrayal winded her. Candace had a notorious reputation at the hospital for trying to pair up people. But because of their shared pain and shared past, Amelia had never expected her friend to practice that annoying habit on her. "You're matchmaking. With *me*. How could you?"

Candace's gaze softened. "Honey, Neal is dead. You're not."

Amelia flinched. "You don't need to remind me. I loved your brother. I still do."

"I loved him, too. And he loved you. You made the last year of his life better. Amelia, we don't have to forget him, but he's been gone three years and we have to move on. You spend most of your time alone in your apartment, reading romances or watching sappy old movies. You need to get out more."

"Not with Toby Haynes!"

"He's the only guy you've dated since Neal."

"We didn't date. We had sex."

"So you skipped a few preliminaries. Big deal. Besides, Vincent wants us to keep an eye on him."

"On Toby? Why?"

"Because of the wreck."

At a loss, Amelia shook her head. "What wreck?"

"The one last weekend that gave Toby a grade-three concussion. Vincent claims Toby's one of those alpha males who refuses to admit to any weakness, so he asked Toby to fly over here and keep an eye on us. But we're really watching him. Sneaky, huh?"

Vincent wasn't the only sneaky one. Amelia stabbed her fingers into her hair, yanked and silently screamed, *This cannot be happening.* "He looks fine."

"And since you worked in neurology before transferring to the burn unit, you know how deceiving head injuries can be. One of us—preferably you, me or Madeline—should be with him whenever he leaves the hotel, since we know what postconcussion syndrome looks like," Candace said. "And I have the name of a Monaco neurologist. Toby's supposed to check in regularly." She dug in her purse and offered a business card to Amelia.

Amelia took it with about as much enthusiasm as she would an open test tube of the Ebola virus. "I'm surprised you didn't ask me to share his suite."

"I was hoping you'd volunteer."

Amelia narrowed her eyes. "You'd better be joking."

Candace gave her an enigmatic smile.

"I could hate you for this."

"No, Amelia, you can't. We were almost family, and you can't hate family."

Ha. Shows what she knew. Amelia's parents detested each other. Their virulent screaming matches were legendary in the neighborhood. Her father might not be able to walk, but he sure could bellow and curse. And her mother didn't take his verbal abuse silently. More often than not, she provoked it.

"If he's so bad off, why did the doctors clear him for travel?"

"To keep him away from racing. There's some rule that says if a sick or injured driver can make one lap around the track and then hand the car off to a relief driver, he can still earn points. Or something like that. Vincent didn't want to risk Toby trying to make those laps when he's unstable."

Which only confirmed Amelia's opinion that adrenaline junkies didn't know what was good for them. If the man had to be forced to take time off when he was incapacitated—

"Consider taking shifts managing the best man as one of your maid-of-honor duties," Candace stated firmly.

If she didn't love Candace so much, she would tell her to take her maid-of-honor tribute and insert it like a suppository. "I *really* could hate you for this," she repeated.

"Nah, you're just miffed because you can't keep running. And because Toby makes you feel something."

Amelia didn't want to feel anything. Numbness was safer. It allowed her to make logical decisions instead of impetuous ones. If the right man ever came along to replace Neal, then he would gently coax her emotions back to life. He would not turn her into a quivering mass of screaming nerves on her coffee table, her floor, her bed and in her shower.

Toby had turned her into a stranger that night ten months ago. Someone passionate, impulsive, impractical and without restraint—a combination guaranteed to result in disaster.

Someone she never wanted to be again.

"Feeling lucky tonight?"

Amelia startled and gasped at the sound of Toby's low-pitched voice rumbling in her ear. His warm breath stirred the fine hairs on her neck.

How did he sneak up on her that way? He'd done so numerous times during the days when Vincent had been in the hospital. She wouldn't even know he was on the floor and then—bam!—he'd materialize behind her, whisper something outrageous in her ear and rattle her nerves like leaves in a hurricane.

She turned away from the craps table. Surprise stole her words and glued her feet to the carpet. Gone was the jean-clad invitation to sin she'd come to know and avoid. In his place stood a man sexier than any other in Le Sun Casino. Correction: sexier than any man in the entire Monte Carlo Casino complex. Maybe even in all of Monaco.

Toby had tamed his golden hair and shaved his stubborn block of jaw. He looked dashing, debonair, suave…all those words she'd read but never used.

Like the blond James Bond. Only better.

He certainly left her shaken *and* stirred. "I—I don't gamble, so luck doesn't come into it."

"No?"

"No, but that doesn't mean I don't enjoy trying to figure out how different games work." With a flip of her hand she indicated the black tux adorning his tall, broad-shouldered athletic frame to *GQ* perfection. "I thought you'd lost your luggage."

"I did, but our helpful concierge pointed me toward the shops when you refused."

She didn't feel guilty for that. Well, maybe just a twinge, given his concussion. She scanned the brightly lit circus decor of the room, looking beneath the colorful carousel dome in the center, past the numerous slot machines and other games of chance and over the finely dressed guests. She didn't spot her suitemates.

"Where's Candace?" The bride had agreed to take the first Toby-watching shift. Amelia had broken away from the group to wander around looking for celebrities before Toby joined them. She adored entertainment magazines, and

Monaco—the casino in particular—was packed with famous faces. Too bad it would be tacky to collect autographs.

"Candace said something about the three of them heading to the Café Divan for dinner and sent me after you. Hungry?"

"Not really. You go ahead."

His silvery-blue gaze coasted from her French-twisted hair to her bronze silk evening gown with its bust-enhancing lace bodice and chiffon godet skirt that gave the impression of curves—curves her matchstick figure didn't naturally have. He finally reached her ridiculously high heels and then took a leisurely return trip. She felt as glamorous as a Hollywood starlet in this gown—doubly so when Toby's appreciative gaze returned to hers.

"You look good, sugar. Good enough to eat."

Her skin scorched. Memories bombarded her. She snuffed them and mentally searched her barren brain for a polite way to send him back to Candace before she weakened. "Thank you."

But then she noted the groove between his eyebrows and his slight flinch when a woman beside him squealed over a win. "Do you have a headache?"

He shrugged. "S'probably jet lag."

Compassion she did not want to feel invaded her. Postconcussion syndrome often included headaches. "It's too soon for jet lag. That'll hit tomorrow or the next day. You should get out of these bright lights and away from the noise."

"Not leaving your side. Bride's orders."

Amelia stifled a frustrated growl over Candace's blatant matchmaking. She would chew out her meddling friend later for ditching her shift early, because there was no doubt what this was—a handoff.

Amelia nodded toward the exit. "Let's walk outside. The

fresh air might help your head. If it doesn't, I have acetaminophen in my room."

His lips quirked. "Inviting me to your room already?"

Smacking him wouldn't improve his headache, so she restrained the impulse. Barely. "You can wait in the hall."

"First let's find a quiet restaurant somewhere," he said. "I could eat."

Hope kicked in her chest. Ditching him couldn't be as easy as passing him back to Candace, could it? "Why don't you join the others? I heard the food's good."

"No point in staying in the casino. I don't gamble either."

Which was an odd thing to say given his occupation was a huge gamble *with his life*.

Within moments he'd handed a message and a big tip to a casino employee to inform Candace, Stacy and Madeline that he and Amelia were leaving. He guided her out of the building with a warm hand on her waist that she couldn't outrun no matter how fast she toddled on her heels.

The cool night air enveloped her. She struggled with her wrap. Toby lifted the filmy fabric. His fingertips brushed her nape and then he smoothed his palms across her shoulders and down her arms in a wide, warm nerve-tingling swath. She silently cursed her telling shiver and hustled down the sidewalk.

Twisting to dislodge the hand at her waist, she glanced back toward the postcard view of the building. "The casino is my favorite landmark in all of Monaco, especially when it's all lit up like this. It looks like a giant wedding cake."

A line of expensive cars circled the Place Du Casino, the kind of cars she'd only seen in movie magazines and on her long-term male teenage patients' hot-rod calendars. She shifted her gaze to the man walking so close beside her that their shoulders and hands bumped. Not surprisingly the Ferraris and Lamborghinis and other overpriced and overpowered toys held his attention.

His gaze caught hers. "Nice wheels."

"Testosterone, tires, trouble. Those three T's are the bane of the burn unit."

"Is that why you hate drivers?"

"I don't hate drivers," she answered quickly—too quickly, if his skeptical expression was an indication.

"Sugar, you were the frost queen to every driver who visited Vincent in the hospital."

"I was not."

One arched golden eyebrow argued silently.

"Okay, so I don't see the point in needlessly risking your life for sport. It's just…stupid."

His chuckle surprised her. She'd insulted him and his profession. Why would he laugh? "So that's why you're playing hard to get."

"I am not playing at anything."

He took her elbow and guided her past the fountains and sculptures of Casino Square and across the street. The warmth of his firm grip weakened her knees.

"Most women want me because I'm fast on the track and slow in the sack. But not you, Amelia. Since the driver thing doesn't flip your toggle switch, then it must be me that starts your engine. So what's the draw? My buff bod or my Southern charm?"

The teasing twinkle in his eyes made her pulse skip. A laugh gurgled from her throat before she could block it. "It's certainly not your humility."

"It's only ego if you can't deliver the goods. I can."

"Oh, *puh-lease*."

He pulled her to a stop on the sidewalk beneath an iron

lamppost. His gaze locked on hers and his big body loomed above her. "I did. And I will."

The intent look in his eyes stole her breath. He was going to kiss her if she didn't move fast, but her muscles seemed sluggish. Toby tempted her to ignore every last vestige of common sense and self-preservation.

Last time she'd fallen into bed with him looking for comfort, but instead of solace she'd found passion—passion far beyond anything she'd shared with Neal. And her body's betrayal had alarmed her. If she could feel so much for a man she didn't love and wasn't even sure she liked, how devastated would she be if she let herself come to care about him and then had to live through his self-destructive behavior?

She'd be her mother all over again.

She had to get rid of Toby Haynes. The sooner, the better.

He lifted his hand toward her face. Amelia ducked out of reach at the last possible second. Her brain thanked her. Her body did not. Her skin tingled and her breasts ached with the need to be touched. "Maybe we should go back to the hotel."

A salacious smile slanted his lips. "Now you're talking."

"And eat in the dining room." She gave him her best don't-mess-with-me glare, the one that snapped even the most quarrelsome patient back into line, but at the same time she noticed the lines around his mouth and eyes had deepened. He was dead on his feet, most likely with fatigue—another post-concussion symptom.

At times such as this she wished she'd chosen nursing for the paycheck. But, no, caring for others wasn't just her job, it was her vocation. Somewhere deep inside her an empathy switch engaged any time she saw someone in pain. That meant she couldn't walk away from this man and potential disaster no matter how loudly her internal warning sirens blared.

She took his arm and steered him toward the hotel. His bicep tensed beneath her touch, and she released him immediately. Glancing sideways at him, she asked, "Doesn't it ever get old?"

"What's that, sugar?"

"The come-ons. You're exhausted, Toby. If I accepted your invitation for a night of nooky, you'd be hard-pressed to follow through."

He looped an arm around her waist and pulled her close to the radiator-hot length of his body so fast she didn't even have time to gasp. "Try me."

Darn. There went that blip of her pulse again. She flattened her palm on his chest and tried to make light of the situation. "Not tonight. You have a headache."

Her flippant reply made the corners of his lips curl…and there went her toes, doing the same. Why, oh, why did a man so totally wrong for her have so much power over her libido?

And then he kissed her. She stiffened with shock at the initial contact with his mouth. Her stubborn muscles ignored her order to retreat and loosened. His lips were soft. Hot. Insistent. Persuasive. His tongue stroked her bottom lip, slipped inside and tangled with hers. Long fingers cradled her nape, trapping her—not that she'd managed to work up the strength to protest yet.

But she would.

In a second.

Or two.

His other hand painted a trail of goose bumps down her back and settled at her waist. His leather-and-lime scent invaded her lungs and his warmth invaded her body. Her reasoning powers left through the same open door.

Why him? Why did Toby Haynes—daredevil extraordinaire—have to be the one to sweep her off her feet? Why couldn't he be as gentle and considerate as the other men she dated, men who asked before each kiss and caress? *Because then you'd turn him down. Right?* Why did her body revel in his high-handedness?

She really had to stop him. But one kiss melted into two and then three. She clung to the lapels of his tux as her thoughts spiraled out of control. This wasn't wise. But he tasted good, felt good, smelled good. Every cell in her body hummed to life.

Toby shifted, leaning back against a nearby building and pulling her between his thighs. As if she weren't hot enough already, heat radiated off the stone wall, making her skin tight and dry. The lace of her bodice rasped her sensitive nipples with each shuddered breath. His hand slid lower, cupping her bottom, heating her flesh and pulling her closer. The hard ridge of his erection scorched her belly through the thin silk of her dress, shocking her into awareness of where she was, what she was doing and with whom.

Oh, God. Not again. Didn't you learn anything last time?

She planted her palms on his chest and wrenched her mouth free. His heart thumped fast and steady beneath her palm. Backing away, she wiped her damp mouth with the back of her hand as if that would wipe away the mistake she'd made.

"Find another playmate, Toby. I'm not interested."

His gaze raked her face, her body, lingering on her breasts, and then returned to her eyes. He didn't say a word, but his expression—and her racing heart—called her a liar. He slowly eased himself away from the wall.

She hugged her wrap around her and walked toward the hotel. Even if she were foolish enough to overlook his profession, she'd heard the other drivers who'd visited Vincent

joke about Toby's short attention s~~p~~
legendary number of conquests.

Toby was all about temporary. She wanted t~~o~~
she wanted forever without fear or conflict. Un
her neglected hormones didn't understand the ~~~~pt of
choosing wisely.

She had to find a way to avoid being alone with him or else her month in this fairy-tale kingdom would feel like an eternity running from the castle dragon.

"I'm sorry," Madeline replied on Tuesday morning.

Disappointment wrapped around Amelia like a boa constrictor. The rapidly descending elevator left her stomach behind. "It's okay. I understand."

She hoped her suitemate didn't hear the dismay in her voice. "You have fun with your tour guide. And, Madeline, if a vacation romance with him is what you're after, then I hope it works out for you."

She turned her attention to Stacy, the third occupant of the elevator. Amelia had only met Stacy a few times before this trip and she didn't know her very well, but she had to enlist aid while Candace wasn't around to interfere and she couldn't be picky. "Stacy, any chance you'll have some free time to take a Toby-watching shift?"

Stacy tilted her head. "Explain to me what you meant when you said you 'accidentally' slept with him."

Amelia winced. Leave it to Candace's accountant to want a logical explanation instead of the sketchy facts Amelia had offered—namely that Toby was trying to pick up where he and Amelia had left off ten months ago and she wasn't interested.

"I'd had a rotten week. That Sunday I'd lost a long-term patient who left behind a grieving pregnant fiancée. Tues-

...ay was the anniversary of the day Neal and I had planned to get married. And then Wednesday Candace and Vincent announced their engagement. Don't get me wrong, I was— *I am*—thrilled for them, but it was just too much all at once, I guess. That night Toby asked me to go to dinner after my shift, and against my better judgment I accepted and…well, you know the rest."

Stacy nodded and her turquoise eyes filled with sympathy. "All three incidents reminded you of what you'd lost, and you didn't want to be alone. Toby was there, and you're attracted to him so—"

"Believe me, I don't want to be attracted. He's totally wrong for me. He's reckless and overconfident and—"

"I don't think he's overconfident," Madeline interrupted. "Look at him. He's rich, gorgeous and successful. He certainly knows how to make a woman feel good. You could do worse. Candace is right, Amelia. You've been mourning too long. It's time to get back in the game. I wouldn't expect forever from Toby, but you should consider him for a vacation fling. You know, to oil your rusty hinges."

The idea both titillated and repelled her. "No, thank you. I'm not the fling type."

"Honey, anybody can be the fling type given sufficient motivation," Madeline said.

Stacy touched her arm. "I'll do what I can to run interference, but remember I'm not a medical professional. The only thing I know about concussions is what I've seen on the Discovery Channel, and that's not much."

"I'll tell you what to look for."

"Stacy, don't forget your delicious French chocolatier," Madeline added. "Franco might have something to say about how you spend your time."

Stacy blushed and ducked her head.

Amelia struggled to hide her grimace. From what she'd learned last night when the women had returned from the casino, both Stacy and Madeline had met men who might monopolize their non-wedding-planning hours. That meant Amelia would be on her own most of the time, because Candace certainly wasn't going to help her avoid Toby. In fact, the bride-to-be seemed determined to do the opposite.

The elevator doors opened. Dread knotted Amelia's stomach, but she squared her shoulders and walked with the others toward the small, private hotel dining room for the wedding-cake sampling. She could handle this. She wasn't emotionally fragile anymore. The anniversary of her nonwedding didn't hurt as much these days, and she'd avoid alcohol—both contributing factors to her stumble into Toby's arms.

She blamed her overzealous reaction to his kiss last night on the element of surprise combined with strolling down the moonlit sidewalks of Monaco—a magical place where princes really did marry commoners.

Even fairy tales have flaws, her practical side interjected. Monaco royalty hadn't exactly lived a charmed life.

Being swept off her feet was fine for fantasies and fairy tales, but choosing a mate for practical reasons instead of letting her hormones and pheromones rule gave her a better chance of having a successful marriage.

In the meantime, she'd simply devote herself one hundred percent to the wedding arrangements. A man's man like Toby Haynes would avoid the girlie stuff the way he would a full-body wax. Sure, he'd agreed to carry out his best-man duties, and he and Amelia would have to work together on the Jack and Jill shower and the wedding-party luncheon, but she'd bet her trusty Camry he wouldn't be caught dead sampling wedding cake, picking out flowers or choosing bridesmaids' dresses.

All she had to do was keep busy with maid-of-honor tasks and he'd stay out of her way.

And then Amelia stepped into the dining room and her plan imploded. Toby stood beside the linen-draped table, talking to Candace and a chef. He looked perfectly comfortable and devastatingly attractive in pressed khakis and a pale blue polo. His jaw gleamed from a recent shave and his hair was still damp from his shower.

His gaze met hers. He toasted her with a crystal glass, and one corner of his mouth lifted in a knowing smile.

She gulped. So much for Plan A.

Plan B, where are you?

Three

"You can run, sugar, but you can't hide." Toby stuck his boot in the gap before Amelia could shut the door in his face Wednesday morning.

He pushed his way into her suite. She'd given him the slip after the cake thing yesterday and gone shopping with her suitemates. Today he'd stick to her tight little tush like a tattoo.

He gave her the once-over. Twice. She looked adorable in her prissy white ruffled nightie with pink cheeks and bedhead. He'd always found bedhead kinda sexy—especially if he was the one who'd caused it.

"Toby, it's early. Why are you here?"

The early-morning huskiness of her voice revved his engine.

"Found a couple of places for the parties. You need to see them before I sign contracts. The car will be here in thirty minutes. Need help dressing?" He didn't expect her to say yes, but if she did, the car would have to wait.

"I haven't even had coffee. Go away and come back in an hour." Shoving her hair away from her face with both hands, she wandered deeper into the sitting room. The sun streaming through the wide window made her long gown damn near transparent. He bit back a groan. Granted, Amelia didn't have the *Playboy*-bunny curves of most of the women he dated and bedded, but the curves she had were in all the right places and looked mighty fine at the moment.

Without looking away from the mouthwatering view, he unclipped his phone from his belt. "I'll ask the driver to have coffee waiting in the limo. C'mon, sugar, move your tail—unless prancing around in front of that window in your sexy see-through gown is an invitation for me to spend the day here with you."

She gasped, looked down and crossed her arms over her breasts and torso. "Go. Away."

"Not happening. Get dressed or undressed. Either works for me."

The flush on her cheeks deepened and her fingers fisted, but she didn't move.

"Need help making up your mind?" He stepped toward her.

She whirled on her heel, hustled through one of the four doors opening off the main room and shut the panel—hard.

He grinned. He could always count on Amelia doing the exact opposite of his usual women. Most would have dropped the gown—if they'd been wearing one when they'd opened the door in the first place—and invited him to spend the day naked.

She was hell on his ego but a good outlet for his frustrated competitive nature.

He made a quick call to order her breakfast and considered calling home to check on his teams, but he calculated the time difference and returned the phone to its clip. Nobody would be in the shop this late on a Tuesday night.

Thinking about the shop made him antsy. He started pacing.

He'd hired a relief driver to keep his car on the track and keep earning owner points. Daily e-mails from his crew chief kept him up to date on the kid's progress. But it wasn't the same as being there. With his teams. In the driver's seat. In the groove of the track. In the winner's circle.

But Vincent—damn his friend's sorry hide—had threatened to pull Hôtel Reynard's twenty million sponsor dollars not just from Toby but from Haynes Racing's other two teams if Toby didn't stay away from the track until the neurologist cleared him. Toby could find another sponsor, but he wasn't willing to lose Vincent's friendship. Especially when his buddy was right. Toby had no business risking himself or other drivers by getting behind the wheel when one little bump could upset his equilibrium and put him and anybody near him into the wall.

One of his laps around the sitting room carried him past the dining room table. A calendar caught his eye and halted his steps. Each square listed the wedding-planning activities for each bridesmaid by time and location over the next four weeks. Hair appointments, dress fittings, manicures, massages…

Toby pulled out his PDA and noted each of Amelia's assigned tasks. If she dodged him again, he'd find her. He'd barely stuffed the electronic organizer back into his pocket when her bedroom door opened.

He turned and his whistle died on his lips.

A white eyelet sundress with string straps crisscrossed

her chest, with a narrow ruffle leading from the V-neck down and around the hem, which hung just above her knees. A waist-high bow on her side cinched in the fabric and reminded him how delicate she'd been perched above him. Long, lean legs. Small, round breasts. Slender enough he'd thought he might snap her in two. And then she'd taken him inside and he hadn't been able to think at all.

If he pulled that bow, would her dress open for him? Would she be wearing plain white cotton panties like last time? And no way could she be wearing a bra under there. His pulse raced.

A matching eyelet headband kept her hair off her face, and low-heeled white sandals revealed shocking-pink toenails. Funny, before Monaco he'd only seen her two ways: Naked and in hospital scrubs. She'd even worn scrubs the night he'd taken her to dinner because he hadn't given her time to go home and change—her clothes or her mind.

He'd never pictured her in street clothes. But that was probably because he spent most of his time picturing her naked. She'd been so efficient on the job that her girlie-girl attire was a surprise. "Nice."

The white bangles on her wrist tinkled as she fidgeted with her purse. "Thank you. Where are we going?"

"Hôtel de Paris and a private villa."

"Why a private villa?"

"Thought the brunch should be relaxed instead of formal. We'll have it catered." He opened the suite door, motioned for her to precede him into the hall and then followed her out. "There are beds at either place in case somebody has too much champagne and needs to sleep it off."

"That's probably a good idea." She hustled to the elevator as if trying to outrun him.

He stepped in the cubicle beside her and braced a shoulder against the wall. As usual, the rapid descent caused the floor to buckle and pitch beneath him. Damn, he hated this. He didn't even want to consider what he'd do if the doc was wrong and the vertigo didn't go away.

It will go away. It has to.

"Are you okay?" she asked.

"Fine."

"Then why do you have a white-knuckle grip on the railing? Are you claustrophobic?"

"Sugar, I spend hours strapped in a race car. Drivers can't be claustrophobic."

She fixed him with her patented get-over-yourself stare.

"Balance problems," he admitted grudgingly several seconds later.

"From the wreck?"

"Yeah."

"Is it just sudden movements or all movement? Up and down? Or lateral, too?" She'd kicked into nurse mode. It turned him on.

Sad, Haynes. Sad.

"Sudden. Whichever way."

The elevator doors opened. She linked her arm through his elbow. "Lean on me if you need to."

He wasn't about to tell her the dizziness had passed— not when he had her close enough to smell the flowery scent of her hair and feel the warm softness of her breast against his arm. "Car should be out front."

Her sandals clicked-clacked across the marble floor. Another first. He was used to her in those god-awful ugly but silent nursing shoes. The tap-tap-tap of her heels danced along his already attentive nerves, jacking his awareness of her up another level.

The driver he'd hired opened the rear door to a black

Benz as they approached. Amelia's steps slowed. "You weren't kidding about the limo. I've never ridden in one. I guess you have?"

He shrugged. "Racing's a fast life. Not just on the track. Limos, jets, helicopters are all part of the deal."

"Rented, right?" Her voice sounded tight. Her hazel eyes couldn't get any wider. She stared at the car as if she expected it to bite.

"The limos are rented. The rest we own."

The shocked gaze bounced back to him. "You own jets and helicopters?"

"Haynes Racing Inc. owns two private jets and a chopper plus an assortment of haulers and motor homes. We keep pilots and drivers for each on salary."

"That seems a little…extravagant."

"Getting to and from racetracks and appearances is part of the job, and a lot of business is conducted during the ride. Most teams are similarly equipped. It's just transportation, Amelia. You get used to it."

"Teams? I thought you were just a driver."

Just a driver. His muscles knotted. She knew nothing about him. And she sure as hell didn't know about his old man's prediction that Toby would never amount to anything.

You're just a pretty face, Tobias. You'll never be nothing else. And when yer looks and charm dry up you'll be just a outta-work bum like me.

A drunk outta-work bum with a mean streak a mile wide and a razor-sharp tongue despite the slurring words.

Toby shook off the bitter memory. He'd scrapped and fought to make sure he wasn't "just a" anything. His talent, interests and finances were carefully diversified. These days you couldn't pick up a sports magazine without finding an article about him between the covers, and stories about HRI filled the pages of racing magazines and a few business journals. He loved every aspect of his business, from push broom to promotion.

Fans and fame had their perks, but he had to admit it was nice to be an unrecognized regular guy—for the most part—in Monaco. "I own HRI. We run three race teams and drivers."

Most women would be impressed with the wealth and power involved in being a team owner as well as a top driver. Apparently not this one. Amelia's lips pursed as if she'd sucked a lemon. She blinked and eyed the hotel as if considering going back inside.

He unhooked their arms and stroked a hand down her spine, stopping an inch short of her butt—not because he wanted to but because she was skittish. He nudged her forward. "Breakfast is waiting. Climb in."

She entered the limo slowly, her head turning every which way, as if she were afraid she'd miss some minute detail. He tended to take a comfortable ride for granted. There were always people to get him where he needed to go, and since he couldn't drive until his head cleared up, having a driver in Monaco was a necessity.

Amelia settled on the bench seat and caressed the dove-gray glove-soft leather slow and easy, as if committing each inch to memory. The way she'd stroked him that night. His muscles clenched. He released a pent-up breath on a silent whistle and followed her in, but instead of sitting beside her he settled across from her so he could watch her captivated expression.

"Sir?" The driver's voice forced Toby's attention away from Amelia's killer legs. Louis extended a tray with two coffee cups, a carafe and a plate of éclairs.

Toby took it from him. "Thanks, Louis."

"You're welcome, sir." Louis closed the door and circled the car to climb behind the wheel.

Toby sat the tray on the seat beside Amelia. The suck-a-lemon look replaced the enchantment on her face. "It won't work."

"What?"

"Trying to soften me up with my favorite foods."

Okay, so he wasn't above using whatever leverage he had to woo her back between the sheets.

"Just ordering something you said you liked." He filled the coffee mugs and then slid back to fasten his seat belt. "I'd rather be serving you breakfast in bed."

She rolled her eyes, buckled herself in and then reached for a china cup. "Give it up, Toby. I'm not going to sleep with you again."

"Ever hear it's not wise to challenge a driver? We're a competitive bunch."

The car eased away from the curb. She pinched off a corner of an éclair and popped it between her lips. The blissful expression on her face had him shifting for a more comfortable position, but the slow glide of her tongue sweeping her icing-covered lips convinced him there wasn't one. His pants were cutting off circulation to one of his favorite parts. He straightened his legs in the space between the seats.

Her gaze found his. "Why can't you accept that I'm not interested and give up?"

"Because you strip me naked with your eyes every time we're in the same room."

She choked on a bite of éclair, chewed rapidly and gulped coffee. *"I do not."*

Her scandalized whisper sparked another flashback to their night together. "Sugar, you can tease me all you want, but don't lie. Not to me. Not to yourself. You want me."

She opened her mouth to argue, closed it again and then frowned at him. Her fingers fussed with the ruffled hem of her dress, and each pleating fidget lifted her skirt an inch or two and flashed him a glimpse of smooth upper thighs. "I do not tease."

He couldn't help laughing. He nodded to her restless fingers. "You do it without even trying. And, sugar, you slay me. Every time."

Her gaze dropped to her lap. She flattened her hand and then looked at the bulge behind his zipper. Her eyes widened and her lips parted. She ducked her head and focused on finishing her pastry with the intensity of a brain surgeon at work.

How could a woman be so totally unaware of her appeal? And why did this scrawny little gal turn him on with zero effort when others couldn't do so with a bag full of tricks?

He'd find out. And once he did, like any magic trick, she wouldn't impress him once he knew the secret.

Toby Haynes was her worst nightmare.

An adrenaline junkie.

Times three.

It wasn't enough for him to drive at breakneck speeds. He enabled others to do so, too.

She couldn't get back to her suite fast enough and hustled down the carpeted hall with one goal in mind—putting a wall between her and her tormentor. She just couldn't figure him out. Why her? And what was up with this morning?

The staggering opulence of the villa and the Churchill Suite at Hôtel de Paris—the places Toby had chosen as possible settings for the luncheon and bridal shower—had set her romantic heart aflutter, but what rattled the most was how effortlessly Toby had fit into both places. He'd strolled into each venue wearing his faded jeans, battered boots and what felt like a silk shirt and looked right at home, whereas she'd been afraid to touch anything for fear of breaking something.

She stopped outside her door and scowled up at him. "You never had any intention of having a keg party, did you?"

His smile turned wicked and she knew she'd been had. Again. During those months visiting Vincent in the hospital, Toby had apparently relished getting a rise out of her. He'd provoked her at every opportunity.

"Is your good-ole-boy shtick just an act?"

"I grew up dirt-poor and barely made it through high school. Don't let a little spit shine fool you." He plucked her key card from her hand and opened her door. And then he put *her* key in *his* front pocket.

"Give me my key."

"Later. Let's hit the pool." He forced her into the suite by the simple act of moving forward. She could either hold her ground and end up plastered against him or get out of the way. A tiny reckless part of her wanted the former. Of course, she ignored that annoying, foolish voice and moved.

He closed the door, sealing them into the suite. All four bedroom doors stood open.

"Hello? Anybody here?" she called out. Silence greeted her and her heart sank. Her suitemates were out. So much for her plan to turn Toby over to one of the wedding party. She faced him. "I have things to do this afternoon."

"What could be more interesting than spending time with the best man?"

"I'd like to go sightseeing. Alone."

"I'll set something up. Tomorrow."

"I don't want to go swimming." Lovely. Now she sounded like a fractious child.

She hadn't visited the pool and rooftop garden yet, and while she'd like to, she'd prefer to save that experience for later, when Toby wasn't in the building. Or the principality. Wearing a swimsuit seemed half-dressed—and half-dressed was almost naked. And naked was not something she wanted to be around tempta—*ahem*—Toby.

"Not much point in having a private pool and hot tub if we never use 'em. And the sign says Clothing Optional." His eyebrows waggled.

Her jaw dropped open. She snapped it closed. He could *not* be serious. "Not interested."

He checked his watch—an expensive-looking ultrathin gold piece. "Lunch will be served on the patio poolside."

She folded her arms and stubbornly shook her head.

A muscle twitched in his jaw and his unblinking stare pinned her to the carpet. "I'm not supposed to swim alone."

Her molars clicked together on that blatantly manipulative statement even though he looked as though he'd rather eat worms than admit it. Duty sucked and Candace would pay dearly for this. Amelia wasn't sure how yet, but her friend would definitely pay.

"I will have lunch with you because I'm hungry and I'll sit in the garden while you swim *with your trunks on*. I have to deal with naked men at work all the time. I shouldn't have to suffer them on my vacation."

Wait. That didn't sound quite right.

And watching Toby's buff body wouldn't exactly be an arduous chore. Unfortunately. Keeping her common sense and hormones separated would be the real challenge. She needed to build a mental Wall of China between the two warring factions of her brain.

"Spoilsport." He winked. "But I'll make you a deal. I'll wear my suit if you'll wear yours."

She bit back a frustrated growl and barely resisted the urge to stomp her feet like the spoiled daddy's princess she'd been before her father's injury. "You are a master manipulator."

That smile—the toe-curling one she detested—slid across his lips again. "I'm a master of many things. As you well know. Making you sing, for one. How many orgasms did you have that night? A record-breaking number, didn't you say?"

Seeds of her mother's infamous temper cracked open inside her, and tendrils of fury sprouted, shooting for an outlet—her mouth. Her teen years had been filled with hurtful words shouted through the house, and it frightened her that she wanted—no, *needed*—to bellow and throw things at Toby. But she wouldn't. She had more control than that. But just in case, she turned on her heel, stomped into her bedroom and shut the door.

A knock sounded before she could lock herself in the bathroom. "If you're not by the pool in twenty minutes, I'm coming back and hauling you out. With or without your suit."

She threw her sandal at the door and then stared aghast and pressed her hands against her cheeks. She never had tantrums. Ever.

Toby Haynes brought out the worst in her, and that was why, no matter what he said or did, she could not afford to get involved with him again.

But how could she avoid certain disaster?

Focus on his injury.

Treat him like a patient.

You never have sex with your patients.

Amelia had ditched him again.

Ticked off, frustrated and determined to track her down, Toby exited her empty suite just as the elevator chimed.

Amelia stepped out of the cubicle and scowled. "Were you in my room?"

"Yep. Went to get you. Said I would." He took in the filmy black fabric covering her to midthigh, her bare legs, the sparkly sandals on her feet and the shopping bag in her hand. She'd changed into her swimsuit. Score one for the Haynes team. "Where have you been?"

"I had to buy sunscreen and get a new key since mine was stolen."

"Borrowed." He pushed open the door to the pool area and the sharp tang of chlorine filled his nose. "Water's waiting."

But Amelia didn't move. She tilted her head, sending her hair gliding across her shoulders. His gut clenched in memory of the caress of those silky strands.

Great. Now he had a hair fetish to go with his AWOL equilibrium and a ban from the track.

"You thought I'd stood you up, didn't you?"

He refused to reply.

"Not used to women saying no, Toby?"

No, he wasn't. In fact, he received more offers each season than an entire football team could handle—and he was usually the one who said no thanks.

"I want to swim. I may be sidelined from racing, but I still need to stay in shape." And according to the doctor, he needed a babysitter to do it. That irked the hell out of him, but if he wanted to make up lost ground when he returned to the track, he'd need to have his A-game ready. No slacking off in his training schedule. His balance issues meant most of his favorite sports were out of the question. Temporarily. He had to stick to swimming and working out in the hotel gym with a trainer.

Amelia's gaze, more green than gold at the moment, coasted over him, lingering on his bare legs. Every cell in his body sparked to life. She slipped past him though the door. He deliberately crowded her, savoring her gasp, her flowery scent and the brush of her body against his.

"You work out?" Her voice sounded a tad breathless. Good.

"Every day. Driving's more than just turning the wheel. A guy needs stamina—which I'm sure you recall is good other places besides the racetrack. What about you? You gonna be able to keep up with me, sugar? Here in the pool, I mean. We both know how well you handle me in other places."

She took off across the flagstones like a driver putting the hammer down in a qualifying race against the clock and called over her shoulder, "I can swim. How is your head? Any pain?"

"I'm fine. Looks like we have the pool to ourselves." Excellent.

She stopped ten yards away beside the deep end and faced him. "Does the bright light bother you? Are you having any other problems, like a decreased sense of smell?"

Her nurse voice clued him in, but still he asked, "Why?"

"Those, along with a compromised sense of taste, are common side effects of a concussion."

"I'm fine. But if you want to play doctor, I'm more than willing."

After giving him a disgusted eye roll, she turned a full circle to inspect the area. "This is beautiful. You'd never know we're on top of a building. It's more like an oasis, and with those tented double loungers I almost expect to see a sheikh stroll past."

Toby scanned what he hoped would be a setting for seduction to see what put that dreamy, awed note in her voice. Citrus trees and flowering plants overflowed from giant pots around the patio. The retractable roof had been opened to let in the sunlight. Despite being surrounded by four walls—walls you couldn't see because of the dense foliage—a gentle breeze rustled the leaves and stirred the air. Probably a well-concealed fan. It didn't do much to cool his overheated skin.

"Sheikh fantasies trip your trigger?"

Her nose lifted. "My fantasies are none of your business."

He loved it when she got snippy, because in the sack she was anything but uptight. He liked the contrast of the prim-and-proper nurse and the sensualist lover. "Wrong, sugar. Making your fantasies come true is my sole ambition."

He peeled off his shirt and tossed it on a lounger and then kicked off his leather flip-flops and rubbed his hands together in anticipation of caressing Amelia's pale, smooth skin. "Take off your top and let me help you with that sunscreen."

She stilled, and then a slow, smug little smile curved her lips as she deposited her bag in a chair, then reached into it and withdrew an aerosol can. "No, thanks. I bought the spray-on kind."

Sneaky. But he could get around that, especially since he knew she wanted to get her hands on him. Even now she checked out his pecs and abs and a flush darkened her cheekbones. His nipples and groin tightened.

"Then you can rub in mine. I love the feel of your hands on me." Hell, he craved it. He'd lost count of the times he'd woken up hard in the past months from dreaming about her touch. Not even other women had blunted his need.

But that was only because Amelia had ended the affair before he'd had his fill of her. It was like leaving pit road with less than a full tank of gas or only two new tires. You'd have to come back sooner or later.

"I'll loan you my spray." She unbuttoned her cover-up. Each released button jacked his tachometer up another notch. By the time she shrugged off the concealing shirt his heart was racing and close to redlining.

Have mercy. Her chocolate-brown halter tankini didn't show much skin, but that top offered up her breasts like an all-you-can-eat buffet. He couldn't wait to take a bite.

She stepped out of her sandals and bent to place them neatly beneath a lounge chair. His libido burned rubber in his gut at the sight of her butt in the brief bottoms. He clenched his fists on the need to cup her curves, ease the fabric down and slide into her slick heat from behind.

"I wish the food was here," she said as she straightened. "You could test it and tell me if your taste buds are altered."

He wanted to eat, all right, but food wasn't exactly what he had in mind.

"Don't you nursing types know you're not supposed to eat right before you swim?" His voice sounded hoarse. Eager to get his hands on her, he closed the distance between them. "Food's coming later. C'mon. Let's get wet together."

An irritated gurgle rumbled in her throat. She parked her hands on her hips, revealing a tempting sliver of pale skin between her top and bottom. "Do those ridiculous lines actually work for you?"

Yes, they did. Extremely well. Usually women giggled themselves silly over his good-ole-boy wit. But not Amelia.

Why was she playing hard to get? Despite what she'd said earlier, he didn't believe she only slept with guys offering the picket fence and the gold ring, because she'd slept with him before. Not that they'd done much actual sleeping that night. That could explain why he'd been comatose when she'd slipped out on him without a goodbye other than that cold note.

Did she like the chase? Had she dumped him so he'd have to pursue her again? Because there was no doubting she wanted him. She studied him the way a rookie does his first ride—with quick, shallow breaths, hungry eyes and twitchy fingers.

What game was she playing? Not one for which he had the rule book, that's for damn sure.

"You look good in that suit. Bet you look even better out of it."

She reached for him. Finally. Hallelujah.

But instead of twining herself around him she planted her palms on his chest and shoved. Toby wobbled and fought for balance. He caught Amelia's wrist and held on. If he was going in, she was coming with him.

The cool water closed over his head, muffling her shriek. For a second, the sudden movement disoriented him, but the silky tangle of her legs with his and his feet hitting the tile bottom centered him. He held her close and stared into her surprise-widened eyes through the clear water.

Tightening his arms around her, he pulled her close and kissed her. A hard press of his lips against hers. Nothing openmouthed or as hot as he wanted, because he didn't want to drown. At least not before he'd made Amelia Lambert pay for making him want her and walking away.

Four

You don't drown your patients, nitwit.

And you don't kiss them.

Amelia broke the surface, gasping for air and wondering where in the devil she'd left her common sense. Toby Haynes had once more goaded her into foolish behavior.

And that kiss… She wasn't going to think about it or how she'd almost coiled around him and kissed him back.

Toby surfaced a few yards away.

She tried to ignore her tingling lips and treaded water. "I'm sorry. I shouldn't have pushed you. Are you okay?"

"C'mere." He swam toward her with a predatory glint in his eyes.

Uh-oh. You're in trouble now.

She sculled backward toward the ladder with her gaze locked on the man pursuing her. "Toby, I don't think horseplay is a good idea for a man in your condition."

"You started it." He kept coming.

"You needed cooling off. I thought you wanted to exercise."

"I do. But right now I want payback. You pushed me. You owe me."

"Oh, *puh-lease*. I agreed to lunch, not to be mauled by you." Her hand bumped the ladder. She gripped the cool metal tubing, but before she could swing around and climb out, Toby grasped the rails on either side of her body, caging her between the steel of the ladder at her back and his equally hard body in front. His strong legs trapped hers beneath the water. Warm. Hairy.

"Mauled?" He practically growled the word. His eyes narrowed to silvery-blue slits. "I remember you liking my hands and mouth on you. 'Touch me everywhere,' you said. Correction—you begged."

Yes, she had. Shamelessly. Heat pulsed through her. Gulping, she kept her eyes trained on his face despite the temptation to grasp his broad, muscular shoulders, press herself against his chest and relive that night.

Provoking him wasn't her best move. And reminding him that sleeping with him had been a mistake didn't seem like the wisest course of action at the moment either. As much as he liked challenges, he'd probably insist on proving her wrong.

Get a hold of yourself, Lambert, and get out of this. He may be sexy, but he is also hazardous. To himself and to you.

But how? A challenge?

"I bet you can't beat me in five laps. Or should we make it one? Are you up to a race at all?"

His nostrils flared at the implied insult. "Yes."

"If I win, you lay off the tiresome cliché macho come-ons for five minutes."

"And if I win…" His eyes narrowed. "I get five minutes."

She frowned. "Five minutes of what?"

"Whatever I want."

Her heart rat-a-tat-tatted like a snare drum. She shook her head with enough force to send her wet hair flying. "No."

"I'm not talking about screwing you, sugar. Even at my worst I take longer than five minutes."

A fact she knew all too well. She shivered despite the warmth of the water and the bright sun shining directly overhead.

She didn't gamble, but this was a safe bet. Toby might have a size advantage, he might even be in good shape, but she'd been on the swim team in high school and during her first two years in college. Since then she'd maintained a gym membership and still swam a mile three times a week. His powerful legs would give him a better push off, but if sudden changes of direction were a problem, she'd beat him in the turns. Surely he'd be eating her wake long before five laps?

"You'll keep your hands and penis to yourself?" His hands had wreaked havoc on her control that night. As had the rest of him.

"If you insist."

"I do." She prayed she wouldn't regret this. "Okay. Deal."

He rolled onto his back, displaying his calendar-hunk chest, muscle-gridded belly and narrow hips in brief black trunks as he swam toward the shallow end. "Need a head start?"

"No." She wouldn't take that much advantage. "Do you?"

He chuckled. "Nah."

She breaststroked after him and realized that for the first time she was pursuing him instead of running in the opposite direction. The idea amused her.

Aroused her.

Worried her.

"Trying to psych me out, Amelia?"

She neutralized her expression. "Would it work?"

"Sugar, I play with the big boys. It's going to take more than an itty-bitty nurse to mess with my head."

She couldn't wait to humble him by beating him.

He reached the shallow end and stood. Water streamed from his body and glistened in his chest hair, reminding her of their shared middle-of-the-night shower ten months ago, of chasing droplets across his flesh with her tongue, of him doing the same to her. Goose bumps raced over her skin. Her breath quickened and her muscles tautened. She rolled her shoulders as she walked to the end of the pool, trying to shake off the time-robbing tension that could slow her pace.

Instead of lanes painted on the bottom of the pool to draw boundaries between her and Toby, the beautiful mosaic of tropical fish looked like a living coral reef beneath her. She knew from her guidebook that Monaco royalty had been heavily into oceanography since the 1800s. The legendary Jacques Cousteau had been director of the principality's Oceanographic Museum at one point. As soon as she could escape Toby, Amelia intended to tour the museum this afternoon. Without one irritating driver.

"Sure you're up to this?" she asked and placed a hand on the smooth rounded tile edge. "Five laps is a good distance."

"Chicken?" he countered, mimicking her crouch, and when she shook her head he said, "On three. One. Two. Three."

Amelia exploded off the wall. Toby bumped into her— not hard enough to hurt but enough to knock her off course. She sensed him stopping, standing, and heard him ask if she was all right, but she corrected her course and plowed onward without wasting precious seconds to reply. She wasn't an overly competitive person by nature, but this time she had to win. *Had to.*

He reached the first turn several lengths behind her, but by the second he was closing in. A quick turn and push and then—boom!—he bumped her again. Two things registered. First, she'd underestimated his swimming ability. And second, the turns knocked him sideways and into her path. She adjusted by widening the gap between them.

By the end of her third lap, allowing him five minutes of *whatever* started looking like a real possibility. A nightmare of possibility. She put everything she had into beating him. Her arms and legs protested her furious pace. Her lungs burned. But still he stayed abreast. She couldn't shake him—and she had to. Now. On this final stretch. But with the finish line in sight, he pulled ahead and she knew she was in trouble. She touched the side several seconds after him and slowly stood on rubbery legs.

What had she gotten herself into?

Toby leaned against the tiles, chest heaving, with a smug smile on his face and a promise in his blue eyes. The victor.

And she was the victim of her own foolish overconfidence. "The turns messed you up?"

"Yeah. You want to cry foul?"

"No." He would have beaten her whether he bumped her or not. "Okay, do your worst."

"I never do my worst."

The ego again. She sighed. "What's my forfeit, Toby?"

Before he could answer, the door opened on a pair of uniformed servers pushing a linen-draped table. Lunch had arrived.

"You'll have to wait and see." And with that he launched himself out of the pool in a rippling display of muscle, leaving her anticipat—*dreading* what was to come.

* * *

The fastest car didn't always win the race.

Toby's years in NASCAR had taught him that winning took patience, skill and strategy. Knowing when to hold your ground and when to make your move often meant the difference between first and forty-third place.

"Sure you want to stick with that no-hands rule?" he asked as he laid his cloth napkin on the table. His body idled like a perfectly set-up car waiting to be unleashed on a superspeedway.

Amelia's spoon clanked against her gelato bowl. "Yes."

"I'm good with my hands."

She inhaled deeply through her nose and exhaled again with exaggerated patience. "I know."

"And even better with my—"

"I *know*," she interrupted. A flush flagged her cheeks, and her hazel gaze skidded away from their romantic alcove.

The servers had set up the table in the shade of one of the tents tucked beneath trees and then discreetly departed, exactly as Toby had requested. A breeze stirred the gauzy drapes and strands of Amelia's drying hair.

His taste buds had gone on strike, but not because of his concussion. He'd been too busy thinking about her slender figure beneath that bathing suit and debating how he'd get her naked without using his hands.

He deliberately rubbed his bare feet against hers again beneath the linen tablecloth just because he liked hearing her breath hitch and watching the color rise under her skin. Unless memory had failed him—and he hoped it had—Amelia was easily the most responsive lover he'd ever had. Instead of little hidden pockets of pleasure, her entire body had been one contiguous erogenous zone. No matter where he'd touched, she'd responded. He wanted her to again.

He dragged his big toe along her instep. She abruptly jerked her feet away and shoved back her chair, but the tightening of her nipples rewarded him.

He didn't doubt he could get her back in the sack with a little effort. Probably within the half hour if he used all his tricks. But he didn't want to have to chase her again tomorrow. This time he wanted to get her into his bed and keep her there until he was ready to let her go. That meant revising his plan, taking it slow and steady instead of pedal to the metal.

She'd be a delicious distraction from what he couldn't have, a race he could win and a hunger he could satisfy. God knows he needed a distraction from being away from the track and HRI.

"Toby, I have things to do today. What's my penalty?"

"I haven't decided yet. What are your plans for this afternoon?"

"Nothing you'd be interested in."

"Like?"

"Tourist stuff." She rose and shrugged on her cover-up. "Museums."

It stung a little that she didn't think he'd be interested in museums. Had she, like his father and countless others, written him off as a dumb jock? "I'll have the car waiting in thirty minutes."

"That's not necessary." She gathered her belongings. "And just for future reference, most women take more than thirty minutes to get dressed."

"Not you. You don't waste time caking your face with tubs of makeup that a guy's only gonna smear. After the museums we'll have dinner at the Italian restaurant Vincent's mother booked for the rehearsal dinner. She made reservations based on someone else's recommendation and she asked me to check it out and make sure it's suitable."

Resignation settled over Amelia's face, puckering her brows and tightening her mouth. He had her up against the wall and she knew it.

"Fine," she snapped through barely moving lips.

Strategy worked every time. Pretty soon Amelia would be his. But not today. Today he intended to enjoy the chase.

If anyone had told Amelia she'd enjoy the company of an egotistical, thrill-seeking, smooth-talking ladies' man like Toby Haynes, she would have suggested they have their head examined.

Her pulse skipped as he seated her at a corner table on the colonnade outside the dining room of the ritzy Italian restaurant. Her irregular heartbeat had nothing to do with the brush of Toby's lightly calloused fingers against her nape as he lifted her hair over the back of the chair and everything to do with the breathtaking sunset over the Italian Riviera.

Who do you think you're fooling?

She sighed. Toby's seemingly incidental touches had tantalized, titillated and tortured her in the seven hours since they'd left the pool.

Seven hours. And not once had she wanted to smack him. She couldn't believe it. He'd apparently been on his best behavior, and if she was on edge, it was only because she kept waiting for him to collect her five-minute debt. She didn't doubt he would or that it would be physical. *Intensely* physical.

He might not have aggravated her with an unrelenting stream of flirtatious banter this afternoon, but he'd watched her. The way a predator watches prey it wants to consume. The way a man watches a woman he intends to bed.

The Oceanographic Museum and Aquarium had been

as fascinating as she'd expected. But a museum she hadn't intended to visit—one Toby had coerced her into—had been the highlight of her day. Prince Rainier's extensive collection of antique cars and carriages had entranced her, reminding her of royal processions, old movies and Hollywood glamour. There had been the traditional Mercedes-Benzes and Rolls-Royces she'd expected as well as more exotic cars she'd never heard of. Toby's knowledgeable commentary had only enhanced the experience.

He settled across the table from her. A crisp white shirt stretched over his broad shoulders, accentuating his tan. Fine tufts of golden-blond curls peeked from his cuffs and open collar. "Tomorrow we'll tour the Venturi factory."

She startled when the waiter opened her napkin for her and laid it in her lap before handing her a menu. You didn't get service like that back in Charlotte—at least not in the restaurants she frequented. "What makes you think I'll spend tomorrow with you? You're not my tour guide."

"Because Vincent sent me over here so the bridal party could babysit me, and Candace has dumped me in your lap."

Surprised by his perceptiveness, she shifted in her seat. "You figured that out, huh?"

"Doesn't take a rocket scientist. Vincent wants me away from the track—and he's not averse to calling in a few favors to get what he wants."

Did Toby also realize Candace was shamelessly matchmaking? The idea was too humiliating to contemplate. "What's Venturi?"

"Venturi is a sports car manufacturer here in Monaco."

"Can't stay away from gas-guzzling big engines?"

He leveled a patient look on her and she had to look away. Okay, so she'd been needling him. But she didn't want to like him and today…today she'd enjoyed his company a little too much for comfort. Dangerous territory.

"Venturi has built GT racers for twenty years, but the model I'm interested in is an electric sports car. I want to see how they packed performance into a battery-powered vehicle. I can't test drive it, but you can. I'll ride shotgun and you'll tell me how she feels."

"Do I even want to know how much this car costs?"

"Six hundred."

"Thousand? Dollars?" He nodded and she gulped. "That's a few too many zeros for me. I'll pass."

"You'll love it." The wine steward arrived and Toby asked, "Wine?"

"No, thank you." She didn't dare weaken her willpower with alcohol. He sent the steward away without ordering.

"You shouldn't let me stop you from having wine with your dinner, Toby. Candace said Mrs. Reynard chose this restaurant specifically because of its famous wine cellar."

"I don't drink."

She frowned. Teetotaling didn't fit her image of the fast-living adrenaline junkie she knew him to be. How had she missed that ten months ago? "Why?"

"My dad was a drunk. A mean one. Don't want to turn out like him." He stated it matter-of-factly and opened the menu.

A fissure formed in her preconceived notions of him. "I'm sorry. I didn't know."

"I don't advertise it."

"Did he…hit you?"

"Until I knocked him on his ass."

Sympathy squeezed her heart. You couldn't work in health care and not deal with physical abuse at some time, but it still disturbed her. No matter how fiercely her parents had fought, they'd never hit each other or her. Thrown things? Definitely. But not at anyone. Verbal arrows were their weapons of choice, but even those had been aimed at each other and not Amelia.

"And your mother?"

"Got tired of his abuse and left the day I turned fifteen."

She struggled with the urge to comfort him even though he hadn't asked for it. In fact, his brusque manner discouraged it. "Not a great birthday gift."

"Better than watching him smack her around." Toby signaled the waiter, who immediately rushed over, thereby killing that line of discussion. "Brave enough to let me order for you?"

"I…okay. But I won't eat anything weird or icky."

His smile said *Trust me*, and then he ordered in Italian, his voice deep and shockingly sexy. The waiter departed and Toby answered her surprised gaze with a shrug. "I have an Italian Formula 1 guy working on my engine team. He taught me enough to get by."

"I'm impressed." That wasn't a lie. Unfortunately.

"Good." His eyes narrowed. "Bet you had a mom, apple-pie and homemade-cookies childhood."

Amelia blinked at the quick change of subject. "You'd lose that bet. My parents married because my mother got pregnant with me. By the time I turned twelve, Mom had decided to make good on her repeated threats to leave my father. We were due to move out the week dad had his accident. Mom stayed to take care of him."

"What kind of accident?"

"My father was a firefighter. He went back into an inferno to save a fallen comrade. The other firefighter died, and my father ended up paralyzed from the waist down. Mom can't forgive him for putting his coworkers ahead of his family. And she makes sure he knows it every single day."

Stunned by her confession, Amelia ducked her head and studied her knotted fingers. Why had she told him that? She'd never discussed her dysfunctional family with anyone. Not even Candace, her best friend, knew the whole truth or Amelia's shameful secret.

For most of her teen years Amelia had secretly wished her mother would pack up and move out instead of staying behind to martyr herself caring for her injured husband. Life would have been much more peaceful if she'd left Amelia with her father.

But that was a boat of guilt she'd rather not row tonight.

Toby reached across the table. She abruptly leaned back in her chair to avoid contact. Accepting comfort from him had landed her in trouble the last time.

He narrowed his eyes. "You chose nursing because of your father."

"I liked helping him and making him comfortable." Looking after her father after school and on weekends had given her mother a much-needed break from being caretaker and her father a break from her mother's acid barbs and tantrums.

"Do you ever hear from your mother now that you're famous?" she asked Toby in an attempt to change the subject.

"She called. Once." The single hard-bitten word discouraged Amelia from asking for details, but it didn't stop her.

"What did she say?"

"She wanted money. What else?"

"I'm sorry."

The server placed their drinks and antipasto on the table and then left.

Toby nudged her foot beneath the table and winked. That invitation-to-sin smile slanted his mouth. "Hey, you're sitting across from NASCAR's sexiest driver. Lose the long face before you ruin my reputation. Unless you want to blow this joint and head back to my suite...."

The playboy had returned. That wasn't disappointment weighting her stomach, was it? Toby was a lot easier to resist when he was trying to get her naked than when he was being nice.

And then something clicked. She'd asked about his mother and opened a door—a door he clearly wasn't ready to let her pass through. "Do you act like a jerk to keep people at a distance?"

His head snapped back and his nostrils flared, confirming the accuracy of her statement. Something flashed in his eyes but passed so quickly she couldn't identify it. And then his expression turned salacious. "So we're gonna play head doctor? My couch or yours, sugar?"

She tried to rally her exasperation but failed. The damage had already been done. She'd had a peek past the charming facade Toby Haynes wore like armor and seen vulnerability. Seeing his pain made her want to help him.

For the first time in her life she cursed her compassionate nature. And she hoped it wouldn't get her into trouble.

Safety lay on the opposite side of that door.

Conflicting emotions tumbled in Amelia's head and agitated her stomach. She turned outside her suite with a quick but cool thanks-for-dinner-and-good-night hovering on her lips, but those words froze at Toby's closer-than-expected proximity. Her spine thumped into the jamb as she jumped back. He'd invaded her space while she'd been busy formulating a plan to escape unscathed.

Toby lifted a hand and leaned closer, but he only planted his palm on the wall beside her head. Scant inches separated their bodies, and his breath swept softly over her overheated face. But he didn't touch her. His gaze held hers, slid slowly to her lips and then returned to stare intently into her eyes for a dozen heart-pounding moments.

Would her five-minute punishment be a long kiss good-night?

She didn't want him to kiss her. His kisses muddled her thinking and made her act rashly. And yet she couldn't seem to persuade her leaden limbs to move her out of his way.

Her mouth dried. She swallowed.

His scent, a lethal combination of musky male and cologne, teased her nostrils. Warmth radiated from him, permeating the thin fabric of her dress.

Just do it. Make me pay already.

She wanted it over. The kiss. The embrace. This stupid fascination. The madness.

He reached past her with his other arm. She closed her eyes and steeled herself for the impact of his hand on her waist and his lips on hers, but instead of the heat and strength of him pulling her into his arms, her sluggish brain registered the hum and click of the electronic door lock. Her lids flickered open. Her key cut into her palm. That meant he must have used his—the one he'd stolen earlier.

He pushed the door open an inch and then shifted his leg to plant his shoe in the gap. The movement pressed the inside of his thigh against the outside of her hip. Hot. Hard. She vaguely registered the quiet cadence of the television coming from the sitting room. At least one of her suitemates was in.

He lifted her hand and wrapped her fingers around the knob. "Hold on."

And then he stroked a finger along her jaw and down her neck to trace the shoulder strap of her dress. Back to front. Scapula to clavicle. His slightly roughened skin raised goose bumps on her arms and shoulders, and her heart nearly battered a hole through her ribs.

"Be ready at nine tomorrow, sweet Amelia." Lowering his hand, Toby eased back and then he turned on his heel, strolled down the hall and disappeared into his own room. His door clicked shut behind him.

Her lungs emptied in a dizzying gush and her fingers contracted on cold metal. She sagged against the wall.

He hadn't kissed her.

She wasn't disappointed.

No. Uh-uh. She wasn't. Not even a little bit.

Just because she'd seen a less jerklike side of Toby today and she'd actually enjoyed his company for once didn't mean she liked him or wanted him to kiss her. Not tonight. Not ever again.

Liar.

She sucked in a sharp breath and plunged into the suite. Candace sat on the sofa surrounded by a rainbow of fabric samples.

"He knows," Amelia blurted. "Toby knows Vincent asked us to watch him. And he knows you've dumped him on me. His words. Not mine."

Candace's wily smile made Amelia's skin prickle. "I always thought Toby was smarter than he let on. That man can play good ole boy better than any Oscar-winning actor when it suits him. But he's smarter than that. If he weren't, Vincent wouldn't invest twenty-million bucks in his race teams every year."

"Twenty million?" Amelia squeaked. At Candace's nod, Amelia's purse slipped from her fingers and bounced on the coffee table. Toby lived in an affluent world she couldn't even begin to imagine. "One of you needs to take a turn with him tomorrow."

"We're all tied up. You're the only one free."

Amelia's temper stirred. "You have no intention of taking a turn, do you?"

"I'm busy. I have a wedding to plan."

"I'm your maid of honor. I'm supposed to be helping you."

"You are helping me by watching Toby. Vincent loves him like a brother. I can't let anything happen to him. And you're the one most qualified to ensure that it doesn't."

"Not fair. Madeline is a physician's assistant. She's had more training than me."

"Madeline has embarked on a holiday affair with her tour guide. Amelia, you know her ex did a hatchet job on her self-esteem. She needs this time to heal."

Unfortunately Amelia knew and agreed. Madeline's ex-fiancé, a doctor who'd worked at the hospital with them, had publicly humiliated her friend and destroyed Madeline's confidence when he walked out of their six-year engagement. Madeline deserved whatever happiness she could find.

The fight drained out of Amelia and an ice block of dread crystallized in her stomach. "I know she needs a boost right now. But, Candace, Toby's just like—"

She stopped. *Just like my father.*

This should be the happiest and most exciting time of Candace's life. If Amelia dumped her pitiful family history on her friend, she could ruin that. Could she live with being a wet blanket?

"I'm pregnant," Candace confessed before Amelia could make up her mind.

"What?"

"It's a secret. Please don't mention it to anyone. I'm avoiding Toby because I'm afraid he'll figure it out and tell Vincent before I can. I want to tell Vincent he's going to be a father in person, and that means not telling anyone until after I can do that. Can I count on you to keep my secret, Amelia?"

"But Vincent won't be here for weeks. He's tied up at the new hotel."

"Right. It's going to be hard keeping this quiet. I haven't been sick much, but I do sleep a lot. And—gag me—I am craving sardines. *Eeew.* It's like eating cat food, but I can't seem to get enough."

Amelia forced a smile. As happy as she was for her friend, she could feel a rising tide of panic. She'd been saddled with a man who could totally wreck her plan for a peaceful life, a man who'd already made her do impulsive and intoxicating things she regretted. A man who made her want to do those things again.

"Nobody will hear your news from me. Congratulations."

Candace stood and hugged her. "You're the best."

"That's what friends are for. But I will need some relief from Toby."

"I'll see what I can do."

But Amelia suspected whatever Candace arranged wouldn't be enough. She was on her own and in serious trouble.

Five

Toby Haynes had the machismo, charisma or whatever it was that sucked all the oxygen out of a room the moment he entered. The small confines of the car only intensified that effect.

"Are you crazy?" Amelia whispered as Toby folded himself into the passenger seat. "We can't just take a six-hundred-thousand-dollar vehicle and leave the country."

"It's insured. And the dealer knows where we're headed. He even recommended his brother's bistro for lunch. Work for you?"

She tightened her already white-knuckle grip on the steering wheel. "I can't think about food. My stomach is tied in knots. This car costs almost as much as I make in a decade."

"I've got you covered. Just enjoy the drive."

She wanted to. Impractical as it may be, she'd fallen in love with the adorable sports car on sight. The smell. The bold cobalt paint. The way the leather seats cradled her body like a spooning lover.

Don't go there.

The total absurdity of the price made sitting behind the wheel feel more like fantasy than reality. Forget Cinderella and her fancy pumpkin coach. *This* was a ride to be envied. Too bad Amelia had always been and always would be the sensible-sedan type when it came to actually purchasing a vehicle. And she never would have dared to test-drive a car she couldn't afford.

Toby leaned across her. His shoulder pressed hers and his springy hair brushed her chin. The clean tang of his shampoo combined with his nearness to make her head spin. He grabbed her seat belt and strapped her in and then turned his head. Scant inches separated their mouths.

Her breath caught and her skin tingled. "But—"

"Sugar, if you're as crazy about celebrities as Candace says you are, then you know you want to see Cannes."

"Well, yes, but…" She wanted to match her handprints to the ones in Allée des Stars, the French version of Grauman's Chinese Theater, where celebrities who'd attended the famous Cannes Film Festival had left handprints in concrete. But she'd planned to travel by train. Alone. Without the temptation of a man and a car she couldn't afford. And darn Candace for revealing her plans. "It's an electric car. What if the battery dies?"

"It's less than forty miles. We'll make it." He sat back and fastened his seat belt. "Quit making excuses and drive."

She bit her lip and wrinkled her nose. "You're not going to let me weasel out of this, are you?"

His eyes twinkled and his teeth flashed in a wolfish smile. "Not a chance. Let's go."

Part of her wanted to do as he suggested and live a little,

but her sensible side kept her foot on the brake. "They drive fast in Europe."

"A hundred and thirty kilometers per hour sounds fast, but it's only eighty-one miles per hour. You can't tell me you've never driven eighty on an interstate." His palm spread over her bare knee and squeezed, sending shock waves of sensation through her. "Amelia, I have every confidence you can handle this car as well as you handle me. C'mon, take me for a ride. You know you want to."

Take me for a ride. You know you want to. Heat imploded inside her. He'd said those same words ten months ago after rolling on his back and dragging her on top of him.

That night she'd ridden him until her thighs burned. And then, sated and drained, she'd melted over him like ice cream on hot apple pie.

She could not think about him and sex and still drive. She picked up his hand, returned it to his side of the console and put the car in gear. Her foot slipped on the clutch and the tires squealed. She flinched.

"Now you're talking. Let's see what this baby will do." He patted the dash.

She shot a worried glance at the salesman who'd given them the tour of the production facility and then the car keys. The man smiled and bowed as she left the parking lot, acting as if people drove away with six-hundred-thousand-dollar cars they hadn't paid for every day. Maybe the rich did. But she wasn't rich, and driving a vehicle that cost as much as a McMansion parked her heart in her throat and made her palms sweat on the leather-encased steering wheel.

Toby read the driving directions the salesman had provided, and all too soon Monaco faded from her rearview mirror and they merged onto A8. The car handled like a dream, and within minutes she got over her initial panic and relaxed. She felt a little like a butterfly breaking free of her cocoon. While she drank in the scenery of southern France, Toby focused on the dials and gauges and asked a steady stream of questions about how the car handled.

"Give her some juice," he prompted after they passed the exit to Nice. "Get a feel for her and then I want you to push her to the edge."

Amelia's heart stuttered. "The edge of what?"

"Control. I want to see what she's made of."

Something in his voice drew her attention. She glanced at him and saw a yearning in his eyes before he turned away. "You really miss this, don't you?"

He wiped a hand down his face. "Yeah. And it's killing me not to put her through her paces. But I wouldn't risk you, me or the other drivers on the road by getting behind the wheel before I'm cleared."

That didn't sound like an adrenaline junkie who never considered the costs of his actions or like a man who'd had to be forced out of the country to keep him off the racetrack.

Stealing quick peeks at him, she nibbled her lip and accelerated. Had she misjudged him? No. His career said it all. Drivers died at racetracks. And the NASCAR fans she knew watched for the excitement of the wrecks.

Car racing was a dangerous sport. Look at Vincent. He'd be scarred for life as a result of a racing mishap—and he'd been an innocent bystander. Toby had chosen a dangerous profession and he didn't even have the benefit of saving lives as her father had had to offset that risk.

They rode in silence past town names she could barely pronounce, and then she asked the question that had been nagging at her since she'd found out about his injury. "Have you considered what you'll do if you can't drive again?"

"No need to think about it. Doc says I'll be ready for qualifying in four weeks."

But the idea had occurred to him. She could see the concern furrowing his brow and tightening his mouth.

"Cars are like women," he said. "Some are loose. Some are tight."

And the playboy rides in again with a change of subject. This time she instantly recognized the defense mechanism for what it was, but she let him get away with it because maybe he wasn't ready to face the idea that his career could be over. In all likelihood, his concussion would resolve itself. But head injuries were tricky. There was a chance he wouldn't improve or that he wouldn't heal as quickly as he hoped.

Patients often had trouble coming to terms with learning that sometimes no amount of medical intervention or wishful thinking could return things to the way they used to be. Her father had fought for years before admitting he'd never walk again.

"Explain your sexist comment."

Toby chuckled. She wished he wouldn't. That low rumbling sound made it difficult to concentrate on anything but the man beside her.

"Racing lingo. Loose means her rear end wiggles. She slides out from under you on the curves. Tight means she won't go where you steer her. She's unresponsive. And like a woman, you need to read her every move and adjust your approach to get the most pleasure and performance out of her."

A disgusted noise climbed her throat. "Must you make every conversation about sex?"

"Sugar, I'm talking about the car. If you're thinking about sex, it's because you're fixated on that night. Same as me."

Gulp. Guilty. "Maybe you're giving yourself too much credit."

"Nah. You want me." Cocky. Confident. *Correct*.

She could lie and deny it, but what was the point when they both knew the truth? But this time she wouldn't let her wants make her forget the possible consequences.

She followed the signs to Boulevard de la Croisette and followed Toby's directions past palm trees and parks, luxury hotels, galleries and designer boutiques. According to her guidebook, this is where the stars shopped—and for a moment, riding in her borrowed carriage, she felt almost as if she fit in.

She found a parking space near the restaurant, pulled in and turned in her seat. "Wanting you is irrelevant. I told you—I'm looking for a husband and I refuse to marry someone with an occupation even more dangerous than my father's."

Toby's gaze held hers. "Nobody but you mentioned marriage. Amelia, you're hot, the hottest woman I've been with in a long time, but I'm not ever going to get married. A racing career's hell on a marriage. Drivers spend more time on the road than at home. Even if it weren't so tough, I don't exactly have a great example to follow. That doesn't mean we can't have a good time in Monaco. You can look for Mr. Picket Fence when you get home."

She should be offended. Seriously offended. He'd just admitted all he wanted from her was sex. Most guys at least tried to fake interest in more. Other than Toby, she'd always been one of those women who had to care deeply for a man before she slept with him, which meant—whether they faked it or not—there hadn't been many men in her bed.

But now that she suspected Toby used tired lines and

clichéd come-ons to keep his distance, she couldn't seem to muster outrage. Instead the temptation to do exactly as he suggested and dive into an affair tugged at her.

How totally unlike her pragmatic self.

She wouldn't consider his suggestion.

No. She wouldn't. Not even for a minute.

So why did the idea bedevil her like a bad case of poison ivy?

Amelia would have whiplash before she finished her dessert, Toby concluded.

Framed photographs of celebrities lined the restaurant walls. Movie and TV stars. Musicians. World leaders. Royalty.

An American sitcom star and his babe du jour occupied a table a few yards away, and in the back corner of the crowded beachfront restaurant an aging rock star was putting the moves on a woman young enough to be his granddaughter. Amelia's eyes were wide and awed as she tried to gawk without being obvious.

So why did these people rate the star treatment when she had no problem shooting him down? He could use a little of that hero worship if it meant getting her back into the sack.

On second thought, it was because she didn't brownnose and she hadn't slept with him because of who he was that he liked Amelia Lambert. Not that there weren't plenty of other reasons to be attracted. Such as her killer long legs, her sexpot mouth and her cute little butt.

Movement drew Toby's gaze away from the woman causing his blood to drain from his brain, and he spotted the restaurateur—the car salesman's brother—approaching with a camera.

Being a NASCAR driver meant being accessible to the fans no matter what you were doing or which continent you were on. The only place Toby had guaranteed privacy was inside his locked and gated estate. He pushed his empty plate aside and switched into promo gear.

"Monsieur Haynes, could I beg you for a picture and an autograph?"

"Happy to, Henri." And he meant it. Every fan, every autograph request rewarded him for years of hard work and sacrifice.

The man glanced at Amelia. "You and mademoiselle?"

"No, I'm not his girlfriend," Amelia answered too quickly for Toby's liking.

He dragged out his trademark grin. The camera flash temporarily blinded him. Even before the spots faded he accepted a black marker, signed the autograph-covered menu the manager put in front of him and then passed it back. He looked back at Amelia in time to see granddaddy rock star's hand descend on her shoulder. She stiffened and so did Toby. Her wide-eyed gaze bounced from Toby to the long-haired, big-lipped guy and back.

Toby's gut clenched and his lunch turned to battery acid in his belly.

"Great to see you, Toby," the musician said without bothering to introduce himself. "Nasty crash. You had me worried when you didn't drop the net and climb from the car. Glad to see you up and about. Used some of your footage in my last video."

"Right. I saw that. Good CD. We play it in the shop." But he'd take a sledgehammer to the disk if the guy didn't get his veiny, age-spotted paw off Amelia. She was his— for now—and he wasn't sharing.

"When will you be back on the track?"

"Chicagoland. I'm taking some personal time till then."

"I can see why you would." The guy's fingers squeezed Amelia's pale flesh and his lecherous gaze looked down her top.

Toby wanted to slug him.

What? Are you jealous?

Hell no. But he didn't like the guy looking at Amelia as if she were some groupie who could be had.

"I'll be watching the race. My money's on you." The guy returned to his jailbait chickadee.

"You know him?" Amelia whispered, her hand covering the area where the guy's had been. In adulation? Or was she wiping away the creep's touch?

"Never met him."

"But he seems to know you."

"That's the way it is in the public eye. People read about you and think they know you."

She bit her lip, lowered her hand and her gaze.

He remembered her fascination with entertainment rags and wanted his bitter words back. But he couldn't erase what he'd said, so he tossed a handful of bills on the table and stood. "If you want to see the handprints before we head back, we have to get moving."

The TV guy waved. Toby nodded but kept walking toward the exit. Several other patrons' heads turned as if they were trying to figure out who he was. Or maybe they were looking to see who *his* woman du jour was.

God knows he'd had his share of flashy, willing females on his arm, but he didn't like the idea of anyone shoving Amelia into that category and he didn't want the tabloids printing her picture or exposing her to that kind of talk. Most of the women he escorted wanted the exposure. He'd bet HRI Amelia wouldn't enjoy the attention.

She glanced toward the actor. "Do you know him?"

"No." As much as he wanted to get her away from public scrutiny and speculation, he realized star sightings were probably a big deal to her. Although he couldn't picture her yanking up her shirt and asking a guy to sign her boob. Toby had signed more cleavage than he could count. Fans asked for autographs on the damnedest things. "Did you want an introduction or autograph?"

"No. I don't want to intrude. Let's go." She didn't speak again until they'd walked a couple of blocks from the restaurant. There was a speculative quality to her gaze when she looked up at him. "I guess I never considered you one of them."

"Them?"

"A celebrity."

"Does that mean you want to jump my bones now that you do?"

The familiar gurgle of disgust burst from her lips, making him smile. He'd grown attached to that sound. He'd lain in bed too many nights thinking of ways to provoke it and then to turn it into that whimper she made when she climaxed.

"In your dreams."

"Every night, sugar." Sad fact—that wasn't a lie. His smile faded.

"Do you meet a lot of stars?"

"Enough. Drivers make appearances for their sponsors. NASCAR's big on fund-raisers and charity events."

Her eyebrows shot up. "Charity events? You?"

She didn't think much of him and that bothered him more than it should. Since his father, he hadn't worried about anyone's approval except his own. So why her? Why did this uptight nurse's opinion matter?

He didn't have the answer. The only thing he knew for sure was that his patience for getting her naked was shrinking fast while other parts of him weren't. Taking it slow and easy wasn't getting him anywhere in his quest to get her into his bed and out of his system. Maybe it was time to scrap that plan and turn up the heat.

"I support several charities besides the Haynes Foundation. I came from nothing. It's my duty to give back."

The sun beat down, reflecting off the sidewalks, glass storefronts and car windshields, driving shards of pain through his head.

"That's a really nice thing to do, Toby."

The approval in her soft voice made him feel ten feet tall and bulletproof. He wanted to kiss her so bad he couldn't see straight. Hell, he wanted to drag her into the nearest hotel and lose himself inside her long enough to forget the races he was missing and the fear that he might not be back in the car for Chicagoland. Or ever.

Amelia took his arm and steered him toward a shop. "The sunlight's bothering you. You need to buy some sunglasses before you get a headache."

Nurse mode. His engine revved. As much as he hated hospitals—and he'd seen the inside of several—it was disgusting how easily her efficient take-charge demeanor turned him on. But it was more than a sexual turn-on. Amelia looked out for him. In the casino, the elevator, the pool, here. How long had it been since a woman—including his mother—gave a damn about him except for what she could get out of him? But he didn't dare let himself come to like or expect it, because in the end she'd let him down the way women invariably did.

He should cut his losses and push her away.

But he couldn't. Not yet.

Not until he'd relieved this itch. And he intended to start scratching it.

Tonight.

"I want my five minutes."

Toby's words stopped Amelia in her tracks. Her hotel key card flipped out of her hand and tumbled, as if in slow motion, to the carpeted hall floor. Adrenaline raced through her veins, flushing her skin and quickening her breaths.

Buying time, she took advantage of Toby's slowed reflexes and knelt quickly to retrieve the card before he could. And then she straightened ever so slowly before meeting his gaze. "Now?"

"Now."

She tried to gauge his mood by his tone and failed, tried to guess what her penalty would be from his expression with no better luck. His set jaw and level gaze gave nothing away. Nor had he said anything on the drive back to Monaco to hint at his intentions. In fact, he'd been unusually silent.

She wanted to fabricate an excuse for why this wasn't a good time, but the creative side of her brain was too busy running amok considering what he could do with five minutes to come up with logical reasons.

Making that wager had been stupid. Stupid. Stupid. *Stooopid*. She didn't gamble, didn't bet. Heck, she'd never even joined the nurses' pool to buy lottery tickets. But she'd foolishly made an exception by wagering with Toby because she'd believed winning a sure thing.

And now she would pay for her recklessness.

"I, um…guess you could come in. I don't know if my roommates are in or out or—"

"My room."

Her mouth opened, but she couldn't speak and could barely drag a breath into her constricted chest. He strolled down the hall, extracted his key from the pocket of his khaki pants, unlocked his door and pushed it open. A tilt of his head indicated she precede him.

This was a mistake. But a promise was a promise. Wobbly legs carried her forward. Doubt sucked each step like deep mud.

Entering cautiously, she scanned his sitting room, noting the earthy Tuscan colors that were so different from the lighter, more feminine decor of the suite she shared with Candace and the bridesmaids. She halted beside the cognac-colored L-shaped leather sofa separating the sitting and dining areas. A wide balcony and a door leading to the bedroom were the only exits—neither a viable means of escape.

He stopped behind her, close but not touching. Her mouth dried. She dampened her lips and focused on the blue sky beyond the glass balcony doors. "What's my penance?"

"Eager, sugar?" The words were low, barely audible, like the rumble of thunder in the distance.

The fine hairs on her body rose as if an electrical storm crackled nearby. "Eager to get back to my room, yes."

"Drink?"

"No, thank you." She clutched her purse tighter. The lace edging the scooped neckline of her teal top rasped against her skin like a calloused fingertip with every shallow breath, and the hem of her denim skirt teased the back of her thighs like a lover's caress.

She'd been wearing this outfit for eight hours. Why had it suddenly become a source of tantalizing friction?

Because Toby was right. She'd fixated on that night, her mind rutted in a treacherous path that could only lead to trouble. Being alone with him made her think of sex. Of intense pleasure. Of impulses best ignored.

He reached around her, took her purse and tossed it on the coffee table. Her fingers fisted and her muscles tensed. She was a mature twenty-seven-year-old woman who dealt with life and death on a daily basis. She could handle five minutes of whatever Toby Haynes dished out.

She cleared her tight throat. "Do you have a timer?"

The air stirred as he shifted behind her and then she heard a click and a metallic chink. Toby's muscled forearm, tanned and sparsely dusted with dark golden curls, entered her peripheral vision. He offered his watch. His other arm encircled her and he pointed at a tiny button.

"Push that button when you're ready to start."

She took his watch in her hand. The gold carried the warmth of his body and burned her palm like a hot ember. "Y-you promised no hands and no p—"

"I remember." He lowered his arms and moved closer. Heat blanketed her back even though he didn't make contact. "Whenever you're ready."

She'd never be ready.

"Couldn't I just do your laundry or something?"

"Hotel does that."

Her thumb trembled above the button. *Five minutes. Get it over with.* His leather-and-lime scent surrounded her, and his breath stirred her hair. *Do it.* Her thumb contracted, starting the second hand. She concentrated on that tick-tick-tick and willed her heart to slow to the same steady beat. No such luck. It hammered three times as fast.

Toby's breath teased the sensitive skin beneath her right ear and his chest molded her back. The barrier of clothing did nothing to lessen the transference of heat. Sparks scattered through her bloodstream.

"You smell good."

"Um, thanks," she croaked. "Toby, this is not a good idea."

"Five minutes. Of whatever I want. You agreed." He nuzzled her temple, pressing his face to hers. His late-afternoon beard scraped deliciously against her cheek, contrasting with the smoother skin over his cheekbone. Soft lips teased the shell of her ear. The nip of his teeth on her earlobe startled a gasp from her.

Damn that promise. But if she held her ground and quit running, then maybe he'd quit chasing and give up the seduction attempts.

She kept her eyes open and tried to remain rigid and unresponsive as he trailed feathersoft kisses down her neck and across her shoulder. But she couldn't stop the tendrils of desire winding along her synapses. He painted a design on her skin with his tongue and then blew on her damp flesh, sending a shudder undulating through her.

Her lids grew heavy. Forcing them back open, she bent her head to check the watch. Only sixty seconds had passed.

He burrowed his way beneath her hair to nibble her nape. Goose bumps raised her skin. Her breasts tightened. Ached. She wanted to lean against him, to surrender and turn in his arms. Instead she clamped her bottom lip between her teeth, stiffened her spine and lifted her chin to study the smooth ceiling.

His tongue laved the pulse point on the opposite side of her neck. He sipped from her jaw, the hollow of her cheek. She wanted to turn her head, wanted to join her lips to his, because heaven knows the man was a champion kisser. He stepped away, saving her from making an enormous mistake. And then he circled in front of her. His hunger-filled gaze devoured hers.

With his hands fisted beside him, he closed the gap between them, sandwiching the hand she'd clenched around his watch between her navel and his erection. She shifted her hand away from the burning contact, unintentionally stroking his length. He sucked in a sharp breath and then leaned forward and kissed her brow, her nose, the corner of her mouth.

Her lids fluttered shut. He was really, *really* good at this. She longed to touch him, to twine her arms around him, pull him close and surrender her mouth.

You're weakening. Restrain your impulses.

She turned her head and forced her sluggish brain to look at his watch and calculate time. It wasn't easy. Two minutes left. She needed something to concentrate on besides the magic of his touch. She started counting down the seconds. One hundred twenty. One hundred nineteen. One hundr—

Soft hair brushed the underside of her chin and then his tongue traced the lace edge of her top from one collarbone to the other, dipping low to lave the cleavage created by the push-up bra Candace had insisted Amelia buy. A moan slipped past her lips.

Um…one hundred, um…seventeen. One hundred sixteen. One—

He bent lower and nuzzled her nipple through the fabric of her top. His teeth scraped the sensitized tip and his breath heated her flesh. She felt the caress deep in her womb and her thoughts scattered. The strain of resisting the urge to hurl herself into Toby's arms and his bed made her tremble.

She lost count. Where was she again? One-fifteen? One-ten?

And then he straightened. Time's up already? A sigh of relief—and maybe just a twinge of disappointment—gusted from her lungs, only to be dammed by his mouth. He kissed her hard enough to force her head back, granting him deeper access, and then he angled his head and swept his tongue between her lips to tangle with hers. Slick. Hot. Ravenous.

Her heart stumbled into a sprint. His chest scorched her breasts. The cool metal of his belt buckle stamped her belly above the hot column of his erection. His thigh pressed between hers, creating a delicious friction against her center. She shifted her hips and pleasure bolted through her. Heat poured from him into her every pore, flooding each cell with hunger.

She wanted him. Wanted his touch, his possession, more of the driving need pulsing against her abdomen. No other man had ever aroused her to such an intense craving. No other man had ever wanted her with such obvious restrained hunger.

An annoying bleep penetrated her desire-fuddled brain. She ignored it, but Toby slowly lifted his head. She blinked, trying to gather her wayward thoughts, and tracked the sound to the watch in her hand—the hand currently tucked in the small of Toby's back.

He wasn't holding her and hadn't needed to. She'd wound her arms around his middle and plastered herself against him.

She didn't even remember moving. She snapped her arms back to her sides. Toby pried the watch from her numb fingers and silenced the annoying alarm.

Horrified by her lack of control, she staggered backward gasping for breath. One step. Two steps. Three. The coffee table bumped her calves, halting her.

"I—I have to g-go."

Toby's chest rose and fell as rapidly as hers. His dilated pupils almost obliterated his silvery-blue irises, and moisture from their kisses dampened his lips. "Stay."

She wanted to. Dear heavens, she wanted to. But she

couldn't risk letting her hormones make her decisions. Shaking her head, she skirted the table, scooped up her purse and backed toward the door. "I can't do this."

"Amelia—" He lifted his hand and moved forward.

She clutched the doorknob so tightly her knuckles ached. "You're too much like my father, Toby. And I, apparently, am too much like my mother. Trust me, that is a horrible combination, and I won't end up like them."

Six

Amelia had barely slept. How could she when she'd realized she was no better than her mother at controlling her impulses?

If Toby's watch alarm hadn't gone off, she would very likely have ended up in his bed, and that would have carried her one-hundred-eighty-degrees away from her goal of finding a gentle lover who would cherish her forever, one who wouldn't undercut her self-esteem with low blows and cutting insults or thoughtlessly risk his life.

And this time she couldn't blame her lack of restraint on alcohol or a disastrous week. This time the weakness lay solely within her.

She sat at the table in her suite Friday morning sipping café au lait and staring blindly at the Mediterranean while waiting for her roommates to join her. She loved their morning gatherings. As an only child, she'd experienced nothing like the camaraderie she'd found with Candace, Madeline and Stacy. Would she have felt a little less like the rope in a tug-of-war match if she'd had siblings to share the load?

Doesn't matter. The past is over. Focus on the future.

Candace wandered in looking pale and queasy. "G'morning, Amelia. You know, mothering us is not a maid-of-honor duty, but bless you for calling room service."

"Good morning." Amelia poured her friend a cup of steaming hot chocolate and pushed it across the table along with a plate of toast. Candace sipped with her eyes closed and then cautiously nibbled her bread.

Once Candace had regained some color, Amelia asked, "What's on the agenda today? I didn't see anything on the calendar except my massage this afternoon."

"We have to make a final decision about bridesmaid dresses this morning. Afterward we'll go to the Oceanographic Museum and then have lunch. Afternoon's your own. We'll meet up again at midnight for an excursion to Jimmy'z, the dance club in the Monte Carlo Sporting Club. The place is famous for celebrity sightings. You ought to love that."

"Sounds fun." Even if she wasn't exactly the clubbing type.

"You've seen the museum. You can skip it if you want."

"Will Toby be joining us?"

"He's spending his morning with Vincent's personal trainer. I don't know about tonight, but I'd guess with his equilibrium issues, dancing will not be high on his agenda."

An entire day without temptation. Tension drained from Amelia's limbs. "Then I'll join you. The museum is worth a second visit."

Stacy wandered in and headed for the coffeepot. "Hi."

The women chorused a greeting. Seconds later the outer

suite door opened and a sweat-dampened Madeline entered wearing her running gear. She lifted her hand in a silent wave and crossed to the minifridge for a bottle of water.

"Working up a sweat with your sexy tour guide?" Candace asked.

"No. I was running off some of the rich food we've been scarfing down."

"That's too bad. I was hoping—"

Madeline groaned. "Please don't start matchmaking. Not everyone is looking for hearts and flowers and a husband."

Candace shook her head. "How can you not believe in love in a place like this?"

Madeline sipped her water. "I never said Monaco's not a very cool place. I can see why Vincent likes living here when he's not away on a job. But, despite the castles and princes, I'm not going to get caught up in the fairy tale."

"You could fall for your sexy tour guide," Amelia teased.

"Not a chance."

Amelia's heart ached for her friend. "Madeline, I hate to see you give up on love just because of one bad experience."

Madeline pointed the bottle in Amelia's direction. "Before you condemn me for not believing in forever, look in the mirror. You don't do long-term relationships either. In fact, you are the queen of short-term."

Taken aback, Amelia blinked. "What are you talking about? I was engaged."

Madeline flashed an apologetic smile toward Candace and then settled across the table from Amelia. "You know I love you like a sister, right?"

Uh-oh. Anything following that preface wouldn't be good. But she'd known and trusted Madeline almost as long as she had Candace. Bracing herself, Amelia set down her coffee cup. "Yes."

"I see a pattern in your relationships that I'm not sure you recognize."

"A pattern?" she parroted.

"You knew Neal's poor prognosis before Candace introduced you and yet you fell for him."

"Well, yes, but—"

Madeline held up a hand. "And you knew the Navy recruiter you dated before Neal was due to be reassigned in six months. We know you're not going to move away from Charlotte and your family as long as your father's alive, so a future as a military spouse was a no-go."

"*Okay,* so that's two, but—"

"Before the lieutenant you dated a visiting university professor who was only in town for summer session. And don't get me started on the guys you dated in college. You only went out with the ones scheduled to graduate and move out of state soon."

Amelia fought the urge to squirm in her chair. Was it true? Had she unintentionally sabotaged her relationships? Of course not. She wanted happily ever after and she'd been actively searching for Mr. Right.

"I believe in love and marriage," she protested.

"And yet you repeatedly chose dead-end relationships."

"She's right," Candace added, shocking Amelia further. "I didn't see it until Madeline pointed it out, but you've always chosen guys who aren't going to be around long-term."

Panic seized Amelia's throat. "No. She's not right. I believe in fate, destiny, kismet and all that stuff. There's a soul mate out there for everyone, and I'm actively searching for mine. I've just been…unfortunate."

"I think you're afraid to commit," Madeline speculated.

"I'm not afraid. I'm careful. Love comes from the head first and then the heart follows. You have to find a person who's like you in temperament and goals, one who wants the same things out of life, and then you carefully move forward. Like Candace and Vincent have. Like Neal and I did."

"What about opposites attracting or sexual chemistry?" Stacy asked.

Amelia's parents had been opposites. The working-class jock and the pampered honor student who'd tutored him in high school. Her mother's dream of attending a private college and then medical school had died when she'd accidentally become pregnant. Amelia's father had gone on to have the firefighter career he'd always wanted. The inequity had caused friction in the marriage.

"Once the novelty wears off, the things that initially attracted you will begin to annoy you, and love will turn to hate when the sacrifices become too great. Sexual attraction blinds you to those irreconcilable differences."

"Are you saying you'd marry someone without sexual chemistry?" Candace asked in a carefully modulated voice.

Amelia tried not to cringe. She wouldn't discuss her and Neal's disappointing sex life with his sister. Besides, it hadn't been Neal's fault. He'd been dying, and you couldn't expect a dying man to be good in bed. She selected her words carefully. "I'm saying sex is not the most important thing."

"It's in the top three, right behind love and trust," Candace insisted. "If the sex is bad, the rest falls apart."

"Franco and I have, um…chemistry," Stacy said with a blush, and Amelia wanted to kiss her for drawing the fire to herself and away from Amelia. "But we've agreed our… er…relationship will only last as long as I'm in Monaco. I've never had a relationship based solely on sex before. It seems…" She shrugged.

"Safe?" Madeline suggested. "You'll have a great time

and he won't break your heart because you know it's going to end here. It's a win-win situation."

Stacy chewed her lip. "I guess so."

Madeline's emerald gaze skipped between Stacy and Amelia. "You two may be going about it in different ways, but you're both protecting your heart with short-term affairs. Same as me."

She covered Amelia's hand. "You say you believe in romance, but I see you making sure no guy sweeps you off your firmly planted feet. There's nothing wrong with that as long as you recognize what you're doing."

Could Madeline possibly be right?

Her friend rose and pitched her empty water bottle into the trash. "Amelia, we all know Toby's a player, but you two strike enough sparks off each other to light California. The way I see it, you have a choice. You can either live in the moment and enjoy the electricity while it lasts or play it safe and hold out for a fairy tale that might never happen. The question is, which one will you regret the most?"

Amelia didn't have an answer and she suspected she resembled a goldfish with her mouth opening and closing but nothing coming out. She wanted to argue, to prove Madeline wrong. But a rebuttal wouldn't form. Doubts, however, bloomed like wildflowers after a desert rain.

"How do you know we strike sparks off one another?"

"Because I stepped off the elevator Wednesday night when you and Toby were standing outside our door. You were so engrossed in each other I don't think either of you heard the elevator ding or saw me in the hall. Rather than get zapped by the current between you, I got back on and went downstairs to the bar, where I hooked up with Stacy."

Madeline held her palms up by her shoulders like balancing scales. "Live or dream? Fun or fantasy? What's it going to be, Amelia?"

Naked and alone, Amelia lay facedown on the table and squirmed under the sheet covering no more than an eight-inch-wide swath across her bottom.

She'd never had a massage, and the idea of someone other than her doctor getting up close and personal made her uncomfortable. But this "treat" was a gift from Candace, and her friend had promised when she'd scheduled appointments for each bridesmaid at Hôtel Reynard's top-rated spa that a massage would be a relaxing and rejuvenating experience.

A little stress reduction couldn't be a bad thing, Amelia admitted. Having to fight the illogical push-pull of her attraction to Toby all week had been challenge enough. Combining his tempting presence with Madeline's eye-opening evaluation this morning threatened to make the knot of tension between Amelia's shoulder blades a permanent fixture.

Yesterday's kiss hadn't helped. If Toby's watch alarm hadn't gone off—

Don't go there.

She'd excused herself from the bridal party after lunch and headed directly for the spa rather than risk bumping into Toby in the upstairs hall. She couldn't face him with her mind in turmoil. But when the receptionist had escorted her into this candlelit room, told her to strip, lie down and cover only her buttocks with the sheet, she'd almost decided she'd rather deal with Toby than expose herself to a total stranger.

Better the devil you knew…

Three things had kept her from chickening out. One, it would have been inconsiderate to cancel at the last moment and to refuse Candace's gift. Two, Candace would be charged for the expensive massage at this late date whether Amelia had it or not. And three, Madeline's accusation that Amelia was playing it safe was a little too accurate for comfort.

Exhaling a series of long, slow breaths, Amelia willed her limbs to loosen. *Relax. The masseuse is a professional. He or she doesn't care what you look like naked.*

She'd almost convinced herself when the door opened and a draft of warm sage-scented air swirled over her skin. Her muscles clenched all over again. She pressed her face firmly into the horseshoe-shaped pillow. If she concentrated on visually tracing the veins in the marble floor beneath the table and didn't look at the masseuse, then maybe this wouldn't be as embarrassing. "G-good afternoon."

"Back atcha, sugar."

Toby! She jerked her head up just in time to see him drop the towel encircling his hips. Her lungs seized and her heart stuttered. It's a wonder he couldn't hear it knocking against the table. His gaze caressed her face, her naked back and her legs before traveling back up to linger on her upper torso.

She flattened her breasts against the table. "What are you doing here?"

His penis thickened, lengthened and rose from his dark golden curls, drawing her attention the way a new intern attracts nurses. Her internal muscles contracted.

"Massage. Same as you. Keep looking at me like that and I'm going to have trouble lying facedown."

"Then leave." Shielding her breasts with her arm, she forced her gaze back to his face. "This is a private massage."

"A private *couple's* massage," he corrected. "You and me, side by side, being rubbed in all the right ways. I changed the reservation."

She could kick him…and herself. She'd thought it odd that the room contained two tables, but she hadn't asked for an explanation. If she had, she could have avoided this. "Do not turn this into something sexual, Toby Haynes."

"I dare you to lie there while the masseuse does her thing and know that I'm naked right beside you getting the same treatment and not get turned on. By the time we're done you'll be wishing it was my hands on your body and that we could lock the door and finish each other on the table."

She did not need that image in her head—the one of Toby pulling her to the padded edge and plunging deep inside her the way he had on her coffee table. And if her cheeks were half as red as they were hot, then he'd know how strongly his words had affected her.

She glanced at the door. No lock. Good. That meant she wouldn't be tempted. Not that she was. Not even a tiny bit.

He sat on the table beside hers, knees splayed, palms planted beside his thighs, which left his privates at eye level. He made no attempt to lie down or cover himself with the sheet. The man had absolutely no modesty.

With a body like that, who would?

And she was trapped. She couldn't get up and leave without giving him an eyeful. She averted her gaze from his long, thick shaft. "Go. Away. This is supposed to be relaxing."

Mischief twinkled in his eyes. "Do I make you tense?"

As a bowstring. "If Candace sent you, I will strangle her."

"Lucky for her, joining you was my idea. I'd hate to have to explain to Vincent that the maid of honor knocked off his bride because Candace was matchmaking."

He knew. She wanted to crawl under the Egyptian-cotton-draped table. Could she possibly be more humiliated? Nope. "Joining me was a bad idea. And cover up, for pity's sake."

His grin widened. "If you insist. No need to get prissy. It's not as if you haven't seen and tasted everything I have."

Her cheeks erupted with a fresh wave of lavalike heat, and her mandible locked. "That. Night. Was. A. Mistake."

"So you keep saying. But repeating the words doesn't make 'em true. And your eyes…well, let's just say lying's not one of your talents." He picked up the sheet and lay down—carefully. She tried not to ogle his perfect honeydew-melon rear before he covered up. Tried and failed.

He rolled onto his side, propped his head on his hand and sought her eyes. "Ever had a massage?"

She couldn't help following the line of hair bisecting his abdomen and disappearing beneath the sheet. "No. Have you?"

"Yep. Occupational hazard. Loosen up or the massage won't feel good."

She shoved her face into the pillow and muttered, "I could do that a lot better if you'd leave."

"We could always cancel and take this upstairs to my suite. I give one hell of a good massage."

"No doubt you've had lots of practice," she grumbled in disgust. "Forgetaboutit."

"You don't know what you're missing. No wait—you do. Am I too much for you, A-mel-i-a?" There he went again, stretching out her name like an orgasmic groan. "Because I could have sworn you were with me every second of that night. Sure felt like it when your body was contracting around mine and squeezing me so tight I thought my…*brain* would explode. And I could've sworn I heard you say—"

"Roll over and shut up or I'm leaving." She lifted her head enough to glare at him. If blood could simmer, hers would. From anger but also from arousal. Which only made her angrier.

"Nah, I don't recall you saying that. It was something more along the lines of—"

The door opened before she could make good on her threat to leave. A man and a woman entered and introduced themselves as Lars and Nina. Amelia tensed and chewed her bottom lip. She hoped the big blond guy was Toby's. But Lars crossed to the shelf at the head of Amelia's table, and her hopes crashed and burned.

The abstract idea of having a strange male massage her hadn't bothered her too much, but actually having his crotch inches from her eyebrows and his hands preparing to touch parts of her the sun never saw made her *extremely* uncomfortable. She wanted to bolt.

"No," Toby barked, making Amelia jump. His jaw muscles looked like marbles beneath his tanned skin. He pointed to Lars. "You're over here. Nina's over there."

Lars shook his head. "Mademoiselle Meyers specifically requested me for Mademoiselle Lambert."

"I'm overriding that request," Toby insisted. "Switch or Mademoiselle Lambert and I are outta here."

She really ought to object to his high-handedness. But her lips remained sealed.

The spa employees exchanged a look, then changed positions. Relief sagged through Amelia. And then a peculiar idea slipped under her skin like a hypodermic needle. Toby didn't want the guy touching her. His possessiveness sent a thrill through her. And wasn't that insane since she didn't want him to be possessive? But the tingles in her extremities couldn't be denied.

Maybe he'd seen the panic on her face and had done the gentlemanly thing. Warm fuzzies joined the tingles.

Or was he one of those guys who fantasized about two women and a ménage à trois? Her lip curled in disgust. The tingles and warm fuzzies evaporated.

She dropped her face into the pillow with a silent groan. She'd better cling to the last idea if she wanted to keep her distance from Toby Haynes.

Do you want to keep your distance?

She chewed her bottom lip. Before this morning the answer would have been an easy and unequivocal yes. But Madeline's comments haunted her.

Had she sabotaged her search for Mr. Right by only dating Mr. Right Nows?

Looked that way. And how could she not have noticed that?

Did the short-term nature of her relationships mean she hadn't cared about the men she'd been involved with? No. But she had to admit she'd never pictured herself sharing side-by-side rockers at the retirement home with any of them.

Not even Neal.

That disturbing revelation rattled her so much she barely registered the warm oil on her shoulders or the firm hands working it into her skin.

"Go easy on her. It's her first massage," Toby said.

Amelia turned her head sideways and found Toby watching her. His back glistened with oil. Lars's big hands dug deep into muscle, but Toby didn't flinch.

For ten months she'd been running from Toby Haynes and the passion she'd experienced in his arms, and yet avoidance of a problem had never been her style. She faced difficult issues head-on. The way she had her father's paralysis, her mother's subsequent caregiver-stress issues and Neal's debilitating disease.

If she didn't get a handle on her aberrant feelings, her desire for Toby could devastate her future plans. He was everything she *didn't* want in a man. Except physically. And yet he'd monopolized her thoughts for an entire year. There was something terribly wrong in that.

Toby lifted his hand, reaching across the space between their tables.

Amelia hesitated. Perhaps Madeline was right and dealing with her illogical attraction here in Monaco, the land of fantasy and fairy tales, was the answer. Toby didn't want a future with her any more than she wanted one with him, and if she let her passion for him burn hot, it would quickly burn out because it wasn't based on anything more substantial than lust.

A nice, controlled burn. That's what she needed. And when she returned to the real world—work, home and family—her problem would be solved and she'd be one step closer to finding a gentle, caring partner with staying power.

She reached across the intervening space and linked fingers with her temporary obsession.

And prayed she could contain the blaze.

If he got any harder, Toby figured his erection would jack his hips off the massage table like a race car waiting for a two-tire change.

No doubt Lars, of the meat grinder hands, knew it. Why else would the guy have tried to mulch Toby's muscles into hamburger for the past thirty minutes? The jerk was probably pissed he'd missed out on feeling up Amelia.

The second the door closed behind the departing masseuses Toby tossed off the sheet, swung his legs over the side of the table and sat up. Rolling his shoulders, he checked for permanent damage.

He studied the back of Amelia's head, the way her silky cinnamon hair parted and trailed over the table. After holding his gaze and his hand throughout the massage, the minute the massage ended she'd planted her face in the pillow.

"You okay, sugar?"

Amelia's back rose as if she were taking a deep breath and then she pushed up on her elbows, giving him a tantalizing glimpse of one pale breast. His dick twitched in appreciation.

"I'm fine." White teeth dented her bottom lip. And then she sat up—sans sheet—making no attempt to conceal a single delicious inch of creamy skin from his view. His heart and groin pulsed in tandem. She noted his roll-cage-hard condition, averted her face and licked her lips—which only increased his discomfort.

Her nipples puckered, begging for attention. He wanted to taste them and then trace every sheet-wrinkle impression across her thighs, belly and breasts. With his tongue. The curls between her legs had been tamed into a tight, tiny triangle since their last encounter. Sexy. Oh, yeah, definitely sexy.

Her hands fisted in her lap. "Can we go upstairs now?"

"Your suite or mine?"

Her gaze didn't get anywhere close to meeting his. "Yours."

He nearly fell off the table. He'd expected her to red-flag him and blister him for delivering yet another line. But he wasn't dumb enough to question his luck. All right, he was dumb enough. But he could wait till later for his answers.

Not wanting to give her a chance to change her mind, he stood.

She slid off her table more slowly, snatched up a towel

and covered herself. Her movements were jerky instead of the smooth, efficient and graceful ones he'd come to associate with the slender nurse.

"Amelia."

She paused and, clutching the ends of the Turkish towel to her breastbone, stared at his chin. Tension tightened her features and a white line cinched her lips. She looked pale and anxious instead of flushed and aroused.

He threaded his fingers through her soft hair and tugged until she met his gaze. Her lashes quickly descended, shielding her eyes, but not before he made a surprising discovery.

She's shy. And nervous.

Something inside him softened, and for the life of him he couldn't think of anything to say to ease the situation. No lines came to mind. No come-ons. No flirtatious, teasing banter. He drew a complete blank. A first for him. As Amelia had accurately guessed, words were his tools. He used them to draw people in or push them away. Now he had none.

So he did the only thing he could think of. He kissed her. Her eyelids. Her cheeks. Her nose. Restraining his hunger, he sipped from her lips until her mouth softened beneath his and the stiffness eased from her muscles—and invaded his.

She leaned into him and then her hand curved over his naked hip, jolting him like a jump-started battery. He lifted his head and sucked air. He wanted to act out every fantasy that had starred her and had disturbed his nights, but he didn't want to be interrupted and he couldn't guarantee that here. So even though letting her go was the absolute last thing he wanted to do, he stepped away.

He yanked a thick hotel robe off the rack by the door and draped it over her shoulders. While she slid her arms into the sleeves, he stuffed his into a second robe and loosely tied the belt. After lacing his fingers through hers, he towed her out of the massage room and into the dressing area. His heart beat faster with every step, as if he were climbing a rock face instead of walking a flat floor.

Eight louvered doors surrounded a splashing water fountain designed to instill tranquility. In his case it failed. Big-time. "Grab your gear and let's go."

"Shouldn't we shower off the oil first?" she asked as she paused by the door of the room beside his. He ducked in, scooped up his clothes and rejoined her.

"We'll do it upstairs. Together." Because if he didn't get her out of here, he was going to lose what little patience he had left. Who was he kidding? He'd already lost it.

"On second thought…" He advanced, backing her into the six-by-six cubicle, and kicked the door shut. He flung his bundle of clothes in the corner, yanked her into his arms and covered her mouth with his. Craving the sweet taste of her, the slickness of her tongue, he delved deep without preliminaries.

He opened her robe, found her satin-soft skin and tightly beaded nipples with his palms. It wasn't enough. He needed more. Her skin. Against his. He ripped open his robe and pulled her close. Hot. Oh, man, she was hot. She whimpered into his mouth at the press of flesh, and he'd bet his trophy case steam poured from his ears.

When his lungs threatened to explode he lifted his lips a fraction of an inch. "Can you be quiet this time?"

She blinked and then her eyes widened. A flush painted her face and neck. She glanced at the closed door and ran her tongue over her damp, swollen lips.

"You mean you'd—we'd—*here?*" The last word was little more than a squeak.

Desire choked him. He jerked an affirmative nod.

Her gaze bounced to the door again and then back to him. "B-before we, um, do this I need to make something cl-clear."

"Shoot." Hell, he'd agree to practically anything to get inside her right now.

How did she make him this crazy when no other woman had? He cupped her waist and walked her backward toward the padded bench.

She splayed a hand on his chest, lighting five fires with her fingertips. "I—I'm not looking for a long-term relationship with you, Toby. This affair ends the minute we leave Monaco. You can't call me or try to see me after we get home."

His steps faltered. She was giving *his* speech. And being on the receiving end was about as much fun as a rectal exam. *He* was the one who set the limits on his affairs.

What does it matter who says the words as long as you both abide by the rules?

"Deal."

Amelia inhaled deeply, squared her shoulders and then met his gaze. "Okay, then. I'm ready."

So was he. Ready to blow, that is. He wanted her that bad.

That wasn't good. *Get a grip, man.*

He skimmed his palms down her back and over her smooth buttocks. He cradled her thigh and lifted until she rested one foot on the bench. Stepping into the V of her legs, he stroked his erection against her damp curls. Her welcoming slickness had him whistling air through his clenched teeth.

"This is gonna be fast. Hard and fast. Are you still on the pill?"

She planted both hands against his ribs. "Yes, but don't you have a condom?"

"Not with me."

Her face and body tensed, her withdrawal obvious even to his lust-fogged brain. "I won't take chances. Especially not with a man like you."

A man like you. The words hit him like a sucker punch. What in the hell did that mean? She didn't think he was good enough? She thought he dipped his stick indiscriminately?

"I'm careful and I'm clean."

"The pill isn't one hundred percent effective. I'm not willing to risk a pregnancy."

Pregnancy? Neither was he. He never intended to get married or have kids. He refused to risk letting anyone down the way his folks had him. God knows he didn't know how to be a father.

"Then we're good to go, because neither am I. But we'll have to take this show on the road. I have what we need upstairs."

Seven

She was going to have sex with a man she didn't love. Amelia wasn't even sure she *liked* Toby Haynes.

Oh, sure, her body craved his. But her body wasn't in charge here. She wouldn't let it be. And once this series of encounters ended she'd go back to being her sensible, practical self.

Yes, he made her feel good. But she'd keep her head this time.

Averting her eyes from the dressing room mirrors, she tried to ignore the naked man bumping elbows and hips with her as she buttoned her top in the cramped space. She reached for her panties, but Toby snatched the pale pink cotton out of her hand and stuffed it in his front pocket.

Amelia stared at the tiny bump next to the much larger bulge of his erection. She blinked and then met his gaze. "Give those back."

"You don't need 'em."

"You expect me to waltz through the hotel without my underwear?"

His wicked grin made her insides fizz like a shaken soda pop. "Yeah."

"You're wearing yours."

"That's so you can peel them off. Later. Real slow." He captured her hand and stroked her palm over the thick, hard denim-covered ridge. Her heart skipped wildly. "See how much I'm looking forward to that?"

She tugged her hand away, but the residual heat spread from her palm to her cheeks and then pooled where her panties should be. She pulled her skirt over her bare bottom. The button and zip challenged her uncooperative fingers, but finally she managed to get the job done.

She couldn't help second-guessing her decision. About this affair. About leaving this dressing room semidressed. About…well, *everything*.

Toby Haynes was too much like her father. But this wasn't about forever. This was about fitting the last piece of the puzzle in place. As soon as she found Mr. Right her life would be perfect.

But first she had to deal with Toby.

The last time they'd slept together she'd been weak and needy and allowed herself to be swept away on a storm surge of emotion and impulse. Impulses were mistakes. But this wasn't an impulse. This was a calculated plan designed to eradicate all traces of her attraction to this egotistical, thrill-seeking, smooth-talking ladies' man from her system the way an antibiotic does an infection. She was stronger now. Strong enough to hold her own and cure this temporary obsession.

Toby's big hand captured hers. With a feeling of inevitability she followed him out of the dressing room. This encounter had been brewing since she'd first set eyes on him in the hotel foyer.

No, she admitted grudgingly. Since the first night she'd gone toe-to-toe with him in Vincent's hospital room.

She'd informed him visiting hours were over and he'd have to leave. He'd said, "Not unless you carry me out. My buddy needs me and I'm staying."

Vincent had been heavily sedated at the time and probably hadn't even known Toby was there. She should have called security and had Toby removed. But Vincent's family hadn't arrived yet, and she'd have hated for her patient to awake alone and in pain. Add in the concern lining Toby's face, and she'd bent the rules. She'd let him stay.

She hated to admit it, but his loyalty to Vincent in the months following the accident had impressed her. When he wasn't on the road for a race, Toby had been by Vincent's side, keeping his friend entertained and motivated through each stage of recovery and every setback.

Toby led her out of the spa and across the vast lobby. Amelia felt incredibly naked, as if everyone around them knew of her underdressed state. Her skin burned. Her palms dampened, and it shamed her to admit they weren't the only part of her growing moist.

They stopped in front of the penthouse elevator. Toby's eyes found hers. The hunger straining his expression dried her mouth and weakened her muscles. He drew circles in her palm with his thumbnail, scraping up arousal from deep inside her and distracting her from her pantiless predicament—but not so much that she didn't wonder if the concierge who acted as a gatekeeper to the upper floor couldn't guess she and Toby were headed upstairs for sex.

The brass doors opened. Toby towed her inside, propped

himself in a corner and pulled her into the crook of his arm. Would he kiss her again on the ride up? Would he do more than kiss her? Did she want him to? Her pulse pounded a resounding *yes* in her ears and much lower.

Just before the doors closed, a third occupant entered the cubicle.

That meant no kisses. She wasn't disappointed. Not at all. Uh-uh.

Liar.

The Mafia-dark burly guy wore a suit and an earpiece microphone thingy. Was that a gun under his coat? Hotel security? A bodyguard for someone famous? His probing gaze inspected both her and Toby from head to toe. Supremely conscious of her nakedness Amelia squeezed her thighs together and fought the blush she was sure must be creeping up her neck. And then the man backed into the opposite corner and faced the doors.

Had Toby noticed the weapon? Amelia sought his gaze and the bottom dropped out of her stomach. If a man could undress you with his eyes, then she'd be stripped bare and they'd be making love in the elevator. Had that been his intention when he'd stolen her panties? She wasn't wearing a bra—almost never did. What was the point when she didn't need support? That meant only two pieces of fabric separated her from his touch.

Her skin tingled and her internal muscles clenched. For a split second she wished they were alone, but then reason reasserted itself. There were probably security cameras in the elevator, and the last thing she needed on this trip was to be arrested for indecent exposure and who knows what else. Not to mention the lack of a condom.

Tell that to her moistening parts and desert-dry mouth. What felt like an eternity later, the elevator opened on the penthouse level. The suit exited first and headed down the opposite end of the hall. Toby straightened—carefully, Amelia noted. She followed him out. She had to take two steps for each of his long strides, and each quick tread sent a teasing draft up her skirt. He inserted the key card into the lock and then shoved open the door of his suite.

Last chance to change your mind.

No. This plan would work. It had to.

Scraping her courage together, Amelia put one foot in front of the other. She'd barely crossed the threshold when Toby palmed the door shut and leaned against it. He snagged her waist with one hand and hauled her between his splayed legs, fusing her hips to his. The fingers of his other hand speared through her hair, bringing her mouth to his in a hard, brief and blistering-hot kiss, a tangle of tongues, a gnashing of lips and teeth.

Her head was spinning before he swept her off her feet and stalked toward his bedroom. She snaked her arms around his neck and struggled to regulate her breathing, but it was a lost cause. He dipped. Believing him about to drop her, she squealed and tightened her arms, but instead he grasped the spread with the hand beneath her knees, ripped it back and then laid her in the middle of the cool Egyptian cotton sheets and followed her down.

His thighs separated hers, hiking up her skirt to an indecent level, and then his denim-covered erection pressed her bare center. The rough fabric abraded her tender flesh in a delicious way, and when he flexed his hips, a bolt of pleasure shot through her, stealing her breath. He braced himself on straight arms above her and then, biceps bulging, slowly lowered his torso until he blanketed her with heat, stopping with his mouth a scant inch from hers.

"Save the screams for when I'm inside you."

His ego truly was astounding. "You think you can make me scream?"

"Guaran-damn-tee it."

And she was just as determined to make sure he didn't. This wasn't last time. Her will wasn't weakened by alcohol or grief.

His mouth feathered over hers in the briefest of teasing kisses. She tried to arch up for more, but his chest held her down. He touched down for another butterfly sip and then rolled to her side, leaving one leg thrown across hers. A big palm spread across her navel and swept upward to the buttons of her lace blouse.

"I like your girlie clothes. I like getting you out of 'em even better."

He started at the bottom, releasing one button, folding back the plackets and then exploring the exposed triangle of skin with his lips, with his tongue. He painted a damp trail along the waistband of her skirt and then blew. The shocking contrast of hot tongue and cold air elicited a wave of goose bumps. The second button gave way. Her rib cage received the same sip-lave-blow treatment with equally mind-melting results. The third button opened. He nibbled a tantalizing path along the underside of her breasts, and her nipples tightened, tenting her thin blouse.

The fourth and final button slipped free, but he didn't hurry to claim his prize—if her small breasts could be considered a prize. His chin, covered in afternoon stubble, scraped a shiver-inducing line along her sternum. She arched her back, lifting herself toward his mouth.

"Something you want, sugar?"

He knew what she wanted. Why make her ask? "Touch me."

"Where? Here?" He nipped her jaw, her earlobe. "Or here?"

He had to feel the pulse in her neck pounding beneath his lips. She fisted her fingers in his short hair and urged him in the right direction. "My breasts."

A quick rasp-rasp across her chest as he shook his head made her want to growl in frustration, until she realized he wasn't saying no. He was nudging fabric out of his way with his chin. His stubble lightly scraped her nipple once, twice. He circled her areola with a sandpaper caress.

She groaned and squirmed as heat and tension spread through her. "Yes. There. Please."

He rewarded her request with the hot, wet suction of his mouth, making her hips bow off the bed as desire yanked deep inside her. He settled her with a big, warm palm on her thigh. And then that hand climbed higher, approaching her exposed sex at a snail's pace. *Faster, faster,* she wanted to cry, but his teeth snagged her nipple, holding it captive for the flick of his tongue, and the words vanished.

He switched to the opposite side, giving equal attention to her neglected flesh, sucking, laving, scraping. And then his hand reached her curls. He gave a gentle tug and she gasped. How could pulling hair be sexy? And yet she was about to come unglued. He traced her damp seam, down, up and then back again and again, approaching but always stopping just short of the spot that could send her over the edge. She dug her fingers into his muscle-corded shoulders and rocked to meet his fingers. She couldn't help herself.

He lifted his head. "In a hurry?"

She licked her lips and tasted him. "Aren't you?"

"Oh, yeah." His killer grin twisted her insides and her toes contracted.

He bent his head and covered her mouth. His tongue found hers at the same instant his fingers struck gold. Orgasm crashed through her in wave after wave. The thigh he'd thrown over hers held her captive for the onslaught, and his kisses muffled her cries.

She dissolved into the mattress, sated and yet still wanting. Wanting him. Too much. So much it scared her. So much it reminded her that she was losing control.

A little foreplay was a good thing, necessary even, to make sex comfortable. But too much was…dangerous. Uneasiness crept over her like a spider web. She struggled to gather her shattered composure.

He flicked open the button of her skirt, lowered the zip and then tugged the garment down her legs and pitched it onto the floor. His heavy-lidded gaze caressed her, making her feel sexy instead of skinny. No other man had ever looked at her that way—as though she was the woman he wanted instead of the one he could get.

He cupped her breasts, thumbed the pebbled tips and then shifted his body back between her legs. His broad shoulders held her open and exposed, and then he lowered his head and did with his tongue what his fingers had done seconds before. He drove her out of her mind, carried her high and then pushed her off the edge.

And she couldn't stop him.

Even before the aftershocks faded, he rose onto his knees, pulled his shirt over his head and reached for the waistband of his jeans.

Time to regroup. She arched up and covered his hands. "My job."

The fabric stretched tight over his distended flesh. Determined to torment him the way he had her and to shift the balance of power back where it should be, she trailed her short nails across his chest, circled his tiny nipples and then raked up and down his fly.

Toby's jaw muscles knotted. His back bowed and his fists clenched. "Be quick about it," he ordered in a strained voice.

He'd made her weak, and she had every intention of returning the favor. "What's the matter, Haynes? You can dish it out, but you're not man enough to take it."

He scowled. "I can take it and I can take you—which you'll find out as soon as you get these damn jeans off."

She lowered the zipper one tooth at a time and then slipped her fingers into the opening to cup and stroke cotton stretched over rigid heat. The cords of his neck tightened visibly. She eased his pants over his hips and then wedged a fingertip beneath the elastic band of his briefs and circled his waist to tease the crevice of his buttocks.

His thigh muscles knotted, trembled. He muttered a blasphemy.

Easing the elastic out of the way, she uncovered the engorged head of his penis and glanced up to find Toby watching her. He gulped and a surge of power filled her. Ever so slowly, without looking away from the need in his eyes, she parted her lips, dampened them with her tongue. His breath hitched. She lowered her head and licked him. Air whistled through his clenched teeth. But he didn't blink.

She shoved his briefs to his thighs, curled her fingers around his thick shaft and licked his satiny length, bottom to top. His hands cupped her head, fingers tangling in her hair. Again and again she bathed him and then took him into her mouth.

"*Yesss,*" he hissed.

She'd never met a man who didn't like this. The difference was this time she liked it, too. Liked his taste. His scent. His heat. She liked making Toby shake, making him swear—which he did more creatively with each swirl of her tongue. She relished pushing him to the edge more than she ever had before.

"Stop." He uttered the word so low and deep she barely understood him. His fingers tightened on her scalp, pulled. "Stop," he repeated louder, clearer, when she ignored him.

"Dammit, stop." He caught her shoulders and forced her to release him and then tumbled her backward onto the bed and slammed his mouth over hers. The kiss bordered on savage. He took her mouth, took her breath. But he didn't take her. His erection scorched the inside of her thigh. She was open and wet and protected from pregnancy. He could have plunged deep even without the condom she'd insisted upon. But he didn't.

Finally he released her mouth and vaulted from the bed. "Witch."

The approval in his tone and in his hot blue eyes belied the insult and sent a thrill through her. Had any man ever wanted her with such naked hunger before Toby? No. And the intensity of his need both excited and worried her. Worried because she felt it, too.

He shucked his clothing in record time, yanked open the bedside table drawer and retrieved a condom. After sheathing himself, he climbed back onto the bed, hooked her knees over his bent arms, yanked her hips forward and impaled her.

Her lungs emptied on a rush as he filled her. Barely giving her time to adjust to his size, he withdrew and then drove deep again and again, taking her on a wild, fast ride. The pleasure was too intense. Too unrestrained. She struggled to rein it in.

She caressed the supple skin of his chest, his thighs, his buttocks—any erogenous zone she could reach.

"Stop," he groaned again.

But she didn't. Arousal tightened inside her, so she redoubled her efforts, mapping his body, seeking out his pleasure points until he cursed and released her legs only to grab her wrists and pin them on the pillow beside her head.

He leaned down, his gaze drilling hers.

"Don't. Rush. Me." He punctuated each word with a hard thrust and then stilled deep inside her. He swiveled his hips, creating a delicious friction against her sensitive flesh. She felt her control slipping and rallied to regain the upper hand by arching her back and taking him even deeper.

He dipped, captured a nipple between his teeth and tugged just hard enough to make her gasp. The love bite reached deep into her womb. Again and again he tormented her breasts and swiveled his hips, until she lost the battle for control and a tsunami of an orgasm slammed through her. He pounded into her as successive waves of ecstasy robbed her of strength and reason. His groan barely penetrated her overwhelmed state. And then all was still except for their gasping, shallow breaths.

Sanity slowly returned and she realized she'd done it again. She'd lost it. Completely. She'd always focused on bringing her partners pleasure and had never really worried about her own. Making them lose control first meant she didn't have to worry about losing hers. Toby refused to let her sacrifice her satisfaction for his.

Sacrifice.

An invisible icy finger dragged down her spine and everything within her froze except for the panicked thump-bump of her heart.

Sacrificing and martyring were two sides of the same coin.

A martyr.

When had she started emulating her mother?

* * *

"Want to tell me what that was about?" Toby's husky drawl yanked her out of her shocked stupor.

"What?"

"Trying to get me off before you finished."

Her barely cooled body filled with uncomfortable prickly heat. She must have drawn the wrong conclusion. And as soon as she could get to her room she could analyze this…encounter and figure out what was really going on.

She focused on his square chin. "That's crazy. I had orgasms." She wiggled, but it was like trying to slide out from under a boulder. "Let me up. I have to dress for dinner with my suitemates."

Toby didn't budge. His hands and hips kept her pinned to the bed. "You had two alone. You needed one with me. Inside you."

"A technicality. Now move." Still avoiding his gaze, she bowed her back.

"You were trying to get me to lose it while you lay there cool as a cucumber, pushing my buttons. Same as last time."

And just like last time, he'd refused to give up until she'd lost it. Her cool. Her control. Her mind. And this time she couldn't blame her lack of inhibitions on booze or grief.

She needed to get out of here. Needed to think. She struggled again to no avail. He held her down as easily as he would a butterfly. His grip didn't hurt, but it was inescapable.

"You're mistaken. Now please get up."

"Sugar, I'm not getting off you until you level with me. And if you don't quit squirming, we'll be here till breakfast. Maybe longer." He rocked his hips. His thickening erection knocked the breath from her lungs—in surprise and in a shocking burst of arousal.

"I need to use the bathroom," she lied.

"Then talk fast. As soon as you tell me why you don't like coming I'll let you go."

She wanted to be somewhere else. Anyplace else. "I never said that."

"The women I know like getting off. With me. Without me. Whenever and wherever they get a chance. Why do you fight it?"

"I don't."

He leaned down, aligning his nose with hers and forcing her to look into his eyes. His hips pistoned again, and her breath hiccuped as a bolt of unwanted hunger shot straight to her core. "It'll take me less than two minutes to prove you're lying."

The man was cocky, confident…and very likely correct.

She could continue fighting and suffer the consequences or get this over with.

"I don't like losing control," she admitted reluctantly.

"Isn't that the whole point of sex?"

She'd known he wouldn't understand. Nobody would. That's why she'd never tried to explain her conflicting emotions about her dysfunctional family.

She bit her lip and struggled to formulate an acceptable—if not quite accurate—explanation. Toby threaded his fingers through hers still pinned to the pillow, withdrew from her body almost completely and then slid back in. He set a slow pumping pace that kept her brain from forming coherent sentences.

"I can't think when you do…that."

"Don't think. Just talk."

"I thought men didn't like to talk after sex."

"In case…you didn't notice…we're not finished. And I'm not most men. Talking fine-tunes…performance. I talk to my crew…when I drive…and my partner in bed. That way…everybody's…on the same page…and we all get…what we want." His shortened breaths made the words come out in choppy bursts.

Her extremities tingled and her toes dug into the luxurious sheets. Another release hovered disgracefully close, and she trembled with the effort to shut it down. *How does he do that?* She had to get rid of him before she became addicted to the way he made her feel, and the only way to do that was to give him what he wanted—the ugly truth.

"My parents hate each other. My mother has a temper. When she lets go, the whole neighborhood hears."

"She hit you?"

Given his upbringing, she wasn't surprised he'd ask that. "No. Never."

"Stating the obvious—you're not your mother." The tendons of his neck corded. His arms trembled.

"But I'm m-more like her than I want to be. Especially in bed with you."

He swiveled his pelvis and her insides wound tighter. A muffled moan slipped between her lips. She couldn't believe they were having sex and talking about her parents simultaneously. The ick factor should be grossing her out, but the powerful surges of Toby deep inside her kept her too distracted with wave upon wave of arousal to maintain rational thought processes.

And *that* was exactly the problem.

"Genes are there. But you have control. Over decisions. Over choices. Don't have to repeat…her mistakes. You choose…to race clean…or dirty."

A drop of sweat rolled from his forehead down his lean cheek. It dripped from his jaw and landed on her breast. He dipped and lapped it up—only he didn't stop with that single sip. His tongue circled her nipple, teasing but not hitting the sensitive center. The opposite breast received the same neglectful attention. Her nails dug into the backs of his hands. She wanted to scream in frustration. But she wouldn't.

"I don't like her when she loses control," she confessed in a rush and immediately wanted the shameful words back. What kind of person didn't like her mother?

Toby's body stilled, but instead of looking repulsed by her admission, his expression softened. The understanding in his eyes tugged at something deep inside her.

"You don't have to like somebody to love 'em, Amelia."

He knew. He knew what it was like to have a parent you both loved and hated. In that instant she felt a connection with Toby that she'd never experienced with anyone else. Not even Neal. The realization sent a frisson of alarm skittering through her.

How could someone who embodied her worst nightmares understand the emotions tormenting her? It wasn't fair. Her eyes stung at the injustice of being so in tune with a man she didn't love and could never trust her heart to because of his daredevil personality.

"And bed is the one place it's okay to let go. Let go for me, sugar." Then Toby's mouth slanted over hers, and the ride turned as fast and furious as the past five minutes had been slow and steady. Her reeling senses welcomed the desire distracting her from her tumultuous thoughts, and when he released her hands to cup his under her buttocks and drive deeper, she wound her arms around him instead of pushing him away.

Another orgasm burst upon her like a flash fire. Slowly the embers cooled and the haze cleared from her brain, and then she discovered a heartbeat too late that she'd miscalculated.

Her plan for a careful, controlled burnout of the passion between them was in danger of going up in smoke.

She was falling for Toby Haynes.

And she had to stop it. Right now.

Eight

She'd hung him out to dry. Again.

Toby had never met a woman he couldn't figure out. But Amelia Lambert stumped him. As crazy as she apparently was about celebrities, she wasn't impressed with him. That irked him, for some damn fool reason. Did she have any idea how rare it was for a guy to accomplish what he had and at his age? How hard he'd worked to make HRI a force to be reckoned with in racing?

She wasn't interested in having her picture taken with a NASCAR driver, in bragging rights of having screwed one or in boosting her career via his. And he'd had dozens of women try to squeeze a wedding ring out of him. Amelia wasn't one of them.

So what did she want from him? And why did she act as though being with him was a chore? Sure, he knew she'd been assigned to babysit him. But, c'mon, she wanted him—a fact made clear by every heart-revving glance she sent his way and that round of set-the-sheets-on-fire sex.

For a second this afternoon something intense had flared between them. *Too* intense. He didn't *do* intense. Except in racing. The vulnerable look in her eyes had driven him from her arms and her warm, flushed body immediately after sex. He'd retreated to the bathroom to fill the big whirlpool tub for round three. And his cell phone had rung.

By the time he'd finished talking to his team manager, Toby had needed to distract himself with mind-numbing sex, but his sheets had been cold and Amelia long gone.

He scanned Jimmy'z. The club was packed. Before the crash, he'd have enjoyed losing himself in the music and dancing. But tonight the noise reverberated off the walls loud enough to make his eardrums vibrate the way a pounding rubber mallet does a dented fender. And he couldn't dance without falling on his ass.

It had been two weeks since the crash and his balance wasn't any better. Would it ever be?

He shut down that line of thinking. He hadn't achieved this level of success with a negative attitude.

It took him fifteen minutes to locate Amelia on the crowded floor beneath the flashing multicolored lights. Watching her move to the insistent beat in her gauzy flapper-style dress gave him an instant hard-on.

All he wanted to do was forget her. Instead she kept sucking up more and more of his brain space. He'd had her. So why did he still want her? Why wouldn't any other good lookin' woman in the club do? But his radio was tuned to her station and he couldn't change it. God knows he'd tried.

He cut through the crowd, taking a straight line toward his target. Guests in various states of inebriation gyrated around him. He'd been in places like this before, where you didn't need a partner to get on the floor and dance. Women outnumbered the men, and a guy could find himself in the middle of an adolescent fantasy—surrounded by willing women who wanted to party. Not his scene. But he knew plenty who practiced the more-the-merrier method of recreation.

Amelia had her back to him and didn't see him when he stopped behind her.

"This cat-and-mouse game is getting old, sugar." He struggled to keep the anger out of his voice. Her ditching him again had pissed him off that much. If not for the concierge, Toby wouldn't have known where to find her tonight.

She whirled around with a hand to her chest. She had on another one of those push-up bras that gave her the kind of cleavage he wanted to bury his face in.

"Toby. What are you doing here?"

"Looking for you."

The women she'd been dancing with opened their circle to include him, but Amelia planted herself between him and her companions. Hunger flickered in her eyes burning a trail over his black shirt and pants. She wanted him and she didn't want to share. The knowledge made his pulse beat as hard and fast as the bass drum throbbing from the speakers. But then she blinked and the reserved nurse returned.

He'd be damned if he could untangle her mixed signals. She alternated between burning his brain and freezing his johnson.

Someone jolted him from behind, knocking him off balance. He struggled to regain his equilibrium. Amelia's hands curled around his biceps and steadied him.

"Could we…?" She nodded toward a dark corner.

Screw that. He needed to get off this floor before he fell like a drunk and out of this noise before his head exploded.

He headed toward the nearest exit and found himself in an enclosed and mostly deserted courtyard overlooking the Mediterranean. The doors closed behind them, muffling the racket inside.

Amelia released his arm, took a deep breath and then blew it out again before meeting his gaze. "Toby, I thought this…thing between us would work. But it won't."

His eyebrows lowered like a slamming garage door. Green flag. Red flag. What was her deal? "We're good together, Amelia. Like it or not, I flip your toggle switch. And you sure as hell flip mine."

"But I don't think I can—"

Her protest lit the fire of anger and frustration that had been stewing since the phone call from Earl, his team manager.

"Don't give me any crap about your mother. She may have a short fuse, but she at least cared enough to stick around. Mine didn't. And if you've been trying to insult me by comparing me to your father, then you missed the mark. The man's a hero. Mine was a drunken, out-of-work bully. Yours had a job ninety-nine-point-nine percent of the population doesn't have the balls to do. He risked his life to save others. Mine—"

"You're wrong. My father was an adrenaline junkie who thought of nothing but getting his next fix. He never thought about his safety, his family. *Me*." Her eyes widened. She slapped her fingers over her mouth and then slowly lowered her hand. "I'm sorry. I don't know where that came from and I shouldn't have said it."

His anger deflated like a sliced tire. "Sounds like your mother's not the only one who can't forgive him for getting hurt."

"I'm not angry with him. *I'm not*." But she was. Toby understood. He'd been there before.

He stepped closer, close enough to catch a hint of her perfume on the cool night air. Close enough that the need to take her into his arms almost got the better of him. He settled for skimming his index finger down her stiff spine. She shivered. "It's okay to be angry, Amelia."

"No, it's not. Anger isn't productive or healthy. And it always leads to—" She shook her head and looked away.

"Am I gonna have to nail you to the bed again to get you to talk?"

Her gaze jerked to his and a shocked laugh burst from her lungs. "Leave it to you to make this about sex."

"Then make it about something else. Finish what you started."

"It's complicated."

Why did he care? He didn't need to be drawn into the drama of Amelia's life. He had enough drama in his own. Especially now. Maybe that was it—he wanted to think about someone else's problems for a change. "I had a concussion, not a lobotomy. My brain still works. And I'm not going anywhere until you explain."

She bit her bottom lip and then resignation settled over her face. "My mother and I have never been close, but before the accident my father and I were. I was his…princess, for lack of a better description."

"And you became his servant."

"It wasn't like that. I wanted to help. And my mother—"

"Your mother…?" he prompted when she clammed up again.

"My mother suffered from a severe case of caregiver depression. Some days she couldn't get out of bed, and when she did it was usually to lose her temper and shout obscenities at Dad. And he gave as good as he got. When they got going, they'd cause wounds they couldn't fix."

"Sounds like you had to become the adult in the family." Something they had in common. "How did you manage school?"

"I just did. It was kind of a refuge, you know? And it wasn't Mom's fault that she fell apart or that she and I didn't get along. I think she saw me as the reason none of her dreams came true. She was only seventeen when she accidentally became pregnant with me. She had to give up her plans for college and medical school. Her parents sent her to one of those homes for unwed mothers where they try to talk you into giving up your baby. She ran away to be with my father and refused to speak to her parents again."

"How did you manage financially if neither of your parents could work?"

"Dad had disability insurance from the fire department and another policy with the bank that paid off the mortgage if he couldn't work. It was enough for a while, but then he contracted pneumonia and spent a month in the hospital. The medical bills piled up. We couldn't cover them. When I was sixteen, the hospital's collection agency put a lien against our house.

"We were already dancing around social services intervening and putting me in foster care. I had to do something. I had never met my mother's parents before, but I found them and begged for help. I didn't know what else to do. They got Mom the psychiatric help she needed to get past the depression and helped with the bills. They paid for my education. Otherwise I never would have been able to afford college."

Amelia was a fighter. Another thing they had in common. The last thing he needed was something else to like about her.

"And you think sleeping with me will land you in the same boat as your mother?"

She nodded. "I don't want to get stuck with a guy who takes stupid chances. It turned her into a really ugly person."

Well, that was honest. Unpleasant. But honest.

"One, you won't get stuck with me. Two, I may not have a wife or kid depending on me, but Haynes Racing has four hundred employees who count on me to keep roofs over their heads and food in their family's stomachs. I have no intention of letting them down. That's why I *don't* take stupid chances.

"I'm betting your father didn't either. And it sounds like he did everything he could to look out for you financially in case something happened to him.

"Accidents happen, Amelia. Bad things happen to good people. Cheaters profit and innocent bystanders get hurt. Sometimes life sucks. The only thing you can control is the decisions you make."

The words sank in a half beat after he said them, and he realized they didn't only apply to Amelia. He'd been riddled with guilt over Vincent's accident even though a NASCAR investigation had cleared him and his crew of any wrongdoing. Toby had done everything within his power to make his pit as safe as possible. *Accidents happen. Innocent bystanders get hurt.* Vincent didn't blame him. Maybe it was time for Toby to quit blaming himself for Vincent's injuries and move forward. The weight on his shoulders eased.

He refocused on the woman beside him. "I doubt your father went into that fire hoping to come out paralyzed. Most men I know would rather die than become dependent on the ones relying on them."

He shoved his fists into his pockets and stared at the lights outlining the three jetties of Larvotto Beach below. "The last time most of my team saw me, I was unconscious and being airlifted from the infield. My team manager told me today that morale has hit rock-bottom at HRI. The team is falling apart and making stupid mistakes. Somebody's gonna get hurt. And I can't do a damned thing about it because I'm cornered here like a kid in time-out."

He huffed out a heavy breath and tried to rein in his frustration. His exile wasn't her fault, but his team was his responsibility. He had a job to do and he didn't know how he could do it from here. "They need to know I'm okay."

"You want to get back in your car," she said quietly.

"Hell, yes." He faced her and saw the worry pleating her forehead. She claimed she didn't care, but not even the dim lighting in the courtyard could hide the concern plain as day on her expressive face. He wasn't sure how he felt about that. Part of him liked it. Part of him wanted to run. "But I'm not ready. And, contrary to what you think, I don't have a death wish. I won't drive again until I'm cleared."

If he was ever cleared.

"Why don't you go home?"

"You're just trying to get rid of me because I make you hot."

A smile flickered across her mouth and her cheeks pinked in the milky moonlight. "Maybe."

"I'm supposed to be watching the wedding party. Even though we both know that's bull."

"Vincent asked Franco—Stacy's…um…boyfriend—to watch over us, too, so it's not like we wouldn't have someone to turn to if problems cropped up. You could go home for a few days, reassure your teammates and then come back. Vincent would never have to know."

The idea sounded plausible. Doable. "I don't lie to my friends. I'll run it by him. If he agrees, I'll go." He needed to go.

He curved his hands over her smooth shoulders, savoring the warm satin of her skin. "While I'm gone, do you think you can dig up some of your father's courage and find the guts to admit you want me instead of blowing hot and cold?"

She stiffened. "I don't want to want you. I'd give anything not to want you."

That hit hard and low. "A driver's not good enough for you?"

She winced at the harsh tone of his voice. "It's not you, Toby. It's me. I don't like who I am when I'm with you."

"A sex goddess who blows my—" he cocked an eyebrow "—mind?"

She blinked, blushed and then shook her head. "An impractical, impulsive, out-of-control stranger."

"We've covered that. I told you bed's the one place it's good to lose control. And I like losing it with you." He tucked a windblown strand of hair behind her ear and then cupped her cheek. The hitch in her breath sent him flashing back to the sounds she'd made hours ago when he'd been deep inside her, but something soft and warm in her expression warned him to paint the boundaries. "What's wrong with a little sex between friends?"

Her eyes widened. "Friends? Is that what we are?"

If not friends, then what? He had nothing more to offer. "I like you, Amelia. But neither one of us wants this to end at the altar. You in my bed in Monaco—that's what I want. What we both want. You're the one who laid those ground rules. And I guarantee you will not get stuck with me."

She tilted her head back and bit her lip. A string of emotions—caution, worry, desire—chased across her face before she blinked them away and met his gaze. "Okay. We'll have Monaco."

She needed an intervention, Amelia decided Sunday night. Because she'd lost her mind.

There was absolutely no other way to explain why she'd agreed to Toby's risky proposition.

As soon as she'd agreed to his terms Friday night, he'd whisked her back to the hotel and into his suite, where he'd made lo—*ahem*—had sex with her for hours. Amazing, lost-count-of-how-many-climaxes-she'd-had sex.

By the time she'd awoken Saturday morning, Toby had already left the hotel. She'd run her hand over his empty pillow and wished he didn't have a self-destructive streak a mile wide. Sure, he claimed he didn't take unnecessary chances and she'd seen a few hints of rational behavior. But she'd also seen the yearning in his eyes when he talked about getting back in his race car. And it had only been weeks since his last crash.

Amelia knew from experience that daredevils never changed their ways. She'd had too many run-ins with frequent flyers—the patients who swore they'd never repeat the risky feat that had landed them in the hospital only to have them return later. She didn't trust mere words. Seeing was believing.

The scary part was that for one foolish moment this morning she'd wanted to change Toby, to ask him to take up a safer occupation. But for years she'd watched her mother try—and fail—to change her father.

A relationship with a man like Toby was akin to walking a high wire without a net. Sooner or later she'd fall and the landing would be painful. Probably crippling.

Getting involved with him was complicated on so many levels. Besides her dysfunctional family, there was Neal. She'd already buried one man she loved. She couldn't handle burying another. She couldn't—wouldn't—let herself love Toby. She could be his "friend" for her remaining time in Monaco, but that was where she absolutely had to draw the line.

And since she couldn't count on Candace or Madeline to be voices of reason, she'd decided to launch her own intervention.

A tap on her bedroom door yielded Madeline. "Are you sure you don't want to go with Stacy and me to Le Texan? I've heard everybody who's anybody hits their Alamo Bar for margaritas."

The chance to do more celebrity watching tempted her, but Amelia had more important plans. One way or another she was going to cure herself of this ridiculous crush she had on Toby Haynes. *And a crush is all it is.*

"No, but thanks for asking. You two have fun. I'm going to kick back, watch some TV and catch up on sleep."

A valid excuse since they'd been keeping late hours and Toby had kept her awake most of Friday night.

Stacy joined Madeline and asked, "You're sure?"

"I'm good here. I might even try one of those decadent desserts the chef specializes in. Have fun."

"Okay, then. G'night."

Amelia wiped her damp palms on her jeans and reached for the remote. Assignment one: witness every hair-raising lap and crash of today's NASCAR race. Assignment two: bury herself in Internet research and bombard her brain with race wreck and fatality statistics. Assignment three: a clean, swift break.

It didn't take long to find an American sports network

broadcasting the race live. Her stomach knotted and her pulse quickened as she watched the pace car circle the Michigan race track.

Toby was there. Somewhere. In the crowd. He might not be driving one of those cars today, but he would be as soon as he could be.

And she was going to sit through this race if it killed her, because she needed to remind herself what he did for a living.

Toby Haynes risked his life for sport.

"Hey, buddy, switch?"

Amelia's heart and feet faltered at the sound of a familiar deep Southern drawl. She stepped on Prince Dominic's toes, winced an apology and jerked to a halt in the middle of La Salle Des Étoiles, the location of *Le Bal de L'Été*, a charity ball held in the Monte Carlo Sporting Club.

Toby, with Madeline as his partner, stood beside them. The other dancers flowed past their little quartet.

Dominic released Amelia and bowed. "Certainly. Thank you for the dance, Amelia."

"Um…you're welcome, Your Highness."

Madeline, looking none too happy over the exchange, paired up with Prince Dominic. The irony of the situation tweaked Amelia's funny bone. Madeline, the one who'd sworn just days ago that she wouldn't fall for the magic of Monaco, had discovered her vacation lover was an incognito prince. A *real* prince with a crown, a kingdom and the whole shebang.

With more than a little reluctance Amelia moved stiffly into Toby's arms. Anger simmered beneath the surface. She didn't want to dance with him and kept as wide a distance as possible between their bodies, but there was no denying the pulse-accelerating effect of his warm hands resting on her waist and enclosing her fingers. She numbly followed his lead.

His silvery-blue gaze rolled across her bare shoulders, down her yellow tulle dress and back up to her face and upswept hair. "You look good."

Amelia glared at him, but her body tingled as a result of his thorough scrutiny, and her breath caught at the hunger in his eyes when their gazes met. Worse, her own hormones kicked into action.

"Let me guess. This is a booty call?"

His eyes narrowed. "Come again?"

"You could have phoned." She instantly wanted the bitchy words back. She sounded like a nagging wife, and that was something she'd vowed to never become. But after his big show of "friendship," Toby hadn't called or e-mailed once in the seven days since he'd left.

Wasn't it adolescent of her to have hurt feelings?

For a moment Toby looked as if he had something serious to say and then the playboy facade dropped over him as clearly as the curtain had closed after the play she'd attended with her suitemates Thursday night.

That killer smile curved his lips. And there went her toes, dammit. "Miss me, sugar?"

Yes. Dammit squared. "Your ego astounds me."

"That's not the only thing." A naughty glint lit his eyes and her pulse took off for the races.

She was annoyed with him for not calling and even more irritated with herself for jumping each time the hotel phone rang or the message light flashed.

She hadn't known if or when he would return until she'd looked up ten minutes ago and spotted him at the entrance of the ballroom, standing beside Vincent Reynard, the groom-to-be. For someone who'd been eager to get rid of

Toby two weeks ago, Amelia had been alarmingly happy to see him tonight. And then a bevy of beautiful, fawning females had surrounded him—the same way they had on the race shows she'd watched. At least none of these elegantly gowned women had whipped out a Sharpie and asked him to autograph bare skin the way the race fans had.

She was jealous, she realized with jaw-dropping shock, of the groupies and the ball beauties. She didn't have the right and didn't want the right to object to the company Toby kept. No, sir. Uh-uh.

But the overly attentive women raised her hackles.

Clearly her intervention hadn't worked as well as she'd hoped.

"Excuse me." She tried to pull away, but his hold tightened. He yanked her against the hard, hot length of his body. The lapels of his tux jacket scraped against her sensitive breasts, making her gasp as sensation shot straight to her core, and every cell in her body shouted, *Welcome home!*

That wasn't good.

"What kind of hello is that for a man who's flown across an ocean to hold you?" he murmured against her temple.

Her breath hitched and a tingle raced through her. She wrenched free without thinking and then noticed her sudden movement hadn't left him unsteady. "Your equilibrium has improved. You'll be returning to the track soon."

"Hope so. Let's get out of here."

"What if I want to stay and dance?"

You're being contrary, Amelia.

He glanced over the crowd—many of whom were staring back at them since they stood in the middle of the dance floor.

"I can manage a few slow ones while you hunt for famous faces."

Her temper cooled enough for her to notice his pallor beneath his tan and the strain tightening his lips. "Toby, are you okay?"

He shrugged. "I've been poked and prodded, X-rayed and MRI'ed from one end to the other this week. I've put out fires, done interviews and personally reassured each HRI team member and every sponsor. Reynard Hotels is only one of dozens we use. What I really need is to get horizontal. Preferably with you beside me."

Anticipation fizzed over her in a wave of goose bumps. The scary thing was that beside him was exactly where she wanted to be.

That definitely was not good.

Nine

Amelia had never had a date fall asleep on her before. Should she be insulted?

But Toby wasn't exactly a date. He was her temporary lover and the last obstacle to overcome in getting her life back on the right track.

Although the hotel was barely a mile away, traffic moved at a crawl compliments of the vast number of people wanting to celebrate the opening of the Monte Carlo season. Toby hadn't lasted five minutes in the dark car before his big body tilted against hers.

She liked the warmth and solid weight of him against her side. Turning her head slightly, she buried her nose in his soft hair to inhale his scent. Desire curled deep in her abdomen. How could she want him this badly? Which twisted Fate had cursed her to finding sexual satisfaction with the one type of man she'd sworn to avoid?

But was Toby really an adrenaline junkie in the sense that she'd come to know and despise through her job?

She'd spent countless hours on the Internet over the past week, learning more about NASCAR than she'd ever wanted to know, and what she'd learned had surprised her. Safety was apparently a priority for the organization, and the rules and regulations intended to keep the drivers safe were overwhelming.

Car racing wasn't bungee jumping, but she'd always dumped them in the same category. Reckless. Pointless. Stupid.

The articles she'd read about Toby from *Business Week* to *ESPN* had all been complimentary. They'd praised his driving skill, his coolheadedness, his business acumen and his determination to make his organization one of the best. In fact, one of the magazines had proclaimed Haynes Racing Inc. a rising star among NASCAR's top dynasties.

Was she wrong about Toby? She suspected she might be. Without a doubt he had an ego, but it looked as though he'd earned the right to be proud. And maybe she had been prejudiced.

Was she also wrong about her father?

As a child, she'd only heard her mother's side of the story. The slurs had only increased in frequency and viciousness after her father's accident. These days Amelia tuned out the words when the tone turned ugly. But until Toby had pointed it out, she had never considered the financial side. Her father *had* planned ahead and he *had* provided for them. If not for his pneumonia and long hospital stay, they would have managed without her grandparents' assistance—not that she'd ever wish Gran and Pops out of her life. She adored them both, and if not for them holding the fort, Amelia couldn't be in Monaco.

People who lived for the moment didn't plan ahead. They acted impulsively, foolishly and without thought for others. Despite his risky job, her father didn't fit that description.

Neither did Toby.

Or was she just fooling herself? Had sexual attraction impaired her ability to think logically?

She studied Toby in the darkness of the limo. Each flicker of light from passing cars and buildings accentuated the tired lines on his face. He looked softer somehow and more boyish without the playboy facade or the competitive edge sharpening his square jaw and prominent cheekbones.

Struggling with the need to trace the shadowy smudges beneath his eyes, she tightened her fingers around his where he'd linked their hands and rested them on his thigh and shifted her gaze to the designer boutiques, sidewalk cafés and posh hotels outside the windows.

Of the trio of her, Candace and Madeline, Amelia had always considered herself the together one. She was the one who knew where she was going and had a plan to get there. Or so she'd thought. She had a job she loved, a comfortable home and great friends. Before Monaco, she'd been convinced the only thing keeping her life from being perfect was the right man to share it with.

How could she have been so wrong? A man wouldn't fix what ailed her. She needed to work on herself. And why had it taken Toby and a trip abroad to show her the error of her ways? She'd learned more about herself in the past two weeks than she had in the previous twenty-seven years.

She'd been sabotaging her search for Mr. Right, emulating her mother's martyrdom and harboring a secret resentment toward her father for an accident that probably hadn't been his fault. She was a psychiatrist's dream pa-

ient. He'd hear her pathetic tale and see the dollar signs
years of therapy would generate.

The question was, where did she go from here?

Amelia didn't have the answer when the limo stopped
at the hotel entrance. She braced herself for another dose
of Toby's magnetism and then gently shook him. "Toby,
we're here."

He jerked upright, blinked and then his eyes zeroed in
on hers. How could he look alert so quickly? "Sorry. Too
many twenty-hour days."

"That's not good for you—especially with a concussion."

"Did I ever tell you your nurse voice turns me on?"

Heat seeped through her veins like an IV narcotic, leaving her flushed and dizzy. Luckily Louis opened the door
at that moment, giving her a few minutes to recover.

Toby helped her from the car. "Night, Louis."

"Good night, sir." He nodded. "Mademoiselle."

"Good night, Louis," she replied as Toby's arm looped
around her waist. He led her into the hotel and straight to
the elevator. For some foolish reason Amelia's muscles
tightened with nervousness. "Should I congratulate you on
your team's performance last weekend?"

He turned sharply. "You watched?"

"Yes. And the race shows afterward, too." Her stomach
burned and churned. "I saw you on the pit box. You're
quite popular with female fans."

The brass doors opened. The hand at her waist urged her
into the cubicle. Toby leaned a shoulder against the wall
and appraised her. "Jealous?"

Yes. She focused on the seam between the doors. "I would
like to think for safety's sake that we are exclusive during
this…affair."

He caught her chin and forced her to look at him. His

eyes were direct and sincere. "I barely slept while I wa gone. When I did, I slept alone."

She shouldn't feel relieved and hated that she did. If he' tomcatted around, she'd have the perfect excuse to end thi before it was too late. "I couldn't blame you if you did Those women are beautiful, built like Barbie dolls and—"

"Easy."

She frowned. "Are you saying I'm not? Because I fel into bed with you faster than I ever have with anyone be fore. Then and now."

He laughed. "Sugar, you wear me out with all the chas ing. But that's okay. I like chasing you. Great view."

He accompanied his words by patting and then caress ing her bottom. Her internal muscles squeezed. Backing her against the wall, he lowered his head. Shamelessly eager for his kiss, Amelia lifted her chin. His breath swep her lips and her knees weakened.

The elevator opened with a ding. Toby withdrew, leav ing her unsatisfied. He linked his fingers through hers and towed her down the hall to his suite. There was no question where she'd spend the night and she didn't play coy. Fo better or worse, she wanted this, wanted him.

She stepped inside and stopped abruptly. Two lamps li the sitting area and a torchière illuminated the space i front of the windows where the dining room table used t be. "What is that?"

He banded his arms around her from behind, sandwich ing her between the warmth of his hands on her belly and the press of his lean body blanketing her back. His lips grazed her bare throat, making her hot and trembly. "Ping Pong table."

"I can see that. But why do you have one in your suite?" She gasped as he nipped her earlobe. His hands rose at a snail's pace to finally cover her breasts. For a man whose claim to fame lay in speed, he could be incredibly, torturously slow at times.

"We're going into training tomorrow. But tonight we're gonna make up for lost time."

The latter statement made her heart stutter, but she focused on the former. "What kind of training?"

"Eye-hand. Reflexes. Reaction times. Endurance." He shifted his hips, and the hard length of his erection pressed the small of her back. "Ever play video games?"

"Um…no."

"I'll teach you. Loser plays naked."

"I don't think so."

He had no problem with eye-hand coordination, if the thumbs simultaneously circling her breasts were any indication. And endurance… Her train of thought jumped the track as he pinched and rolled her nipples through her gown. Oh, yeah. Endurance had never been an issue either.

Desire knotted inside her. It wasn't fair that Toby could make her ache when the two men she'd loved enough for intimacy hadn't even scratched the surface.

He nudged her forward with a bump of his hips. They crossed the room and stopped with the side of the green table pressing inches below her mound. Toby released her without stepping away. The air shifted as he moved behind her. Out of the corner of her eye she saw his tux jacket hit the floor. His shirt followed. And then he unzipped her dress. His warm, slightly rough hands brushed her shoulders, sweeping the spaghetti straps down her arms until the yellow fabric pooled on the table. The cut of the dress hadn't allowed for a bra.

He sucked a sharp breath and ran a finger under the elastic of her plain white cotton panties. "These are so damned sexy."

He had to be joking. She wanted to turn and look in his eyes, but Toby held her captive between his hips and the table. "Don't most men prefer Victoria's Secret thongs or something sheer?"

His bare chest scorched her back and his hands recaptured her breasts. He caressed, plucked the tight tips and licked, sucked and nibbled her neck for excruciating moments before answering, "I'm not most men. I like these—" he snapped the elastic, and the slight sting below her navel was about the most erotic thing Amelia had ever experienced "—because they're straitlaced. When I get you between the sheets, you're anything but. You burn me up."

Had it not been for the table digging into the tops of her thighs, she might have collapsed. Leaning forward, she flattened her palms on the cool table to keep herself upright.

"Got a problem with that?" He pushed her panties past her hips, bunching them with her gown at table height. Slipping his fingers into the cleft of her body, he found her wetness. His growl vibrated against her nape and down her spine.

"No," she whispered. Desire arrowed straight to her core as he caressed her. Her fingers and toes contracted. She was incredibly close to climax and he hadn't even kissed her mouth yet.

She tensed, trying to maintain control, and he bit her neck, not hard enough to leave a mark but enough to make her drop her guard.

"Let go for me, Amelia," he ordered.

One hand teased her breast. The other delved through her damp curls with devastating, unrelenting accuracy. His teeth grazed a trail along her neck and shoulder as he relentlessly rushed her over the edge. She shuddered in his arms as release racked her far too quickly.

She needed more. Needed him. Inside her. She pushed her bottom against his erection. "Toby, please."

He grasped her waist, spun her around and lifted her out of her dress to sit her on the table. A quick movement stripped her panties down her legs, but he left her stiletto sandals behind. He stepped between her thighs. Clamping his hand behind her neck, he yanked her forward for a slap of her breasts against his chest and a ravenous meeting of mouths. His tongue thrust deep, tangled, stroked. His hurried hands raked her back, her bottom, her legs.

Impatient, she tugged open his belt and pants and cupped his erection through his briefs. What had he done to her? When had she become a woman driven by her desires?

He swore when her fingers delved beneath fabric to surround him, shoved his hand into his pocket and retrieved a condom and then let his pants fall to his ankles. Amelia took the packet from him, ripped it open and rolled the latex down his steely shaft.

He gritted his teeth and inhaled deeply through his nose, and then his hands curled around her hips and pulled her forward. She guided him into her center, where he plunged deep in one sure stroke. His heart pounded hard and fast beneath her palm and his chest hair tickled her skin.

He speared his hands into her hair and then muttered against her lips as his hips pistoned. "Hair. Down."

She reached up and released the single clip. Her hair tumbled in a cool tangle against her shoulders. His fingers stabbed into the strands, dragging her back until her spine pressed against the cold table.

The table was hard. Toby was harder. Hotter. He pounded into her. She tangled her legs around his waist and arched to meet each hurried thrust. This wasn't like before. This need was stronger. Deeper. More intense. Her muscles

quivered as passion built swiftly. The control she valued
so highly was nowhere to be found. Seconds later, release
rocketed through her.

Toby's groan mingled with her moan as he shuddered
above her and then stilled. His labored breaths steamed her
neck. His lips and hands soothed as if to make up for the
frenzied lovemaking.

Slowly he eased upright, bracing his weight on one arm.
His gaze met hers and his palm cradled her cheek. "For
what it's worth, I missed you, too. Didn't want to. Didn't
have time to." He shrugged. "But that's the way it is."

Her stomach swooped as if she'd plunged over the peak
of the highest roller coaster. And there in the least romantic
place in the entire world—flat on her back on top of a Ping
Pong table, for pity's sake—Amelia realized this wasn't a
crush.

She'd done the unthinkable.

She'd fallen in love with Toby Haynes.

And there was no chance at all that he'd ever return her
feelings. Or that she'd want him to.

Whoever had come up with the line "Out of sight, out
of mind" was full of crap.

Toby stared at the ceiling, unable to sleep despite the
fatigue chaining his body to the mattress. But instead of
rising and dealing with the mountain of race weekend work
waiting on his notebook computer, he stayed where he
was with Amelia tucked against his side and her head on
his shoulder. Warm. Soft. Asleep. Her sweet-smelling hair
teased his chin and her soft puffs of breath stirred his chest
hair. One silky leg snaked across his.

She'd been antsy as hell to leave after that embarrass-
ingly fast encounter on the Ping-Pong table, but he'd bull-

dozed her into the shower and then back to bed for a slower round. He had to make it up to her for going off like an inexperienced kid beneath the high school bleachers.

What in the hell had happened tonight?

He'd been looking forward to surprising her at the ball, to telling her about his medical progress and his crazy week and hearing about hers. But the moment he'd spotted her in the prince's arms he'd wanted to kick some royal ass. Knowing the guy was her suitemate's lover hadn't made a bit of difference. Toby had wanted blue blood on his knuckles.

Because of his father, Toby didn't do violence. He let his driving do the talking instead of his fists.

And he didn't do jealousy. He had never made a fool of himself over any woman and never would. But he'd felt more than a twinge of possessiveness tonight. Amelia was his. For now. He'd worked damned hard to get her back in the sack.

It hadn't helped that he knew she deserved a man who could give her the royal treatment and fulfill all her silly romantic notions. God knows she had a surplus of those.

Despite having the Atlantic Ocean and a seven-hour time difference between them, she'd monopolized his thoughts all week. He'd driven himself to exhaustion day after day, but every night he'd fallen asleep thinking about her. She'd invaded his dreams and been his first waking thought each morning—a result of the morning boner those dreams had generated, he assured himself.

He'd wanted her no-nonsense opinion on this medical test or that one and he'd wondered what she'd think of the other drivers' wives. Some were in it for the money and attention, but there were a few stickers he thought she'd like.

Did Amelia have what it took to be a sticker? To stand by her man through good times and bad?

Probably. But it didn't matter. He didn't do long-term relationships.

He had to nip this thing he had for Amelia Lambert in the bud before he wasted any more time picturing her naked on the king-size bed of his motor coach.

He had two weeks left to get his fill of her, and the only way to do that was to saturate himself with her company and her body. Starting now, he'd stick to her as tight as the decals on his race car.

And then it would be over and he'd be free of this obsession that had haunted him for months.

"Where are you going?"

Amelia winced at the sound of Toby's sleep-roughened voice behind her. "To my room."

She gave up on the stubborn zipper and reached for the doorknob. She'd hoped to escape his suite without having to face him. The discovery of her feelings was too new and raw.

She heard him cross the room, and then his warm fingers brushed her spine as he finished zipping her dress. "Stay. I'll order breakfast."

Her nerve endings danced beneath a tent of goose bumps. She didn't want to turn around. Didn't want to look him in the eye. If he guessed her feelings, he might pity her, and she'd had a lifetime of pitying looks from the neighbors after each of her parents' shouting matches.

Or, worse, he might paste on that professional face he wore when approached by autograph-seeking fans. There was nothing wrong with that face if you didn't know him well enough to see the walls behind the smile. But she did.

That brash smile hid a really nice guy. One who was loyal to his friends and his employees. One who'd been abandoned by his mother and hurt by his father but had still managed to turn out all right. Better than all right. And it was those moments when she'd glimpsed past the cocky attitude that had landed her in this trouble.

"I need clothes. I can't wear my evening gown all day."

The pale yellow tulle showed signs of having spent the night on the floor. Last night the gown had made her feel like a wood nymph. Today it looked more like crumpled litter.

And she needed space. To think. To decide how to fix this mess she'd gotten into. *If* it was fixable.

"I'll lend you a shirt." His arms banded around her, pulling her stiff body against his. From the intensity of the heat, she guessed he'd climbed from the bed naked to come after her. "You'll look sexy as hell in my shirt."

"I don't want to miss Candace's morning meeting."

"Vincent hasn't seen her in weeks. He'll keep her occupied."

"You don't know that for sure."

"Yeah, I do. Last night he told me he planned to take her to his place and keep her in bed for a week." His bristly chin prickled deliciously against her jaw, and his hands stoked the fires that should have been extinguished last night. "Sounds like a good plan."

"Toby—" Her breath hitched as he cupped her mound through the wispy layers of fabric. "I can't find my panties. Last night's or the ones you stole the other day."

"I'm holding them for ransom." She felt his smile against her cheek and heard it in his voice.

His fingers worked magic, pooling heat beneath his palm. If she didn't get away soon, she'd cave. She twisted abruptly and pulled out of his arms. He looked sleep-rumpled and sexy with his hair standing in golden spikes and a morning erection that begged for attention. *Dangerous territory.*

She focused on the tiny scar on the bridge of his nose rather than his eyes or his gorgeous body. "I want my own clothes."

He swiped a hand across his chin. "Yeah. Okay. Bring a couple of days' worth while you're at it."

"Why?"

"You'll be spending your nights here."

Internal alarms clanged. "That's not a good idea."

"You like sneaking out every morning?"

Not really. "Sharing your room is too…domesticated."

"It's convenient."

She gathered her courage and met his gaze. Her resistance wavered, but she soldiered on. "Have you ever lived with a woman before?"

"No."

"And I've never lived with a man. I don't think we should be each other's firsts for something so important."

"It's only for two weeks."

"It would still feel like a commitment to me. And you said…you didn't want one of those." She hated the slight rise in her voice, as if she were asking instead of stating a fact.

His expression closed. "Monaco only. That's our deal."

Her heart sank a little. Yes, that was their deal. One she'd readily agreed to. How could she have known her feelings for Toby would change? But his hadn't. And just because she'd fallen for him didn't mean she could ever be comfortable with his hazardous career.

That being the case, she couldn't and wouldn't let herself get used to playing house with Toby. It would make ending this relationship even more difficult.

His eyebrows lowered. He looked ready to argue but shook his head as if deciding against it. "Today's race day. I want to show you what I do when I'm not in the car. One of my techies did some space-age stuff and rigged up my laptop so I can communicate with the team live. You can listen in on the radio."

His excitement was palpable and curiosity got the better of her. "Okay."

"We'll start after we work out. Bring clothes for today and tonight, too." He turned and strode back into the bedroom.

Amelia stared after him, both stunned and amused by his assumption that she'd comply without question. He'd soon see otherwise.

And as inevitable as sunrise, she'd soon see heartbreak.

Who was this impostor and what had he done with Toby Haynes? Amelia asked herself as she paced Toby's suite Sunday night.

The seductive playboy had vanished, and in his place sat a sharp, decisive, no-nonsense businessman. Even his body language had changed. Instead of a casual you-know-you-want-me-come-and-get-me posture, Toby looked commanding and every inch the multimillionaire force to be reckoned with the magazines declared him to be.

He communicated with his teams via a headset microphone and watched the race live through his laptop. Beyond the computer screen on the coffee table, a big flat-panel TV hanging on the far wall also played the race. Toby watched both with an eagle eye and juggled comments and responses to and from the three race teams he had running today as easily as he'd recite his alphabet.

Frankly Amelia found this new persona incredibly sexy. And she hadn't had many complaints with the previous one.

For the past two hours he'd analyzed and discussed how to run this race from thousands of miles away. When time permitted, he'd turn off the microphone and explain some of the goings on to her.

Amelia had expected to be bored. She wasn't. The difference between watching this race with Toby and watching last weekend's alone was like night and day. In fact, this behind-the-scenes view fascinated her and had taught her a very important lesson.

Racing wasn't about the wrecks. It was strategy. Like chess. Only faster. And with more at stake. Sure, most of the technical lingo streaming through the speakers zipped right over her head, but from what she gathered, rocket-science calculations influenced every decision, from when and how many tires to change to when to stop for gas and how much to put in the tank.

She'd had no idea driving in circles—or in this case, on an irregularly shaped road course—could be so complicated.

A string of curses erupted from the computer. She recognized Toby's substitute driver's voice. The young driver was a hothead. It wasn't the first time he'd gone off.

"What happened?" she asked as his car pulled out of line. Several vehicles passed him.

Toby silenced the mic. "He got hung out to dry." At her confused frown he explained, "The car behind Jay's bumped him out of place. He lost the draft. It slows him down and he falls back in the pack."

The driver made a few erratic moves on the track as if he wanted to sideswipe someone.

Toby said, "Jay, if you bend my car on purpose, you're out of a job. Shake it off. The best revenge is finishing ahead of the dickhead, and if you keep your cool, you can be a contender. We're not looking for a win. Just a top-ten finish."

Another surprise: winning wasn't everything. Consistency ruled. A bunch of top-ten finishes triumphed over a few number ones in the NASCAR scoring system.

"I'm going to take him out," the driver replied.

"If you try, you run the risk of cutting a tire, hitting the wall and taking yourself out. Play it safe. Be patient."

Play it safe. Be patient.

She never would have expected to hear those words from Toby's lips. She would have expected a risk-taking adrenaline junkie to encourage retribution. Instead Toby calmly talked his guy out of anger. Again.

Energy rolled off Toby in waves—waves that filled Amelia and made sitting still difficult. He'd been focused so intently that, other than talking to her, he hadn't taken a break since before the race began. His voice was beginning to get husky. She crossed to the minibar, poured him a glass of iced water and slipped in front of him.

He winked his thanks and her heart hiccuped. Two weeks. She had two weeks left and then he'd be gone. Back to his races. Back to his female fans.

Another pair of cars bumped. Smoke filled the air surrounding them and sparks arched off the pavement. "Caution flag's out, Jay. Settle down. Be ready to move on green."

Toby flipped up his microphone, caught her hand and pulled her into his lap. His thighs were hard beneath her bottom, his palm warm on her belly, her need instantaneous.

"Having fun yet?"

"Yes." And she meant it. She marveled at the change. In him. In her. Instead of viewing the race as forty-three men trying to kill themselves, she'd caught Toby's excitement.

Omigod. Surely with her aversion to dangerous sports she wasn't becoming a NASCAR fan?

He massaged her nape. "When we get back to the States, I want you to come to a race."

Amelia gasped in surprise and hope surged in her chest. Was he saying he wanted more than Monaco? And if so, could she live with knowing each day he went to work might be his last?

She didn't know. The only thing she knew for sure was that she didn't want to become a nag like her mother.

As if he'd read her mind he said, "Just one race before we say goodbye."

Her hopes plummeted. Apparently this race—her race to win Toby's heart—was all about the crash.

Ten

Some butts were made for bicycle shorts, Amelia decided Wednesday afternoon as she watched Toby climb from his bike at the top of the hill outside a village perched on the side of a mountain.

She'd enjoyed every bit of the scenery on today's ride from Monaco into France, including the jagged cliffs, olive groves and cypress, pine and mimosa trees. But she'd especially enjoyed following Toby's tush in skintight black Lycra.

The week while he'd been in the States had dragged, but the four days since his return had flown past. When Candace didn't have her working on the wedding, Toby had kept her occupied for the remainder of the days and nights. She hadn't had a moment to herself.

With his equilibrium returned, Toby had exercised and played at a furious pace, but always with the proper safety gear and always including her. If she'd ever doubted his safety-consciousness, then he'd shown her differently. He'd practically armored them both to go mountain biking today and Jet Skiing yesterday. He'd made her wear eye and hand protection and a mouth guard to play handball. A mouth guard, for pity's sake. That had to be the least sexy thing she'd ever worn in her life.

Boy, had she been wrong about him being reckless. That didn't help her situation. If he'd been careless just once, it would have made pulling back easier.

She dismounted and walked beside him. "So where are we and why are we here?"

"Roquebrune-Cap-Martin has a tenth-century castle. Since you're into that stuff, I thought you'd enjoy a tour."

She fell a little deeper in love with him in that instant, as she had done a half dozen other times this week. Like when he'd surprised her with a snow globe of the Monte Carlo Casino, her favorite building, or when he'd taken her to dinner and a couple of clubs where celebrities hung out and let her gawk her fill of famous faces. And now a castle tour.

"We'll leave the bikes here and climb." He gestured first to a modern bike rack and then to the historic-looking, steep stone steps.

She pressed a hand to her heart while he secured the bikes.

Would he go to this much trouble if he didn't care about her?

He shoved his sunglasses into his hair and pulled a bottle of water from his knapsack—a bag that included everything from sunscreen to a first-aid kit. She knew because she'd watched him pack it.

"Thanks." She twisted off the cap and sipped. The chilled water cooled her parched throat. A rivulet escaped her lips and ran down her chin.

Toby reached out and caught it with his thumb—a

thumb that caressed her jawline and eventually paused over her rapidly beating pulse. His silvery-blue gaze locked on hers and heated.

She gulped and offered him the bottle when what she needed to do was dump the cool liquid over her overheated body.

He raised the plastic to his lips. The simple act of drinking behind her seemed as intimate as a kiss, and it, combined with the promise in his eyes of passion to come later, stole her breath and dried her freshly moistened mouth. Sexual energy crackled between them.

Toby recapped the bottle, dropped it back in his pack and captured her hand. With each step she took into the past down medieval stone streets and steeple-covered alleyways Amelia became more determined to make her affair with Toby last as long as the ancient castle walls around them.

She couldn't be happy with just Monaco anymore. And maybe it was time she fought for what she wanted.

"I should have known men would bring sex toys and gag gifts to the shower," Amelia said to Candace Thursday night in the Hôtel de Paris's luxurious Churchill Suite.

Candace flashed a wicked grin. "And I hope you and Toby enjoy your party favor."

The bride-to-be had given each member of the wedding party a set of "lovers' dice." One die had a body part on each side. Face, lips, breast, genitals… The other had commands. Caress, touch, lick, bite… The players were supposed to roll the dice and do whatever the cubes commanded.

The hot look Toby had flashed Amelia when he'd opened his gift had nearly incinerated her on the spot. Without a doubt he was looking forward to using his new toy, but not because he needed help being creative in bed.

Amelia shook her head to clear the haze of arousal clouding her thinking. "Candace, you have to stop match-making."

"You must admit I did a stellar job this time. You guys are perfect together."

All Amelia had to do was convince Toby of that. And she intended to try.

A knock on the door yielded the porter towing a lug-gage trolley.

"Would you please load up the gifts and carry them to the limo waiting downstairs?" Amelia instructed.

He went to work and Amelia turned back to Candace. "I could wring your neck for lying to me—to all of us—about this pregnancy. Not only was it *not* a secret, you've been us-ing your morning sickness like a get-out-of-jail-free card."

"Oops. Busted." Candace gave an unrepentant shrug. "Tonight was truly amazing. I can't thank you enough. You and Toby make a great team."

The Jack-and-Jill shower had been a success not only because the menu Amelia and Toby had chosen had been delicious and the setting spectacular but also because the naughty gifts and commentary provided by Vincent's friends had kept everyone entertained.

"And that video roast Toby put together for Vincent with the other NASCAR drivers was a hoot. I laughed so hard I almost wet myself. He's definitely a keeper, Amelia."

"Enough already. Message received."

The porter finished and headed for the door.

Candace kissed Amelia's cheek. "That's my cue. I'm going to take this loot to Vincent's place. If you see him before I do, tell him he owes me for skipping out early. I know he and Toby had to talk business, but this is a huge haul. I'll see you tomorrow."

Smiling at a job well done, Amelia shut the door behind her friend and scooped up the last of the wrapping paper. She stuffed it into a trash bag and glanced at her watch. Room service would be here with dinner in just over an hour. She scanned the suite one last time. Maid service would clean up tomorrow, but Amelia wanted to get the worst of it before Toby returned. He'd disappeared somewhere with Vincent about twenty minutes ago.

Early-evening sun streamed through the wall of windows at her back, casting a golden glow across the parallel white sofas. She tilted her head and considered the fireplace centered in the dark wainscoted wall. Was it too warm to have a fire? She'd never made love in front of a blaze. It would be a first, one of many she wanted to share with Toby.

When room service arrived, she'd ask them to light the logs. Happy with her decision, she set the trash bag by the door and headed for the bedroom.

Her blood raced in anticipation of the night ahead—one of only ten they had left in Monaco. Because he'd reserved the room for the entire day and night, Toby had suggested she pack a bag and plan to stay here tonight instead of returning to Hôtel Reynard.

All week Amelia had stubbornly refused to move into his room despite his repeated requests. Tonight she had a surprise for him. She'd not only packed, she had some sexy ammunition that she'd picked up when she'd bought Candace's negligee at the designer outlet. The teddy was easily the most decadent piece of lingerie Amelia had ever owned.

Convincing Toby he wanted to continue their relationship beyond Monaco wouldn't be easy, but she couldn't give up without a fight. She had every intention of using this sumptuous suite and luxurious bath to further her seduction. If she was lucky, he'd return in time to join her in the oversize tub.

She reached for the zipper at the back of her dress, but the sound of male voices coming from the balcony outside the bedroom stilled her hand. The door was partially open and the gauzy curtains undulated in a gentle breeze.

"I can't believe you did it."

She identified Vincent's voice and the smell of cigars and smiled at his compliment. He'd enjoyed the shower even though Candace said he'd protested that real men didn't attend bridal showers.

"You melted the icy nurse and got her into bed."

Amelia's blood ran cold. *Icy nurse?* Were they talking about her?

"It took you a year to do it," Vincent continued, "but you won the bet, man. I owe you a grand."

"You don't owe me anything," Toby replied.

"Yes, I do. None of the other guys will believe you succeeded. If I hadn't spotted Amelia coming out of your room this morning, I wouldn't believe it myself."

Amelia's pulse roared in her ears. Her knees weakened and her head swam. Cold formed inside her like an expanding snowball. Gasping, she leaned against the wall to keep from falling.

A bet. Toby had seduced her on a bet.

And she'd fallen in love with him.

Anger replaced humiliation. Outrage quickly followed suit. She wanted to throw something. To scream. To rant. To curse him. But she reined it in. She'd always had her mother's temper, she realized. The difference was Amelia knew how to control it.

She marched across the bedroom, shoved the sliding glass door wide open.

The men spun to face her.

"You jerk."

Toby dropped his cigar in the ashtray and slowly rose. "Amelia—"

"You used me."

Toby's jaw muscles bunched and his lips flatlined. "I didn't."

"How dare you make sport of my feelings? But then, you make sport of *your life*. I guess breaking my heart is no big deal." She held up a hand when he tried to speak. "I'm entertainment? A joke between you and your buddies?"

"It isn't like that."

"Did you or did you not make a bet to have sex with me?"

She saw the truth in the guilty flush on his face. She'd wanted him to deny it. Pain engulfed her like an avalanche. Cold. Hard. Fast. It pummeled her and left her dizzy.

"That was a long time ago." He strode toward her, reached for her.

She flinched out of reach. "Don't touch me."

"Sugar—"

"I'm not your sugar. I'm not your anything. All I am is another easy lay for NASCAR's poster boy."

"You're not easy. You're—"

"An idiot. An idiot who fell in love with the man I thought you were. Clearly I was deluded." Her eyes and throat burned. Terrified she'd break down and cry in front of him, she backed away. "And you're an even bigger idiot than I am, Toby Haynes. Because I loved you despite your enormous ego, your dangerous occupation and the fact that you're convinced every woman will leave you like your mother did."

She gulped a series of breaths and fought to regain her slipping control. "I would have stayed. No matter what."

He just stared. Silently. The man who talked all the time—even through sex—remained mute.

"You lose, Toby. We both do." A sob forced its way up her throat. She turned on her unsteady legs, snatched up her purse and overnight bag and ran from the suite like a coward.

This was one battle she wasn't strong enough to fight.

"That wasn't pretty," Vincent said.

"Shut up," Toby growled and tried to make sense of the sucking void opening inside him.

He ought to go after Amelia. But he didn't know what to say. He'd done the crime. He had no defense. Even if wanting her had stopped being about the bet a long time ago.

"I'm sorry she overheard. I thought she'd left with the rest of them."

Unable to untangle his thoughts or his tongue, Toby turned and looked at his friend.

Vincent's head snapped back as if Toby had punched him. "Shit. You fell for her."

"Of course not," Toby denied automatically. But he wasn't sure if the words were true. He wasn't sure of anything except that he'd hurt Amelia, and the pain in her eyes shredded him.

She'd said she loved him.

Past tense.

"You fell for her. And I screwed it up. Candace is going to kill me. She's been trying to get you guys together forever."

Vincent raked a hand down the unmarred side of his face, and for once Toby couldn't muster the guilt he felt every time he saw the scars caused by a freak accident behind his pit wall.

He couldn't feel anything. Numbness invaded him.

He'd made Amelia cry.

During the months he'd hounded her at the hospital he'd seen her lose patients and deal with hell on earth, which is how he'd come to view the burn ward. But he'd never seen Amelia cry. Until now.

He'd hurt her. And he had to fix it.

But he didn't know how.

Or why it mattered so much.

Thank God she'd caught them.

Amelia raced out of the hotel and right up to the limo as the porter loaded the last of the shower gifts into the trunk. She handed him her bag and joined Candace by the door.

Candace turned. "Did I forget something?"

"Get me out of here."

"What about your plans to spend the night? And why are you crying?"

Amelia put a hand to her cheeks. Wet. She hadn't even noticed the tears. "In the car. Please. Let's go. Hurry."

"Sure. Okay." Candace glanced back toward the entrance and then followed Amelia into the plush interior. "Start talking."

Amelia took a fortifying breath. "Toby slept with me on a bet."

"Oh, please. He's crazy about you. And the way he looked at you when he opened his dice…" She fanned her face. "I almost had an orgasm for you."

"I heard him, Candace. I heard Vincent say it and Toby didn't deny it." She accepted a tissue from Candace and blotted her face. "I fell for him and all he wanted was to score."

The teasing smile faded from Candace's face. "I'll skewer his nuts and Vincent's, too, if he was in on this."

At the moment, her petite blond friend looked capable of doing exactly that.

"Candace, I can't go back to Hôtel Reynard. I can't

look Toby in the eye and know I meant nothing to him. I just…I can't. I need time."

"Then you're really in love with him?"

Amelia's throat clogged, preventing speech. She nodded.

"Amelia, I've never seen you as happy as you've been this past week. Not even with Neal. Don't you want to give Toby a chance to explain?"

"I did. Please—help me find another place to stay or I'm going to have to go home."

"The man is an idiot. He doesn't deserve you."

As much as Toby had hurt her, Amelia's hackles rose at the insult. "He's not the idiot. I am. We agreed on a temporary affair. Monaco only. I'm the one who had a change of heart. You can't blame him for not loving me."

"Of course I can." Candace pulled out her cell phone. "I think I know of a place where you can stay. One he'd never think to search—assuming he has a conscience and decides to find you and apologize. If he does, you'd better make him grovel."

But Amelia knew that wasn't going to happen. She'd been nothing more than a game to Toby.

Game over.

The woman was like a ghost, Toby decided at the brunch he and Amelia were supposedly cohosting. One minute she was there and then, when he tried to reach her, she vanished.

On Friday she'd dodged him at the engagement party held on the world's largest privately owned yacht, which happened to be moored in Monaco's harbor. The yacht owners were friends of the Reynards and had expressed interest in sponsoring a race team. Toby hadn't managed to give a damn. He'd been too busy thinking a person could only run so far on a boat and yet Amelia had escaped him.

Saturday she'd avoided him at the cathedral when the wedding party had met with the officiant for an explanation about the differences between American and French ceremonies. The people of Monaco followed French law and that required a civil service. But Candace and Vincent wanted a religious blessing, too. That meant getting married twice. Toby couldn't imagine marrying once let alone repeating the mistake.

Talk about double jeopardy.

For an hour he'd sat two yards across the aisle from Amelia. He might as well have been on the other side of the Atlantic. She wouldn't look at him or speak to him.

When he'd tried to corner her after the preacher wrapped up his long-winded spiel, the bridesmaids had closed ranks and whisked Amelia away on some bridal errand.

The standbys he used with other women weren't working. He'd tried sending flowers, chocolate and jewelry, but each gift had been returned to his suite. He didn't know what else to do. He'd never had to work hard with women. Before Amelia, that is.

The schedule he'd copied from Candace's calendar weeks ago must have been scrapped, because Amelia hadn't been anywhere she was supposed to be.

The past two days, he'd taken to loitering in the lobby near the penthouse elevator, hoping to catch her when she stepped out, but this morning the concierge had informed him Amelia had moved out of the hotel. He couldn't say where she'd gone, and none of the bridal party or Vincent would talk.

Toby's only option was to ambush her at the brunch today, but so far his plans had been thwarted. He hadn't been able to get close enough to apologize. Amelia had managed to keep herself on the opposite side of the wide flagstone terrace earlier. And then, when they'd come inside to eat, she'd seated herself twelve feet away at the far end of the long dining room table.

He stared at her, willing her to look up, and ground his teeth in frustration. He could work his way through a pack of cars at almost two hundred miles an hour, but he couldn't get through two dozen guests.

But they were in a private villa, and he'd be damned if he'd let her escape again without talking to her.

Halfway through the meal, one of the servers stepped to Amelia's side and whispered something. Amelia nodded, rose and followed the woman out of the room. Toby saw his opening and headed after them. Out of the corner of his eye he saw Candace stand and Vincent pull her back down into her seat. He'd thank his buddy for that intervention later.

"Yes, that's fine. You can serve it with chocolate ganache and fresh raspberries instead of whipping cream," he heard Amelia say as he neared the kitchen, and then her heels clicked in his direction.

He ducked into an archway of the nearby study and then snagged her arm as she passed and reeled her into the room.

She squealed in surprise and then recognized him and jerked her arm free. "You scared me."

He shut the door. "I wouldn't have to sneak up on you if you'd quit avoiding me."

He missed her, dammit. Missed her sappy romantic notions. Missed her snappy set-downs when his ego got out of hand. Missed her touch. Her kisses. Her bony knees, for god's sake.

"I've been busy. What do you want? I have to get back."

He studied her pale face and the shadows beneath her hazel eyes that even heavier-than-usual makeup couldn't disguise. "I'm sorry."

Her chin lifted. "Sometimes sorry isn't enough."

"Dammit, Amelia—"

"What do you want from me, Toby?"

"I…don't know. But…not *this*."

She folded her arms across the top of a sleeveless lavender lace dress that outlined every single one of her delicate curves to mouthwatering perfection. "*This* is of your own making."

He didn't want to fight with her. He wanted her back in his bed wearing a sheen of sweat, a satisfied smile and nothing else.

But that wasn't what she wanted to hear right now.

"I won the bet when we slept together the first time."

"That makes me feel *so* much better." Her sarcasm cut deep.

"I won and I didn't tell anybody because I—" He scrubbed the back of his neck. "Because I didn't want them to know."

She studied him in silence. Waiting? For what? He didn't know. He inhaled, exhaled, searched in vain for the answer. "You were giving drivers frostbite left and right. Vincent was facing setback. One of the grafts didn't take, and they'd just told him he might never regain use of his right hand. He was pretty torn up."

"I remember."

"I was trying to give him something to think about besides another round of debridement and more surgery. But one of the other guys overheard and news of the bet spread like stomach flu."

Her face softened. But he didn't see forgiveness. And that was what he wanted, he realized. He wanted her to forgive him. "I never intended to hurt you, Amelia."

"It was still a rotten thing to do."

"Yeah." He shoved a hand through his hair. "But we

would have ended up together sooner or later. This thing between us—"

"It's over, Toby."

He couldn't accept that. She reached for the doorknob, but he wasn't ready to let her go. He splayed his palm on the wooden panel, holding it closed.

"The neurologist I've been seeing over here has cleared me to drive." He'd found out this morning and he hadn't told anyone. Not Vincent or even his teammates, who had vested interests. But he'd wanted to tell Amelia.

"Congratulations," she replied in a flat tone.

"I'll be flying back home immediately after the wedding reception Saturday to try and make the race. I'd have to start in the back of the pack since I'll miss qualifying, but it'll be worth it to get behind the wheel again."

"Driving with jet lag would be stupid."

"You're the one who said jet lag kicks in later. It shouldn't hit me until after the race."

She looked ready to argue. Instead she bit her bottom lip and shrugged. "It's your life."

She tried to step around him.

He cupped her shoulders and felt the muscles bunch. "Amelia, I am sorry."

Her eyes, more green than gold at the moment, met his. The sadness in the depths hit him like a head-on collision. "So am I."

She ducked away and left him. And he didn't feel any better.

The most romantic wedding in the world was going to be absolute torture.

Amelia fidgeted with the silk wrap of her strapless dress, the flowers in her upswept hair and then her monochromatic bouquet. Multicolor bouquets were considered in poor taste in Monaco, so Candace had chosen all white flowers.

Madeline came up beside Amelia to study their reflections in the big gilt mirror, and the phrase "Misery loves company" sprang to mind.

"We're a pitiful pair, aren't we?" Madeline whispered.

They were dressed similarly but in different shades. Candace had been determined to squeeze color into the ceremony somewhere and she'd done so with the bridesmaids' gowns. Madeline's dress was the palest green, Amelia's a soft-blush pink.

Madeline shifted a long, dark curl. "What were we thinking?"

Amelia met her friend's gaze. Madeline's vacation affair with the prince had also blown up in her face. They'd commiserated last night over drinks after the rehearsal dinner. Amelia still felt a teensy bit hungover.

"We weren't thinking. That's the problem. And you were right—my taste in men sucks. I couldn't find true love with a map." Amelia glanced at Candace on the far side of the room with the photographer. Her friend's wedding gown—an exquisite creation of a hand-beaded bodice and a silk douppioni skirt that hid her pregnancy—made Amelia's heart sigh. "And Candace deserves better than two wet-blanket bridesmaids, so slap a smile on."

"I will if you will."

Both forced smiles at their reflections and then grimaced. Amelia shook her head. "Not very convincing."

Stacy glided up. Her gown was pale blue, her smile genuine and blindingly bright. "It's not over until you leave Monaco."

"It's over," Amelia and Madeline chorused simultaneously. Toby planned to leave Monaco immediately after the reception, which would end in—Amelia glanced at her watch—four hours tops. The difference was that she now trusted his judgment. If he said he was ready to drive, then he was. He wouldn't take unnecessary risks. But that didn't stop the apprehension from tensing her muscles. Just because they couldn't be a couple didn't mean she didn't want him to stay safe.

"You two shouldn't give up so easily. You still have a chance for your dreams to come true." Stacy's lover had proposed last night at the dinner after the civil ceremony, and the accountant's face glowed with as much happiness as the bride's.

Madeline's laugh held no humor. "And I thought Amelia was the romantic of the bunch."

Amelia shook her head. "Not me. As you pointed out, even though I didn't know it, my feet have always been firmly planted on the ground. And I plan to keep them there. The blinders are off. No more temporary men."

The music swelled outside the antechamber and someone tapped on the door. Candace snapped to attention. "That's our cue."

She gathered the folds of her gown and floated toward them in a cloud of rustling silk. "Before we go, I want to thank all of you for making this day—heck, this entire month—unforgettable."

"If you make me cry and ruin my makeup, I will never forgive you," Madeline said but blinked furiously.

Amelia laughed her first genuine laugh in a week. "Ditto. Let's go tie this knot before your groom realizes your bridesmaids intend to vacation at your villa in Monaco every year for the rest of their lives and changes his mind."

Candace grinned mischievously. "That's the beauty of the French system. We tied the knot with the civil ceremony last night. There's no stress of wondering if he'll change his mind and bolt today. It's too late. I've already hooked him."

She grabbed Amelia's and Madeline's hands. "Today is just for fun. So try to have some."

Not likely, Amelia thought as she followed Stacy and Madeline toward the nave. Stacy walked down the aisle first, followed by Madeline. Amelia took her place and looked up.

Mistake. Her gaze found Toby's. He wore a black tux, a stark white shirt and black tie. His golden hair gleamed in the candlelight, and he was so handsome he took her breath away.

Her heart pounded. Her knees locked. Her stomach knotted. This would be the only time she'd ever walk down the aisle toward this man, the man she loved.

"Go, sweetie," Candace's father prompted from behind her.

Amelia blinked, refocused on Vincent and headed toward the altar a few beats behind schedule.

Had someone leaded the soles of her designer sandals?

Vincent gazed beyond Amelia, his attention no doubt on his beautiful bride. The love in his eyes brought a lump to Amelia's throat. Would a man ever look at her that way?

Neal hadn't. No, the look in Neal's eyes had been more like…gratitude, she realized. He'd been thankful to have her, but he probably hadn't loved her. Why else would he have kept postponing their marriage?

And she hadn't loved him either. Not the way he truly deserved. Amelia missed a step at the discovery. She'd wanted to love Neal because he was perfect in every way— except for his terminal illness. Gentle. Reserved. Predictable. Despite that, she hadn't been able to make herself love him wholeheartedly or make herself desire him.

Desiring Toby had come all too easily, starting at that

first meeting. Loving him had sneaked up on her, and that unexpected blow had made it all the more powerful.

At the brunch he'd said he hadn't meant to hurt her, but that wasn't the same as loving her.

She reached the end of the aisle, took her place and lifted her eyes to find Toby's silvery-blue gaze focused with unwavering intent on her. She saw want and regret and frustration in his expression, but she didn't see love. And his love was the one thing she wanted more than anything else.

She blinked and turned away.

The service began. Amelia barely heard the words. And if a tear or two slipped down her cheek, she hoped everyone would attribute it to tears of happiness for her friend.

She wasn't going to sleep with another man unless he loved her. She deserved that, didn't she? And if that meant she either had to do without sex or had to buy herself a battery-operated boyfriend, then that's what she'd do.

From now on it was all or nothing. No more dead-end affairs. No more men who couldn't commit.

If she couldn't have the kind of love she saw shining on Candace's and Vincent's and Stacy's faces, then she'd rather be alone.

Alone. And empty.

Amelia followed the steward carrying her luggage off the yacht. The owners who'd hosted the engagement party had been kind enough to offer her refuge after she'd fled Hôtel Reynard.

The rest of the wedding party had already left Monaco. Vincent and Candace were on their honeymoon. Franco had taken Stacy to his French family estate. Even Madeline's prince had come through. He'd surprised them all with a proposal during the wedding reception yesterday and then he'd whisked Madeline off in the royal jet to his country in the South Pacific to meet his family.

Amelia was happy for her friends but a little saddened, too, that she hadn't found what they had.

A limo longer than any she'd ridden in during her stay in Monaco waited at the end of the jetty. This one would easily carry ten or more people. The driver climbed out and opened the rear door for her.

"Louis?" *Toby's Louis?* But Toby had flown out yesterday. Vincent had probably arranged for Toby's driver. He'd also arranged for Amelia's.

Coincidence. Get in the car, Amelia. It's time to go home.

"Good afternoon, Mademoiselle Lambert. I trust you enjoyed your stay in Monaco?"

"It is the most romantic country in the world," she dodged. There was no way to explain the range of emotions and personal discoveries she'd made here in the past month.

Louis smiled. "That it is."

"Could I have a minute?"

He nodded and then joined the steward to help him load her luggage in the trunk.

Amelia turned a full circle for one last look at the harbor, the Mediterranean and the jagged landscape. She'd teased Candace about coming back to visit every year, but Amelia wasn't sure she could handle the bittersweet memories. She'd have to if she wanted to stay in touch with her friends—and she did. Candace had said she and Amelia were almost family.

Louis returned to her side. "Mademoiselle?"

"I'm ready." She climbed inside the dim, cavernous interior and the door closed behind her. It took a second for her eyes to adjust. The first thing she saw was a bouquet of roses on the nearest seat. A dozen *red* roses.

A shuffle of sound drew her attention. She turned her head and saw Toby in the back. Her stomach tumbled to her toes. "You're supposed to be in Daytona."

"Next week will be soon enough to get back on the track." He wore a blue silk shirt the exact shade of his eyes, navy pants and sunglasses. Her own panicked face reflected back at her in the lenses. "Sit down, sugar."

She wasn't ready for a tête-à-tête with Toby, but the car started rolling before she could reach the door handle, and diving out…not a good plan. She scrambled for a seat, the farthest one from him, and buckled up.

Toby stayed where he was a good six feet away with his fingers laced in his lap. The pose looked casual until she noticed how tightly his fingers were knotted and searched his face.

"What's going on?"

"You were right," he said. "I use the bravado to keep people at a distance. That's because the last woman who saw the real Tobias Haynes didn't like him enough to stay. Plain ol' Toby, a serious kid who loved anything with an engine, wasn't good enough."

A kid? "Are you talking about your mother?"

"Yeah."

"Toby, she fled an abusive relationship. She did the right thing in getting out."

He hesitated and then said, "She should have taken me with her."

She couldn't imagine the heartache he must have felt. "Yes, she should have."

"The point is, I'm not always charming, witty or fun."

Where was he going with this? "This is news?"

He stiffened. "Hey—"

"Toby, *the point is,*" she repeated his words, "when you

cast off the playboy-jerk armor and quit trying to get into my pants you're a very likable guy."

"Yeah?" He sounded surprisingly unsure.

"Yes."

"You like it when I get in your pants."

She sighed. "Toby—"

"My father called me *To-buy-ass* instead of Tobias." Toby glanced out the window. His jaw looked rigid enough to snap. "He said I was a worthless piece of crap and once the Haynes charm and looks faded I'd have to buy my women like he did."

Amelia's heart squeezed at the pain he couldn't quite conceal beneath the clipped words, and anger stirred toward the man who'd hurt him. "I don't think I'd like your father much."

"Not many people did." He faced her again. "He kicked me out when I turned eighteen. I hitched a ride to Concord and begged until somebody let me push a broom in a race shop. I had a knack for engines, and that got a little attention. I worked my way up from there. It took years before I could convince somebody to let me get behind the wheel."

She'd read some of this online, but not the part about his father. Details of Toby's life before NASCAR had been impossible to find. She knew because she'd searched.

"Racing…what I've accomplished…it all proves my dad wrong."

"You should be proud. You worked hard and earned your success."

His jaw shifted. He sucked one deep breath and then another. "I'd give it up if you asked me to."

Shock rippled through her. "What? Why would you do that? Why would *I* do that?"

She hadn't even noticed the limo stopping, but Louis

opened the door, so it must have. Moments ago Amelia would have given anything to get out of this car. Now she wanted to stay and find out exactly what Toby was trying to say. "Toby—"

"Immigration is waiting." He came forward, climbed from the car and then offered her his hand.

"You can't drop a bomb like that and then walk away." And then she stopped and studied the unfamiliar surroundings. "This is not the Nice airport."

"No. It's a private strip. We're flying back on the HRI jet."

"But I have a ticket."

"It's been canceled." He hustled her into the small building and through the formalities.

Afterward, she looked up from tucking her passport back into her purse and found him holding a blue velvet box.

A jewelry box.

A *ring* box.

Her heart skidded to a halt and then pounded like a woodpecker on speed in her chest.

He'd removed his sunglasses, and for the first time today she could see his eyes. But she couldn't read them.

"For you. No matter what happens, this is yours to keep."

Don't get your hopes up. He's commitmentphobic.

Her hands shook so badly she could barely hold the box. She took a bracing breath and lifted the lid and saw a ring.

A key ring.

Disappointment weighted her shoulders.

What did you expect?

"What is this?"

"Keys to that little blue car you fell in love with. It should be waiting in your driveway when you get home."

Her mouth dropped open. "Toby, you shouldn't have. It's too much."

"You take care of everybody else. Somebody needs to spoil you."

"I—I don't know what to say."

"*Thanks* should do it. And maybe a kiss. Or two."

Did he expect her to resume the affair at home? "What do you want from me?"

He hooked his hand around her elbow and guided her toward the doors leading to the runway. "I've been giving some thought to that crazy idea of yours."

"What crazy idea?"

"The one about the dog, the kids and the white picket fence."

"There's nothing crazy about—" The glass doors slid open and the words died on her lips. Two parallel rows of white picket fencing created a four-foot-wide path across the asphalt. About thirty feet from the terminal the fencing took a right-angle turn behind a big metal storage box.

"Maybe it's not such a dumb idea after all," Toby said beside her.

Her feet moved numbly forward. This seemed a little *Wizard of Oz*-ish, like traveling the yellow brick road.

Toby pulled her to a stop before she could look around the corner. "Let me give 'em to you."

A mixture of emotions tumbled through her brain. Confusion. Hope. Caution. "What are you saying?"

His eyes warmed and her breath caught. She blinked, convinced that she was mistaken in what she thought she saw.

Toby cupped her cheek. "I'm saying that standing in that church I realized I wanted to hear you saying those words, making those promises to me. And I wanted to make them to you. I want forever with you, Amelia. The kids, the dog, the porch swing. The whole deal."

A tremor started in the pit of her stomach and worked

its way outward. Her lips quivered. Her throat closed up and her eyes burned. She closed her gaping mouth, opened it again, but no sound emerged.

Toby thumbed a tear from her cheek, one she hadn't even noticed escaping. His lips turned up in a clearly forced smile. "But not the cat. The cat's a deal breaker."

A laugh bubbled from her chest. She could tell the joke was a nervous one and part of the carefree facade he wore like protective armor. "Oh, Toby…"

He pressed a finger to her lips. "HRI is strong enough to survive whether or not I ever climb back in the car. I have to finish this season because I'm contracted to my sponsors, but after that I'll give up driving if you want me to. What matters is having you by my side."

He cupped her shoulders and turned her around. The picket fence path led to the stairs of a small white jet. *Marry me, Amelia* had been written in huge red script down the side of the plane. She could only gape. Happiness swelled within her. She tried to contain it. He hadn't said the most important words yet, and she refused to settle for less.

And yet he'd offered to give up driving for her. That had to mean something, didn't it?

"It'll take about a mile of this white stuff to circle my property. Lucky for you, I can afford it."

She faced him. He held another ring box, this one open to display a gorgeous heart-shaped diamond on a wide gold band. Her lungs failed. She pressed her fingers over her mouth.

"You're into the hearts and flowers and stuff, so…" He shrugged. "If you don't like it, we can get something else."

He tipped up her chin, forcing her to meet his gaze. The love she saw in his eyes, on his face, made her dizzy with oy, and no matter how many times she blinked, it didn't go away. She wheezed in a breath.

"I always swore I'd never let a woman get close enough to hurt me. I never guessed that letting the right one—*you*—go would hurt more. I know I acted like an ass. But if it's not too late, please give me a chance to earn your love again.

"I didn't tell the guys about our night together because I didn't want to share. It was special. At the time I didn't realize how special. And then you dumped me with that cold note and I knew I had to get you back. You started out as the one who got away. A challenge I had to win. But then you stole my heart and became the one I can't forget."

He dropped to one knee. "I love you, Amelia. Marry me. Please."

"You love driving."

"I love you more." He stated it simply and without hesitation.

She reached out a tentative hand and stroked his hair, his cheek. "I would never ask you to give up something that makes you so happy."

"Then don't make me give up you."

Those perfect words sent a shiver of delight through her. 'It's not too late, Toby. I couldn't stop loving you that easily. Even though I did try.

"You've shown me time and time again you're not the daredevil adrenaline junkie I thought you were. I trust you to not take foolish risks. And I don't want you to give up driving until you're ready to quit.

"Yes. Yes, Toby Haynes, I'll marry you."

She bent and gently pressed her lips to his. He rose swiftly, crushing her into his arms, sweeping her off her feet and deepening the kiss.

She wound her arms around his neck and smiled against

his mouth. If anyone had told her a year ago that her knight in shining armor would ride in a race car instead of on a white stallion, she'd have told them to have their heads examined.

But this time she was more than happy to be wrong.

* * * * *

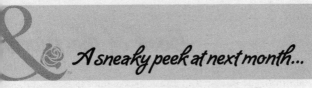

A sneaky peek at next month...

By Request

RELIVE THE ROMANCE WITH THE BEST OF THE BEST

My wish list for next month's titles...

In stores from 16th March 2012:

☐ Claimed by the Italian – Diana Hamilton,
Christina Hollis & Kathryn Ross

☐ Reasons for Revenge
– Maureen Child

3 stories in each book - only £5.99!

In stores from 6th April 2012:

☐ Capturing Her Heart – Nina Bruhns,
Caridad Piñeiro & Kathleen Creighton

Available at WHSmith, Tesco, Asda, Eason, Amazon and Apple

Just can't wait?

Special Offers

very month we put together collections and
nger reads written by your favourite authors.

ere are some of next month's highlights—
nd don't miss our fabulous discount online!

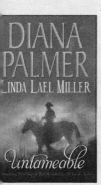

n sale 16th March

On sale 16th March

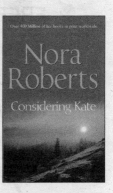

On sale 6th April

Save 20%
on all Special Releases

Find out more at
www.millsandboon.co.uk/specialreleases

Visit us Online

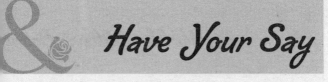

Have Your Say

You've just finished your book.
So what did you think?

We'd love to hear your thoughts on our
'Have your say' online panel
www.millsandboon.co.uk/haveyoursay

- Easy to use
- Short questionnaire
- Chance to win Mills & Boon®
  goodies

The World of Mills & Boon®

There's a Mills & Boon® series that's perfect for you. We publish ten series and with new titles every month, you never have to wait long for your favourite to come along.

Blaze®
Scorching hot, sexy reads

By Request
Relive the romance with the best of the best

Cherish™
Romance to melt the heart every time

Désire™
Passionate and dramatic love stories

Visit us Online
Browse our books before you buy online at
www.millsandboon.co.uk